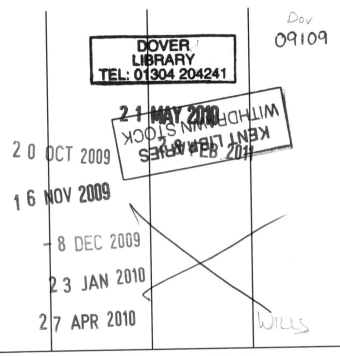
Please return on or before the latest date above.
You can renew online at *www.kent.gov.uk/libs*
or by telephone 08458 247 200

CUSTOMER SERVICE EXCELLENCE

Libraries & Archives

00884\DTP\RN\07.07   LIB 7

FINDING AVA

Ava Dimato has never felt quite comfortable in her privileged life among Boston's élite. As the only daughter, her life is controlled by the protective men of the Dimato clan, but on her father's death, she discovers she is not who she thought she was. Her quest to find her true identity sends her hurtling from the arms of her married lover and her comfortable New England life into the murky past of Catholic Ireland and Boston's seedy underbelly. The truths she uncovers are difficult and disturbing, but only in discovering where she came from can she truly come home...

FINDING AVA

FINDING AVA

by

Kathy Rodgers

Magna Large Print Books
Long Preston, North Yorkshire,
BD23 4ND, England.

British Library Cataloguing in Publication Data.

Rodgers, Kathy
    Finding Ava.

    A catalogue record of this book is
    available from the British Library

    ISBN   978-0-7505-3006-4

First published in 2007 by Poolbeg Press Ltd

Copyright © 2007 by Kathy Rodgers

Cover illustration © Marcus Appelt by arrangement with
Arcangel Images

The moral right of the author has been asserted

Published in Large Print 2009 by arrangement with
Kathy Rodgers, care of Poolbeg Group Services whose agents are
Dorian Literary Agency

Magna Large Print is an imprint of Library Magna Books Ltd.

Printed and bound in Great Britain by
T.J. (International) Ltd., Cornwall, PL28 8RW

Acknowledgements

So many good people need to be available and so many things need to be in place to enable my writing and me to escape from my glass jar to the book-reading world. My appreciation of the support of these people, including those who buy my books, cannot be overstated. Without this support there would be no book for the reader and without the willing reader there would be no room for the writer.

A special thanks to:

Paula Campbell and all the staff at Poolbeg Press, especially Niamh, Lynda and Conor, who gave me my start and continue to back me in this competitive world.

Gaye Shortland for her boundless faith and empathy with the writer and her knowledge and insight that transform 'nice idea' to 'good book' and, occasionally, 'something needing a lot more work' to the bookshelves! I'm sure that many writers have silently thanked Gaye as they've trod past their work in the bookstores – I know that I do.

My agent Dorothy Lumley for her patient and diligent pursuit of the snowed-under publishers on my behalf.

Mary Carelton-Reynolds and all the staff at Longford Town Library who support, indulge and sometimes endure my wild dreams and frustrations. I had a wonderful book launch in Eason's where Maureen Sullivan did a terrific job launching it. Also to Noel O'Connor, Alan, Mary and all the staff who did a wonderful job in catering to all our needs. I hope a great night was had by all and a special mention to family members who travelled from Mayo and Dublin to it.

Audrey, a fellow-writer of no little fame here in Longford, for her insatiable interest and support and more so her ability to help me see put-downs and knock-downs as challenges and steps. If she were a boxer, the rest of us could all throw in the towel.

And then there is family…

My boys Kevin and Shane, who now know that each acceptance of my work is a signal that a celebration or treat is due. Not forgetting their cousins Kate, Áine and Maeve. I can't forget a few grown-ups that lend a hand, Éamonn, Ann and Thomas. Also, Audrey (R), Nana Rodge, Nana Josie and Papa. Last, but by no means least, the O'Sullivans in Sydney and London and the Rodgers in Rome and Perth.

To my grandmother, Mary Gray.

It was down her lane that the scribbling first began.

1

The booming voice of Ben Dimato echoed down the vast hallway as he dutifully ushered the last sympathisers from the house.

'Thank you very much, Mrs Vernon – watch out for Al there – poor Joe's bourbon seems to have gone down very well with him over the evening.'

'Yes, Ben – of course – I'll take care of him.'

I shut my eyes at the sound of Barbara Vernon's saccharine-sweet tones.

'Hush now, Senator,' came her husband's drunken voice. 'Me and Joe broke open many a bottle in our day, 'specially when he came to Vancouver for our hunting trips. It's only fair that I should warm my belly for my – eh, our – return flight with one last dose of his hospitality. He wouldn't have minded.'

Listlessly I rubbed specks and crumbs from my black trouser suit. This suit had served me well. It had bailed me out on three occasions over the past five years – my mother's funeral, my son Ethan's and now Joe Dimato's, the man I had always regarded as my father. Until recently – very recently.

'I think you should look out for Ava, though,' Barbara went on. 'She looks really cut up about it all – she and her dad were so close – she's going to find the going very hard trying to do that job by herself. Poor Joe – he never let go of the reins

– couldn't really. It's a task for a man, Ben.'

That's really most kind of you, Mrs Vernon, I reflected grimly. With women like you on our side, we'll surely win the battle. I can imagine you lapping up Joe's stories when he took himself out of Boston to de-stress by shooting at some poor innocent animal. I can see you nodding your dyed head in agreement. Yes, me and Al could see that Ava was always too soft – she'd be much better with a small boutique of her own, maybe interior design. She's always had wonderful taste, hasn't she – but when you're hiring and firing, you need something more. You need to be tough, to be able to judge character – suss out the no-goods. That's what Joe Dimato would say – you need to be able to identify the right people for the right job at the right time. I grimaced as images of 'bad eggs', as Dad would call some of my selections, surfaced in my brain. Not that I needed to recall right now, what with Barbara Vernon doing it for me.

Why don't you take yourself and your drunkard husband back off now to Vancouver, Barbara, where you can nurse him and pander to him until he's up to another boys' day out?

That morning, my brother Chad had jabbed pointedly at me across the funeral parlour. Eventually it had dawned on me that my choice of funeral attire was causing him problems. There it was, neatly pinned to my tailored black jacket: *Ava Dimato, Head of Sales, Dimato Pharmaceuticals.* Just in case somebody didn't know I was the grieving daughter – or maybe it was my rebellion, me telling my fretful brother that I was well up to coping with the challenges at the office,

14

despite all of his recent insinuations. Uncle Ben had taken his turn too and now the gruesome 'Barbie Doll Vernon' – as if I needed to be reminded further of all my career blunders at their precious company. No, I reflected grimly – this black suit might be first into the sack to be dispatched to the charity shop on my next visit. But I'd be keeping the name-badge and the job and the begrudgers could go to hell. It was enough to have them whispering and smiling knowingly at Dimato Pharmaceuticals – it was too much to hear the word had spread to Canada, to a patronising old cow who needed some other focus once the TV listings confirmed that there was to be no *Oprah* or *Sopranos* that day.

The mourners were stalling at the front door. Fresh air was whirling in, chilling me to the bone. I shivered and automatically hugged myself for warmth. Chad caught my eye and quickly looked away. Oh, Uncle Ben, would you please get rid of them, I begged silently.

What was it that my friend Frieda used to say? Death is so final. One minute they're with you – then nothing. That emptiness, the unbearable, almost dizzy lightness I felt the day they lowered my little boy Ethan into his final resting place, the weight of his little body never again to burden my arms, the normal comings and goings of family and parents that formed part of my day ... gone ... removed ... permanently.

You only got it half-right, Frieda. It's not that the weight of it all disappears – it's just transferred, straight into the head.

Mine was thudding right now with sadness,

anger – and questions. Yes, loads of questions. None of that finality you mentioned. Why won't Chad, Uncle Ben – anyone – talk to me about it?

My uncle's voice interrupted my thoughts. 'Joe lived his life to the full.'

'Yes, he did. He was a wonderful man,' Barbara Vernon replied.

Go, please just go, I silently urged. I was having a hard time keeping my composure. I willed myself not to start crying.

'Goodbye, Ben, and thank Ava and Chad for me. I'm glad in ways that his dear wife Maria went before him. This would have devastated her – she wouldn't be able for it. Men and their toys – what possessed them to go off flying like that against all the weather forecasts?'

'Stubbornness, Barbara, nothing more than that – Joe thought he was invincible. Kept him hanging on for the past six weeks. He's off now to join the others and they can accuse and blame each other until the dinosaurs return to earth. Me, I don't want to see another funeral until my own – too many recently. Whoa there, Al, you'll topple over and hit your head! Get a grip!'

'Not so easy for a man in politics to be missing funerals, Ben,' Al slurred. 'Real vote-catchers they are – but you're not going to run for office next time out, are you? D'you think Chad will make it? Stop dragging outa me, honey! I'm well fit to walk.'

'Take care now. And thanks again for coming.'

The door clicked shut and Ben's heavy footsteps thudded purposefully down the hallway.

I looked at him resentfully as he strode into the

living room. No chance of getting information from you now, is there? Too long in politics, too polished, patronising. 'We all go through life enduring something we cannot understand, Ava,' he would say before he'd divert to some shallow reminiscence about some trivial event in his own life. You might be sixty-nine, Ben, but it has been one long political charade. I've already been through more than you will ever experience. Now the last of the mourners are gone, you can give yourself a pat on the back for being an old hand at these things, did it properly and all that. The way your brother Joe, my 'father', would have wanted. Can't you hear me pleading with you? I've just found out that Joe Dimato is not my father. Okay – so you haven't the faintest idea what I'm talking about. Then there's nothing keeping *you* here now that you've done your bit. Fuck off, Uncle Ben!

'That's the last of them gone – I'm whacked. Now, don't forget – your father's will is being read at three o'clock tomorrow. He nominated me as executor and I want you both there. Do this for him, Ava. I know it's hard for you right now, but you can't airbrush your family out of your life because of this – you've got responsibilities. They've been with you, behind you, for the past thirty-seven years. Joe was a father to you for every one of those years – he loved you and you know it. Chad, you'll be okay, won't you?'

I sat silently with Chad in the sitting room as Senator Dimato's chauffeur-driven BMW purred quietly down the driveway into the Boston night.

After an eternity Chad shuffled towards the door, coughing artificially as he went.

17

'I will be there, anyway,' he said in a voice at once both resigned and defiant. 'Listen, I've got to give Martha a lift across the city – she's finishing up in the kitchen. I'll be straight back to stay over for the night. You won't be alone, Ava.'

I found myself suddenly saying, 'That's fine, Chad, but you take yourself off to bed. Look at how much you've drunk – I've already agreed with Martha to take her off home.' I could just about hear the alcohol slurring my speech.

Martha Jones had lived on the edge of the Dimato family for far too long. If my uncle and brother were going to shut down communications with me, then Martha – having lived in the bosom of the family for forty years – was next best bet. I was in the kitchen before Chad could react.

'C'mon, Martha – I'm taking you across to Jamaica Plains. The rest of the cleaning can wait until tomorrow – I'll finish it off myself – you've already done more than your bit.'

I could feel Chad starting to mouth an objection in the background but I had Martha's coat draped round her in an instant and we were in the car before my brother could thwart my sudden inspiration.

2

'You really need to come in and have some coffee, Miss Ava. That police officer – I was sure he was going to give you a traffic violation. I could have taken a cab. Thank the Good Lord he knew Ben.'

'Yes, Martha,' I said disinterestedly. I didn't want to be reminded that my uncle was my unwitting saviour on this occasion. I had more important things I wanted to talk about, questions to ask.

Some forty years back Martha had arrived penniless from Jamaica to be taken in and exploited by my uncle – and his brother, my dad, Joe Dimato. Ben didn't always need a full-time housekeeper, spending so much time out of state. On these occasions, Martha would be dispatched over to Beacon Hill to cook, clean, baby-sit, whatever it was that needed doing. As a child, I looked forward to the times that Ben would leave town as it meant that Martha would be coming over to stay awhile. She had a seemingly endless selection of bedtime stories and a storytelling style to accommodate them all. She'd giggle when I'd suggest she should be on stage – she was very conscious of her weight and was grateful for the anonymity working as housekeeper for the Dimatos gave her. She was terribly distressed during Ethan's funeral and it brought on one of her asthma attacks. I'd sat with her a couple of days later in her tiny little apartment, touched by her genuine grief for my little boy, glad to find a haven from the wooden mourning of my family. Martha was now sixty-four and finding it harder by the day to haul herself about.

Right now, I was looking back nervously at my gleaming new jeep and the gangs of youths loitering on corners. Martha picked up on my apprehension immediately and called one of them over. He looked no more than fourteen and she was pressing a ten-dollar bill into his hand.

'Breslin, I want you to look out for this lady's car and, if anybody comes near it, you holler as loud as you can. Martha will come out – you hear?'

The boy studied the money in his hand without speaking, looked at his watch and then at me. Probably keep him there for all of fifteen minutes, I felt. I reached into my bag and took out twenty dollars.

'You give Mrs Jones her money back, Breslin, and take this. I won't be too long.'

Inside her apartment, my eyes came to rest on the wall-mounted photograph of Martha and a teenage boy. Linford, where are you now, I pondered – prison maybe?

Obviously nowhere good, otherwise your mother wouldn't have gone all quiet about you again. I don't have any good reason to remember you with fondness either, do I? My mind flashed back to one of my many mistakes at Dimato Pharmaceuticals...

'Open the trunk of your car, Jones,' Joe Dimato

had growled menacingly.

Two silent, burly security guards hovered above Linford, leaving him in no doubt that they would smash it open and him too if he didn't co-operate.

'Come here now, Ava, so you can see,' came the patronising voice of my father as he began to mimic my own. 'Sure, there's no harm in giving him the job of janitor – he's been clean for two years. Just not caught until now. Do they look to you like the laptop computers and cell phones that have been going missing from supplies?'

It was humiliation time for Mr Dimato's daughter and there was little I could do but glare silently and accusingly at Linford. Martha cried for weeks and I felt like an accomplice, as I had fought to get him the job. It couldn't have been easy for him, parted as a baby from his mother in Jamaica for over two years until they managed to reunite in America. No mention of a father. Linford would be past forty by now and he'd had so many chances. My eyes shifted to another picture – Martha and her two grandchildren, Chantelle and Hugh. At least he did that for her, I conceded sarcastically as I reflected on Martha's delight and pride in the pair.

Time to get back to the present as Martha entered the room with hot coffees and the obligatory packet of chocolate cookies.

'Now, Miss Ava, you were saying on the way over that you need to ask me some questions about your mother?'

'Yes, it's a bit embarrassing – it's about me too. I know you won't talk to anyone else about it but

21

the best way to tell you is to plunge right in. I'm not Joe Dimato's daughter, Martha – can't be – and I was hoping you might know something about it.'

Hours later, I sat nursing a drink in the kitchen at Beacon Hill, listening to the sounds of Chad shuffling restlessly upstairs as if confirming the charged tension that had developed between us. It was a waste of time – I should have let you drive Martha over, Brother. Thinks I was born in Scotland, that's how much she knows. I reproached myself for my surge of anger towards her and had to remind myself that this could be one person's secret – my mother's. Somehow the lethargic Maria Dimato had escaped the attention of everybody to indulge herself in extra-marital sex and I was the result. It would have been almost credible but for the laid-back reactions of my brother and uncle. It just didn't match up to first-time news for them – surely they would have been at least a little bit surprised and angry to boot?

I'd prompted gently at first.

'You've been with us for forty years, Martha. By my count, that's three years older than me and I have an American birth certificate, not a Scottish one. I really want you to think hard back to then – see if there's something you can remember. My mother had to be having an affair. Someone knows something – only they're not saying. I can feel it though, for sure.'

Martha Jones hung her head limply as she listened to my pleading.

'Really, Miss Ava – I don't know. You're forgetting that I started off as your uncle's housekeeper and he lives the far side of Boston. Back then, I didn't go over to Beacon Hill at all. You were, I think, three when Mrs Dimato first got bad with her nerves and she went to the hospital. It was then that I started coming over to help out at your house–'

'Martha,' I interrupted, 'what about all your stories about when I was a baby – the time I first walked?'

'Yes, yes, and they're true. Mr Joe, he'd bring you and Chad over to Ben's a lot. It was there one day that you got up and walked – where you hit your head against the chair. I don't like this because I don't know anything about it – and I don't like talking about your dead mother like she was some bad woman. She wasn't – there has to be some mistake.'

Now, back at Beacon Hill, the wine bottle was empty and yet I couldn't recall finishing it off. It had been a long day but I had got through it. I ached for a comforting hug and the reassuring words from a loved one that it was going to be okay. I found myself staring at mother's favourite armchair where she loved to sit and read her books. My legs felt weak as I walked across the sitting room and poured myself a small bourbon from my father's decanter. I was on my own.

'Cheers, Dad, wherever you are!' I winced as the whiskey burned my throat. A toast to 'family' – my mind flashed back to the Christmas Eve drinks parties we'd have in this very room. Joe would be in congratulatory mode – telling Chad and me that the company's success was all down to us. A few drinks later, he would say it was all down to him and my brother would wink conspiratorially across the room. It was harmless really – even my normally teetotal mum would partake by supping a few Yuletide sherries.

The thought brought a tiny smile to my lips. 'To bed, lady,' I whispered quietly in the stillness of the room.

I was tempted to knock on my brother's door. It would be nice to talk, maybe claim back the old relationship we had before Uncle Ben had taken my impressionable brother under his wing. Chad was here because he felt duty bound that night, not because he cared. If Joe Dimato wasn't my real father there was always the possibility that he wasn't Chad's but he didn't want to know.

'It's not a problem for me to stay the night, Ava. Isabel and the kids, they understand,' were my brother's parting words before going to bed.

I smirked manically as the beep-beep in the next bedroom signalled the delivery of my text.

'Chad, I won't be going to the will-reading to-morrow. I've got another appointment. Whatever way it goes, it will be okay.'

I sat up in my bed and peered at the luminous clock figures as they silently taunted me that the night was going to amble along at its own pace. Yes, 5:30, Ava, and it'll be 5:55 when you look at me in a few minutes' time. Yes, you're right, it is true that most big cities never sleep these days and Boston is no exception. But the people you want to talk to are sleeping, Ava, and you're just going to have to wait, aren't you?

My thoughts drifted to my brother in the room next door and the phone call that began it all, the slide towards the shocking reality that I was not the flesh and blood of Joe Dimato. Damn Chad for being so stoic and aloof. Even when he left that message, the toneless formality of his voice.

'You need to get down to the Mass General, Ava. It's Dad – he's been in a serious accident, a plane crash. Ring me when you pick up this message.'

I got there in time to hear the nurse talking to Chad as he nodded grimly in agreement. Third-degree burns, just managed to get out before the aircraft was engulfed in flames. The others were in the morgue. Sit with him, talk to him. Her tone and eyes told me that she was merely going through the motions, procedure. After all, I'd been there before, hadn't I? Part of hospital protocol, keeping up the hope, the pretence right up to the point of confirmation that it was time to ring the undertaker. Dad was gone from us and the only thing that was delaying his departure to the afterlife was the machinery surrounding him.

That evening it was my turn to watch and when I exhausted myself evoking and replaying all the pleasant memories of our entwined lives, I resorted to staring blindly at his medical chart as if this would somehow resuscitate him. God, you're back at this again, I reproached myself. Didn't work for poor Ethan, my baby, did it – the fantasies you played out as you sat beside your sleeping baby right here in this hospital, willing him to hang on, live, flourish. All in vain, those dreams, Ethan going to kindergarten. Ethan going on his first play date. Ethan going to high school and college. It was not to happen – my little boy's body returned to the soil scarcely past two years old.

My father's chart swam in front of me and I blinked back my tears.

Suddenly a piece of harmless information shot a lightning bolt towards my brain, thrusting me outwards into the hospital's corridor.

'Nurse, I need you to come quickly, there's been some mistake! The blood sacs, they're the wrong grouping, you're giving my father the wrong blood!'

Much later, I was to sit in the muted lighting of the private bedroom, assured that there was no mistake. Except that there was a bigger mistake looming ... one spanning nigh on four decades.

'Blood Group O – you are not my father, Joe Dimato,' I said aloud to the empty room. 'You told me you were A – like me, A – you even joked about it – A for Ava, you said. You lied. Why?' I knew why. My mother Maria was Group O, of that I was sure. And O plus O equals O when it comes to blood inheritance. Not A. Not Ava. Squinting, I studied the contours of his face, tentatively brushing my fingers across his as if I was touching some unknown, mysterious species for the first time. I looked away from the log of blood transfusions recorded as the doctors fought despairingly to revive his battered body. God, Ava Dimato – Ava Somebody, you cannot be your father's child.

Waves of panic and queasiness swept over me as a piece of a jigsaw suddenly clicked into place. I could only be the result of some illicit liaison Maria Dimato had while Joe's back was turned. Imagine, my lifeless, tablet-sustained mother going out to play with the boys while her main boy was away. It was scarcely credible and it felt so cheap, tawdry. Some opportunist stud had laid Maria Dimato down and departed smugly into the night, his seed nestling safely inside her preparing to grow into the sleepless woman that now lay waiting impatiently for morning to come. Surely, Joe Dimato could not have known – my brash, proud father would not have accepted another man's child? I sighed as I battled against the reality that this was one secret that was likely to rest in the graveyard with my mother – maybe my true father lay silently elsewhere; maybe he walked but did not know.

Joe Dimato's blood group might have meant nothing to me had I not learned so much about such matters during the saddest days of my thirty-seven years. I mean, I know that many an unsuspecting creature ventured forward through life blissfully unaware that their beginnings were not exactly as Mum or Dad described. Try it – ask someone you know what their blood group is and most likely they'll grimace helplessly while looking at you like you were some form of vampire to be avoided at all costs. However, I got to understand these medical matters in the cruellest of ways.

'Mr and Mrs Prefontaine – can you come in? Doctor Benjamin will see you now,' said the neatly attired fifty-something lady.

I'd later become very familiar with Carla Lane.

Several pairs of eyes swept across us as others waited to hear the judgements and solutions to whatever brought them through the door of this renowned specialist.

'I'm afraid the news is not good. Your son Ethan is suffering from a rare blood disorder. It's usually hereditary, not always though – he will need a bone-marrow transplant at a future date. A sibling is the ideal donor but, in the absence of that, we'll need to look at the family, both sides – get some more information on who might be able to help out if they're needed. It's treatable and we're optimistic ... but we have lost some over the years. Hopefully...' His voice trailed away.

Bruce Prefontaine, my husband of eighteen months, stared blankly at the floor as my mind raced frantically for escapes and denials of what we had just heard.

The months that followed quickly ruled out Bruce's family – his parents and an elderly aunt were unsuitable as donors and he had no brothers or sisters. One by one, members of my family who came forward with help were rejected.

'There's something that just doesn't fit,' Bruce would say angrily. 'Can't you get your family to be assessed by another specialist – surely some fucking one of them has got what's needed to save our baby?'

'I've tried, Bruce, honestly I have. They have volunteered, been through the same tests as your family and Doctor Benjamin says no – he cannot use them. There's nothing more I can do. Can't you just go back to bed – you're only upsetting Ethan with your yelling.'

I would stand outside on the balcony of our third-floor apartment in Charlestown, holding little Ethan, until his pitiful wails eventually gave way to a silent breathing as he looked outward, transfixed, at the Boston lights, upwards to the Bunker Hill Monument until his head eventually sagged. Your dad's gone back up the monument, little guy, I would say. Yes, all two hundred and ninety-four steps, thinks it will help you – leave him be. Someday you and me will walk up there, the pair of us – maybe Bruce too. Gently I would prise open the tiny fingers that clung to mine, laying him down in the little cot at the bottom of our bed.

Two years later the words of Doctor Benjamin echoed coldly across the gloomy graveyard where my son lay. 'We have lost some…' No, Doctor, *I* have lost some … Ethan … soon Bruce. He can't get past blaming my family for this.

3

Eventually, the digital lights on my clock started to fade and gave way to the Boston morning that seeped through my curtains. Thoughts of Doctor Benjamin had kept me awake throughout the night and he was to be my priority for the next day. He surely wouldn't be able to claim blissful unawareness like my family and Martha – he would have seen straight away that I did not belong to Joe Dimato. I was beginning the day with a firm resolve that someone was going to answer my questions and was able to blank out any hung over feeling and fatigue that last night's drinking would normally bring. I alternated my en-suite shower between hot and cold until I felt tinglingly refreshed. I'd cast aside my black mourning suit in favour of a tailored navy trouser suit and, once downstairs, fortified myself with coffee and toast.

Chad looked around the doorway.

'Ava, I got your text – you'll really have to reconsider. You must be there to hear Dad's will being read out. What will the Fairbanks think?'

'They're a law firm, Chad. They only think when they're paid to do it and they won't get anything for worrying about where I am this morning. What time are you doing it at anyway?'

'Eleven thirty. Ben rang to tell me it's brought back to this earlier time as he has to fly up to Washington to some meeting in the afternoon. What are you doing that's more important?'

I snatched up my keys from the table, glancing at my watch. 'Mm ... eleven thirty, who knows? You might get to see me over there. Gotta go now, Chad.'

My brother's protests receded into the background as I shut the door firmly on my way out. If my uncle could suit himself, so could I.

'Mrs Prefontaine, you cannot go in there. Doctor

Benjamin will not see you,' the normally demure Carla Lane blustered frantically.

Carla, the super-secretary, always followed you in the door before plonking your medical file dramatically on the doctor's desk. The grovelling to her boss – 'If there's anything else you need, I'll be right outside' – before departing officiously back to her reception desk. You'd wonder if she had a framed portrait of him back home, wherever that was – no rings, I'd often noticed. This eminent man the centre of her pathetic little universe from nine to five, at least.

'It's *Ms Dimato*,' I said. 'We're down to one in the Prefontaine family these days so what's the point? And I'm going in to see the doctor. You're not going to block me. He's in there and I'm seeing him.'

'At least let him complete his business with his patient.'

I sat, staring transfixedly at the floor as memories of our visits a few years back started to surface – Ethan, Bruce and me. Carla would have the play-bricks out once we showed our head around the door and Ethan would sit right there on the floor building them up until they toppled over. Whoops of joy would follow and he would look towards me for approval. Towards the end, he lost interest in his little game and preferred to nestle in quietly with his mother.

Changed the carpet, I observed, blinking back the tears.

Some minutes later, I stood facing the doctor.

He looked flustered, with his collar undone, and was sweating profusely.

'I was so sorry to hear about your father's death, Mrs – I mean Ava. I'd hoped to go to his funeral but...'

I eyed the man with cold fury. 'I didn't come in here to talk about Joe Dimato's death. I'm here about my Ethan – I've been phoning over the past week and you haven't returned any of my calls.'

'Yes, I'm sorry – things have been very hectic. Could you keep your voice down, please?'

'You'll have a lot more to worry about than the pitch of my voice if I don't get some answers. I'll be citing you for professional misconduct.'

'There has been nothing of the sort from me. I assessed all the people who came forward and they were not suitable. I was blue in the face telling that to Bruce.'

'Yeah, but I now know why and *you* had to know all along that Joe Dimato was not my father! You let my Ethan die – had I known I could have got it out of Mum who my real father was. We could have saved him!'

'No, you don't understand – we couldn't have saved him. But I can't discuss this. All of the people we brought in are entitled to their own confidentiality regarding their medical history and personal lives. Let it go, Ava, it's no good.'

'Confidentiality – you mean fucking secrets! Are you saying that you *know* – that my mum told you who my real father is and you're not going to tell me?'

Doctor Benjamin's hands were visibly trembling as he struggled to compose himself. All of his confidence and assuredness seemed shattered, his expertise seeping shamefully down the sewer. I clenched my fists tightly as if to stop myself racing forward to throttle this revolting creep who had let my son die. Expert indeed.

'God, Jesus, no. Mrs Dimato really wanted to help – but she just didn't know who the father was herself.' The doctor stopped suddenly as if the words had come out despite him.

My own manic laughter echoed back to me. I swallowed hard past the salty tears that were building up inside me.

'Oh, for Christ's sake, are you saying my mother was getting it off with so many that she couldn't say who the father was? That's not how I remember her. You're talking in riddles – bullshit!' I slammed my fist violently on his desk.

'Please, Ava. You're going to have to calm down – no, just go, you'll have to leave.'

'I will not go! There's no doubt in my mind but that you knew this all along – you couldn't but have. Don't stonewall me – oh, I wouldn't be at all surprised if my family, maybe Uncle Ben, are putting the frighteners on you, telling you not to talk to me. Please, doctor, at least tell me what you know – it can't save Ethan now, but I need to understand.' I could no longer hold back the tears.

No words passed for minutes, just the quiet sounds of my crying and the doctor trying to clear his throat as if he wanted to speak but it wouldn't quite come.

'I shouldn't tell you, Ava – but you're right. I've had Ben Dimato visit me recently. And he'd get me struck off, maybe even bumped off, a lot sooner than you could. Believe me, there are things you have to leave alone. Let it go.'

Tears of desperation stung my eyes as I surrendered to the hurt and helplessness of it all. I must have fainted, as suddenly I was sitting on the floor, drinking from a glass of water offered by Carla.

A hushed silence descended and Doctor Benjamin eventually spoke in a faltering voice.

'I'm only going to say this once and then I will deny that I ever said it. You deserve to know. Mrs Dimato took vast pain and despair to her grave – you'll know all the tranquillisers and anti-depressants that were part of her life. She couldn't help you, she really couldn't. Maria Dimato was not your mother, Ava.'

4

Ava Dimato-Prefontaine always was a mouthful, I reflected bitterly. I would need to get my office nameplate changed, again. First it was *Ava Dimato*, then it was *Ava Dimato-Prefontaine, Head of Sales*, then back to my 'birth surname' once my divorce from Bruce was finalised. Should I place a further request now – *Ava Whatsername?*

I'd gone to the good doctor's surgery to vent my anger at his deceit and in the faint hope that he might have some information on who my straying mother's lover was. These feelings were instantly deflated and rendered meaningless, my

34

whole existence to date exploding as one terrible lie into my face. I was too stunned to ask the obvious questions but Chris Benjamin rendered them all needless.

'I don't know who your real parents are, Ava, honestly I don't. I tried to get Joe Dimato to tell me but he wouldn't. Do you want me to arrange a lift home for you – you still look very pale?'

I'd waved his offer away, getting out onto the street as quickly as I could in order to get some air. Now, here I was in the nearest cafeteria calling for endless refills of coffee as I tossed trivia regarding surnames about in my head. It was as much as I could do right then. I'd gone from the comfort zone of knowing to zero in two dramatic steps – nobody's child. Was it karma, not the weather, that brought Joe Dimato's plane down from the sky and kept him alive long enough for his daughter to stumble upon his awful deeds? And what were those deeds?

My watch said twelve thirty. Inspiration and anger suddenly hit me – my beloved uncle and brother would most likely be still over at Fairbanks Attorneys going through the motions of feigning surprise and approval as each line of Joe's will was read out. Maybe would even adjourn to lunch with their legal eagles to con-gratulate and patronise each other further. My hunch about Ben knowing had proved right and I'd bluffed Chris Benjamin into confirming it. Damn my uncle – I was going over to Fairbanks right away to confront him, challenge him to tell me the truth. I ran back towards my car in the parking lot but not quickly enough to catch my cell phone before it rang out. Six missed calls. I started listening

'Ava, it's Chad, again. Can you please return my calls? Uncle Ben is blazing mad with you for not being here today – you really should have come. We're still over here at Fairbanks – just a few things to wrap up, some papers to sign. Dad looked after us both very well. I hope you'll be back at the house later on. I'd like to see you before I go back over to Cambridge.'

Damn you, Chad, I thought. Dad ... brother, it was nauseating. Just how much did he know? Well, I was coming over to find out. A cab was inching its way out of the parking lot, no passengers. Best take it, I thought – the cabbie would navigate his way through Boston's streets in a fraction of the time it would take me.

'Could you take me to Fairbanks Attorneys – they're near the Onyx Hotel down Portland Street?'

I'd got a silent one and I was glad. Needed time to think. Somehow, I felt my news was not going to be a surprise to my brother either.

'Get over it, Ava,' Chad had said the night I'd told him what Joe's medical chart had told me. 'Dad is dying. He has been your father for the past thirty-seven years. Okay, let's assume that there's someone else out there, maybe he knows, maybe he doesn't ... maybe he doesn't give a damn.'

Insensitive bastard, I thought. Careful with that word, Ava. Men! Why can't Chad see that I'm craving for another baby but am so afraid? Can he not see that knowing my past might help me? Well now, Brother, things have moved on since

36

that night at Mass General and, if I'm not part of Joe and Maria Dimato's biology where did you come from at eighteen months my junior? I hope that this news will make you sit up and take notice. Do you really think that being godmother to your two children is any substitute for my Ethan?

'My dad says I'm going there when I get big,' six-year-old Sam had said while pointing out a photograph of Harvard University. 'Gonna major in law and economics. Then I can help Grandpa and Dad at the office.'

Yes, Sam, sure, I thought – Chairman of Dimato Pharmaceuticals, go for it. Have you ever heard of a childhood or children's TV – *Barney*, maybe *The Simpsons?* How can I continue to pretend that you're Ethan when you talk like this? Now, I realise that you're not even my nephew.

My phone rang again.

'Ava, it's Gayle Fairbanks. I just felt I should give you a ring when I didn't see you at the will-reading today.'

'Oh, hi, Gayle.'

Gayle was one of my school-friends and had handled the paperwork for my divorce. Her father had made her a partner in the firm when she was in her twenties and the fact she'd got a powerful father and three brothers to compete with in the family firm gave us lots of common ground to moan about when we got together over several glasses of our favourite white wine in one of the many bars surrounding the Government Centre. Though, in fact, by now the inferiority complex in this Boston firm was on the male side, as Gayle was not one to be outshone by anyone.

She continued: 'Ben and Chad and our boys are gone up to the Onyx for lunch. I didn't sit in on the will – just looked round the door once to say hi to you, but no sign.'

'No, Gayle – I had other things to do. Can we talk again soon? I'm just caught up right now.'

I didn't want her about when I tackled the Dimato men.

'Ms Dimato,' came the voice from behind as I peered around the hotel dining-room. 'Table for one?'

I could not put a name to the familiar face. 'Eh, no – I was going to join up with my uncle and brother here but I can't seem to see them...'

'They left a little while back – are you sure I can't offer you anything?'

I was already walking away, shaking my head in reply

I dialled my brother.

'Chad, we need to talk – urgently. It's very important. I'm here at the Onyx – where are you? Are you going back to the office?'

'No, something else has come up. I suppose you want to know about the will now. Well, it'll have to wait – you should have been there, you know.'

I bit back my anger at his indifferent formality. The way he saw it, I'd missed a business meeting that I could have attended. Bury the reality that I would have been sitting in on the reading of a stranger's will – and with strangers. Well, I wasn't

38

going to let it go at that.

'Chad, I really need to talk with you – can you come over this evening, please?'

'I'm afraid I can't, sis. I need to do something for Ben right now – it's to do with congress. Then, I need to get back home this evening. Sam has been bombarding my phone all day long.'

'And what about your other child, Sabrina, she might want to see you too,' I said stiffly. 'Only she's female and disposable – like me. One minute you're pinging away at my phone demanding that I get straight back to you and now you can't even tell me when we'll run into each other again. I thought you were all geared up to recite Joe Dimato's last wishes to me. What's changed?' I couldn't call him Daddy any more.

Silence. Then: 'Ava, you were with Chris Benjamin this morning, weren't you – when I was trying to connect with you?'

I stiffened suddenly, recalling the doctor's terror of Ben Dimato. I was not going to tell my brother the rest of it just yet, though I sensed that it wasn't going to be a surprise. I wanted to be face to face with him when I told him.

'Are you having me followed, Chad?' I asked. 'And what might he tell me that seems to be unsettling you so much?'

'What he might say wouldn't bother me at all, Ava – it's how you react to it that worries me. You got new information about Dad recently and it's affecting you. It's only natural. But sit with the information for now – don't go doing anything silly.'

The edge to his voice convinced me that I could no longer wait.

'It's not just about Joe Dimato any more – it's about Maria, too. There was no other man.'

The pause was agonising. Damn you, I thought – why don't you lead off for a change?

'Okay, Ava. So, let me see – if Benjamin told you the full of it, you'll now be able to conclude that you're adopted. Isn't it better to know that they both wanted you instead of thinking that you were Mum's sordid secret?'

'Chad, I'm done talking with you. I have a birth certificate naming Joe and Maria Dimato as my parents. There's something wrong here. You seem to be in denial – fobbing it off as adoption. You know something and you're lying.'

'They are your parents. I couldn't care less about your birth certificate – I'm sure Dad did what was best at the time. Okay, I can see where you're coming from – he might have broken some rules. But he took you on as a baby because he wanted you – that's adoption to me. Now, do you want to hear about his will?'

But you *do* care about birth certificates, Chad. *Your* birth certificate is very important to you just now. You're going for election, aren't you? And you need to be an American citizen for at least seven years. Otherwise, you won't qualify, don't even get to start...

'It's not top of my priorities right now,' I answered. 'I guess you get to take over as head of Dimato Pharmaceuticals and I get to keep my job, the family home, a share of the company, maybe twenty per cent of the profits...' I stifled an impulse to yell out at my brother – how often had we both sat silently as Joe Dimato patronised us with his boring narration as to how the family jewels would be carved up when he departed to his rewards in the sky. Stop talking about when you're dead, Joe, mother would say while placing the bourbon decanter and glass on the coffee table in front of him. It was if Joe Dimato's death was always destined to be the Main Event. Nothing about his wife's succession rights – what if she outlived him?

Chad's silence confirmed that I'd got the gist of it about right.

'Have you not considered, Chad, that people mostly adopt or take other people's children because they cannot have their own – you're younger than me. Where does that place you?'

I recoiled abruptly as his voice came back instantly, laden with menace.

'I'm moving forward, Sister, not looking left, right or backwards. You hear that? You keep probing, but if it affects me or anyone else in our family – I'll make sure you pay for it.'

Yes, Chad was moving forward all right. He had November 2004 in his sights for some time now – the day he would secure that seat on the House of Representatives. Congressman, the Right Honourable ... really should have made it last time out. It wouldn't help if some wayward woman, particularly his sister, were to send the wheels crashing off by exposing sordid family secrets.

'Fuck off, Chad! How dare you threaten me?'

The phone went silent and the chill of fear I felt

41

seemed to propel wintertime Boston swiftly towards the Arctic Circle. Seems you knew all along, *Brother*, I laughed silently. You're a mushroom, Ava. Kept in the dark for ages and then smothered in shit. Yeah, a mushroom – that's about it.

5

Standing in the kitchen of Priscilla Compton's house, I looked out onto the gardens that I knew intimately from my childhood days. Images of Frieda and me surfaced in my mind.

'We're playing families, Mum,' she would announce impishly when her mother came to enquire about the missing bedclothes. 'This is Meg – she is Ava's baby; and this is Wayne – he's mine.'

It was clear that Frieda's mother doted on her. 'Okay,' she always conceded.

'Coffee, dear?' I jerked back instantly from my reverie.

'Yes, please, Priscilla, I'd love some. I'm just admiring your garden – you've never changed it.'

'Hardly at all – you've had some fun out there. Frieda was on earlier. She and Nigel have been down in Rio on vacation, but you know that.'

I had phoned ahead to tell Priscilla what my visit was about. She had seemed a little reticent, I thought.

The Comptons had lived down the road from

us for as long as I could remember. Their daughter, Frieda, was my best childhood friend and it was a friendship that survived through our teens, graduations, marriages, my divorce. There were two older brothers, much older than Frieda, so her mother was getting on when she was born. 'A gift from God and so unexpected, just when Mum needed it' – that's what Frieda would say proudly about herself as she regurgitated her mother's words. Her youngest brother, William, was aged sixteen when she was born and both brothers were in university by the time we became friends. The boys never paid any heed to us, some gentle teasing apart. It was like the Comptons had two families – that thought suddenly jerked me back to present. They weren't the only ones, were they? And that was why I was at their house right now

We sat down at the breakfast bar, a large bowl of polished apples between us.

'I've been replaying the past over and over since you rang, Ava. I don't know if I can help. I thought of you as nothing other than Maria and Joe's child all these years. This is a hell of a shock.'

'It's that all right.'

'And your birth certificate seems like a regular one, with their names down as parents and no indication of adoption?'

'No, no indication whatsoever.'

'Well, perhaps that's the practice abroad.'

'Abroad?'

'Wherever you were born – Scotland, wasn't it?'

'Scotland?' There it was again. Martha had said the same.

'Well, we always assumed it was Scotland. Around the time you and Chad came along your father was expanding into Europe. He was setting up in Scotland – Edinburgh, that's where it was. By the time they came back, you and Chad were in tow.'

I tried to suppress my exasperation at her innocence. As a mother of three, couldn't she see the absurdity, the coincidence of it all? Maria Dimato didn't like to travel; she had no curiosity about the world at large, found it hard even to leave the house. Suddenly she gets a fondness for roaming – when she's pregnant, of all times? It just didn't add up and I cursed myself for not seeing the light earlier – the people with the real answers could no longer speak.

'Priscilla, we both have American birth certi-ficates – we couldn't have been born anywhere else but here.'

'Oh! We never knew that, Ava.'

'Did you never ask? Did my parents never make a single reference to the matter over the years?'

'Ava, I just accepted that your mother was very private – no, reclusive. She never mentioned and I never asked. Maybe there were things I should have noticed but Frieda was just a baby and my attention was all taken up with her. Joe Dimato didn't like questions either – people around here knew that and left them alone.' She paused for a moment. 'You could ring the local registry office – the certs might be forgeries. I–' She paused again, a look of uncertainty on her face.

'Yes?' I prompted.

'There is one thing, Ava, but I'm almost

44

reluctant to mention it, it's so odd–'

'What is it?' I asked, my heart beating faster.

'I rang Robert while you were coming over. I don't know if he's rambling, but he's now saying he was never convinced that your mother went to Scotland. Joe came back once a month but nobody saw Maria, except my Robert – that's if his eyes were seeing right. He says that he saw Maria passing our house in Joe's car a couple of times during that period. Of course he couldn't see if she was pregnant or not. Imagine him coming up with this after nearly forty years! He could be right that she never left America though ... she suffered from agoraphobia ... people who get it bad rarely leave their houses, let alone the country.'

And there it was. As easy as that. The lead I was looking for.

It struck me then how much my mother had been robbed of in her life. It was true – she never went out if she could at all avoid it. She existed in her husband's shadow. Why the hell didn't she fight back? An old familiar rage erupted inside me. Childhood memories came flooding back: me rushing home to tell Mum that Mrs Compton was mad and her husband Robert was kind of strange too. She used to go on the swings and see-saws with Frieda down at Franklyn Park, get herself covered in sand. And Robert, once he climbed so high in a tree he couldn't get back down. Trying to retrieve a football for some boys in the park. Then, aged six, I used to cringe at the possibility that *my* parents would ever behave like that. The Comptons have never grown up, I thought, they still think they're children. Why wasn't Frieda embarrassed at them? She seemed so unfazed by it all, even giggling at the zoo-keeper's disapproving looks as we passed through his turnstiles – 'Probably thinks we're tramps sleeping in the park,' she'd say. My nanny would stare condescendingly at them when they dropped me back at the house from the play-ground. 'Always keep your clothes clean. Look at the dirt of the parents, the example they are showing their daughter – how will she grow up?' Mum giving them a vacuous wave from the living room as they drove away from the house. How it finally dawned on me that the Comptons weren't mad at all and that it was me who was missing out. Chad and me. The pleadings, the tears.

'C'mon, Mum, it's really fun, I know you'll like it. We can have a picnic too ... it doesn't matter that you can't drive – Mrs Compton said you can go in her car.' No, Doctor So-and-So was coming over later and Mum would get in trouble if she wasn't there. I usually got to the playground dollar-laden and with bags of candy but no Mum. Some of our nannies were good and joined in the fun and I would merely nod when some unsuspecting child called them Mrs Dimato. Couldn't do that with Martha Jones, though, all the way from Jamaica and dogsbody to Ben Dimato for as long as I could remember. She was my favourite.

'I'm sure Robert did see her, Priscilla. That's the answer. It was a set-up. She never left home.'

I bit my lip as I battled with the notion of forgery. Happened all the time with driver's permits and passports. Even experts found it hard to tell the difference sometimes. Home birth.

'What does Chad have to say about it all?' Priscilla suddenly asked.

'Eh, he doesn't know.' I reddened at the ease of my deceit. This was a no-go area with my brother – on this one, he was something like that silly illusionist who enclosed himself in a box for weeks. Impregnable, unreachable, Chad had mapped out the next two years carefully. Congressman in 2004 and ready to assume his uncle's mantle when he stepped down from the Senate two years later – he had it all worked out, it was his destiny. I shuddered at his coldness. It just wasn't the Chad I knew.

I got to my feet.

'If you think of anything else, you will let me know, Priscilla, won't you?'

'But of course. It's just that I'm not sure there's anything else to be added. Robert will be home soon. You can wait for him, if you like – but that's all he has to say about it in any case. I must say I was astonished when he said he suspected something funny was going on all along. Never breathed a word to me. Trust a man not to bother to mention something so vital!'

'You're telling me,' I sighed. 'Well, Priscilla, I'll run along now – maybe ring Frieda later. I'll let myself out.'

'Hi, this is Bruce. I'm not available right now, but if you leave a message–'
I ended the call. Better to talk direct to the man – my man, I thought wistfully. Five years and no

47

contact. He could be married again. Amazing though. The same message, most likely the same phone. Eventually, sleep overcame me and visions of Bruce Prefontaine began to creep beneath the duvet, working their way up from my toes towards my thighs until they seemed tinglingly real, alive...

It was the summer of 1994 and Bruce had just joined Dimato Pharmaceuticals as a sales executive. Dad was 'grooming' me, as he called it at the time, to be Head of Sales or Human Resources. Couldn't make up his mind what I was best at, he'd say. Oh, he had great patience in showing me the ropes but both Chad and me quickly realised that as long as he could walk, he would not let go of his role as the decision-maker, the final say-so. Experience was to teach me ways of getting around this: get the thing done, Ava, if you think it's right – tell him afterwards. A grunt usually signalled his grudging approval that I had done okay, that he wasn't needed for all the decisions, that it was possible that someone other than him could steer his beloved company through choppy waters. It was when you got it wrong that you were treated to his rage and conviction that he was the only one who could do anything right.

It was the spring of 1994 when Joe Dimato passed me a list of people to be interviewed.

'Honey, will you take charge of this? We need two – no more. And, remember, you're not a social worker – I don't want you falling for crap from another no-hoper. I'd really do it myself, but I just can't fit it in – anyway, you have to ground yourself again, take some responsibility here.'

I gritted my teeth silently. The disaster with Linford Jones was too fresh in my mind and the retraining in interviewing skills that Dad had forced me to do. Another dirty job for Ava, I thought. I will be saying no to at least eight people on this list and will be able to see the despair registering in their eyes. Sales always attracted egotistical people who hid their insecurities underneath layers of bravado and bullshit.

Dad had beaten a quick retreat before I could object. I bit down on the urge to chase him, suggest that Chad get involved – get stuck in, be given his share of the dirty jobs for a change. I'd only be accused of cowardice, opting out. My brother would probably be wining and dining some affluent customer, maybe another foreign trip. He was welcome to it, boring farts – but it was being taken for granted that hurt.

My interview with Bruce could only be called hilarious. It wasn't that I found him instantly attractive – he would barely reach my eyes in his stockinged feet. No, it was just that he was funny, seriously funny.

'Ms Dimato – Ava,' he said, squinting at my name badge, 'this is your opportunity to take your company to the next level. Corporate advertising. The World Cup is being held in America this year.'

'I know that, but it's soccer, Mr Prefontaine – what's so exciting about that? Come August, most of America will have forgotten about it and it will be back on the minority channels, in the graveyard slots.'

'In America, maybe – but we're talking world-wide here. Can you imagine, we'd have your name up in lights around the globe!'

'How could a game of soccer possibly increase the sale of medicinal products? This is absurd.'

'You've got to have belief – faith, Ms Dimato.'

Bruce made the final cut solely because his exuberance stood out against the dullness of his opposition.

'Your office will be on the second floor, Bruce. Remember now, there is a six-month proba-tionary period and your job is to support sales in America. We'll plan your holidays for the World Cup. That way, you can take in some games and maybe work off this fantasy regarding medicines and football.'

There was an unexpected flutter of excitement when I saw Bruce standing at my office door a few days later.

'Hold on, Chad – look, I'll ring you back. What is it *now*, Bruce? Lost your way again? This is the fourth floor – your office is on the second.'

'I know, I know, Ava – but this is your lucky day. I've got two tickets for the Giants Stadium: Italy and Ireland. I've checked it out – we can get a flight down and be back up before the night's out. You can't let this one pass – you've got to come.'

I surveyed this jack-in-the-box, hoping that I did not look too much like Joe Dimato when he disapproved of something. Couldn't the guy take a hint? I didn't date my employees. What was he, five-five at best? Neatly cut brown hair and you had to look very closely to see if he needed to use a razor. Suits came from the major chain stores – Bruce had not yet made it so big that he could walk down Boylston Street and flash his credit card in some designer boutique. Quite suddenly, the words appeared to tumble involuntarily from my mouth as if controlled by some magic celestial force.

'Okay, then – I'll come. Let's hope it will shut you up for good about this football.' I felt my cheeks burn at my own folly. God, what would I do if the staff found out? My father, worse still. He looked little more than a boy.

'Michael J Fox, when are you coming back to my future?' Laura had giggled at her own little joke when Bruce first appeared in the company canteen.

This was part and parcel of indoctrination into the headquarters of Dimato Pharmaceuticals and some more timid employees were known to regard it as mobbing, bullying. You had to learn to 'cut it' quickly or you would otherwise be submerged.

Bruce passed the test with flying colours.

'Coming right away, princess! Now – how was that?' he responded, eventually allowing a stunned Laura some air from his lingering kiss.

The chorus of approval went up immediately as the office prick-tease was silenced for once. Bruce, alias Michael J Fox, had arrived and was now 'one of the boys'. Later attempts by Laura to rename him 'Prince' sagged like a lead balloon.

Bruce had established his ascendancy and he was not giving it back.

His passion for soccer was later explained. In his own words, he was a promising left-winger whose budding career was curtailed by serious injury. He'd even been over to England, the 'world powers' at this game, he would say. It was at Portsmouth that he snapped his cruciate ligament.

It took a fair bit of posturing from me to feign interest in all of this. I probably had one of those 'cruciates' in my leg too but there was little fear of me snapping it as I nursed my way gently from treadmill to Jacuzzi to hot spa in the Marriott Long Wharf gymnasium.

'Faggot's game,' Laura said a little unconvincingly as we sipped our coffees one morning in the staff canteen. 'Look at them, their ponytails and all that. Give me a good quarterback any time.'

A voice came from the table behind us. 'Aw, Laura, c'mon! Why don't you just screw him and have done with it – I mean, look around you, he's the only one you haven't – sorry, just joking.'

Laura turned to face Melissa, the newly hired temp. Her stinging retort appeared to become stuck suddenly in her throat as she paled and kicked out at me under the table.

'Don't lash out at me, Laura, it wasn't me that said it.' Too late I saw the reason for her kicking and now he was looming large over me – Joe Dimato. And, in the time it took to say the words *my* company, my father and I had the canteen to ourselves.

'You must think I'm running a fucking charity here. It's not just about you lounging about painting your nails – the staff take their lead from you, follow the example set for them. You've been in advertising, finance and now here. But the same pattern continues – I'm telling you, Ava, sometime soon, I'm going to blot out the fact that you're my daughter and you won't be involved here any longer.'

He paused to signal at the canteen assistant hovering nervously in the background. 'Bring me the usual,' he barked out authoritatively.

Red-faced, I saw my opportunity to divert him. 'Look, Dad – I'm sorry but you really need to cut down on the greasy food. You've been piling on the weight.'

'Yeah, the rule-book says you start with a good healthy breakfast – except I can't get any food where I live in the morning. Tell this to your mother. And as for you – you're changing the subject. That file you lost – have you found it yet?'

I rose from the table. 'Still looking, Dad.' It was time to get away, try to reassert myself with the staff. The whispers would already be spreading. Daddy's little girl gets it in the neck – again.

Back in my office, I looked at the Italy scarf that Bruce had left behind. Clever boy, this guy. Joe Dimato was very proud of his Italian roots and his brother Ben played this card expertly when consolidating his support base in the cut and thrust of politics.

I picked Bruce up at his apartment in China-town.

'You don't mind, do you?' he had asked. 'I'm still getting physiotherapy on my legs and I've been told to keep away from the driving – it can stiffen you up all over again.'

'Poor baby!' I said mockingly. 'Which one is yours?' Then I noted the vacant space reserved for Apartment 203.

'Garaged, right now. Blown head gasket, at least that's what my mechanic says.'

'Look, Bruce, maybe I'll park here outside your apartment. We can go down by the subway, maybe take a cab. I can pick it up at the end of the evening.'

Bruce manfully tried to educate me in the rules of soccer during the game. He didn't need to. Winning or losing was the name of the game and the faces of the Italians as they left the Giants Stadium told its own story. The Paddies had won out.

'Mightn't be such a good idea to go to Pizza Hut, now?' he asked.

'Not at all. I'm well used to solemn Italians in my home. We'll go.'

Bruce did not try to kiss me as we parted later at his apartment and I felt a tinge of disappointment at not being invited in. Naturally, no girl with Italian blood would have given him his way on the first date ... but I was curious. How did this little enigma live? Apartment in the cheapest part of town. Maybe he was bluffing, didn't even own a car. It would have been nice to poke my nose about the place for just a little while as long as he didn't take it as a signal that he could get into my pants on our first date. How did he eat –

what'd be stocked in his fridge? Did he keep the bathroom clean – sleep in a double bed? Maybe some photographs would enlighten me?

Not tonight. We said our goodbyes outside his apartment and he turned suddenly as he made his way up the path from my car.

'Maybe we could do this again ... take in a show or something?' he said, shuffling his feet expectantly.

'Yeah, I'd like that. Only, keep it out of the office.'

'Understood,' he said as he bounded away up the steps.

The first kisses arrived soon after, although I still hadn't got past Bruce's front door. Previous experience had taught me that boys generally let you know quite quickly what they were after but not my Bruce. *My Bruce.* What's happening here, I had to ask myself? I was acting like a teenager – the secrecy of it all. It was scarcely credible that I was falling for this guy – yet I could not deny it was happening. Was it Ava's rebellion against the stuffy protocol of her family? Sure, he hasn't even registered his interest – just hanging out with the boss's daughter makes him feel good. That was until the night of the lost file...

'Ava, Chad here. Dad is going wild up here. The Carney file is still missing. We've checked all the offices, but no sign. That leaves the vaults and he wants it found before tomorrow. He said he reminded you about it two weeks back. We can't let Maurice Carney win his case against us – it'll set precedent and we'll have a flood of litigants against us if some information in that file makes its way into the public domain. You know how careful we need to be after the Woburn case and all that. I'd love to help but I have a meeting later this evening. Can you bail me out on this one?'

'When you put it like that ... you owe me one, though, Brother. I've been taking fierce abuse from Dad about this – and we both know it was you that had it last only I didn't record the switch.'

It took just a mention of Woburn to get Dad quaking in his boots. The extraordinary incidence of leukaemia occurring in that area had led a number of families into the courtroom with a major chemical company that they held responsible. Dad would selfishly curse the families involved and linked even the most genuine and minor complaint to opportunists piggybacking on the hysteria prompted by Woburn.

Purists and nitpickers, as he would call them. Yeah, and litigation addicts also, too lazy to get up off their butts and go out to earn their own money. Much better if you get some wise-guy lawyer to pounce on the most harmless discrepancy and blow the thing up into a 'Woburn Balloon'. And Woburn was much too close to Boston... It all became too much one stormy night on Beacon Hill as Dad's volcanic temper disintegrated and bedlam took over.

'I'm home, honey,' came the boisterous voice at the doorway.

It was *that* voice, the one that confirmed that Dad had dropped into the Sevens Ale House on Charles Street on the way home. It usually indicated that there was some mini-crisis afoot in Dimato Pharmaceuticals and Dad had retired to the bar at the end of it all to vent his frustration and launch into a cognac-fuelled tirade at the imbeciles who had spoiled his day.

What he was to find when he got home was to overheat the cauldron completely.

'What is it you're watching, ladies? I could really do with a coffee and a club sandwich, if anyone is offering. What ya watching?'

The housebound Maria Dimato whiled away her languid days by reading and TV-watching. Her choices were invariably linked to some social injustice issue or, if you preferred Dad's opinion, people with 'chips on their shoulders'. She had her own little DVD stash and social crusades such as *Twelve Angry Men* and *Erin Brockovich* were among her favourites. It soon dawned on Dad why he was going to have to make his own sandwich.

'That's that fuckah Travolta and his propagandist junk about Woburn ... turn the fucking thing off and get me some food, woman!'

Maria was lost in her film and barely recognised his presence. It was time for her daughter to intervene.

'The movie, it's called *A Civil Action*, Dad, and I happen to be watching it too. Now will you calm down – or go off to your bed and sleep it off.'

'Don't you tell me to calm down, you little bitch! The man's a dancer, not an actor. Strutting his stuff in *Grease* and what's that other one – *Saturday Night Fever* – and then disappears into

57

nowhere once he gets too fat for his dancing shoes. Then he resurfaces with a new faith and this bullshit and expects all of America to sit up and listen. Yeah, a dancer, that's what he is and now he wants people to accept him as an actor. If it weren't for gullible women like you pair, he'd still be squeezing into some dancing costume, lining out with the faggots in some backstreet playhouse. I'm not having it. Switch it off! Now!'

Joe Dimato was not the only one about with an acid tongue, who could give it a lash when the going got tough. There were two sides to our relationship and my meek acceptance of his ritual humiliations at work contrasted sharply with my fierce resolve to resist his bullying nature spilling over into life out of the office. I often cursed myself for not being more focused at work – then I could really tell the Dimato men to stuff it: Ava was taking no more of their abuse and sarcasm.

Right then, I felt my pulse racing, the nerve ends tingling. I was scared stiff of my father but I'd be damned if I would allow him to talk to my mother like that.

'Faggot... I knew there was something I needed to tell you and now you've gone and reminded me. Thank you. You're to ring your brother the minute you get home. You could always take the phone up to your "bachelor" room upstairs and leave your wife and daughter to get on with it here.'

There it was, two in one go – the whispers about Uncle Ben that wouldn't go away and the aging Lothario that was my father reminded of his own retreat from the marital bed.

My father went crazy, smashing furniture, hurling insults. My mother started to sob and I put a protective arm around her. This seemed to enrage him further. Crystal glasses came crashing towards us. I scrambled across the wooden floor, splinters of glass cutting into my palms. I made it into the hall and I heard his laboured breathing as he chased me up the stairs. I ran as fast as my legs would carry me into my bedroom and locked the door. Should have left out the innuendo about his beloved brother, Ava – he'd have just about coped with the rest of it. He started to kick the door down as I dialled the police number.

An hour later, the MSPD car departed from Beacon Hill with the words of the rookie police officer ringing in my father's ears.

'You're not above law, Mr Dimato, regardless of your money or your senator brother. Go back indoors now. You've got your wife to thank that I'm not taking you in on a public order offence and you won't bully me from doing my job. Go back inside, Mr Dimato.'

The smashed TV screen lay on the floor as an uneasy peace was restored. Mum assured me she would be okay and I made my way back to Lewis Wharf, stung by the savage cruelty of my father's words.

'I suppose next thing you'll be inventing is that Ethan was poisoned by that water! Get to fuck out of my house! You were always a bitch.'

The 'morning-after' apology came all right but it could not remove the stain, that further confirmation of the smouldering intolerance of anything and anybody that did not fit in with the way the Dimatos viewed the world. And the cruelty they would use to enforce it.

6

Maurice Carney's grievance was about the instructions on one of our medicinal products. He claimed that he was alerted by a change in the leaflet, suggesting that the drugs involved should not be taken by him. While he had no evidence of any physical consequences, he was claiming for worry and distress and would not let go easily.

I made my way to the vaults in the late evening and, bingo, the wandering file was located with surprising ease. I was about to ring Chad when I felt a hand reach out to touch my hair.

'Bruce, I'll kill you – what are you doing, coming up behind me like that? You scared the hell out of me. I'll–'

'Hush,' he said, placing a finger across my lips while moving downwards with his free hand. Straight into my pants.

'What the – stop it, you hear – right now,' I heard my voice say, though my legs were parting slowly.

'*You* stop me – I can't – I've been waiting too long for this.'

The order never came and in seconds I was reaching backwards to seek out his manhood, bringing it quickly to a hardened state. Then he was in me, clutching my breasts, caressing, talking.

'Of course I can feel it, Bruce – but hurry on,' I panted looking out at the light in the corridor. 'What if someone walks in on us? Gosh, it's lovely, but please come quick.'

'Aaaaah!'

A little later, I turned off the highway in the twinkling light.

'Where are we going?' Bruce enquired, stroking my hair.

'To my place, see what more surprises you've got. No need to keep you a secret any longer.'

'Let me get this right. You've hired this new fella for sales six months ago and now you want to marry him? We hardly know him – God knows where he came from. Can you not rethink this – give us all a little more time?' Joe Dimato mopped the sweat from his brow.

'No, Dad,' I said firmly. 'I'm marrying Bruce. It's as simple as that.'

Dad looked at me over the horn-rimmed spectacles that he used for reading and seemed to be considering my spirited defiance. He'd sampled it before when I jilted Kyle Wahlberg a matter of days away from the altar.

'But you can't do this,' he had said at the time. 'Dammit, Ava – all the arrangements are made. People are coming from everywhere. How am I going to stop them?'

'If you had been listening, you'd know that I

wanted none of this fuss. I'll help with the phone calls and all that. Perhaps you'll have to entertain some guests that are already on their way.'

Kyle had taken the news much better than I had dared to hope. I thought he was secretly relieved. We were both only twenty-one and had allowed our families to dictate the pace of our relationship. Neither of us was ready. The Dimatos might have come from Italy three generations back but the culture was still omnipresent. I resolved that minute that Ava Dimato would make her own decisions from there on.

Two years later, Dad and I were to clash again when I told him that I was buying an apartment in the city. Three hundred thousand dollars. I had raised two and I wanted him to loan me or give me the balance. Preferably give. He was to sit, head in hands, completely outraged, silently trying to comprehend all of it. In his world, parental wealth was passed on when occasions such as marriages and deaths took place. In the meantime, you were provided for, everybody looked out for each other. This did not include a single daughter leaving the family home without reason.

But I had reached a point where I felt wholly suffocated by Mum's illness and melancholia – any sort of meaningful exchange with her was out of the question. I comforted myself with the thought that Mum had retreated to a safe place where Dad could no longer hurt her. Joe Dimato survived the atmosphere, using a diet of extra–marital affairs, late homecomings and early morning departures from his bachelor bedroom. Best not to disturb her... the insomnia... even though she could do enough sleeping for the rest of America. That's how he protected himself, avoided acknowledgement of his wife's state. Keep her at home – we'll all muck in. That was his solution – I did not need to be told that his true motivation lay in not having a member of the Dimato family permanently institutionalised. Keep it in the family. I had to stand my ground firmly – I needed my own space. I was going and two hundred would get me something down near Franklyn Park. Little dangerous down there for a woman, though, muggings, car-jackings and that sort of stuff. Definitely not an address that would allow him to boast about where his daughter was living. Wordlessly he had written the cheque for one hundred thousand dollars, and soon I was signing on the dotted line for Lewis Wharf. Never said if it was a loan or a gift and it was never raised again.

Now, aged twenty-seven, I stood in front of my parents, meeting my father's stare firmly. My mother looked absently out the window, rubbing her foot intensely over some imaginary stain on the polished living-room floor.

'Aren't you going to say anything to your daughter, Maria? You haven't even met this guy.'

'Leave Mum out of this, Dad. It's a bit late in life for you to start taking your wife's counsel on matters like this. Bruce and I are going away to get married. We're going to Rome alone, apart from Frieda and Bruce's friend as witnesses. We can have a small family do when we get back. Is that settled, then?'

Maria Dimato stood barely over five-foot tall and looked much older than her fifty-five years. Depression had reared its ugly head early in the marriage and a lifetime of medication and hospital admissions had taken their toll. She had gained a near-encyclopaedic knowledge of the hospitals surrounding Harvard and doctors and nurses at the Beth Israel and Brigham & Women's Hospital were on first-name terms with her. She was all-American and came from the Cape Cod area of Boston. Her real name was Marie but Dad had his own interpretation of it – so, as he kept saying it, others fell into line over time. Born Marie Keller, now Maria Dimato. Mum married Joe aged twenty and ten years later I was born. Nothing to do with family planning, she said – just how things turned out. Taciturn was how her doctor described her – she never used two words where one would do. Maria would take all hospitalisations and medication changes in her stride but any mention of counselling or therapy was met with a battening of hatches as she foreclosed once more on her emotions. I stopped crying after her fourth admission, not wanting to make a scene in front of Chad. I was twelve, and my crying had a habit of kick-starting my brother, only he'd take it much worse. He'd got so bad one evening the doctor was over with Mum, he'd suggested to Dad that he watch out for his son – maybe get him to a child counsellor.

'I'm pleased for you, dear, if this is what you want,' my mother said in a barely audible voice.

'You leave her alone now, Joe. No more inter-fering, you hear?'

'I suppose I could buy him a bloody car as a wedding present,' Dad said angrily. 'Imagine, at his age – he hasn't even got a bloody set of wheels. I never approved of you buying that apartment – that's where all of this started, isn't it?'

Bite your lip, Ava. At least he hasn't mentioned the money. You're marrying Bruce and Dad's insults won't change that. He'll get used to it – he's going to have to.

At the time, I was basking in the warm glow of our almost nightly passion at my love nest. The one that Dad had part-financed. We used to lie there exhausted, sweating, chatting about silly little nothings before we'd start all over again. Sometimes we'd just take off walking down the Waterfront Park in the middle of the night, holding hands, talking and making plans.

Now, I'd once again got my way with my domineering father by facing him down. He'd just taken one further look at the eyes that burned brightly with determination. Chad was to tell me later that Dad was fazed by what he called my bloody gutsiness once I set my eyes on a target.

'Thank you, Dad,' I whispered as I contem-plated another victory out of the office against the bewildered old man.

Joe Dimato, head of a major international company, owner of property throughout the state of Massachusetts, unable to handle his feisty young daughter at home. The downside was that he'd hover like a predator at the office for God knows how long as he awaited my next blunder. Then it would be payback time. I'd keep it from Bruce until later on. When we were in bed together. Then I'd say yes to his proposal – a lady needs to have a sense of timing, I reflected longingly as the sensations swept through my body.

'You have to marry them to know them.' That's what Frieda would say, repeating her mother's words with conviction. And so it proved.

Once Dad had realised there was no stopping me and that I was going off to Italy to get married, he'd started pushing Naples forward as the place I had to go. Relations still down there, his sister Laverne and my cousins – they'd look after me, make sure I was okay. I had to let him down gently but firmly – I was going to Rome and he was free to invite anyone he wanted to the post-wedding bash. That was the compromise and there was nothing Joe Dimato could do but look helplessly towards his wife in frustration, hoping she would say something that would steer his headstrong daughter towards his course. But it wasn't Maria Dimato's course either and she became an unknowing ally to my cause through her reclusive nature. Suited her down to the ground. She could absorb it as part of any old day without having to step out of her insulated shell.

I wore a knee-length cream dress and a single flower in my hair and Bruce was dressed in a blue linen jacket with beige chinos. Frieda and

Bruce's friend Richard were also dressed casually and we giggled happily as the priest mistook them for the couple exchanging vows. We retired to a discreet trattoria in backstreet Rome where we shared wine, pasta and ciabatta bread. It was simple and relaxed once Richard got the message he would not be parking himself in Frieda's bed on this or any other night.

'Understood, but it's your loss,' he said indifferently. Richard obviously didn't twig or maybe didn't care about the wedding band on my friend's left finger. She and her husband Nigel had flown in on a different flight. He had taken himself off sight-seeing around Rome.

'Let the prick keep on dreaming,' she whispered when he was out of earshot. 'My Nigel will have the bed well warmed up by the time we wrap up on this. Rome is not just for newlyweds, you see.'

We got back to our suite a little later than planned, Bruce going straight to the bathroom.

'Just going to powder my nose' he slurred unsteadily. 'Isn't that what the ladies say?'

And that was exactly what I discovered him doing. Powdering his nose. Cocaine. I had seen it often enough on the social circuit.

'Bruce, I don't like what I'm seeing – where did you get this?'

'It's just a harmless bit of coke, Ava. I'm really bunched after all the travelling and Richard said it would help with – you know,' he said, eying me lecherously. 'It's purely recreational. I'll do you just one line, no more.'

'Okay, you're on. Only, no more secrets, you

should have told me. I won't play the prude tonight.'

We showered together the following morning, making love slowly, tenderly as we sudsed each other over with soap. I felt reassured and warm at this gentle comedown from the frenzied, sweaty night we had just spent, feeling a vague sense of disquiet at the unnatural energy and abandon that had kicked into my husband. At Harvard University, drugs were freely available on campus and you could take your pick right up to heroin. I shuddered at thoughts of students who had succumbed to the temptation. There was at least one suicide, I could not remember her name – but the face, yes.

Then there was Aaron Wilson – everybody knew he was out of it but did nothing about it. Found dead on a sports field at the college, overdosed on heroin. A rambling statement from the authorities about the counselling facilities the college had made available but which Aaron had never come to. Then he was buried and that was it. The resilience of the young – we were all laughing and joking within days. Not a word about Aaron. His family most likely were grieving and distraught in some distant point but there were college parties to be got on with and the smell of cannabis permeated the lavatories. The school would occasionally take a stand by suspending or expelling somebody but a week later that person would be back. A letter saying you were in rehab or attending a counsellor, that's all that was needed – and the students knew it. Somehow, right now, it seemed all wrong.

I wanted Bruce and me to be a family, have a family.

'Promise me one thing, Bruce,' I said later as I lay quietly in his arms.

'You got it,' he murmured.

'Well, it's really two things. Next time you need a booster, I want you to be at least seventy and it will be Viagra.'

'Deal – look, I'll flush the stuff down the loo right now if you want. Honest, it was just a one-off, the excitement of it all.'

A week later, we were back at Logan International Airport and there was Dad, all smiles in the welcome lounge. Damn him, most likely he'd examined my travel tickets before I left. I might have thwarted his plans for a society wedding but he was not going to let his only daughter's betrothal go unannounced. It was all set up, taking place at the Onyx Hotel down Portland Street on Friday. There was a full sit-down-and-be-served menu for two hundred guests early on with evening buffet invitations going out to a few more hundred who were down the pecking order of importance. Very convenient, Dad, right next the State buildings, the courthouses. The fat-cat officials at the main bash, with the pen-pushers surfacing later on, most likely having wound up their working week by retiring to the pubs at lunchtime. Many of them were in the pocket of my Uncle Ben – with their tankards full, they'd be drooling and grovelling to this famous man in no time. I gritted my teeth silently in the back of his Cadillac as he went down the list of people who were attending.

All that was left to be done was for Bruce to contact his family – get them to come over. My new husband nodded sheepishly in agreement – he worked for this guy, what could he do?

As it turned out, it wasn't so bad at all. The man above intervened on the morning of the do and the good senator was rushed to Massachusetts General Hospital with chest pains. The bulletins came thick and fast in the early part of the day. No, it wasn't a heart attack but they were detaining him, just to be sure. It seemed his absence had a liberating effect on the guests. Like they were unshackled, able to be themselves. Only Chad seemed put out – without Ben to do the introductions, he retreated towards his reticent self. Probably sees this as a step backwards in building his political profile, I thought. If only I could make my brother see he was not cut out for the job – that he should stop being an impostor, get his own life, get away from moulding himself so much in his uncle's image that it would become too late for him to rediscover his own self. Anyway, right then he was only twenty-five and it would be at least a few years more before he could throw his hat in the ring to claim the coveted prize: his uncle's senate seat. He would come out of his sulk in due course and a few beers later he was mingling happily with ex-school friends, the political cloak cast away for the moment. It helped that Dad had hired the Victor Mendoza Quintet for the evening. They were one of the more renowned jazz outfits in the city and there was nothing like jazz music to get my normally staid brother to cast off his inhibitions. Even dancing with Laura now. I laughed as I imagined the future boss of Dimato Pharmaceuticals waking up to find the office secretary and tartlet in bed beside him. He'd be mortified, wouldn't he? Chad with his easy smile and downbeat but charming way. Isabel, then his on-off girlfriend, sat stony-faced in the background, her face a picture of indignation. Laura let my brother out of her clutches and she sauntered towards me.

'Hiya, Ava, you look fabulous, how was Italy – did you see the Pope?'

'That I did, Laura, all the newlyweds gather outside in the square each Wednesday to get the papal blessing. I just couldn't fit him into my schedule for a personal meeting. He understood – maybe next time, he said. No, it was lovely. Today isn't half-bad either – thanks for coming.'

'Don't mention it. Say though, just to tip you off. There's a bit of tension out there between your father and your Uncle Jeffrey. I'd watch them if I were you.'

Won't I just, I reflected. Jeffrey was Mum's only brother and he hated Joe Dimato with a passion. 'My sister's name is Marie,' he would say, '*Marie* not Maria. Why does he need to sabotage her name, demoralise her further? What's up with him? Most Italians have moved on from that domination bullshit years ago? It must kill him that neither you nor Chad look a bit like him.' How right Jeffrey was to turn out on that one.

'Bruce, where have you been? I've been looking everywhere for you.'

'Tucking Richard into bed. He's out of it again. Doing lines of coke and drinking Jack Daniels all day.' He was all apologetic. 'C'mon, I'd better bring you over to my parents. They look a little left out.'

'Bruce, I hope you weren't...'

But he was gone from me. I resolved that in future I would keep him away from his sleeping buddy upstairs.

'Ethan – that's what we'll call him. Isn't he just fantastic, all eight pounds of him!' We were both besotted with our baby son. He just missed our first wedding anniversary by one day. It was time we started looking for a home and moved out of my apartment. I wanted Bruce to do it before my father got involved.

'Let's just enjoy our little boy, Ava. The apartment has wagon-loads of space and a rooftop garden. It will be time enough to upgrade to something bigger when he's walking.'

'Bruce, will you just go looking? I'm not having our baby on a third-floor apartment and he's definitely not going up to that garden on the roof. He could easily fall off.'

I surveyed our little bundle of joy protectively and started fantasising about the rest of my life, our lives – Bruce, Ethan and me. Maybe I could buy a place on Beacon Hill, fulfil my dream. And my new home would be so different to the house that I was raised in. It would be a place where peace, joy and children playing would exorcise my memories of my soulless mother casting her dismal shadow of despair across that otherwise beautiful place. Ironic that, the Dimatos making their money from medicine while the matriarch slowly and emptily wound her life down on a cocktail of prescription drugs that numbed her to the house's beauty.

This was not a time to be maudlin or self-pitying, I reminded myself. I was going to be a different mother.

Frieda came over from Cape Cod to do godmother and Chad displaced Richard who was now gone off the scene. 'I am not having him, Bruce,' I said firmly. 'I've seen you with that look on our wedding night and I've seen it many times on Richard since. Not where there's a baby involved.'

Dad was immensely proud of his little grandson, insistent on showing him to almost anyone he could. I kept Bruce as far away as I could from the Dimato social circuit, sensing his suffocation at the overpowering nature of it all. Dad had put promoting him on his agenda, now that he was family. Yet again, I had to ward him off – there was no way I wanted my Bruce to lose his own identity for the sake of the Dimato family. Not like Mum, a poor American girl so besotted that she allowed her birth name Marie to be modified by her husband as he pleased until everyone accepted her as Maria. More Italian, you see.

It was thus that I was quite happy to accompany Bruce to the South End on weekend nights. Jac's Café for food, Wally's for the music, all cheap and cheerful. I was glad to accept Laura's suggestion that her mum would be available to babysit Ethan – it beat dragging him across the city to a grandmother who just wasn't up to the job.

'Ava, I don't want to alarm you – it's probably nothing but that little boy is not gaining weight. You're breastfeeding, aren't you? I'd be inclined to check it out.'

Sitting later in Doctor Benjamin's office, I didn't know whether to curse or canonise Laura's mother for telling me.

I beat a hasty departure home to Mum to break the news, while Bruce went to his family. We needed to gather information quickly, see who could help us out. I was stunned by her numbness to it all, the vacancy of her look.

'Is that all you have to say, as a mother yourself? "Yeah, sure – get me an appointment though I don't think he'll take me",' I mimicked my mother's droning, listless voice. 'Oh, Mum, can't anything get through to you? Why are you so detached from it all? We're talking about my son, your grandson, and you're just treating it as another day out with the medical profession. How can you be like this? Is there anything left on this earth that will get you going?'

'I'm really sorry for Ethan, and you too – but you can't go on abusing me like that. I said I'll help – what more is there I can say? I see you're crying, Ava, and I'm crying too, inwardly, though – not just now but for many long years. God is punishing me for my sins – sins from my past. It's a terrible thing, it really is.'

I looked at her confusedly. Mum confessing that she had feelings? My silent, stoic mother, lost in her own little world as life passed on by? She hadn't said that much in years. It was soon forgotten, though – I was now a mother myself and I simply didn't have the time to be analysing or questioning this distant woman's feelings. Ethan was very ill and he needed me right then – and I needed so much to pull him through this.

It was only the beginning but my mother's words were to resonate cruelly some twelve months later as Mum linked Priscilla Compton's arm as they left the graveyard.

'A terrible thing, Priscilla, terrible, to lose a child like that.'

Resentment towards my mother rose like bile above my despair. She really deserves a cheque in payment, like the priest. Maybe I'll send her one. Make it out to *Maria Dimato, Professional Mourning Services Ltd.*

7

'Hello, this is Bruce Prefontaine. I see you coming up as a missed call on my phone.'

I choked suddenly on my words as the memories came flooding back – the first meeting, the intimacy, joy and then despair. More despair as Bruce plunged headlong down the cocaine circuit afterwards. Still, I'd rung him now and I would have to persevere, get it all out.

'Bruce, it's me, Ava. I really need to talk with you.'

Silence, then sounds of Bruce clearing his throat.

'God, it's you – Ava. Eh, I don't know what to say right now. It's been what ... maybe six years? That's a long time... I'm not sure I would have rung back had I recognised the number. In fact, I don't think this is a good idea at all. We didn't exactly part on the best of terms.'

'How have you been since?' I shuddered as I recalled witnessing the disintegration of my husband in the two years after our son's death.

Looking back, I should have recognised the glazed look as our efforts to save Ethan became increasingly frantic. Sometimes, I'd join him on his *Jesus Walk* up Bunker Hill Monument to see what inspiration he was getting up there, looking out across the city as if this was his penance for Ethan's illness.

'Try holding him for a while, Bruce – he's your son.'

I put it down to tiredness, I looked a right mess myself, but the cruel truth about my husband's decline had yet to come out. The 'white lady' had become Bruce's best friend, his crutch, and experience taught me to recognise that it had been happening right under my nose, even in Ethan's final days.

We'd retreated to the Children's Hospital in Boston once it became apparent that there was nothing we could do except wait for the day that our little boy's suffering would pass. He was too young to say it but it was as if my little boy was deciding for me where he should end it all and it was the spark that lit up in his eyes when he mingled with other little children at the hospital that convinced me. Bruce made no objections, just moped about in a daze, letting everybody else take over.

'Can't you just sit still with him, Bruce, with me – the doctors say it's not going to be much longer,' I pleaded as Ethan's little grip on my thumb became weaker. 'He knows we're here, Bruce, I can feel it. Don't keep walking in and out – hold his hand, stop holding your head.'

He would ground himself for a few minutes but his wanderlust always resurfaced, coming back and forth until even the medical staff became exasperated with him. I just placed my head on the pillow alongside my little boy, not knowing how long I'd lain there until I realised that there was only one hand gripping. I was putting his little hand between the blankets, kissing his still forehead when Bruce returned.

'It's over now, Bruce. It's over for little Ethan and you've missed it. You can sit with him now and explain it, if you like – tell him what's up those steps that's more important.'

It was all I could say as I got up to leave the room to grieve in private – away from the corpse of my little boy and the shell that was my partner.

It was to blow up completely when Bruce ended up in a cell at the New York Police Department courtesy of a complaint by one Joe Dimato. Sixty thousand dollars. Embezzled by Bruce. Right under my nose. His rejection of the promotions that Dad offered him now made more sense – he was quite happy to stay where he was, where he had access to the company's financial account. Where he could be away from the office without being questioned as he slithered off to keep himself 'topped up', as the counsellors would say. It took all of my powers of persuasion to get Dad to drop the charges. Bruce was so badly down the gutter that he wasn't below using the death of our son to escape a custodial sentence.

'Fuck you and your family! They wouldn't help us when we needed it most. I'm not going down for this – your precious family are not without their secrets.'

You got that one right, Bruce, I thought, snapping back to the present as his voice came down the line.

'I'm clean and I want to stay like that,' he was saying. 'Look, Ava, I know you will have a reason for ringing me, but I'd really like to hang up. I have a future now – and my past is not part of it.'

'Don't do that, Bruce – don't hang up on me. I really don't know who to turn to. Something bad has been going on for a very long time and I can't turn to my family ... it might help me, us, understand why our Ethan died.'

'Do we not already know that? He died because he was a very sick little boy and nobody could help him.' The drug-filled venom and bitterness seemed gone. 'That's the way I look at it these days, Ava, the way I need to look at it. Ethan's not coming back.'

Tears welled up in my eyes. So positive about it all, I was beginning to resent him – regret the call.

After an eternity Bruce spoke again. 'I don't

want to turn you away if it's really important but you'll have to give me some idea where you're coming from. Even then, you'll have to leave it with me. I'm not jumping into any quick decisions on this.'

Bruce listened while I filled him in with what I knew.

'Jesus, Ava, do you hear what you are saying? It's not adoption, so it can only be something illegal. Think about it – why did they pass you, maybe Chad, off as their child? Did they buy you, perhaps kidnap you?'

Alone later, I chided myself for ringing him. Selfish one, that – and pointless, too. I mean, Bruce was hardly likely to produce my mother, perhaps my father, from a lucky bag, was he? I had nothing to go on, not even a name. I seemed to be setting out from nowhere and going towards the same place. I looked out into the street from the crowded café. People from all walks of life scurrying by – mothers and children oblivious to the pain of Ava Whatsername. I paid up my bill and trudged wearily back towards the office, contemplating defeat before I even started. I resolved that this was one that needed a long chinwag with Frieda and I was going to set aside some time to talk it through with her – away from the goading presence of the Dimato men, 'moved-on' former husbands. Where I could slow down my fast-racing brain and work it all through with my trusted friend.

But back at the office there was someone waiting to bring up my frenzy all over again.

I eyed Ben Dimato frostily as he swivelled round

in my chair, a photograph of Ethan in his hands.

'I see you've let yourself in, made yourself comfortable, Uncle Ben.' I had no way of disguising the rancour in my voice. 'Could you put my son's photograph down, please?'

'Whoa, Ava, don't let's get off on the wrong foot – I was just passing by, thought I'd drop in. I believe that Chad has filled you in on the details of your father's will?'

'He mentioned what was in *Joe Dimato*'s will all right.' I stared pointedly at the giant figure in front of me. Over six foot and ample-girthed, Ben was at least three hundred pounds. Devoted himself to public office from an early age as a campaigner, congressman and, lastly, senator. Never married, he was now sixty-nine and had announced that he would not be seeking a further term in office. He was bowing out. He had taken Chad under his wing some twenty years back as a spotty-faced teenager in preparation for the day Ben would step back into the shadows. My brother Chad, graduating in law and politics at Harvard University – subjects that he would never have taken had he not come under the influence of the man now sitting at my desk. Your love of art, Brother – languages, travel, all forsaken at the beckoning of this sinister figure. Even my powerful, arrogant father shrank in the presence of Ben's hulking figure – the man's sense of certainty, omnipotence. Born to win, without a doubt. My office felt cold as I recalled Doctor Benjamin's fear of this man who had the key to unlocking the family secrets. A key that he would never hand over to his niece.

80

Ben was talking again.

'You don't need to take this as badly as you have done, Ava. You're right set up for life. Chad is as shocked as you are about all of it but at least he's not being so selfish. Maybe you're over-looking a few things here – Chad could easily see this as an opportunity to be recognised as sole heir but, no – as far as he is concerned, you're his sister in spite of all this. Let sleeping dogs lie – it's not going to get you anywhere.'

'I don't think it's all that simple, Senator,' I said acidly. 'I've been looking at photos of my parents over the years recently. Damned if I can see any resemblance between them and Chad. Now, take Dad. Isn't it well known that he comforted himself in many a female bed while Mum was locked up in the asylum? Wouldn't it be a fine turn-up if we established that Joe had some genuine offspring?' I laughed manically. 'Woweee! Now that would certainly shine a torch on who might be the true heir to Dimato Pharma-ceuticals!'

'You were always the joker, weren't you?' Ben laughed heartily.

'Why was Joe cremated, Ben, and then you and Chad running off suddenly to scatter his ashes – where was it? Cremation – that was unexpected for a man who was so Catholic he never left his rosary beads behind, despite the line of trollops he bedded.'

Ben was struggling to remain off-hand, care-free. 'What's it matter to you? You've got your information from Doctor Benjamin. Do you really think the world out there gives a damn where you came from? You're here, that's what counts.'

'I care and I got the distinct impression the good doctor won't be talking about it to anybody else. Seemed very afraid of you – he certainly didn't volunteer that you'd been leaning on him – I had to get it out of him. You like scaring people, don't you?'

'Naw, I'm just a big pussycat. Do you not remember – I even had you fooled when I dressed up as Santa for the charity bash.'

I grimaced. Didn't I just? Right now, I felt like I needed someone to pass me the sick-bag as my childhood adulation of Uncle Ben came to the surface. More than willing to bring us down to the Public Gardens on a Saturday when Mum wouldn't and Dad couldn't. Always protective, he became my hero when I became aware that he had rescued me from an attempted kidnapping in the park when I was just four. In the newspapers it was – a photograph of me in my pushchair, Ben alongside. The senator, demanding more policing in the park and asking that they be on the lookout for the woman that tried to snatch me. Seize the opportunity, Ben – keep yourself in the limelight, the people's hero. Get that planning-permission hold-up out of the way, more street lighting for mugger's alley, even your niece's trauma. Anything that will keep your name in the *Boston Globe*.

A lightning bolt suddenly shot upwards to my brain. The kidnapper – the woman in the park – she was never prosecuted although she had nearly made it through the gates with me in her arms. I cursed my innocent acceptance of Ben's explanation that she was most likely a random opportunist who had made a quick getaway on the day. I cautioned myself to keep my desire to know in check – no point asking the secretive senator, I'd merely be alerting him, giving him time to muscle out other possible sources of information. No, it would wait.

'I'd safely say that deception has surfaced as the strongest family trait, Senator.'

'Deception is part and parcel of politics but you're crossing the line into something much more profound and dangerous. I'm not sure I'd be able to protect you if someone were to be embarrassed by your spying.'

I could feel my face burning. 'All those stories you told me when I sat upon your knee, Uncle, tucking me in at night when your brother was too drunk to do it. My, you've got to see many countries in your day. Learned anything about the baby trade on your travels?'

Ben was on his feet now. The intimidation hung like sulphur in the air-conditioned office and I felt my hands hot and clammy.

'It may have escaped your attention, what with all that has been going on lately: Chad will be aiming to take his place in the House of Representatives come November and I'll be making sure that he gets it. I'm advising you to back off and you ought to heed my advice. Doctor Benjamin has taken an extended holiday – just to save you the bother of going around there again. I'll let myself out.'

I asked Laura to cancel the morning's appointments and turned the fan on full power as I reflected on the lock of Joe Dimato's hair nestling in an envelope under lock and key. Knowledge is useless unless you have proof and it was Ben who taught me that. I dismissed the idea of going into Boston Police Station to make a complaint about my threatening uncle. No evidence, no witnesses – nothing to report except people's all-cowering fear of the senator, my fear too. I could imagine some bemused officer noting down my experiences, trying to work out where the crime was. A family spat, that's all it was, and what with Ben's cosy relationship with the Massachusetts State Police, he'd know about it before I was twenty strides out the door of the station.

I waved at Bruce as he peered around the coffee shop we had agreed on in the Back Bay. A little off the beaten track, I'd made my way there on the subway. Since Ben's visit, I had a sensation of being followed, occasionally dismissing it as my frayed nerves acting up. Didn't see anyone, just that claustrophobic feeling.

We hugged lingeringly and Bruce broke free first.

'You've obviously been having a terrible time,' he said with genuine sympathy in his voice.

'Tell me first how you've been getting on, Bruce. It was selfish of me to contact you like that, putting myself first.'

'Well warranted in this case. Okay, where do I start? I don't do drugs, I'm a born-again Christian – only joking. No, I'm just clean and it's great.'

I laughed heartily when Bruce confirmed that he still had no set of wheels, could easily see himself as getting through life without them. No sign of any grey hairs and a little fuller than when I last saw him. Eating better, still less than one-fifty though.

'A soccer coach, no less! I shouldn't be surprised. Have you moved on in your love life too?'

Bruce looked at me directly. 'I've told Arlene that I'm meeting with you, and why. I've been with her eighteen months.' He couldn't have made it clearer and I was not going to ask him if there were any little feet pattering around. The wounds were still too raw.

Later he said, 'I've been thinking about what you told me and in some way it all fits. I'd imagine that the only thing that matched Joe Dimato's craving for a child was his ego. Couldn't admit to the world that he was taking on another person's child. No, it had to be full ownership with our Joe, plain and simple. Then you were born and he didn't get the male he wanted, went back and did it again within two years.'

I struggled to comprehend what my ex-husband was saying and found myself resenting this changed man. A wave of self-pity and anger came over me. Poor Ava, whistling around in the dark trying to find out who she is and where she's from – so desperate she's dim enough to call up this weed, this addict, to help her find something, somebody that he cannot possibly find. Better to remember him as the pathetic little creep she dispatched from her life with a paycheck for his treatment bill, the little squirt who discovered an even higher place at the Prudential Centre Skywalk to look down in all his cocaine-filled wisdom on the city below. Yes, Ava, that way you won't have to acknowledge the robust, confident Bruce sitting before you. Doing something he always wanted – new life, new partner. Moving on. No set of wheels but having them can be difficult at times, especially when they're coming off, spiralling out of control. Like my life, I thought as I met his direct gaze.

'That's not a very nice thing to say, Bruce – heck, at the very least he chose me.'

'Mmm, it wasn't meant to be hurtful, but you need to be thinking of all possibilities if you're to get where you want to on this. Maybe he picked your mother and you came along after – if he did it that way, he couldn't control whether he got a boy or girl. Even someone as high as I was on cocaine could see how he treated women at the office. Your mistakes were always magnified – anything went wrong at Chad's end, it was pure bad luck. I'm sorry if this comes across all bad. Look, some people I know in recovery have been through this relative-hunting thing. You seem to have so little to begin with. I'll talk to them – see what can be done to get you started.'

Later, as Bruce was leaving, he turned back quite suddenly. 'Eh, where *do* you want to get to with this, Ava?'

'Don't know. Maybe I'll be able to answer that if I get there?'

'Yeah, maybe – though there might come a time

you'll have to reassess, decide whether it's worth it.' He stopped suddenly. 'There I am, intruding now – I'd best stop giving advice – I'll be off.'

Bruce had changed, of that there was no doubt. For the better too, but not for me. His feet were planted firmly on the ground despite the fact that I felt his sadness when he spoke of Ethan. I felt resentful of Arlene and fought with myself for being like this. You don't even know her, Ava, and Bruce is entitled to be happy. The loss of his little boy seemed a lot simpler from his side of the fence – not less sad, just simpler. I told myself the difference was that he did not have to deal with the all-invasive presence of the Dimato men whether swarming round on a daily basis or merely their threats lurking ominously in the background. The provocation of it all keeping the cauldron simmering for the castaway woman who simply wants to know who she is. Not too much to ask.

Bruce, your parting question was silly – yet the simplicity of it was meaningful. Where could this possibly bring me? It could do nothing for Ethan and it could not alter the gene pool from which I came. These people, whoever they are, gave me away voluntarily – there can be no other explanation. Most likely, I wouldn't want to know them, a cautioning voice thundered in my head. Let go, Ava, let go.

8

During the months that followed, I sat forcefully down on any urges I had to follow through my craving to discover the real Ava. What if I wasn't even Ava, let alone Dimato? Over many long, tearful phone calls, Frieda was my rock during this time. It helped that she was childless herself. I could see myself resenting her if she had any. Nor would she have had the time or energy to indulge me. No, it was good to have it this way.

'Do you remember all the times we played happy families with our dolls, Frieda?' I asked through misted eyes. 'All the make-believe and a much bigger, truer story right there in the background. I can't forgive them, and having to look at them all the time, Ben and Chad – it doesn't help.'

'Have you thought about taking a little time out from the company? You need a break and you can afford it too.'

That was true, I reflected. But money wasn't the problem – stay too long away from the job, Ava, and you might be told you're not needed. It was something about the pitiful weakness of my home-alone mother that kept me battling to keep up there near the helm of the company. And I reassured myself that I was needed there too. I found myself lying to Frieda.

'Yeah, the Dimato money.' I winced at the

cynicism in my voice.

Frieda came back firmly. 'It's money and it's yours, too – send some up here if you feel you have too much. Say, you're welcome to come down for a few days – we're both working but don't let that hold you back: there's lots to do.'

Through these conversations, I got to create images and fantasies of what might have happened all these years back. Some were pure junk – the idea of Mum kidnapping me from some maternity hospital was appealing from a sentimental angle but didn't hold water once the wineglass was set aside. Nothing like the theft of a baby to hold the world's attention. It would be flushed out in no time. The Dimato men – now they could be persuasive and had the money to be so. It wouldn't be too hard to target some desperate girl – she mightn't even have wanted the money, just the secrecy that her plight demanded and, boy, would it have suited them.

'It isn't fair that they are getting away with it, particularly Ben. I just know by his smugness that he was involved – most likely set it up.'

Frieda continued to listen but there were realities that she would not let me evade.

'I really think you need to go to a therapist first, that's if you're going to go through with this. You are also starting in a complete vacuum with not an iota to go upon. Think about the therapist: they do have their place – it'll strengthen you for whatever decisions you need to take.'

'I do have a lock of Joe's hair,' I said conspiratorially.

'Yes, Ava, and I've told you. All that proves is

that you are not his and don't bring up your mother again. Exhuming her now would merely prove what you already know. Plus, your uncle and brother are not even disputing it. It's a waste of time.'

I didn't want to embrace the frankness of my friend's words. It was Chad's identity that needed to be protected. God forbid that this American citizen, aspiring congressman and senator, would have his cover blown by his big sister Ava and her need to know. They weren't even worried about that – it was that her need to *tell* might surface, and if she told, they'd all start to wonder about *him*.

'They're not prepared to put any trust in me, Frieda – I just want to know, that's all. If they stopped being so selfish, they'd easily see that I'm not going to be going round to the *Boston Globe* with news like this.'

'I think they know that. But you're dealing with two men with their eyes on a prize. You might be discreet but what if your real mother, perhaps father, was less so?'

'Why did he cremate Joe, especially when Mum was buried? Running off with his ashes!'

'Well, what does it matter? You already have your evidence – your father's hospital chart.'

'Gosh, you're right – Joe's hospital records – they would show–'

'Ava, the hospital would issue a confidentiality statement – Joe Dimato's records are private. Look, get yourself out of the Dimatos' heads. Stop torturing yourself with all this speculation about their motives. It's very simple – they don't want you to know and they're not going to help you in any way on this one. See that therapist.'

I hated that she was right. Even if I pulled it off, all I would get is revenge. Embarrass and humiliate Ben, Chad – but I'd be no nearer meeting my true needs. It all looked so futile. I winced at Frieda's reminder that there were countless lost souls on the same mission as me and going nowhere. Then there were the ones who found something and didn't like what they saw.

'Yeah, I remember reading about this fella – down in Alabama, I think. Traced his father after a ten-year quest, pulled out a gun and shot him stone dead. Just like that. Has lots of time for reflection now, when his cell door closes at night.'

Later, I laughed at her parable. Could easily be true for all that. I was glad I apologised for my insult that she sounded like Ben, trying to get me to drop it. That wasn't fair. Frieda was merely trying to protect me.

I examined the contents of my fridge, kicking out at it when my frustration boiled over at my hunger yet revulsion at foods that I normally liked. Eat, Ava, you must eat.

Four in the morning, I noticed, as I sat in my unit kitchen, looking out at the lights of downtown Boston in the distance, another little piece from the cheeseboard making its way towards my mouth as I twirled my small knife theatrically like a conductor's baton, waiting to plunge it with rage towards my foes. Where have my taste buds gone to? I feel like a mouse in the dark.

Trudging towards the emptiness of my bedroom, asking myself what Bruce was doing right now. He was a light sleeper back then and, when he woke, things generally began to happen. I needed badly to hold this moment if sleep were to come my way for what was left of the night.

Becky Knox looked up at me and then the clock as I walked across the open-plan offices on the fourth floor. Twelve noon. 'Chad's inside, waiting for you.'

'Thank you, Becky, back with us for a few days again?' I asked politely.

Becky was in her fifties and it was a poorly kept secret at the office that she and the late Joe Dimato were lovers. It was over thirty years since I nearly walked right in on them one evening and heard the groaning behind the door. Only my training in social etiquette and my fear of upsetting my father had saved me from witnessing the whole of it.

'Who's that?' I heard. 'Hang on – don't come in here. I'll be out pronto.'

I waited till he emerged.

'Ava, it's you. You shouldn't be sneaking around the office at this hour.'

'But school closed half an hour ago, Daddy, and you weren't there. You promised to pick me up. What was the noise?'

Right now, Becky was looking back at me defiantly. 'Laura had to take a few days off. Some domestics she had to sort out. I'll just be here for two days. I left a reminder on your desk about the days I worked last month. Accounts say that my payments haven't gone through yet and then I find the paperwork still on your desk.'

I mumbled an apology and grudgingly acknowledged to myself that I was a little too mature to be holding on to blaming the other woman.

'I'm sorry, Becky – that was careless of me. I'll put it all through this evening and include tomorrow too.'

Well, at least he's not sitting in my chair, I thought as I looked round the door of my office. Thirty-five now, I thought, same age as Dad was when I was born. Once he was old enough to sit up, Dad had ensconced him in a real leather swivel-chair in his office. Something about men and their 'sons'... Bruce's words came back with a bittersweet taste. It was no inconvenience for Joe to mop up after Chad's endless pirouettes in the chair resulted in the inevitable throw-up or perhaps a fall on the deep carpet. I had a nanny for such crises. Chad had abandoned sports in high school, having endured one too many disappointments on the reserves' bench. He didn't seem to care – by that time he was besotted with Ben and Dad did not seem to object to the moulding in Ben's image. Chad had few peers in the high-school debating leagues and his research of the minutiae left me exhausted at the thought of it. He sometimes seemed like Bruce, but without the white powder. He was tall, blond and good-looking and girls were not in short supply – but only as a diversion to his main agenda. Politics. Got married aged twenty-eight and even then Uncle Ben managed to tarnish the happy occasion by labelling it as a good political decision.

'C'mon, Mum, let's go for a walk in the gardens,' I would say. 'Do you really want to hear more about disarmament, the third amendment?'

I was usually met with a 'You go yourself, the tablets have me drained' response.

Off alone on my walks with only my cell phone for company to text my frustrations to Frieda.

'What is it you want, Chad? I'm not really in the mood to talk business. And you won't talk family.' Just that minute, I was determined that any ruffling of my feathers by this brother would not let my resentments resurface.

'Nothing like that,' he said quietly. I noted that he had dropped the 'sis' label that had become quite pronounced during recent encounters. Taking care not to rankle. 'I believe Ben has been giving you some grief lately. He means well – I told him he was crossing the line, to lay off you.'

'Is this the bad guy, good guy routine, Chad? You coming in here to soften me up? Forget it – it'll probably please you, though, to hear that I'm not up to caring much about it all right now.' I turned away as I didn't want him to see my tears.

I seemed to be living on a diet of coffee, cheese and wine for weeks, interrupted with snatched sleep and violent dreams. Sometimes it was me doing the violence, coming back as an avenging angel on mothers who abandon their children. Strange that, the mother bit – I couldn't yet dump my anger on the man involved. Couldn't give him any more than a bit part in my exhausting reconstructions of times past. Most likely, he planted the seed, then ran. Isn't that what men do anyway – hit and run, go to ground rather than face up to the responsibility of it all? I just couldn't turn even a small piece of anger away from the woman who most likely carried me for nine months and then left me with the shell that was Marie Dimato.

I so wished that Chad wouldn't shut down so forcibly on the probability that we shared the same boat – I couldn't accept that he had no curiosity, no desire to unravel the past. If he sided with me on this one, together we would wear Ben down – he'd just have to give in to us, tell us what we deserved to know. However, I was letting it go for today and a strong voice in my head was saying that was where it belonged. Every day.

'I'm relieved to hear that, Ava – honestly I am. I've had many sleepless nights too, but I want to get this seat, go on and make senator later on. I've been working towards it for so long. Maybe after the election, we could look at it again...'

I thought of it, five months until election time and the Democrat party had chosen him as their candidate. The posters were already printed, the image consultant was hired and Chad had done his media training. Even had gone into his walk-in closet over at Cambridge while Isabel followed obediently in tow casting *Thou shalt not wear* items into the charity-store bags.

'You'll always have a reason for not wanting to look at it, Chad. Don't come in here building me up with false promises. I've had enough disappointments lately and am leaving it for now. Anyway, with your uncle keeping tabs on me, you'll most likely be first to know if I go back on my crusade.' I had reached the end of the road but saw no harm in prolonging his anxiety a while longer. 'I was thinking of taking some time off work, Chad, I'm really spent – nothing to give right now Maybe go down to Cape Cod to Frieda for a little while.'

'That's okay – there's nothing going on fire here. You will keep me posted where you are, though? I mean, no, this sounds bullshit but we've only had each other for all these years. Knowing that you're all right is important to me.'

I was prompted to reply that what he was talking about was an easing of his conscience but my talk with Bruce had helped. It wasn't just that he might be under pressure from our formidable uncle. He might quite simply be terrified at the thought of facing the realities involved. Look at that guy with the big mop of hair from Simply Red – can't stop himself giving interviews to the world media about how much he hates his mother, leaving him alone and all that. Brosnan too – went back home across the water, looked, found and snapped the book shut.

'I think I know what you mean and I know you care. I'm just sad that you're closing down on all of this. And, don't worry, I'm not taking time off to go foraging. Even if I did, there's nowhere to start other than the Dimatos. Mum and Dad are gone. I'd need to take Ben down to Brooklyn Bridge – hang him up by his feet, and I'd still get nothing. Don't think I haven't dreamt about it, gone though all the fantasies.'

My brother was gone now and his crap about

looking at me for the post of chief executive rang hollow in my ears. Laura had shown me the 'head-hunting' file, the high-profile achievers that Dimato Pharmaceuticals would be chasing once my brother took up his seat in Washington DC and began the second phase of his ascent to power. Had to show his voters that he was there for them. You'd be looking for someone with the right pedigree and the right track record, Brother – not some lovelorn female that couldn't even see when the man in her bed, her husband, was fleecing the company.

9

Bruce Prefontaine had come into my life at the time of the World Cup and was gone four years later when it shifted to France. It was at this time that Dad discovered that he was siphoning money from the company account and he took great relish in contemplating that the would-be soccer star might watch the games from a prison cell. Better still, not get to watch them at all. He was missing the point – Bruce was seeing everything then through a haze of cocaine and it was eighteen months later I wrote the cheque for his rehab. God, he had put me through so much, but a small piece of me clung to hoping that we could rebuild and be a family again. He was the man I had chosen, who'd stirred me, tugged at the heart – something that none of the many young 'suits' and well-honed men that I got to mingle with on the Boston business and social circuit had done. But Bruce had damaged it all so badly. When cocaine lifts its nose off the glass to speak, it can come at you with unbearable cruelty.

'It's on your side that the incurable disease exists... I'm going to get out of this – it's just a passing phase.'

In the end he came to me for help and with great difficulty I set aside my resentment towards him to give him his chance. But he didn't know that the treatment centre had groomed me to be hard on him.

'You have to distance yourself from him, Ava,' the counsellor had warned me. 'Okay, so you're putting up the money for him – but don't let him think it's anything more than that, the last time his wealthy wife will help him out. Yes, I can see you've still got feelings for him but hide them – for now at least. I've sat with this fellow and a lot of his denial and complacency is linked to knowing that Ava will bail him out. In time, you'll see you've done him a favour. Tough love, even coldness – you've got to do it – it's for him too.'

I'd rehearsed it alone. 'This is a one-shot opportunity you're getting, Bruce. There are no conditions other than, when you come out, I will not be involved with you or supporting you in any way. You may not move to the far side of the world, but I do hope you will put *some* distance between us. Even if you don't and decide to live across the street, I'm cutting you out of my life. You're going to leave me alone from here on and if that means unleashing the Dimato boys on you, I won't hesitate.'

Bruce didn't get to see the tears when they came but he'd listened and that was how it worked out as the days, months and years passed since that crisis meeting. My husband descended from his cloud-hunting mission from the vantage points above Boston; there was talk of one of our sales people bumping into him down Connecticut way, but it lapsed. Bruce's name was taboo at the office, forbidden. The forgotten man, his best parts buried deep in my heart, banned from resurfacing because there was one wound too many to allow healing, reconciliation. Life had to carry on.

Laura had one day summoned up the courage to pop a question that nobody else seemed to have the courage to ask. 'What are you doing these days for ... well, you know...'

I smiled inwardly at her blushing face. This wouldn't faze her under normal circumstances but she had lived through my tragedy and I was her employer, sort of. We were out on one of these teamwork-building evenings at the bowling alley. In a strange way they worked. The only rule was that insults hurled at these bashes didn't count and there was no comeback, no retaliation. Joe Dimato had it sussed out that the insults always came from the can't-hack-its, the plodders working off their failures at the last round of promotions. 'Take it on the chin,' he would say to his managers. 'I'm paying you extra for that reason. Keep telling them that they form the backbone, the heartbeat of Dimato Pharmaceuticals. I'm looking at Eastern Europe where we'll be able get the same thing done for a pittance some day. Then they'll know that they had it good.'

'Aw, c'mon Ava, you're holding out on me. You know exactly what I'm talking about – it's the four-letter word.'

'Not on your wavelength at all there, though I am trying. I mean you could be talking about romance, sexual intercourse.'

'Typical, sure sign of the snob coming out. I'm not talking HarperCollins Dictionary here – are you fucking anyone these days?'

Nothing like getting a bit of fun out of Laura first, before you confess.

'Mind your own business. Why do you ask?'

'Well, see that cute guy over there – he's been asking a lot of questions about you lately and he's looking over right now. His name is–'

'I don't want his name, thank you very much,' I replied, meeting the gaze of the man across the floor. Same age as me and that was about all we had in common. I needed to sabotage any match-making ideas Laura had, though I admired her honesty.

'Well, actually – there is – no, conditions, first. You get your walking papers if this comes back,' I said, fingering my glass of wine.

Laura immediately drew an imaginary zip across her lips and I filled her in roughly with what needed to be told. No names, though.

'Geez, Ava, do you think his wife suspects?' was all that she could muster.

Ethan's illness, coupled with Bruce's addiction,

meant that we never got around to trading up from my bachelor-girl apartment. He was out of my bed and apartment for nearly two years by the time he went into rehab and the sheer nuisance he made of himself during that time left me too exhausted to acknowledge that I was missing sex. However, along with the peace came the solitude and I became aware of the unease I felt alone up at Lewis Wharf. On a whim, I went back home but did not sell the apartment immediately. I needed a haven. I did not want a relationship at any cost but there were times when I needed somebody, something – just to hold me together. I was just thirty-one and the burgling of my apartment was to bring me into contact with Paul Briscoe, State of Massachusetts Police Department. A single phone call from Ben had brought the borough's second-in-command to look over my modest apartment.

Paul perfunctorily showed me his State Police badge as I showed him into the rooms.

'I haven't lived in it for a while,' I said apologetically, noticing him twitch his nostrils as his eyes scanned the room. I immediately thought of Gene Hackman, Popeye Doyle in that film *The French Connection* – that was it. A bit unkempt, unshaven, could do with someone to iron his clothes. Supposed to be based on a real character and it could easily have been Paul if he came from that era.

'Alarm switched on?' he asked as he opened and shut doors aimlessly.

'No, there's not a lot of value here, I mean, financial value. I just never thought. What would a thief want with portraits of my family, my little boy?'

'Mightn't want them at all, probably taking them away for closer examination. Or to see if some hundred-dollar bills are stuffed down their backs – you'd be surprised how many do it. Were the frames valuable?'

'Not terribly so. Look – I'll make you a list. Some matter, some don't. I'd really like to get them back.'

'You might think this is a strange question but would you pay to have them returned? This scumbag may be gagging for his next fix – we hate this part of it, but some thefts of personal items cause so much pain to people – we sometimes get results through our network of informants.'

I found myself guessing his age – fifty, maybe. Wondered did he have a woman at home – if he did, getting her man to work well-groomed did not seem to be a priority. Second-in-command – this man looked more like a low-grade detective and yet there was a confidence, an imperturbable air that gave him a feral presence, a charisma. No 'We'll get you your stuff back, Ms Dimato, we know your father and uncle well' patronising from this guy. Untamed by the monotony, the brain-numbing forensic procedures of police work.

'Wait until we see what you come up with first, Officer Briscoe.'

Paul was back within two days. 'Looks like we got all of it back, mostly intact,' he had said. 'Fifteen-year–old girl. Obviously was disappointed with her haul at your place. Walked right into it when she was doing another joint up the road. A right Aladdin's Cave back at her squat. She's already back on the streets – there's no place to keep her. Misdemeanour, that's the word they use. I prefer crime. Anyway, you're happy.'

I liked his laid-back ease at once. Didn't come to pay homage to Ben Dimato, who pulled the strings to get him here. 'Well, thanks, Officer Briscoe, you've done a good job. I'll mention your help to Ben.'

Paul Briscoe's eyes hardened suddenly. 'Just taking orders. If it was left to me, Ben Dimato's interferences would go to the bottom of the pile.'

Different all right, and somewhat interesting. There weren't too many around the state of Massachusetts who would speak ill of the senator. I wondered if he would do it to his face.

'You still came running, though,' I ventured teasingly.

'Curious,' he explained. 'I wanted to see if the Dimato skirts were as obnoxious as the trousers.'

'And?'

'You're okay. Don't mind me. I've just been too long in the system, got cynical. It's not your fault that your uncle is a jerk.'

'Look, I could brew us up a coffee if you like – it'll only take a minute?'

'Why don't you buy me a drink, instead? – coffee only keeps me awake for half the night. I noticed there's a cocktail bar on the bottom floor: I always have at least one to chill out at the close of business – for me that is, not the hoods.'

Paul Briscoe was forty-seven and was getting out of the MSPD at the end of the year. Going into the private sector, security, litigation and all that. Too many manuals recently in the Massa-chusetts State Police, procedures, evaluations, post-mortems Paul wanted a bit of independence, less scrutiny. Had joined up at eighteen, went through training school and was on the beat eager to make a difference. Went on promotion to work in the Organised Crime Unit; spent seven years there. Promotions kept coming until five years ago – Paul had been passed over for Chief of Police three times since.

Time to move on.

I was surprising myself by how easy I found this middle-aged man's company – yet here I was, mildly titillated for the first time since I sent Bruce Prefontaine into the wilderness two years back and put my sex life on hold.

'At least you'll be getting away from the politicians, Paul.'

'Not a bit of it. The bottom line is that money talks and there's corruption out there everywhere. Hey, I'm sort of corrupt myself,' he said, a twinkle coming suddenly to his world-weary eyes.

Paul parted that evening with a backward wave and the words 'we might do this again'. Same words as Bruce after our first date but the similarity ended there. It wasn't even a question. But we did meet, and we soon became lovers. It just sort of fell into place, really – once I'd agreed to a date after the 'thank you for getting my stuff back' drink, it was as if we both knew that it was fated to happen. He seemed in no hurry though and for weeks I'd see him off at the subway across the road from my apartment. I still spent most nights on Beacon Hill but had freshened up the apartment and slept over there the nights I was meeting him.

The announcement boomed out that there was a hold-up on the line and the Massachusetts Bay Transportation Authority didn't know when service would be resuming.

'A suicide, it seems,' Paul explained. 'Decided to inconvenience the rest of Boston while doing it – they won't move him until forensics photograph him all ends up. Look at them all running for the cabs.' Our eyes met. 'Any suggestions, Ava?'

I tried hard to match his calmness, the feigned indifference. 'We could always get a bottle of wine, go back to the apartment – we could ring for a cab when the competition dies down.'

'Or just go back to the apartment?'

'Yes.'

Paul was first to speak afterwards.

'Did you whisper something about two years when we were in the heat of it?'

I nestled my head in on his wiry chest, a bit self-conscious at how aggressively I'd reacted to his teasing foreplay by thrusting myself down on his manhood. 'Mm, could have – but I don't want it to be another two years, for sure. Now, I'd say it'll be at least another hour before you've a chance of a cab. Pity about your age, though.'

'Think I can't rise to the challenge,' Paul asked, moving my hand downwards.

Our eyes met in the muted light and I could feel the sparkle, the fun.

'Looks like you already have.' I lay face down on the pillow. 'Girl's choice this time?'

Paul was married with two grown-up children – he didn't expend any excess energy in keeping our relationship secret but he was discreet. A quick phone call would have me accompanying him from Logan International Airport to a nearby state when he was on a job of sorts and we were back very quickly. It was a relationship that suited both sides – I could not take on a man who wanted children and Paul, well, it was obvious there was a missing ingredient in his life that I couldn't nail down.

'I don't want to contaminate what we have with moans about my wife's bedroom skills or that she doesn't understand me,' he said one night as I lay in his arms. 'We pull well together on most things – we've just been moving in different directions over the years. Why the sudden interest in her? You've never asked before?'

'Oh, I don't know, Paul – we've been meeting like this for a few years. I just bumped into my ex-husband recently. He's got someone new – asked me had I met someone. I said no, but not because I was hiding anything. It's how it feels, though – you're really on loan, that's all.'

'I won't leave my wife, Ava.'

'I'm not asking you to leave your wife but I don't need to be reminded of it *all* the time – the rules, the understandings. Oh, pay no attention – seeing Bruce just reminded me that I don't belong. It'd be nice to belong, maybe not right now but sometime.'

10

Paul didn't know that the Dimatos were not my real parents – I kept it from him. Sometimes, I was tempted to ask for his help, what with his police experience and all that but I quickly dismissed the thought. Despite my assurances to Chad, I was in no doubt that I was being kept under observation and that Ben would not think twice about exposing our relationship if Paul gave him any trouble.

I really needed something to keep my mind occupied and soon I was back on the phone to Chad.

'I'm going down to Frieda the day after tomorrow for a few days.'

He sighed and then added, 'Well, good for you.'

'Another thing, I've been thinking of totally revamping the house, Chad. You know, getting a new kitchen and–'

Chad chuckled good-humouredly. It was like old times when I was trying to talk him round to my way of thinking.

'Well, it is yours, Ava – your home now. I'm really not bothered what you do and I know you've got great taste?'

A fresh start for the house on Beacon Hill was what I wanted. I might not have needed five bedrooms on nearly two acres right then but I'd always loved the place, the gardens, the little stream and wishing well. It was the inside that needed attention – all the bland curios and knick-knacks and Dad's silly stories to go with it. Chad really went for his stories about the men coming down off the paintings on the walls at night. It was me that went to his bedroom at night to tuck him in and reassure him that there was no such thing as ghosts.

Next morning I would get someone from Sweet Peas Home over to help me choose colour schemes.

Chad had one last request before he hung up. 'Do you mind if I drop by – there are some bits I would like to take away for myself, that's if you don't want them?'

'That'll be fine.'

Chad could not fully understand the depth of my love for the rambling house, which became something of an obsession. He had moved to the political hotbed of Cambridge around the same time I met Bruce. Dad had bought a house down Brattle Street in the early nineties where the budding political dynamo could be closer to his uncle. Lot more than the hundred grand you gave me, Dad, I reflected. Still, there was always Beacon Hill. 'This place,' I would tell Dad when he occasionally enquired as to what I found hardest to tear myself away from – where the heart was, sort of. It was a *fait accompli* that the family home would come my way and Chad seemed quite happy with that. Politics aside, it was Dimato Pharmaceuticals that drove him and I knew that his strategy to achieve that involved constant reminders to Dad regarding the values of one captain steering the ship.

He needn't have worried, I thought as I looked out my bedroom window while the late summer evening descended on the gardens below. It was funny really, what with Mum's depression and Dad's absences and affairs, that my resentments never included the house. It was my escape, my consolation where I played out dreams that altered through childhood, adolescence, woman … mother. I never got it out of Mum why our house, unlike others in the neighbourhood, did not have a name. This was to provide the basis for many a game for Frieda and me as we scribbled our ideas during *Guess the Name* charades. The winning name would change with the seasons and might depend on the flowering stages of a particular plant or tree. *Strawberry Fields*, *Chestnut Grove*. Later, I came to understand why I never pushed my parents too hard on the subject. No, it would kill off the fun, the fantasies – I'd name it when it was mine only.

Now, I had it for myself at thirty-seven and I brooded over the sadder motivations that took over in the more recent past. Ah, yes – motherhood. It didn't happen when Ethan was born – my focus at that time was my marriage, my baby. It was not a time when I needed my imagination to sustain me. No, the love affair with this bleak, beautiful house resumed around the time Bruce left my life completely and I was wholly alone again. It didn't matter that Paul Briscoe mostly obliged when my physical needs surfaced and I could not argue against the attraction – but it was the cold habitual nature of the thing, the secrecy, the time management … the contraception.

Doctor Newbury was a rock during this time and constantly reassured me that there was no contradiction between being on the pill and my maternal neediness.

'It's completely natural, Ava. You're bound to have fears that are holding you back but it's eight years since little Ethan. There have been advances since – you've probably heard that they've made a breakthrough where they can clone healthy cells to kill off diseased ones. Gene therapy, they call it, but it's early days yet.'

Early days, I thought grimly as I reminded myself that I was thirty-seven. Still young enough, but I had baulked at all the big decisions over the last few years. Ironic, to look back on my enquiries about adoption only to find myself with my very own identity crisis and nobody to help. I reflected on my promise not to torture myself any more. Move forward, Ava, have that baby. Then you can bring the light that was lacking into the Dimato household. Into each room, the laughter of children banishing the gloom that lurks there.

The shrill ringing of my doorbell jerked me from my slumber on the morning that followed and I raced downstairs. The lady at the door introduced herself, emphasising the words *Interior Design Consultant* so effectively that her name wafted back out the door. Her face dropped when the delivery services van pulled up right beside her. I hadn't told her that I had done my own shopping, browsing the old spots like

Cambridge Antique Market and more upbeat places like Koo de Kir. Even bartered some dowdy, colourless items that only the most fervent antique hunter could appreciate.

Gemma was the consultant's name and it took her a few minutes to recover from the realisation that the commission on this job was not going to be as big as she anticipated.

My new furniture was spaced out on the front lawns and the van was soon full of the castaways, leaving a near-empty interior. She brightened up a little when I told her of a bigger job coming up at the office and it was no harm letting her believe that she was choosing the colours as we moved from room to room.

The formalities completed, I quickly packed my case as I contemplated my upcoming trip to Cape Cod to meet Frieda. I'd go down by bus – no point in wearing myself out, driving for up to four hours on the tortuous roads. Get to sit back, admire the scenery. Convenient, I thought, that a business trip had come up for her husband, Nigel. Typical of Frieda – always one for arranging some quality girl time.

The house phone rang just as I was proceeding towards the doorway. I paused in the doorway as the message-answering service kicked in.

'Ava, it's Bruce here. I've got a name for you on this relative-hunting thing. Her name is Emily. I'll leave her number and email address. She's been down this "relative road". Anyway, here goes…'

But not today, old flame, I thought as I gently closed the door.

The cab driver looked in the mirror expectantly

as I sat into the back.

'South Station, please. I'm off up to Cape Cod, Provincetown to be exact.'

'Okay.' He eyed the jeep in the driveway. 'Nice car, yours. I thought a jeep would be the ideal companion for anyone going to the Cape?'

'Oh, all that's being looked after. I'll just be putting my aching feet up.'

I thought I heard him mutter something about swapping jobs as he pointed his car in the direction of the big urban sprawl that was Boston.

11

I made my way towards the rear of the Plymouth and Broxton bus at South Station, gratefully plonking myself into one of the two remaining seats. The bus was packed with women and young children – little wonder as the Cape was geared up to meet the needs of even the most demanding child. I smiled as I recalled my week-long summer-camps with Frieda at the Cape Cod YMCA – the Fun Club, that's what they called those camps and fun was what you got. We had started going to the camps twenty-seven years back – we were both ten, and a week down at the YMCA was pencilled in as an essential, a must-do for the next five years. As time and childhood faded, we reluctantly conceded we had outgrown the camps but not the Cape and we'd moved onto more sophisticated activities, like the Cape Cod Sea Camps that were so popular during the summer. Got to eye up some of the talent too, the bare-chested beach boys in Bermudas strutting their stuff aboard their mega-rich parents' yachts. Frieda was an avid water-sports enthusiast and she had me windsurfing, parasailing and scuba-diving in no time.

On this occasion, she was to pick me up at Provincetown and she was talking of going whale-watching at Stellwagen Bank.

I looked briefly at the man sitting alone across from me, reading *Fodor's Guide*. You wouldn't need that if you knew Frieda, I thought, smiling to myself. It seemed that she was fated to live along this windswept land of sandy beaches and dunes. We had attended Harvard University together and it was there my lifelong friend met Nigel. Their romance quickly blossomed and I used to rib Frieda mercilessly when I discovered that his family lived down at the Cape.

'Oh, I see, Provincetown. And the father has set some land aside so the son can build – once he's met the woman he wants, of course. And she's had this love affair, this obsession with Cape Cod since she was, let me see, ten. Very convenient.'

She would haughtily dismiss my teasing with a nonchalant wave of her manicured hand. 'Nigel and I are in love – the fact that he's from down there is just coincidence. As soon as we finish our studies, we're getting married,' she said determinedly, before lapsing into an indignant silence, but not for long. 'I'll let you in on a secret! We've already set a date, been down to the Ocean Edge to book our reception. We've gone for low season when the crowds won't be so big. Daddy's picking up the bill.'

And he could, I reflected, as the bus sped along the road towards Provincetown. Robert Compton was a very wealthy man and had made his fortune through property development and snapping up land in places nobody else would buy. Held onto it until the city simply ran out of land in seeking to house its ever-growing population. He was much less ostentatious than the Dimatos and he just sat back enjoying himself the weekend of his daughter's wedding as her friends luxuriated in the oversized hotel rooms and condominiums that he had rented for them. Robert always looked out for me and this was confirmed when the resort receptionist checked my booking for Frieda's wedding. 'Ah – yes, Ms Dimato. Mr Compton has booked a condo with an ocean view for you. Number 135. I'll go get you the keys.'

My thoughts flicked back to Kyle Wahlberg as the bus trundled along towards its destination. Sixteen years since I jilted him close to the altar – he went off to New York immediately afterwards. Yeah, he came down with me for Frieda's wedding. It was immediately following our engagement and we were going to make this occasion a 'first night' for us too. Making love against a background of ocean waves should normally be an exhilarating experience but watching poor Kyle struggle to unroll the condom over his erect penis took the heat out of it somehow. He was hardly inside me when I felt

114

him sag suddenly with a barely audible groan. We both lay there silently, embarrassedly, as my mind strayed back to the night I lost my virginity, aged seventeen, on one of these sea-trips down at the Cape. Said his name was Jason and that was all I ever got to know about him. It was much better, lasted much longer than this, though. More foreplay, more control. 'That was nice,' was about all I could say to Kyle as he manoeuvred carefully outwards, terrified that he might accidentally empty the condom's contents into Joe Dimato's daughter. Yeah, nice – that's what Kyle was and no more.

Going down towards the Cape brought back the memories of our first meeting and how close I came to marrying him...

Two essentials in the Dimato social calendar were to attend the reading of the Declaration of Independence on that famous day and the Italian Festa in late August.

It was 1985 and I was standing in the street listening dutifully to the orator on the balcony of the Old State House as he reaffirmed the sense of selves of all good Americans. Kyle had come up with his parents from Rhode Island and was staying with Uncle Ben overnight. A few sneaky glances and crowd manoeuvrings and he was by my side.

'Ahem, Ms Dimato, I was wondering if you might like to go off somewhere, maybe have a coffee, a latté perhaps? This is a little stuffy, don't you think?'

I looked questioningly towards Dad and he

silently nodded his approval. It was the indoctrination, only a twitch of the eyebrows perhaps but a good Italian girl needed to know. And so I followed this tall, dark teenager as he made his way up towards the Government Centre.

Over coffees and pastries at Seasons, I got to know that Kyle had finished high school and would be coming to Harvard later that year to study law and economics. His mother was Italian and I was later to find out she had a fervent interest in her son maintaining the Italian connection – put it above personal likings and choice. Kyle's mother knew the ropes and I cursed my naïvety later when I saw that we were being set up.

'I was just wondering, Ava, if you'd mind hanging out with me for the first few months at Harvard? I was hoping to go to Bryant down at Rhode Island but Dad insisted.' His face reddened and his voice rose a little. 'It's not fair, all my friends are going to Bryant but because my father wants something else ... him and your uncle are as thick as thieves.'

That was the clincher and I interrupted immediately. I knew the feeling.

'Of course, Kyle, I'll do it, no problem. "Shuah", I'll be looking for the company myself.'

'You will – well, that's just great – I didn't think you'd say yes – it's just great,' he kept saying as his brooding Mediterranean features broke into a broad smile. 'Eh, I think Dad is coming back up for the Festa in August. We might get to meet at it – maybe I could ring...'

116

'That'd be wicked. I'd like that, good.'

'You mean "wicked wasome for shuah" – I hope?' Kyle replied.

'You'll be all right in Harvard if you keep talking like that, Kyle! Maybe it'd be a better "idear" if you took me down to Little Rhody for a "soder" – now that'd be double wicked, wouldn't it?'

And that's how it all began. Kyle seemed to know the rules – it was about hanging out together rather than letting it all hang out. A relationship carved out in both families' image and culture and one at the time I was very comfortable with. Our time at Harvard passed quickly – there was always something going down, whether it be chasing the fortunes of the Red Sox, the Patriots, the Celtics or spending time down at Providence with Kyle's family unwittingly copper-fastening the family-fusion part of the picture. Any release from the sullen morbidity of my mother at Beacon Hill was most welcome and Kyle Wahlberg was my getaway, my escape.

Too late, it dawned on me as I walked away from Lord & Taylor on Boylston Street fingering my engagement ring. My 'retreat' had effectively brought me back full circle to enable my family cement their values whilst giving Ben Dimato the opportunity to firm up his political connections in the Ocean State. Kyle's Dad, Dermot, was on the Rhode Island General Assembly but his political ambitions did not extend beyond the state. Someone for Ben to link up with, use.

Now, on the bus to Provincetown, I cringed as I reflected on how close we came to marrying – we'd only made love twice more after that first time and always with the obligatory condom. I came to realise that the dour Kyle never took chances with anything and that his escapade at the Festa where he snatched some dollar bills off the passing floats was a one-off – nice to be brought down to Salumeria Italiano to fill a picnic hamper of cheeses, meats, the obligatory Italian breads and wines and to scoff it all down in the Public Gardens.

The man across from me had put down his travel guide and our eyes briefly met. He looked immediately away, then shut his eyes as if some great need for sleep had suddenly come tumbling down upon him. He was sweating profusely despite the air conditioning on the bus. You're not really dressed for the Cape, I thought, wondering if he had a suitcase in the belly of the bus. Somehow, I couldn't visualise him in bathing shorts on the Cape's sandy shores – he looked pale, almost ashen, as if he had been in hiding from the searing heat of Boston for some time.

Soon I would be with my friend and I wouldn't have to occupy myself with this trivia. I glanced at my watch – one more hour to Provincetown.

The bus suddenly came to a halt amidst a great big billow of smoke and the driver was soon making crisis calls.

'Yes, yes, I know it's the engine and it has overheated but I am a driver, not a mechanic. Does anybody check these machines at the depot these days for water and oil?'

The crowd chorused in disapproval at the delay, children with their beach buckets and shovels beginning to weep as the scorching heat zoned in on the stagnant bus. An offer of help from a would-be engineer was politely declined – it was insurance, against the company rules. An irascible old man mumbled something about calling up his lawyer once he disembarked.

Frieda's name came flashing up and soon I was outlining my predicament.

'Yeah, I think we're not far from Hyannis. Hold on, there's an empty bus pulling up next to us. I think we're up and running again. You hang on there, I'll see you soon.'

Gradually, and with the help of some quips from the ever-patient driver, a harmonious atmosphere was restored on the new bus as we trundled along to the final stopping-off point, which was Provincetown.

Frieda and I hugged wordlessly as I disembarked. She flicked back her auburn hair. Soul mates indeed, and we were bonded closer by the sad fact that we were both aged thirty-seven and without child. All the times we spent playing mummy with our dolls – the futility of it all. She would admit to feeling sad about it but never dwelt on it. Found out quite early that she couldn't have babies. We cried together about it just once and that was it. She was getting on with her life – didn't she have Nigel and wasn't she having a wonderful time down here? Always busy, she revelled in her role as narrator on the Provincetown Trolley Tours – eternally courteous, deftly handling all queries that came her way as the tourists looked out on the national seashore. During winter, she helped out as a temp at the Hyannis Public Library. Then, to pass the evenings while Nigel was away, she'd be down at the Fiction Workshop or Theatre Company in Provincetown. Frieda had a degree in English Literature and the library manager was always nagging her to take a permanent position. 'You know more about this place than most of the long-term staff and you've got to think of your pension,' he'd say. But this lady was not giving her summers away to anybody and thus all his overtures went in vain.

'Would you let go of me, girl! At least give me a chance to get my case off the bus or you'll be lending me your underwear for the rest of the week. God, it's great to see you and get away from everything!'

Soon we were sitting at a dining table in Mojo's, one of our favourite haunts during our teenage years. Same as it always was, I thought to myself – some of the innkeepers in Boston ought to come out here, recognise the value of keeping good things as they are. No sooner did you find a good place to eat in Boston than they'd change the menu, the décor and the feel-good factor was gone. Not here though. Back then, on our summer forays, we would go for the French fries and pizza but when a girl hits her thirties she has to look after the body, the skin. We confirmed our order to the smiling waiter – fried fish and baked potato for me, tacos and salad for Frieda. And lots of spring water – the wine would have to wait until we were plonked in the sofas of my friend's home. So too the serious conversations, it seemed.

'Wasn't it here you and that Jason came – the night you lost it, you remember? It must be going on twenty years ago, maybe even close to the anniversary?'

Despite the glib, almost naïve innocence of her voice, I could sense her delight at my reddened face, my discomfort. Still self-conscious about it as I approached my forties. It wasn't the act itself – sometime in the future, I'd be able to look back and say that between the dunes at Race Point Beach with the sun setting in the background wasn't a bad place to discover sex, to feel a male erection within you. No, it was the awkward silence afterwards, fumbling to find our clothes, shake the sand from my bra and pants as Jason looked out towards the sea as if he had some great wisdom, could see the meaning of it all. Then he goes and tells me that he's only fifteen. 'Below the age of consent – and you seventeen,' Paul Briscoe would jest. 'That'd be a crime, Ava, you harlot!' Yeah, there was that and the five sleepless weeks I waited, pleading for my period to come.

Frieda continued in the background. 'Yeah, it was the Festival of Lights we came down for, round about Thanksgiving. Gosh, it wouldn't be warm at all around then, would it? Damned if I could be brave enough to let someone take my pants down in the month of November, right out in the open. Brrr!'

A swift kick below the table prompted Frieda to

take this conversation off on a different course. The waiter also arrived just at the right time. I was doing my own mental inventory of my friend's sexual indiscretions, building up my little encyclopaedia of her confessions to me over the years. There was food to be eaten and the fish looked magnificent. Tuck in, Ava, you have lots of time to seize *your* opportunity to make the lady squirm. The waiter passed by our table with a giant burger and fries and I glanced sideways to see who was going to tackle such a mountain of food. The man on the bus, sitting alone. He obviously wasn't visiting relatives, I decided, as he started to tackle his plate with gusto. Probably will wind down at some cheap motel room afterwards, I thought. Hope they have a shower in it for you, sir, I mouthed silently as I recalled the odour of his perspiration wafting across the stiffing heat of the bus.

Dad would occasionally take time out from building up his pharmaceutical empire and grudgingly take us down to Provincetown for the weekend. Mum would come too and we invariably ended up at Napi's, a Mediterranean restaurant on Freeman Street. As children, me and Chad would stare confusedly at the menu – the shrimp feta, the vegetarian dishes – and long to be across the road in Mojo's where you could get real kids' food, burger and fries and the like. That's Napi himself – the owner, Dad would say proudly when he returned from his chinwag with the sombre-looking man at the bar. I doubted that he welcomed my father's intrusions all that much – he would just listen politely, sipping his muscadet, pen poised over the crossword, as Dad regaled him with updates on half the Italians in Boston. Occasionally, he could not resist scribbling on his newspaper while trying to simulate curiosity about my father's ramblings.

'Gosh, I enjoyed that,' Frieda at last said as she surveyed the two cleared plates. 'What's it to be now, girl – coffee or back to the ranch?'

'We'll go back to your place if you don't mind – maybe stop off at that Portuguese bakery on Commercial Street. I can still taste the lovely pastries we got last time out. We can look in on the boutiques another time.' I leaned across the table and whispered, 'I'm starting to tire of looking at that guy across there ... he was down all the way on the bus, sitting opposite me. He really could do with a wash.'

Frieda's hazel eyes narrowed slightly as she surveyed him briefly while he poured the last of his pitcher of beer into his tankard. 'Don't let his look fool you,' she advised. 'All sorts of eccentrics came to Cape Cod throughout the year, most of them millionaires.'

Anyway, there was girl talk to be attended to and who gave a damn if he was curled up in Provincetown's most expensive suite by midnight or trawling the back streets trying to pull a hooker?

Frieda had parked well away from the hectic Commercial Street. We walked to the edge of town, carrying my beloved pastries and wine, and a short drive later we were sitting in the living room of Frieda's unpretentious house on the East End.

'Here, you do this, Ava, will you?' Frieda was struggling to open a bottle of red wine. 'This one looks like it came from the wineries up at Martha's Vineyard, yeah – Chicama – but it's not much use to us if we can't open it. I always give this part of the job to Nigel – he says I just haven't got the knack.'

We had opened our second bottle as I brought my childhood friend up to date with my plan. I was going to have a go at having another baby, see could I get Paul Briscoe to row in with my intentions. It was a now-or-never situation as far as I was concerned and I was going into it with my eyes wide open, prepared to take on all the risks. All I got back from Frieda was listening – no cautionary advice, lectures or warnings. I felt vindicated, reinforced by her unquestioning faith in my judgement.

'I know it might be hard for you to listen to all this, Frieda – but I had to tell someone and I wanted it to be you. I'm selfish but I really want to have a baby.'

The comforting arm on my shoulder. 'Not at all – you don't go around feeling guilty about me. Sure if there weren't more children coming along in the world, I'd quickly lose my job down at the theatre.'

Ah, yes I thought. The Playhouse down at the Vineyard and Nantucket. During July and August, Frieda would take the ferry regularly across to Nantucket, where, once inside the theatre, she could transform herself into the Wicked Witch or Mother Goose as awestruck little faces looked on. Never a hint of self-pity when the children departed with their mothers at the end of the show. Couldn't get Nigel to go down, though – he found it too upsetting.

'Yep, my Nige doesn't say that much but I know he would have loved children. Keeps himself occupied with his computer, drawing up plans for the next big development anywhere between Provincetown and Boston. I always make sure he has an up-to-the-minute copy of *The National Register of Historic Places.* That way if he gets any hare-brained ideas about spoiling the Cape's beauty, I just point out the register to him. He's down at some conference in New York these few days. I pretend to be engrossed when he tells me about it – he says my rolling eyes are a giveaway, though. Would you believe, I don't even know where he's staying – he just rings me on the cell phone twice a day – then we both know the other one is okay.'

That would be Frieda, for sure. Once she set eyes on Cape Cod on her first YMCA excursion, she was destined to come down this way. Almost ran out the gate on her final day at Harvard to tell her dad, Robert, the news. It wasn't that she was unhappy at home – it was the great big city of Boston that smothered her, left her drained and trodden upon. I didn't need to enquire about her and Nigel – her voice said it all: she was as certain about him as the day she first clapped eyes on him at Harvard.

'I'm having him, he's mine, Ava,' was all she said as we left the recreation hall one day after she and Nigel had spent the lunchtime ogling each other across the crowded recreation hall.

Put herself forward for secretary to the college baseball team once she knew that he was involved. Still couldn't understand the scores but it wasn't the game that she was chasing. Yet, once the major league season got underway, she'd be down at Fenway Park in her Red Sox jacket with Nigel, as the team strove to emulate former glories. The intensity of their interest had mellowed over the years as she and her husband became involved in more sedate hobbies. 2004, however, saw them revisiting their lost youth as the Red Sox recaptured the World Series after a gap of eighty-six years. Out came the jackets, the caps, and for once Cape Cod was to take second place as the heady couple hit the bars around Harvard to celebrate the second coming of their heroes.

Over the next few days we lazed on the beaches at Martha's Vineyard and Nantucket and evenings were spent ambling around Commercial Street, browsing in the shops where I picked out some gifts. A nice shirt and tie for Chad and some children's games for Sam and Sabrina.

It was over a mocha coffee and rhubarb-and-apple crumble at Café Edwige that I sensed something was wrong, too much for it to be coincidence.

'Don't look now, Frieda, but it's that man from the bus again, also from Mojo's the other evening. I'm sure I saw him on the beach today also. Sort of stood out in his street clothes. I'm sure he's following me – but why?'

Frieda met his stare briefly before he averted

his eyes to look abstractedly at the newspaper he was holding. 'Yeah, he looks out of place in here all right, like he's waiting for someone or something. Wouldn't be too hard to work out who he's working for either – given what you told me. The only time I hear my dad curse is when he hears Ben Dimato's name mentioned. Always putting the squeeze on people who get in his way, spoil his party. You're probably right – he might be stalking you but I wouldn't worry about him. He's nothing – doubtful if your uncle is paying him more than a hundred a day plus expenses. I'll go right over there and tell him to get lost, if you want.'

'No, leave him be, you're right,' I laughed. 'He's not worth bothering about. What the hell, sure it's Uncle Ben that's wasting his money.'

While I bristled at the intrusion, I took solace at the thought of my big uncle's fear, his paranoia that little Ava might embarrass him. Spineless coward, I thought. Maybe I would lead this fellow a merry dance, go in and out of these places that specialise in tracing ancestry. Entice him, make him think he's onto something big like a pauper chasing a dollar bill down the Cape's windswept beaches. I felt a smug sense of satisfaction. If only Uncle Ben knew that it had slipped down my list of priorities right now. Suddenly, I felt buoyant.

'No, I don't care – he's just some sad man who can't get himself some real work. Forget him – let's order some wine. I'll be going home tomorrow. I think I'll fly back, avoid him. I'd be happier not to be around him. He mightn't be a threat but it's the dinginess of him – it's suffocating. No, I'll take the plane – let Inspector Clouseau sweat it out on the bus.'

'That's the spirit, Ava! Here's to you, me, Nigel and to Paul Briscoe, that he may deliver the goods! Pity you never bring him down this way. He'd actually blend in unnoticed. What with all the dollars flying round this place, older men with younger women is all the rage.'

'Bitch!' was all I could muster.

'Mmm, maybe. Listen, though ... how's about we have a bit of fun with your friend over there. Your phone will ring any minute now and you're going to answer it.'

'Am I? Okay, I gotcha.'

Frieda pushed me into the shop as Sweaty Man came walking fast up the street.

The name above the entrance said *Whiplash* and inside there was a selection of underwear, gadgets and gismos that ranged from practical to erotic to 'should be censored'.

We had spent an entertaining couple of hours leading Sweaty Man on a wild-goose chase through the streets, shops and cafés, with Frieda surreptitiously phoning me at each stop. On taking each call I would fake a tortured expression and try to give the impression that I was being instructed on some weighty matter. Sweaty Man plodded after us in the heat all the way, becoming visibly more exasperated as time went by. Eventually, well-fuelled with the glasses of chilled wine we had consumed at the various cafés, we even dropped into a law firm's office and sat giggling in the waiting room until the Great Man was ready to see us, only to abruptly exit, pretending we had just received an emergency phone call.

Tell Uncle Ben about *that*, I thought with satisfaction, as we emerged to see Sweaty Man busy on his cell phone.

Now, inebriated to the point of silliness, we were spending a huge amount of time in this little sex shop with the cooperation of the shop assistant Jill, a friend of Frieda's.

Sweaty Man lurked outside, walking by and glancing in periodically, hardly bothering to conceal his presence at this point.

Then, a few muttered words from Frieda and Jill hurriedly ushered us into a small storeroom at the rear.

'What are you up to, Frieda?' I demanded as she closed the door, leaving it very slightly ajar.

'Bet he'll come in. He'll think he's lost us. Jill knows what to do.'

We were on the point of giving up when Sweaty Man appeared at the door of the shop. He stepped inside, peering furtively and urgently around. Self-consciously, he brushed some items with his hand, trying to make himself look like a casual browser.

Jill approached. 'Can I help you, sir? What kind of thing are you looking for?'

The beads of sweat were clearly visible as he broke into a stammer. 'No ... I ... eh, just came down with my sister... I thought I saw her turn into this shop ahead of me ... she and her friend?'

Jill smiled sympathetically. 'Look, sir, it's very

brave of you to come in but you don't need to do that "sister" bit. We're very tactful in here. It's best to pay cash, though, that way there's no trace. Makes me sick, though – these government officials with nothing to do but spy on people's comings and goings on credit cards. Voyeurs, that's what I'd call them – it's disgusting, don't you think?'

'No, no, it's not that I want to buy anything. I'm just looking for somebody – I thought they were in here but they must have left. Did you notice which way they went?'

'Mr ... but you don't need to give your name ... I know by the look of you ... you see, my husband Howard is hooked on wearing my stuff, been at it for years. I've lived with *that look* – the moment he sees lace or silk – for fifteen years. And you've got it right now – own up to it!'

Sweaty Man tried to be assertive. 'Look, I'm just looking for two women who were in here right now! Can you tell me which way they went when they left?'

Jill was enjoying herself. 'I think I have just what you're looking for! This contoured lace bra, especially designed for gentlemen. It's a two-piece – you have to take these as well.' She was holding a pair of pink silk panties aloft. 'One hundred and twenty dollars.'

'She'll give the poor man a heart attack!' I whispered.

As Sweaty Man stumbled from the store, it was only right that I should have the last say.

'Jill, you've got another customer – I'm afraid I've wet myself trying not to laugh.'

12

I came back from my vacation with Frieda feeling invigorated and refreshed. That last evening, we took the sunset boat out to Stellwagen Bank to watch the whales. I looked around the boat at the other passengers and it seemed like we had given Sweaty Man the slip. Hopefully for good. The trip lasted about four hours but it seemed to pass in no time. It was exhilarating stuff – those giant creatures arching up from the water against a backdrop of gannets and storm petrels flying dangerously low across the water, seemingly unperturbed at the cavernous jaws lurking below.

Frieda left me at Provincetown Municipal Airport the following morning and I settled back into my seat to conjure up the most magnificent dreams. Let your imagination run riot, my teacher at drama school would say. That was more down Frieda's avenue, God bless her – telling her gave it resonance, meaning, like it was official ... almost. I tingled with pleasure at the certainty of my plans. Nothing like a woman-to-woman chinwag to put things into perspective. You've been hearing it from your heart for years, Ava, I thought. But this was the first time I was prepared to listen. I was coming off the pill, going out there to get myself a baby. It didn't have to be Paul Briscoe if he didn't like it – we'd agreed it wouldn't be fair to trick him – but even then my

131

mental sketch of what was going to happen did not include a reluctant father in the long-term. Just the seed. This was something I was doing for me and Paul seemed the least complicated option – own family, much older, he mightn't even be around to make a fuss. Also because he was available and pragmatic – my biological clock was ticking down fast. The Dimatos may have been driven by their circumstances but it was time for me to go for something that I wanted, something that had taken me so long to give in to. I felt that I was doing the right thing and reasoned that one loving parent was fine – I had more than enough love to give.

Funny how other priorities recede and disappear, I thought as I looked back at Sweaty Man sitting a few rows back on the plane. I had caught sight of him going through the departure gates and I felt daunted by his invasive presence. My plan to avoid him by flying back home had bombed. Persistent, even though he might only be getting a pittance for tracking my movements. I was in no doubt that he was one of Ben Dimato's henchmen but I felt I could afford a laugh at the futility of it all. I'd talk to Chad when I got home – my suspicious uncle might listen to him and believe that I'd given up the ghost and wanted some peace right now. In the meantime, I was going to use it as an excuse for some more fun – face down this persistent bugger, call his bluff.

'Do you mind if I sit with you?' I asked as I approached. 'It's just that I noticed you on the way down alone on the bus, like myself.'

He shuffled nervously. 'I'm not sure they like people moving between seats – can be confusing if they need to contact someone quickly.'

'No need to worry on my account,' I whispered conspiratorially. 'Nobody knows I'm on this flight, so nobody can be looking out for me. Well, to be honest, I'm a little worried. There's a guy a few seats up who has been stalking me. I've been down in Provincetown for a few days with a friend and I'm sure I saw him several times when we went in to the city.'

'Really?' was about all he could muster. He was perspiring heavily at this stage, face flushed.

'Yeah, in coffee shops and the like. Jams a newspaper to his nose the minute you look back at him. Even followed us to the beach and, guess what ... a lingerie store one day ... maybe he's just a pervert.'

'Look, Miss, I really have to–'

'I wouldn't mind if I was Madonna or someone famous. I wonder should I report him or just kick the fucker in the balls? There's lots of ways of dealing with someone like that.'

He refused my offer of a drink, mumbling unconvincingly about a car waiting at the airport. A giveaway that – two empty miniatures in front of him. After a few minutes he retrieved a battered-looking laptop from the overhead compartment. 'I've just remembered some work I need to do. I hope you don't mind?'

'Not at all, Mr ... but then I didn't get your name. Enjoy the rest of your flight.'

I sniggered to myself at his discomfort as I returned to my seat. Sweaty Man was jabbing sporadically at his laptop. He could be preparing a dossier on me right now, updating his report. Or maybe he was an unwitting victim of my paranoia – on touchdown, he'd shoot off to the nearest tavern to tell his drinking buddies he'd been propositioned by a complete stranger. No, the sex shop experiment had proved that, for whatever reason, business or pleasure, he *was* following me.

I'd talk with Ben and then again I mightn't. Didn't really matter, did it?

Chad was to pick me up at the airport but I was greeted by Isabel and their two children in the arrivals lounge. Sam and Sabrina had made up little paper flags with their auntie's name on it and hollered my name loudly. I put on my best artificial smile for my sister-in-law.

She'd done her own psychiatry on what was best for me as I sought to fill the void created by Ethan's absence – baby-sit her children, get me 'out of myself' was what I overheard.

Of course, I was a very handy short-notice option for Isabel and she frequently had need of a short-notice option. She even had the audacity to dump them on Mum once when she was the only sitter available. That time, I had to rush from my office across the city when Mum rang to say she had lost them somewhere in the house.

I almost ran Sam over outside the front gates.

'How come Nana can't play hide and seek?' wept a tearful Sabrina who had got trapped in a small cupboard in the basement.

Maria Dimato looked wordlessly into her teacup.

134

As I tucked them in later that night, I could only tell them that Nana was going away for a rest for a few days.

Her doctor had taken just one look – the usual symptoms, the same solutions.

As for the baby-sitting, of course there was something in it for me too. I could act out my games of make-believe, substituting characters and personalities at will.

But I was enraged to overhear Isabel say one day: 'Ava is so practical, isn't she? I mean, you read about people who go through her trauma. They can become obsessive about other people's children, leads to all sorts of problems. Not Ava, though – she's too well-balanced – I think she's coping very well.'

She was too bloody short-sighted and smug to accept that only the most deranged person would want to hold on to her children a moment longer than was necessary. Then, she'd need to do something about it.

Sam interrupted my thoughts, bringing me back to the present.

'Could you bring me and Sabrina to Cape Cod next time you go, Aunt Ava? Me and Sabrina would love to go there.'

'We'll see, Sam.' I made some excuse about being tired and waved them off at the gate of the house.

The smell of fresh paint tickled my nostrils once I'd opened the house, and freshly cut flowers adorned the pretty new vases I'd bought. Good on you, Gemma – probably supervised it all

135

yourself, really want that job at the office, don't you? I had kept up with my emails on my trip to the Cape and now rummaged through the post. There's nothing much there, I thought, turning my attention to the voicemails.

A few minutes of listening and deleting came to a sudden halt when I heard a familiar voice on the phone.

'Ava, it's Bruce – I don't know if you're in there. Your car's parked outside. I did some more prowling around – talked with a few people who find themselves needing to look for their families. You get your share of those in recovery. Anyway, it looks as though you're not here – I'll call, er, ring again.'

My heart skipped a beat. Beacon Hill was about two hundred kilometres out of the way for him. He had my cell-phone number and he could have rung in this information. He'd sent out clear messages last time that he had moved on. A shiver of excitement ran down my back. Did he still have feelings for me? I looked pretty much the same as when we'd parted, with my hairdresser expertly concealing the only signs of aging to date. The difference between Bruce and Paul and the others was that there *was* a spark once. I was not sure that it could be rekindled, though I chided myself for even daring to think that would be part of my new plan. I rechecked the message, noticing that it was ten thirty at night, four days back. All the jibes about Bruce not having a set of wheels resurfaced. Was he planning a sleepover in the city ... where? Only one way to find out.

'Bruce, you've been around looking for me. I

was visiting Frieda for a few days. Is everything okay?'

'Yeah, I just dropped by – you got my message about Emily?'

'I got that a week back – before I went,' I said pointedly. 'It was late at night you came by – you seem to have put yourself out and you without a car.'

'No, not at all. Emily lives up that way just a few minutes away from you. I've often stayed with her when I go to my meetings.'

Oh. So much for that.

'Say, you seem to have cooled on the idea of looking for your real family – or have you found them?'

'No, it's not that. Look, I've got her number and thanks. I'm just not up to following it through right now, that's all.'

So, Bruce hadn't put himself out. He wanted to help and felt he had amends to make to me. It's the way they do it – in Narcotics Anonymous, that is. One big family. Emily was only a stone's throw from my place and he'd stayed with her. I felt so foolish and angry at my disappointment. Here was a new man, very different from the man I had fallen in love with – I mightn't even like him. Talk about picking up the wrong signals! Bruce had a new life and a new Narcotics Anonymous dictionary to go along with it. It was as if my emotions had gone full circle through the wringer and back again since the truth began to dawn as I sat with Joe Dimato in his final days. 'You can't be moving in all these different directions, especially at the one time,' Frieda had said. 'Finding him, finding her, they, a baby, yourself, and that's not even including the resentments and revenge – and even romance. You're tearing yourself apart.'

She didn't need to add what she was thinking: that I'd go the same way as Mum if I didn't get a grip.

Upstairs, I checked out the bedrooms, noting with approval the pleasant glow of the new colours in the mid-morning sun. A noise from the guest room soon put a halt to my progress and nervously I opened its door only to relax when I saw the big lady herself in the bed. Martha Jones – slave to Ben Dimato and occasionally the rest of the family. She leapt to attention in the bed as I tickled her ebony ears with one of the flowers.

'Miss Ava ... I'm sorry. Chad asked me to come over. Ben's gone away, so I was kind of spare. Just like the old days, I guess, except this weight is slowing me down. I'd just given downstairs a spring-clean. Came upstairs to do the same and saw the bed. I'll get onto the rest right now.'

'You'll do nothing of the sort, lady. I'll skin that brother of mine alive when I get him. You should be putting your feet up – well entitled to it, you are. I'll put the kettle on. You come down when you're good and ready.'

Martha was quickly up in the bed. 'Miss Ava, don't go giving out to people on my account – there was another reason I jumped at the chance to come over here. It's Linford – he turned up the other day. He was looking for money as usual which is bad enough. But it means that I don't get to see my two grandchildren, Chantelle and Hugh, until he's gone. Their mother wants them to have nothing to do with my Linford. He's forty-two now and he makes me so sad – he's had so many chances.'

I felt my anger flaring up as I went downstairs. The neck these men have! Linford, too. Was it not enough that Martha should be hanging out my uncle's laundry for forty years?

I resolved quietly to check out what pension arrangements Ben had made for her. In the meantime, I knew she'd welcome some tea and talk.

13

Paul Briscoe sat quietly opposite me in the near-empty bistro in downtown Manhattan. The waitress eyed us quizzically as she removed our meals, almost untouched, from the table. Paul waved away her concerns – we had no complaints to make. After an eternal silence, he took a further gulp from his wine, bracing himself as if he was building himself up to saying something. I wasn't going to wait any longer.

'Paul, you've been around the block several times in your life – you shouldn't be so surprised. You've shared beds with me in more than a few motel rooms and I've never asked for anything in return. I'm being completely upfront in telling you that I'm coming off the pill and why I'm doing it.' I paused. 'You could still say I'm asking you for nothing – you don't have to be part of it afterwards, if you don't want to. There will be no comeback or hassle from me on that one. Time is running out for me and I want to have a baby.'

I was starting to feel desperate at his continued silence. Being honest with Paul did not include the fact that I was not a daughter of Joe and Maria Dimato – that our child might die. I'd never get him to agree if he knew the full story. Oh, he did know about Ethan but not the detail. It was just too painful a subject to be bringing up.

'Look, the reason I'm asking you is that I know you, and I want it to happen soon. We're good together – you've always said that. I really don't want to go and stand on a street corner or apply to be implanted with some stranger's sperm. I want to able to look my child in the eye and tell him or her when he or she is old enough how they came to be.'

'Can we go for a walk in the park?' Paul said suddenly. 'I don't want to talk here.'

'But there's nobody else here ... okay, if that's what you want.' Jesus, why is he stringing me out?

Eventually, he spoke.

'I've always been a selfish bastard, Ava – always wanting anything important to be on my own terms. I've sometimes found that hard with you, felt lousy when through some kind of pride or independence I couldn't bring myself to admit that I often wanted to leave and set up home with you. I'm sorry for that. What you're asking of me is surely important – a baby – and it would be mine too. I don't know how or what I'd feel if all this came to pass – how I'd react if I saw the face of my own child. I'm fifty-four now. Look, I'm saying yes to it. Don't start asking me am I sure, it's fine – it'll be okay.'

A huge surge of relief flooded through me.

We spent several hours in the park that evening and it felt as if that was the day I got to know the real Paul Briscoe.

'You know, you scared the shit out of me at first – even put me right off my food. One thing, though, if this happens – don't shut me out. I wouldn't be the type who'd be stuck in your face waiting for my turn to change the nappies but I've done okay with my own two. Even their mother says so and she's not one to give me credit if she can avoid it at all.'

I nudged him gently. 'Okay, Dad, give me an example of "good" with your boys. I need a reference in order to consider your request.'

'You're enjoying this right now, aren't you? No, I've always been there for them, even now they're adults. Only last week, I got to know that Brad, the younger of the two, had failed his exams and would have to repeat. Came to an "arrangement" with him, I did. The money for the repeat year is to be a loan – to be repaid when Brad is earning his own money. I'll never see a cent of it but it's about discipline and if it gets him to knuckle down and pass next time, it'll have worked.'

I could see that this was reminding Paul that he was still 'Daddy' – and he liked it. He was talking again.

'Now, take the other fellow, we call him Junior

141

because he's Paul, too. Last year, he was buying his first house and–'

I decided it was time to interrupt. 'You've got the job – in fact can start immediately. God, your chest is bulging with all this fatherly pride! I don't want you keeling over from a heart attack now that you've agreed.'

It couldn't have gone better and I made a silent promise that Paul was going to see a new woman between the sheets as soon as we got down to it. I contained my craving to ring Frieda there and then to tell her that he'd gone for it. Too much talk of this baby thing was bound to be upsetting for her too.

I smiled as I remembered the protests of my interior design consultant a little over a week back.

'I'm not so sure, Ms Dimato' she'd said, surveying the sombre beige of the rooms. 'The replacement colours you're suggesting – they come from the baby catalogue. Do you know that?'

'No,' I lied. 'But I want these colours for this room.'

It was well past nightfall and we were going through the gates of the park, our arms linked.

'You've gone all quiet, Paul,' I prompted. 'I hope it's not about having doubts – I want this to happen.'

Paul looked backwards again. 'No, nothing like that – it's probably nothing. It was just that weirdo in the distance with his camera. Amazing what makes people tick – trying to take photos of the night-time sky – saw him trying to catch a rabbit running by.'

'Didn't see him, Paul – but it's not that un-usual. People who paint sometimes do it – helps them when they're at the easel. Cameras these days are high-quality – they can pick out a lot of detail, even in the dark.'

'You seem to know a lot about these things. Anyway, whoever he is – he could be doing something worse. Like trainspotting – did you ever hear the like?'

'I don't want to talk about him, Paul – I'm just so happy and excited. Now there's a thing – I was talking to Ben the other day.'

Paul burst out laughing. 'You're just after using the words happy and excited and then his name crops up!'

'No, no, it's not about him at all. We just got talking about the woman who tried to snatch me in the park all those years back. Sometimes I just wonder who she was.'

'Well, it's past thirty years now, Ava. I doubt she'll confess at this stage.'

'My Gene Hackman,' I said playfully as we left the park together.

14

I felt like I was walking on air. I went to see Jessica Newbury the next day and she seemed genuinely pleased with my decision. She had been my physician when Ethan was born and shared my frustration regarding Dr Benjamin's deceit and evasiveness. He was really in a hopeless situation, though, she felt, as there was nothing he could do. Just couldn't persuade Joe Dimato to give him the information he needed.

'You'll have nothing to worry about, Ava,' she said. 'You're in great shape and have at least seven fertile years ahead, I'd say – you could clock up a few during that time. It mightn't happen immediately, though – the system takes time to adjust.'

Paul was willing to be the father of my child. I had no illusions that having Paul's baby would bring us closer together. I felt we were as close as we were ever going to get – friends, romantic dinners, able to laugh together and good in bed together. But that was it. My 'arrangement' with Paul had been in place for too long for me to consider or even hope that we would waltz off into our twilight years together. I hadn't given any thought as to whether I wanted it myself. I was just grateful that he was going to help me become a mother again.

The moment I got home after seeing Jessica, I

lit a fire – it wasn't even cold, but I wanted to give a ceremonial burning to my contraceptive pills.

I thought again of ringing Frieda to share my news but decided against it. My friend had done more than her fair share of listening to my maternal urges. But I needed to tell someone – Laura was out of the question, too loudmouthed. I decided to call up Gayle Fairbanks and ask her to come around on the pretext of seeking some legal advice. She had two children and I had other, non-legal, questions I needed answers for.

'I'll come around this evening. We've lots of catching up to do. Anyway, it's about time my beloved dropped his golfing putter and minded his, *our*, children for a change Should I bring a bottle? I doubt legal is your real reason for wanting to see me! Otherwise you'd have been over here for the will-reading. I'll get a cab and maybe Dad can pick me up later.'

It was very uncommon to see Gayle surprised but I managed it that evening. The wine helped to loosen my tongue up as I poured it all out excitedly.

'He went for it, Gayle, he went for it! God, I feel like getting him over right now and ripping his clothes off!' Suddenly I stopped. 'But we usually only get it off once a week, sometimes longer – that won't be enough, will it – and why are you looking so dumfounded?

'Stay calm, girl – I read somewhere that stressed-out women are less likely to get pregnant. You'd never know. How many women even on one-night stands found themselves in the club afterwards?'

'Yeah, you're right. But I want that baby, Gayle. I really have to find ways of sleeping with him more often. I'll do it down country lanes, in parks – I could pretend he's a businessman, bring him into my office, lock the door...'

My mind flashed back to when Bruce made his surprise move on me in the filing room all those years ago. Could I imagine Paul Briscoe, in his fifties, doing it anywhere other than between a pair of sheets?

Gayle was just listening, an amused smile on her face, so I continued.

'How often do you and Michael do it, Gayle? I know it's rude to ask but...'

Gayle was laughing hilariously at this stage. 'Listen to you, Ava Dimato! The campus prude! You'd run a mile at the sight of a dick those days and listen to you now! They used to say that the first guy to lay you would be carried shoulder high through the college. Here lies John Doe, the first man on earth to remove Ava Dimato's pants!'

True, I conceded silently. After my illicit liaison with the adolescent Jason, I kept my jeans firmly buckled for at least the next three years. It took that long to get over the shock of it all, the worrying, waiting for that time of the month to come round again. Imagining days to be weeks – weeks to be months, buying the pregnancy testing kit but too terrified to use it. I even went out to celebrate once I knew the danger had passed – got absolutely plastered. Dad grounded me for a full three months and added another when I wouldn't tell him the pub that had 'put up the beer'. He'd get the senator to close them down, pronto.

'It's not funny, Gayle! Look, I'm sorry I asked about you and Michael.'

'Not at all, I was just winding you up. Well, it depends. Sometimes he'd want it nearly every night, then nothing for weeks. In the early days, I found it strange – wondered was he having an affair and all that. Men, they might be very different, but they're the same as us in ways. The trick is to have the libidos in harmony, clicking together at the one time. Easier said than done, though.'

We sat for hours talking until we heard the sound of a car droning up the drive. Gayle glanced at her watch.

'That'll be Dad – regular as clockwork. He doesn't want his protégée to pick up a drink-driving conviction.'

She hesitated a minute as if she was contemplating saying something or struggling to let it pass.

'Say, Ava – you asked me earlier why I looked so surprised. I'm not at all. I love my two to bits and, in the same situation, I'd go for it. But the name Paul Briscoe took all the wind out of me. And it's been going on for – how many years did you say?'

I could feel myself blushing. 'Eh, six or so – I was hardly going to post a note in the *Globe* that I was seeing a married man. You called me a prude earlier, Gayle – you sound like you're judging me now.' I was beginning to get angry and defensive. Wasn't it Gayle that many of

147

Boston's erring husbands went to when they wanted to keep most or all of their wealth when their suffering wives showed them the door? And boy, could she make even the worst slime-ball smell of roses!

'Oh, Ava,' Gayle retorted, her impatient nature beginning to surface, 'it's nothing to do with him being married. It's the name – Paul Briscoe. Just how well do you think you know this guy?'

'Well enough – I know he's a hard man and all that but he's not like that with me. Why should he faze you – I didn't even think you'd know him?'

'Unfortunately, I do. Maybe I'm going a bit over the top. Our paths have crossed in the past and I just don't like him. No, it's me – I'm prejudiced and it's causing me to overreact. I'm delighted for you, Ava – I really am.' A horn tooted. 'That's Dad getting all impatient. Gotta go.'

Later I sipped quietly on a glass of wine and pondered over Gayle's remarks regarding men and sex. I preferred to banish her reaction to the mention of Paul Briscoe from my mind. Paul didn't achieve his career aim of becoming Chief of the Massachusetts State Police but he was trebling the money in the private sector and was regarded as a very formidable man in matters of security and litigation. Most likely Gayle had a brush with him and lost. She'd find that hard to take from someone who had no law degree. Couldn't she see that they had a lot in common? Neither liked losing. No, that's all it was, I reasoned.

I needed to think about sex and babies. Bruce

was always erratic and, with hindsight, I could tell the nights he had been doing cocaine. Frantic, almost violent. When he came down from it, then nothing for weeks. Once Ethan became ill, I switched off myself. I knew I'd loved Bruce but now my faith in our good times was tainted by doubt as to whether and when his lust was fuelled by the 'white lady'. I held on to the spontaneity of our tryst in the filing room, I just had to.

I'd have to talk to Paul about our agreement about him not coming to my house. What was the difference? I was not trying to rob him from his wife and he once suggested to me that she knew there were 'other women'. Maybe not me, but she knew he was not monogamous – Paul was sure of that.

In the meantime, I had to show some commitment as Head of Sales at Dimato Pharmaceuticals.

The following morning Laura eyed me suspiciously as I breezed smilingly about the place. Normally the sales executives viewed a summoning to my office with some trepidation. My grieving in the aftermath of Ethan's death and my divorce brought me down a road where I devoted much of my energies to keeping Dimato Pharmaceuticals up there with the competition. Maintaining your figures was never enough; the line on the graph needed to be on the rise always – otherwise Ms Dimato had issues and invariably I dumped them on some trembling poor individual fearful for their job. I winced as I recalled some of my behaviour in the early days after my divorce – 'a pure bitch' would be a generous description. It was my way of diverting the sympathy away from me, the 'well-meaners' who'd unwittingly say the wrong thing at the wrong time and I'd end up in the toilet cubicle all over again, hiding my tears from the crowd. I did not realise how badly I was grieving and even Joe Dimato had to tell me to lighten up a little.

'I had Dan Kinsey in with me, Ava – he's always been one of our best sales people. Says he can't work with you any more – bawling him out in front of his colleagues. You shouldn't have come back to work so soon. Take some time off – as much as you need.'

Through gritted teeth I told Joe that I needed to work and otherwise be left alone. 'I don't want their sympathy, yours neither.'

Now I smiled as I overheard one chap who had been in with me talk to Laura outside.

'I'm telling you, she's gone all strange. My figures are down and she merely says try and get them up. Not "get them up", just "try".'

Laura the office flirt had metamorphosed into a conservative mother of two children and was planning on having a third. No teasing the boys these days. No leaning over them with her low-cut blouses and short skirts. 'I'd make sure you improve, Joe – she might not be like that at your next review,' was all she said.

I asked Laura to make sure that the office was clear by five o'clock that evening. There was to be no overtime and I didn't want anyone staying on voluntarily.

'Assessors,' I explained when she looked at me

confusedly. 'I'm thinking of changing the layout of the office. I've had the health and safety people in with me and they have asked for some changes – so I've decided to do a bigger job. The place needs a revamp – this open-plan thing gives people very little chance to do their jobs, trying to out-shout each other over the phone.'

'Well, yeah, but it's going to cost a lot of money. Why not just do the changes recommended by the authorities? And should you be asking Chad about it?'

I waved a hand dismissively. 'Let me worry about my brother, Laura. How are Wendy and Elliott?'

Ten minutes later, I regretted asking that question. Wendy was nine – she was top of her class and playing so many sports that you'd wonder if she slept at all. I wasn't going to ask though. Then there was Elliott, she was really worried about him at first – he wouldn't mix, hung around at the weekend on the PlayStation. Took a stand, did Laura, and it worked.

'The assessors want the place vacant, Laura,' I reminded her firmly at last. 'Right now I need you to get everyone out and take yourself off home too.'

Within half an hour a hush descended upon the third floor of Dimato Pharmaceuticals. Then, the sound of footsteps across the laminated floor. The head of Paul Briscoe appeared around my office door.

'What is it, Ava? I got your message, came over right away. What's so urgent?'

'Did I say urgent, Paul? No, I just wanted to

show you something,' I replied, slowly unbuttoning my dress to show him that I was wearing nothing but a pair of black panties underneath. 'The rest is your choice – you can take them off or leave them on.' I was already moving towards him.

'Jesus, Ava – what if someone comes in? I don't know about this.'

I was now kneeling on the ground unbuttoning his flies. 'Funny, that's what I said to someone many years ago. The only person that's going to come this evening is you, Paul.'

Paul was a bit old-fashioned but, even in his fifties, he was a virile man. It took me no time to have him rigidly erect and I then lay back to take his manhood and at last his sperm to where I wanted it to be.

'Gosh, that was something,' he said afterwards. 'I never knew you were such a vixen – I thought I'd done it all and here I am in my fifties still learning about sex. A vixen. No – a tigress!'

I lay there contentedly for a while despite the hard floor. After a while, I stirred.

'Fancy a few drinks before you go off home? We could go over to Johnny D's on Holland Street, grab a bite to eat at the same time?'

'Yeah, and the music over there too – blues, my favourite. Christ, I'm being spoiled rotten here tonight – how can I say no?'

I knew that Paul frequently went alone to the House of Blues in Cambridge. Being owned by Dan Aykroyd and Julie Belushi, it attracted high-profile people from across the city.

It was too risky to bring a secret mistress to that

place. Almost without fail when Paul turned the key in his car, it would kick-start one of his blues CD collection. It could become frustrating when I just wanted us to talk.

We parted outside Johnny D's about an hour after midnight, with Paul looking backwards towards me as he strode off into the night.

'Eh, just by chance I'm free, sort of loose, to-morrow evening. Are you caught up or anything?'

'No, Paul, I'm not.'

Within minutes, I was sitting in the back of a taxi on my way home to Beacon Hill. Ah, that practiced nonchalance, indifference, Mr Briscoe. Same as the time we first met – always asking as you walk away like it's not a big deal, doesn't really matter. But it does and I felt it in you tonight. You want more – a woman gets to know these things.

The night had gone well. Twenty years on from Jason and the beach, life's experiences had brought me full circle – that time, my heart beat with fear as I begged for my period to come. Now it was beating again but with anticipation, hope. It's going to happen and soon – if I keep on saying it, believing it, I just know it will.

15

Isabel rang that weekend to say that she and Chad were going out. Some social do – important that husband and wife presented as the perfect couple. Vital for Chad's political ambitions. Imagine a brother a congressman, going down to Washington DC to legislate for the greater good of *his* people! He was very young – maybe one day he could go for president. It was okay to dream, wasn't it? That Arnold Schwarzenegger, body-builder, came over from Austria, now he's Governor of the State of Florida – they even talk about him being president – but her Chad had a lot more going for him than that guy.

'You'll have an orgasm over there if you don't come down to earth soon,' I sighed wearily. 'Yes, I'll take Sam and Sabrina for the night. I suppose that's what you were getting round to asking before presidential matters interrupted your thoughts?'

Bloody skinflints, loaded with money – why not pay a baby-sitter? But it was all needed for Chad's campaign and her closet. Anyway, I thought, Paul was away on some job that night and if we kept at it the way we were recently Ava Dimato would have her own baby very soon.

Paul's too, I reminded myself– but it was up to him how much he wanted to be involved. I was happy with what I was getting but, even if we

154

clicked very soon, the age gap between father and baby would be fifty-five years.

On this day, I felt ashamed that I had resented Sam and Sabrina so much in the past. They were only children.

Their mother was a daughter of one of Ben Dimato's lobbyists and she had decided she was going to have Chad come hell or high water. Boy, could she tune in to the vanity of my image-conscious brother – reassure him, flatter him, indulge him! Could even suck his dick when he had his trousers on, I once reflected acidly. Chad could go missing on her for days, sometimes weeks, and she would wait patiently for his return. Where he was and what he had been doing did not matter to Isabel. Occasionally, I likened her to a fisherman sitting by the water as his prey swam up, down, then back again as it fed on things more pleasing while ignoring the hunter's hook. But Isabel was determined to snare her prey. Chad took the bait eventually, the wedding was arranged – and what an eventful few weeks the build-up to the occasion was! I was glad to be able to escape to my apartment but I was fooling myself in thinking that I could escape my father's constant demands for help with the preparations.

'Your brother needs you, I need you – this is no time to be selfish. You know your mother is not well and there's so much to be done. Please, Ava – this is woman's stuff. I'm no good at this type of thing. You'll know the right things to do. I don't want our family to look like geeks, that we've done nothing.' He paused to take some air

155

into his ample belly.

Yes, Dad, I thought bitterly, I know the ropes – I've been through it with Bruce, remember? Have you given any thought to the hurt, maybe envy that I'm feeling right now? The male Dimato striding regally down the aisle of the cathedral, everybody clapping. The women with rings gleaming on their fingers, using the celebration as a fashion parade, maybe hoping to win some imaginary competition. Congratulating each other in the rest-rooms – swapping the names of hairdressers, boutiques, even fashion consultants. All promising to visit the other person's until, out of earshot and fuelled with wine, they'd start ridiculing each other's taste. Eyes would also veer in Ava Dimato's direction – how is she coping? Poor, foolish girl, married that druggie – where's he now? I think she's into her thirties – all she'll get at this stage is someone who knows she's worth a few dollars. She could *try* to look happy for her brother. And that dress! Was she not wearing that at the New Year's Ball?

Dad interrupted my resentments. 'Ava, what's it going to be – are you going to come over here and help me? Jesus, don't keep me hanging on! Maybe I can try to get your cousin Anita to come down but it's going to be very embarrassing. You know that me and your mother's brother Jeffrey don't get on. It would be a real kick in the guts to ask for his daughter to step in and give me a dig-out. And all because Chad's own sister can't help him out!'

'I'll come straight over, Dad,' I said wearily,

angry with myself for succumbing to his clever manipulation.

In any event, the wedding feast passed off successfully and met all the Dimato criteria of glamour and importance. It was even one of Mum's better days, Dr Newbury having ensured that she was a walking pharmacy on the day.

Sam and Sabrina came along quite quickly afterwards.

'I think you were right,' Ben Dimato would say. 'It's a good idea to be a family man when you're looking for votes.'

That was somewhat ironic as Ben was single and there was occasional innuendo regarding his sexual preferences. Nothing concrete, just rumours. One newspaper had to pay him compensation in the seventies for suggesting he was gay and the settlement bankrupted them, forcing them to wind down the business. That left him almost untouchable from a media angle, safe as houses. Nobody else in the press was willing to go to print with anything negative about the senator, risk their livelihoods. It was too costly if you got it wrong.

Chad had just finished renovating his mansion on Brattle Street and new lawns had been sown. The children were forbidden to walk on them until the grass was fully grown and any violations would be severely punished. A great address if you wanted to make quick strides forward in politics, that's how Chad described Cambridge. The colleges, the leading role that the area took in pushing social developments forward for the greater good of Boston. Spit out the dictionary,

Brother, or you'll choke on it.

'Auntie Ava!' the children screamed while running past me towards the trees, the hideaways and the children's play area that Joe Dimato insisted be kept available for them. With Isabel departed, I set up vigil in the kitchen where I could look out as they acted out their games and fantasies.

I was going to have my very own baby someday soon and suddenly I could see Sam and Sabrina in a different light – they weren't really so obnoxious after all. Having a nanny while their parents relentlessly ploughed the social circuit as my brother prepared for his accession to Ben Dimato's throne cannot be easy, I reasoned. What if I had twins, I thought suddenly? Imagination, particularly in my then-expectant state, is a wonderful tool and I was able to peer through that window and simultaneously see Sam and Sabrina as being these twins and Chad and me at the same time.

'Chad, come down, I can't climb that high, I'm telling Daddy – you're not allowed up that tree!'

'Tell-tale, tell–tale!'

Yeah, they're soaking themselves in the pond right now – me and Chad used to do that. Mum would be reading some book, although she never seemed to turn the pages. Dad was brilliant at playing the games with us but he wasn't often around – he just didn't have the time.

'For Gawd's sake, woman,' Dad would say when he returned home to find us shivering cold and wet from our escapades in the garden. 'You don't have much to do, Maria! I eat out, we have a cleaner coming in. Can you not fucking see when our children are at risk of pneumonia? Pull yourself together, woman, even if it's only for a minute to put dry clothes on your children!'

Our children, *your* children. Now don't go that route, Ava. You and Paul are going to have a baby – well, me really, but Paul is going to help me. I looked out at Sam and Sabrina again. It's lonely being an only child, nobody to play with. This baby I'm going to have, if Ethan was here, he'd help ... what would he be ... eight years old now ... he would have loved a little brother or sister ... my tears are streaming. Get a grip, Ava – you were always so *practical*.

At least that's what they all used to tell me. Chad and I quickly got used to changing into dry clothes ourselves – making up our own food. Suddenly, I came to a decision and went out to the garden.

'Sam, Sabrina! Come here, I want to show you something!'

The children stared disinterestedly at the built-in barbecue nestling in the corner of the garden. Chad would not allow it to be used while they were around – they could burn themselves, he would say patronisingly

'You can't play with that, Auntie. We were playing hide and seek.'

'It's not for playing with – it's for cooking food. Do you want me to show you? What would you like to eat?'

It took a little convincing, but soon we were eating frankfurters, burgers and fries with a large bottle of Coke. Dusk was beginning to descend

159

on Boston and with it a hint of chill. I put more logs into the outdoor fire pit as the children watched, fascinated. Fires everywhere, cooking, warming. I was going to hold on to this moment for as long as I could – this was going to become more common into the future. Sam was first to speak.

'Wowee, burnt food tastes really good! Wait until I tell Dad. I'll ask him to buy a barbecue once we're allowed walk on the new lawns!'

Sabrina interrupted. 'It's really a fire, isn't it? I was scared first but I'm not now. Thanks, Auntie.'

We ate quietly for a while. I was enjoying their company while still grieving for my lost son.

Suddenly Sam spoke again. 'Auntie, is it okay to finish school at high school? I mean, it doesn't say you're stupid if you quit then?'

'It doesn't mean you're stupid just because you want to leave, Sam. I wanted to leave myself but I changed my mind and I'm glad I did. You just concentrate on your kindergarten right now and the rest will take care of itself. You don't need to be making decisions for that right now – it's so far away. At least eleven years for you, Sam, and you're the oldest – you'll be seven very soon, won't you?'

There was a brief silence, each looking at the other. It was as if Sam wanted to tell me something but wasn't sure.

'Eh, well, it's not about me ... sometimes Daddy and Mummy shout. She wanted to work in an office but Daddy won't let her. He says she has to stay at home and help him to get Uncle Ben's job. He says she won't get a job 'cos she stopped at high school.'

'I see.'

Sabrina took her turn. 'Mummy shouts back at Daddy, "At least I know where I come from – you don't!"'

I stiffened suddenly and felt my pulse racing. So Chad believed that it wasn't just Ava who was not a Dimato – he was in the same boat too only wouldn't acknowledge it, couldn't. I struggled to compose myself while feeling the menace of Ben Dimato, Sweaty Man on the bus, the plane – the determination to keep me in the dark at all costs. Would I confront Chad again?

Sam spoke. 'I told Mummy that I knew where Daddy was from – Beacon Hill, right here – and not to shout at Daddy. I don't like it when they shout.'

I was in a distant place. 'Yes, that's right, Sam, Beacon Hill, exactly where we are this minute. You were right. Mummies and daddies shouldn't shout at each other.'

I tucked them into their beds later on that night and it was not long before silence descended upon the bedroom upstairs. It seemed even Isabel knew more about the family tree than I did. So Chad was prepared to acknowledge it to his wife but not his sister. I thought about my talks with Frieda and my talks with my inner self. You're going to let that one go, Ava, I whispered to myself. You've had a go at finding out who you really are but it hurts when your nose bangs against the wall. Anyway, I knew where I was going at least and there's lots of people who haven't a clue what direction they're headed, while staring into a hopeless future. I was Ava and I was going to be a mother again. My baby would need a surname and Dimato would do. What did it matter, it was only a name – even had its advantages. I could continue the pretence once I had my baby. I had my soul, my inner spirit – maybe Paul would let me put his name too on my baby's birth cert, get nearer the truth, so to speak.

I drifted off to a peaceful sleep and soon the names of babies danced across my brain. Definitely not Joe or Maria. And hopefully God's providence would ensure that I didn't choose the names of those who had abandoned me.

16

I awoke the following morning to the shrill ringing of my doorbell. I peered through sleepy eyes at my bedside clock. Eight thirty. I would have taken another hour quite easily but somebody with their finger pressed was making sure I didn't. I'd let whoever it was have it when I answered the door – was there Superglue on the bell or something? No, better look out my bedroom window first, see who it was – prepare myself.

Chad's sleek car gleamed upwards at me and simultaneously my 'brother' stepped backwards from the door, looking upwards to see if life had yet begun that particular day for his older sister.

I glared downwards at him and opened my window.

'Chad, what in the name of God are you doing coming over at this unearthly hour? It's Saturday, the kids' day off school – my day off too, come to think of it.' I took note of his immaculately groomed blond hair and Sabrina's account of her mother's insult came back instantly. *At least I know where I came from.* Funny, how I never considered the contrast between his blond hair and fair complexion and my own darker looks before. Always dismissed people who brought it up as boring old farts. Nothing to do except talk about the superficial: looks, the weather, their last or next holiday.

'Are you going to come down and let me in or stay up there hurling abuse at me? Come on down. I'm on a tight schedule – I'll tell you all then.'

Soon I was opening my door and Chad immediately made towards the staircase. I leapt in front of him instinctively.

'What do you think you're doing, Chad – surely you're not going to haul the poor mites out of bed? They're probably exhausted. We stayed up to watch a movie last night. Come into the kitchen. I'll make us some coffee, catch up on things.'

Chad looked at his watch and it was as if for a moment he would lunge for the stairs to haul his slumbering offspring from their beds. 'Well, okay – I can spare half an hour – sure we can make it sort of an informal boardroom meeting, too.'

Soon we were sipping steaming mugs of coffee

163

and the aroma of toast waiting to pop its head up filled the kitchen. I found myself at one time examining and calculating my brother's features – blond-haired, six one, one hundred and ninety pounds, athletic, graceful. Certainly will pick up some votes for his looks alone. What would I be? Five four, dark. Hopefully, I was still below one hundred and twenty-six – that usually was the warning signal that I needed to get to the gym. Paul Briscoe might be the no-bullshit type – but it was not beyond him to compliment me on the firmness of my body.

Chad looked at his watch again. 'Well, Ava, how are things for you? You look a lot more sparky these days. You seem to have got over Dad's death – terrible shock, and then you finding out what you did.'

'Yeah, I'm a lot better now, Chad. It was awful – Dad dying, finding out that I had biological parents out there somewhere. But no, it's gone from a need-to-know to a nice-to-know situation, sort of. I'm looking to the future now – anyway, any chance of my finding out rests in a graveyard and a crematorium.' I paused for a moment. 'That was unusual, don't you think? I mean, I never knew Dad wanted to be cremated – you'd think he'd want to rest beside Mum. What did Ben do with his ashes, anyway?' I was conscious of the lock of hair that I had clipped from Dad's head at the moratorium. I didn't need it as proof for myself but when you were around Ben Dimato long enough, it was wise to look out for your ass. Wouldn't cost him a thought to present you as unbalanced, deranged, if you were getting him hot under the collar of his shirt.

'Dad never did much resting with Mum while he was alive, Ava. It was usually with some other woman. I'm not saying he wasn't a great father – he was – I think anyway. But would you want him as a husband? No, it was no particular surprise to me – haven't given much thought to it really. He's gone and he's not coming back – Ben scattered his ashes at sea.'

Uncaring bastard, I thought – no real grieving there. Wouldn't even listen to Dad who had begun to have doubts about his son and politics. He didn't see how both jobs could be tackled at the same time and had told me as much.

'Damn, Ava – you'd think Ben was his father, not me. I'm getting tired of it all.'

'You should be telling this to Chad,' was my reply. 'I'd love to see him well away from it, too. Talk to him, Dad, he might listen.'

It was kind of strange to witness the frailty, the lack of confidence, in my father's voice. 'I doubt that he would – too far in, dazzled by it all.'

Within days, Joe Dimato's aircraft fell from the sky and he was never to tell his son about the doubts that had surfaced.

Things were falling nicely in place for the man sipping coffee and munching toast in my kitchen and he was probably feeling even happier now that he knew his sister was less likely to upset the applecart by revealing that there were gremlins in this famous, respected family.

'Don't you ever wonder though about yourself, Chad – where you came from?'

I was standing behind him buttering more toast

165

but I didn't need to see his face – the stiffening of his whole body in the chair told everything that needed to be told.

'No, I, don't, and I *could* be Joe Dimato's son – I really don't want to go down that avenue this morning and that's my bottom line. I really should be getting the kids up.'

Only a few months from voting day and my brother's fragile temper was getting more brittle by the minute. He hadn't shown it for some years, but Chad could easily go into overdrive with his fists if somebody really upset him. Once, he'd gone into a fit of rage on campus at Harvard when he saw one of his uncle's election posters daubed *Faggot, the Darling of the South End*. He had tracked down the culprit and put him in the City of Boston Hospital with a broken jaw and collarbone. Miraculously he wasn't censured – but even Ben wasn't impressed. Time for another lesson in politics and how to accommodate diversity. So what if people wondered about never seeing him linking the ladies around – they were voters first, people second.

'Okay, okay,' I said, 'no need to bite my head off. It was just a question – you should chill out a bit. Anyway, I told you that it's not at the top of my list any longer.' I noticed immediately how he settled more easily into his chair.

'And tell me now, Sister – would you be seeing anyone these days?'

I thought instantly of Ben Dimato's surveillance operation and wondered if Chad already knew. I had to suppress a giggle at my stalker's embarrassment on the plane – he never thought

166

I'd have the neck to confront him. God, I must have absorbed some of the Dimato gene – I had the audacity to face down someone who had the nerve to pry into my affairs. No, I thought – they wouldn't really be interested in Paul or if I was sleeping with half the city and I really didn't know if my brother was part of the stalking thing.

Chad might be quick-tempered but was not in his uncle's league when it came to being devious, nasty and downright intimidating. I acknowledged to myself that Chad had always been protective towards me – it was just that my obsession with ancestry scared the shit out of him. You're so vain and attention-seeking, Brother dear – can you not see that you are not cut out for politics? It was sad really, watching my brother pander to and fawn over Ben Dimato. He seemed oblivious to the fact that Ben was a seriously treacherous man who, once he made a decision that there was something to be got or a path to follow, went after it. Didn't matter who got hurt – once Ben got his prize, it was worth it all. Rumours abounded regarding my uncle but nobody was brave enough to voice them aloud – whisper them, maybe in crowded bars in jesting terms – but confront him, put it on the record? No way. You'll be devoured by the wolves when – if – you get in there, Chad, I pondered sadly. Despite recent revelations, I had a deep affection for the man at the kitchen table. I grew up with this hunk – we played together in these very gardens; he comforted me, hugged me when I cut my knees, wiped away my tears. God, Ava, I smiled as I thought back to my childhood days –

what was it Dad used to say? Yeah – if tears could be bottled and sold, we'd make a fortune out of that girl. It was true, the things that I had achieved through crying over the years – toys, candy, getting Frieda over to play – I didn't know whether to cringe or laugh at the woman I had become. If I was to answer Chad truthfully right then, I'd have to tell him that I was getting laid by a married man.

'Oh, nobody in particular,' I answered evasively. 'Listen, I'll stir up the children for you, get you on your way. You're off to a convention or something, was that what you said?'

'Yep, it's a biggie. We can bring the kids and all – they have crèche facilities laid on. The killer with all of this thing – doing the circuit, making the connections, getting your face out there on the billboards – is that I don't get to see Sam and Sabrina often enough. But then I think they'll benefit in the long run – it's important to have the right connections in life. We wouldn't be where we are now without that.'

I was tempted to ask him where he thought that was but resisted. Down at Cambridge, of course. An old saying surfaced – done well for himself in life yet hasn't got a life. It wasn't the time for sarcasm.

'Do you mind if I follow you up – just look out on the gardens, reminisce, sort of?'

'You don't have to ask, Brother – best view is from my bedroom but you'll know that already. Up you go, take a look – Mrs Compton still says it looks the spit of the Garden in the Woods down in Framingham. A miniature model, as least she

says so. I get it tended professionally these days –
All Seasons Landscapes come down twice a
month. I'd love to have the time to do it myself
but duty calls in the city. Betcha if we played a
game of hide and seek right now I'd still win.
Even taking into account all the tricks you'll have
been picking up from Ben Dimato.'

'Now, now – he's not that bad. It's just that you
two don't gel. He's always singing your praises,
how you keep us up there with the competition
and all that.'

Sam and Sabrina tucked into a breakfast of
cereals and yoghurt and I ticked my brother off
soundly for his insensitivity towards Martha
Jones.

'She's near pension age and carrying all that
weight. She's totally bushwhacked half the time.
She's Ben's housekeeper, not mine or yours
either. I hope my uncle's been paying into a
private pension for her?'

Chad shifted uncomfortably. 'I really don't
know – I'll mention it to Ben.'

'Do more than that, Brother. Deal with it. If
you're looking on getting into office, you need to
have these things covered. Wouldn't look good at
all … that's if it came out.'

'She wouldn't, not Martha, would she? I mean
she hasn't said anything to you, has she?'

'Not exactly, but she was rabbiting on about
someone who took a case to the courts.'

I felt well satisfied as I sensed him doing some
mental arithmetic on what it might cost at this
stage. Served my uncle right – if he could afford
to finance some down-at-heel gumshoe to pry

into my affairs, he had no excuse for not looking after Martha. Maybe help her escape the high-rise tenement she lived in.

I waved them off as the car went down the avenue, repeating my promise to Sam and Sabrina that I'd take them up to the Public Gardens next time – go out on the water on the swan pedalos.

Chad was having a house party to celebrate his victory at the primary elections where he had got his nomination, the penultimate battle before his name went on the ballot paper. It was the following Saturday and Martha would be there helping out. Tips were very good, he said – she wouldn't want to miss it herself.

I had the rest of the day to fill in and Paul was coming over that night.

17

Springing that surprise on Paul at the office had really worked a treat. Our sex life was always good but it had lacked something insofar as it seemed to be a controlled act. Precautions had to be in place so that Paul's wife didn't get to know and I didn't get pregnant. I didn't care about the first part but I winced at the influence Joe Dimato used to have on my life – he wouldn't have wanted his daughter as a single mum, would he?

Now he was gone and it didn't matter. I should

have done this earlier. I'd be doing it with Paul tonight – in my own house and in my own bed. What if this was the night I conceived? Funny, it was that tryst at the office with Bruce that really set me out on the path to marrying him and now I'd aroused something on that office floor with Paul that caused him to abandon his cautionary nature.

'Hell,' he had said, 'why not? We'd hardly have felt comfortable before this, what with your father around most of the time.'

It seemed that it wasn't just Chad who was benefiting from the passing of the man we used to call Dad. I kept having to remind myself that all of Paul was not on offer – his bonds, conventions and niches, even with his now adult children, were too strong for him to prise open or risk severing. In the flush of anticipation that I was now experiencing I wondered if I could have loved Paul if he was unattached. Like I did Bruce? Don't be a fool, Ava, I scolded myself. You have things to do today – a meal to get ready, preparations to give Paul the most wonderful experience in return for the most wonderful thing he was going to give me. Enjoy it yourself, too.

I dealt with some emails – yes to some sales executive saying that a family problem had come up and could he have Monday off. I did my shopping on the internet as I really needed to give time to cleaning out my bedroom which was a complete contrast to my clean-desk policy at the office. This was where I let it all hang out and all the clothes and underwear that I had used in the previous fortnight were strewn across the floor, the bed. Make-up, work reports and more personal stuff. Just as well I'd left this room off the decorator's list, the key nestling safely in my pocket when I went down to Provincetown to meet up with Frieda. My bedroom was my sanctuary, my own personal haven, and I wanted to keep it as my own little world where nobody was allowed to intrude. This morning, however, I was regretting my decision as I ran around frantically putting everything in order.

I took a breather and wondered a while at my own bizarre behaviour. I wasn't one to panic – I had handled the worst of Bruce's addiction in a calm, rational way, paying for his treatment and sending him off into the sunset to take responsibility for his own life.

I suppressed thoughts of Ethan – that was different, chaotic, unbearable. I was behaving like a teenager waiting to be initiated that evening – texting Frieda, texting her back and on it went. Looking back it was a combination of happenings – discovering that I was somebody else's daughter, 'Dad's' death, the fact that I was off the pill, going to have my own baby, that had me behaving in this delirious way. It was like I was on one of these giant roller-coasters at the fairground – the fear yet anticipation, the sheer thrill of it all. Would Paul even notice all the trouble I'd gone to? I stopped to think of the first time he had come into my life when the apartment was burgled, the first time I had put the Gene Hackman label on him. Paul grudgingly put on a tie in the mornings and his suits didn't exactly look like they had come fresh from the dry-cleaner's. Same for the overcoat. Though he'd improved once he went into the private investigative field.

'I'm after corporate investigative work,' he would say a little vainly. 'After all, I was second-in-command at Massachusetts State Police. I don't want to be some seedy gumshoe spying on some horny fucker cheating on his wife. Heh, that's rich coming from me, isn't it?'

We laughed together and that was the chemistry between Paul and me – we could laugh together. No strings, just two people meeting each other's needs. The doorbell rang and my delivery of groceries had arrived. I noted the wine and wondered could I lure him into staying the night. He could hardly drive if he accepted a few glasses, could he? With all prepared, I poured myself a glass and settled down to wait – the obligatory blues music poised to start in the CD player. I thought about the times we went to the clubs. Occasionally, he would forget that he was no longer a policeman and he would engage with some decidedly dodgy characters while I sat alone, tapping my feet to the music. It would always be explained away as being for a friend still with the force, inside information, a tip-off on something that 'was about to go down' – and anyway Paul owed him one. I grew to live with it – I had no hope of changing it.

Seven twenty – now that was another irritating thing about this man, apart from the fact that he was married. Around seven he would say – you could never tie him down to saying exactly when.

Right now, he was late. Seven forty-five. Damn him, he has his bloody cell phone switched off. By half past eight, I found myself struggling to hold back the tears and bring up some rational explanation that would enable me escape the dreadful thought that he had opted out – that I was not going to have my baby. Suddenly, the doorbell rang and I rushed down the hallway, fumbling excitedly with the latch as I opened the door.

A man and a woman. The woman in police uniform. Something about a guy called Jed Byrne – the name came across in a blur. His car pulled from the river with him in it. Dead. They'd like to talk with me about it. No, I was not under arrest but they would prefer if they could interview me at the police station. As I walked robotically towards the police car, the clearest thing I could remember was the lady officer saying, 'Have you locked all your doors, Ms Dimato? It's just that this could take a little while?'

18

Jed Byrne – something like that – that's what they said. Jed Byrne. I racked my brain feverishly as I sat alone in the small room where they had placed me. What had this got to do with me? There would be someone along to talk to me soon. I looked at my watch. That was half an hour ago. I wondered if I should look out to reception again and ask when this someone would be along – last time I went out it was clear that I was expected to wait until *they* were ready, sort of go back to your room, sit down and have some patience, Ava. I'll fucking sue them when I get out of here, I vowed silently. Wrongful detention – they said I wasn't under arrest, didn't they? I could have upped and walked out and I was sorely tempted to do it. Yet a sickening feeling told me to hold on and clear up this misunderstanding, whatever it was. I'd taken my coat off in the stifling heat of the car and left it there and in it was my cell phone. I couldn't even call Paul, anybody, to come over and help me.

'Yes, Ms Dimato,' the police officer replied disinterestedly when I came out of the room again. 'Unfortunately, they got called out as soon as they dropped you here. I've radioed them and they should be back soon. You can use the phone behind me if you like.'

'Eh, no thanks, I'll give it a few more minutes.' All of my personal numbers were stored on my phone.

I dismissed the thought of asking for my lawyer. I reasoned that only people who had something to hide did that.

After what seemed like an eternity the door opened and two men came in and sat down on chairs opposite me. I shifted uncomfortably in the hard chair that I had been occupying for near on one hour. It would have been natural for me to scream out at them to tell me what this was all about but this was a surreal situation, absolutely bizarre. I'd wait until they spoke.

One of the men was smallish, rotund and bald – the other thin and wiry but equally small. The fat man cleared his throat.

'Ms Dimato, my name is Detective Dan Jefferson and my colleague is also a detective – Ramon Hawkes. We're investigating the death of Jed Byron. His car went off the road up near Beacon Hill, where you live, straight into the Charles River – about six thirty in the morning. A jogger saw it all. He was there one minute driving in a straight line – then whoosh, he was gone! Just like that.'

Both men were staring at me meaningfully as if I could explain it so that they could mark *Solved* on the manila folder and pack up, go home. Them – not me. My head thudded rapidly. Byron, not Byrne – I still didn't know him. The pointed reference to where it happened, near my home.

'Listen, officer, all I can say is that I don't think I know the man you are talking about. I'm very sorry about what happened to him, but where do I come into all this? What's going on?'

The fat guy spoke again. 'Forensics examined his car. They're fully satisfied that someone tampered with it. The brakes *and* the accelerator – he never stood a chance. Jogger said he could see the poor man's face as he hurtled towards him, terrified – knew he'd been done for, set up. A wife and three children left – most unfortunate – except it seems as if someone planned his bad luck.'

I was beginning to get angry at this probing

little creep. 'Can you get to the point on this so that I can go home?'

It was the thin man's turn. 'Do you mind looking at some photographs of this man – while he was alive, of course – see if you recognise him?'

'Certainly, anything to get out of here.'

I was handed a small wallet containing two photographs. Taking them out, I flicked one over. I jarred with shock. Sweaty Man was looking straight back at me from the photo. The bus, Provincetown, the plane back. A still-life image and now his life had gone the same way. My stalker. By now, I was trembling. Compose yourself, Ava. There's something very strange going on here and you need to keep cool. Then I heard it, my own voice – speaking involuntarily, lying almost in spite of myself.

'No, I don't recognise him – can you please tell me what this has got to do with me?'

The thin man cut in, again ignoring my question. This is the way they must do it, I thought – questions and answers. The person being detained does all the answering but gets no answers. Where are you, Paul? Fuck you! Get me out of this!

'So, let's repeat this – you're saying you've never seen him before?' He turned to his partner. 'Dan, could you get them to turn on the heat in here – Ms Dimato is trembling. I didn't think it was that cold.'

'Yes, that's what I'm saying.' I felt like I was going to faint – trapped, snared by my first, panic-ridden reaction. Lies, they'll always come

177

back to haunt you – wasn't that what I overheard Mum shouting at Joe Dimato late one night when I sat on the stairs as a child eavesdropping on the argument going on in the kitchen? I remembered the fear back then – haunt, the Haunted House – was something terrible going to happen – should I wake Chad, get him out before the ghosts came?

The fat man's turn. 'Mmm, that's very interesting. Ms Dimato – I'm going to show you something and maybe you can help us out on this one.' In one swift movement, he pushed a photograph across the table. One of myself. Frieda and me, yeah – that was when we were in that coffee shop down in Commercial Street. My mind raced frantically – what was I going to say now, would I say anything? This was meant to be the night Paul Briscoe and I were making babies together. Nothing came out. A voice came at me in the distance – I didn't know whose it was – I was beginning to lose track of whose turn it was, it didn't seem to matter any more. I was getting sucked in deeper and deeper. I felt like I could almost reach out and touch the tension in the air – sinister, macabre. I could hear the fat man.

'Ms Dimato, are you okay? You look very pale. Ramon, will you go and get some water? No, we were just wondering, Ramon and me that is, how a photograph of you might come to be in the trunk of a dead man's car? Jed Byron, that's his name – just to refresh all of our memories. Dead. And forensics are saying it was no accident.'

'I have no idea, none at all. I'd love to know myself.'

The thin one, Ramon – I was beginning to get a grasp on their names – returned to the room and I gulped greedily on the water offered. They were talking again in the background, as if I didn't count. Byron was a small player in the overall scheme of things, errand runner and the like – his life most surely snuffed out by someone with something to hide. Probably rich, power-ful...

All of a sudden the pace and tone of the interrogation was to change. The voice of the fat man became hardened, aggressive, accusatory.

'Listen, we're dealing in bullshit here. That photograph was taken down in Provincetown. You took a bus down there and a flight back. Could we at least agree on that?'

For the first time, the face of Ben Dimato flashed across my brain. Me as a child, him lifting me aloft when he came to visit. Always came with presents – toys, candy. Me and Chad were in awe of him and Dad made him sound even more fascinating. Ben is the most powerful man in the state of Massachusetts, he would say. Somehow a shivering feeling was beginning to creep over me – he had to be involved, but why?

'Yes, all of that's true – that photo is of me and my friend Frieda. And yes, I did go down on the bus and back by plane – is there a crime in any of that?'

Ramon's turn, a much softer voice. 'Not at all, but let's rehash, go back over things again. You've already told us that you don't recognise this man, isn't that right?'

'Yes, I don't, I really don't,' I mumbled. I was

beginning to see what was coming and I was desperately looking for an out, an escape route. 'I mean, I could have passed him in the street, not noticed him.' I picked up the photo of Sweaty Man once more, trying desperately to look inquisitive, innocent. 'You know how it is, we go by so many people in the city these days ... maybe...'

Dan Jefferson again, the voice cold, accusatory. 'No, we don't know, Ms Dimato – we don't know at all. What I do know, though, is that you're telling us lies. A pack of lies. Don't know why – yet – but definitely lies and big ones at that. You're an intelligent woman, Ms Dimato, and you'll know that there's CCTV coverage on all planes these days. I'm not going to show it to you now but you know what it would show, don't you?'

I nodded numbly – there was no way out. You fool, Ava – why didn't you say yes, I do recognise him, at the outset? Ramon's voice in the background, soft, caressing. It was as if he was replaying a scene from a play, bringing me back on to that plane.

'The stewardess – the one we interviewed – said you really caught her attention. The way you approached this poor man, Jed Byron, offered to buy him a drink. I don't wish to offend you, Ms Dimato – but her first reaction was that you were a prostitute. Then she heard you accuse him, in an indirect way, of following you. She said she thought it was very intimidating, despite your game of make-believe that you were referring to someone a few rows up. And she wasn't the one it was aimed at, though she could see that Jed Byron, our dead friend here, didn't like it either. He looked scared shitless, that's what the stewardess said.'

'I want a lawyer. I want my lawyer. Right now. I'm not answering any more questions until she's here. Her name is Gayle Fairbanks.'

The fat one, Dan, interrupted. Sarcastically. 'Yes, and we'll call her for you – right now if you want. We do things by the book here – don't we, Ramon? God only knows where she is at this hour. Saturday night. Probably getting laid – no, sorry, I withdraw that, I shouldn't have said that.' He paused for a minute. 'Look, I'll level with you, Ms Dimato – Ava. We can wrap this up quickly so you don't need to call your lawyer. I don't believe that you killed Jed Byron, don't believe that at all. I have to ask you, though. Are you seeing someone these days?'

'Eh, no, I mean yes, I am. But it's none of your business,' I replied haughtily. There was no point denying it – it was obvious they knew. This was the way they lived, the ones not in uniform. Slithering around the place, the pubs and clubs, gobbling up all sorts of crap so that they could extract one useful piece from it all. 'Crack the case' – that was a phrase that Paul often used.

'Spot on again, Ms Dimato. None of our business. Except when it happens to be him, Paul Briscoe. Show her the photo, Ramon?'

Me and Paul in the park together. That was the night he came on board, agreed to help me have my baby. The man taking photos of the evening dusk, only he wasn't really. He was intruding on our special moment – tarnishing it with his prying. And now he was dead and I was in a police station, deep in trouble. I could hear Dan in the background, taunting.

'Now there's a fellow who'd be capable of anything, even murder. One of us, he was. As bent as they come. Nobody knew how he rose to second-in-command. Now, if Jed Byron was going to cause him any grief, like tell his wife you two were having an affair, our friend Mr Briscoe would have no problem dissuading him – permanently.'

It seemed now like they were having a conversation among themselves, as if I was not there, didn't matter. Ramon was talking.

'I know, Dan – but we can't lose track of the fact that Ms Dimato threatened Jed on the plane. Poor Jed was one of our recruits too. Didn't last long. Eighteen months. Totally unsuited. Pathetic really, going around snooping on others for a few measly dollars, thinking he was one of these private dicks you see in the movies.' Suddenly he turned towards me. 'I'm very sorry, Ms Dimato – me and Dan were just reminiscing. We're nearly finished here and you can go. Just one last thing, though. Perhaps you and Paul Briscoe weren't having an affair at all?'

'I really don't know what you mean by that. I've told you earlier it's none of your business.'

'Yeah, and that's fair enough with me. No problem with that. It's just that Paul is a private investigator too. High-class stuff, corporate and all that. Operated at a much higher level than poor Jed. I'm just thinking of Dimato Pharmaceuticals. He wasn't doing any work for you, was he?'

I had been beginning to recover some of my composure only to have it now replaced by anger and doubts about Paul. The reaction of Gayle Fairbanks to his name, his ex-colleagues suggesting that murder was not beyond him.

After all, I hadn't done anything and yet here I was – detained in a police station for hours being interrogated and taunted. I felt invaded and humiliated. I was tempted to mention Ben Dimato but a safety valve inside my head was telling me not to – I'd wait and talk to Paul. I stared icily back at the two men.

'I think you said I could leave and that's what I'm going to do. No, thank you, I don't want a lift back to my house.'

Dan spoke. 'Ms Dimato – you will let us know if you're leaving town or anything, won't you? We may need to talk to you again about this.'

Without answering, I strode purposefully out the door of the police station. I rushed to the rest room of the nearest café and it was then that the tears came.

19

It was 2.30 a.m. Sunday morning and I became conscious that the bathwater around me had become cold. I had taken a taxi back home and the only thing I could think of doing to relieve

183

the trauma of the evening was to take a hot bath. No thought of eating, not even a coffee. I dialled Gayle's and Paul's cell-phone numbers repeatedly, yelling out in frustration as their message-minders kicked in. It just didn't seem to me that I could convey what had transpired that evening in a message, so I left it. Sweaty Man now had a name – Jed Byron – but he didn't need it any longer. I felt saddened that his life had ended in such a violent and undignified way. He looked and sounded like a pathetic character and had paid the ultimate price for the dreams and illusions he held about himself. I hoped and prayed that his untimely end was not connected to me or Paul Briscoe. Surges of anger also surfaced towards him. He was tied up with Ben Dimato and his life had ended in the same sleazy way that he had lived it. I took some Nurofen to relieve my thumping headache but sleep refused to come. Those digital clocks again, their red figures glowing in the dark reminding you of each sleepless minute as it passed. If only Paul would call, ring, do something – and I'd have to talk to him about the nagging doubts that were starting to creep up in my mind. There were too many people that went stiff with fear at the mention of his name and Gayle was not one to go all wobbly unless the threat was real. My wish was soon to be granted but not in the way that I expected.

I heard the purring of a car and looked out to see Paul's car approaching. I rushed out to greet him, hug him, get him to hug me. My gallop came to a standstill when I saw his bloodied, bruised face – he also appeared to be moving towards me with menace gleaming from his eyes. I found myself being pushed violently back into the hallway, my back crashing against a wall. Paul was holding a fistful of my nightshirt, shoved up against my chin.

'Bitch!' he said suddenly 'You fucking bitch, you set me up!' He let go abruptly, pacing up and down the hall, moving towards me then back, as if he was struggling to restrain himself from hitting me.

'Paul, I—'

'Don't talk for a minute – don't even say a fucking word.' Paul suddenly punched a mirror on the wall, shattering the glass. Blood started to seep between the fingers of his clenched fist.

'Stop it, Paul! Stop it! You're hurting yourself!'

'Sure, of course – can't you see my face or are you bloody blind? Do you think that this doesn't hurt too? And all because of you!'

'Paul, they had me in for questioning too – it looks like they really came down on you – they're not allowed to do that, are they?'

'Who – the cops? They didn't do this! But you know that!'

'No, I don't! How could I know that?'

'Bullshit!'

'Paul, could you just settle down even for a few minutes so we both can get a handle on what's going on here? There's things I need to ask you – people are saying terrible things about you.'

'Things *you* need to ask me! Well, get them asked quick, because you won't be asking much of me from here on. It's over. I'm out of here when I get some of my own answers. So, shoot –

and quick.'

I struggled to compose myself, trying to think of ways of asking my man if he was a killer. It was ludicrous to even think that I could manage to do that without provoking him. So I just blurted it out, conscious of my trembling voice and direct gaze. I wanted not just to hear his response – I needed to see the truth in his eyes.

'Paul, did you kill Jed Byron?'

He looked as if he was about to laugh suddenly but his face then set, eyes hardening. 'I shouldn't even dignify that with an answer but no – I never laid a finger on him. You, Jefferson, Hawkes – all of you are crazy. What sort of bullshit did they feed you?'

'I was brought in for questioning about a Jed Byron who had been following me, taking photos – including one of me and you together. This Jed guy is dead, taken out of the river, and the police suspect me, you or both of us did it. That's all I know.' I retched suddenly, rushing towards the toilet bowl as fast as I could.

Paul followed and looked at me quietly for some time before speaking.

'I was brought in for questioning by the police too. Earlier this evening, round about six thirty. That bit was easy. I told them to get off their fat arses and get out there and look for the killer.' Paul stopped for a minute, shaking his head. 'I knew Byron but I hadn't seen him for years – if you exclude the night in the park, that is. Jesus, I should have cottoned on to who he was – but he was just too far away. An insider tipped me off that you were in the station too and I went over towards Lanigan's Bar to wait for a phone call saying you were out. It was on the way over that I got jumped, dragged into a car by three men. I didn't know any of them but they certainly knew a hell of a lot about Ava Dimato.'

The claustrophobia of it all hung heavily in the room as the anger, the accusations came hurtling forward.

'Fuck it, I don't give a shit about Jefferson or Hawkes and I'll make someone pay for these bruises in time, too.' He paused. 'But it's you – you really took me in – setting me up to be the father of a child who was destined to die. How do you think I'd have felt about that? But of course you think I'm a murderer so a little thing like my son or daughter dying wouldn't count. Haven't you spent *any* time trying to get to know me over the last few years? Why did you do it, Ava? Why? Just give me your answer and I'll go.'

I found myself speechless, my voice and throat paralysed. Nothing coming out. The tears began to slide down my cheeks ... Paul's voice coming in the background.

'Right, we have the waterworks now but I want some answers!' He punched the wall violently again.

'Paul ... please ... let's talk–'

'Don't avoid the question, you bitch! I can live with the boys getting the drop on me. I'm in no doubt but that Ben Dimato arranged it for me but that will wait. But there's something that can't wait and you're going to tell me – like it or not.'

Half an hour later, I sat alone in the kitchen, in

a ball against the back door, hugging my legs. Single again with my lover for the past six years gone out of my life.

Paul had calmed down quite suddenly. He hadn't been talking about me setting him up for a beating, he'd told me. I'd set him up for a baby. Sneering bastards. Even as they kicked him, they warned him of the dangers of getting Ms Dimato pregnant. Some rare illness – the child was guaranteed to die. Doctor had advised no more pregnancies. Some story about me suffering from depression, going round saying I was not Joe Dimato's daughter. Making things very difficult for Ben and Chad's campaign. They felt Paul should know in case I was leading him on a wild-goose chase, stirring up dirt where there was none to be stirred. I had inherited the gene, this depression thing, from Maria Dimato and they thought he should know. Very generous of them, he had said as he rubbed at his bruised ribs. They'd prefer if he didn't see me again – this could cause so much pain to his own family if they knew it. Only he didn't want to see me anyway, because I'd duped him.

'Is it true, Ava?' he had asked, almost in a whisper.

My voice was still paralysed. I wanted to tell him that it wasn't true but amidst all the twisting of fact by his attackers stood a stark reality. I was a liar – and one that was prepared to use something he had to fulfil my dreams.

'You're not going to answer me and doesn't that say it all? I'll let myself out,' he had said resignedly. Suddenly he seemed small, vulnerable, as if his fifty-four years had caught up with him.

I sat on, Mum's words preying on my brain. *Lies will always come back to haunt you.*

Much later, I lifted myself from the kitchen floor and slid upstairs, numbed by events and the eerie silence of the Dimato house. Too many deaths, departures and sadness – my unquestioning love for the house on Beacon Hill, my sanctuary from all things bad, was on the slippery slope.

Rest in peace Ethan, Mum, Dad ... goodbye, Paul.

20

Frieda listened attentively over the phone as I recounted the traumas of the previous evening to her. That Sunday morning, I did not want to get from my bed, face the world, talk to anybody, until it suddenly dawned on me that the police might want to talk with Frieda about Jed Byron, maybe had done at this stage. I owed her that at least, to warn her.

Her voice came back impatiently over the phone. 'Yes, yes – I can hear all the detail. There's a man dead in the river, you're under suspicion, spent hours under interrogation and lost your man at the end of it all. It's the way you're telling it to me that has me worried. So matter-of-fact, casual. Like you've just spilt a cup of coffee, or something. Ava, this stuff is frightening, pure trauma. You're in shock. Get yourself over to your doctor, then your lawyer. And in that order – now promise me that!'

'But what if they come after you?'

'I don't care but I have a feeling they won't. Somebody has it in for you, girl. Not me. And we both know who – you get over to your doctor now, you hear me? I'll ring you back later.'

'But, Frieda ... Paul ... you don't think he would have done it, killed Jed Byron?'

I didn't get an answer to my question. Frieda hadn't even met the man. Nothing would be beyond him, not even murder. Those were the detective's own words. My whole body was quivering as I recalled Paul's cold assuredness down at the blues clubs, mingling with the hard-core of Boston's underworld. Totally fearless. But the beating, where did that come in? I ducked under the covers and decided to take no more calls unless the number flashing up was Frieda's. I resolved that I'd deal with doctors and the legal profession the following day. I needed to sleep – there was no way I could face out that day.

The beep-beep on my phone announced an incoming text. It was Chad, reporting from the conference. All was going well down there – he sounded too cheerful to know anything. Either that or he was very, very good at pretences. I switched off my cell phone and silently prayed for God to give me some rest.

I knew Frieda would ring again but I was too exhausted to answer her, to be lectured again about seeing my doctor. Somehow, I drifted off.

Suddenly, I was sitting up in the bed – the drone of a car humming up the driveway, a ray of light flashing through the gaping curtains across my bedroom wall. My house phone rang again. I checked the number. Damn, Frieda, I just can't answer you right now. Two men, one of them was going round the back. Surely not the Mass State Police again? No, they're two different guys. Suddenly, they're back at the front. One of them is pressing the digits on his cell phone. Then talking. The sound of his voice wafted upwards through the open bedroom window in the still night air and I pressed my back against the wall, terrified that my shadow might be seen from below.

'Ben, we drove by like you suggested. She's not here. The house is all locked up. The phone is ringing but she's not answering. There's a car here – a jeep – but it looks like she's taken off somewhere. There's a window open upstairs. Do you want us to break in – check the place out?'

Silence for a minute, the man appeared to be listening while his buddy drew shapes in the gravel with his boot.

'Whoa now, Ben! Don't go dumping this on me. Okay, we've lost her but you told us last night to prioritise Briscoe – that you had her covered.'

A brief interlude. God, I wished I could hear what was going on the other end of the line. The man was talking again, this time with menace in his voice.

'No, you listen to me, Mr Dimato. We don't work for you. The boss said he owed you a favour

191

and we've done you a few over the last few days. It's quits now apart from one last bit of friendly advice – a wise man would back off at this point. You're no longer a priority and you'll find that our employer thinks that way too. Are you a wise man, Senator?' He snapped the flip-phone shut and tossed it into his pocket.

His partner stopped drawing circles on the driveway and they moved towards the car.

'All okay?'

'We're done with this, Leo. Not often the boss takes on trivia like this. As much as said so himself. "We owe him one, but don't go breaking your balls on it," that's what he said. The good senator seems to be in awe of his own power. You going down the clubs tonight?'

'Yeah, I'm on a promise down at Axis tonight. Only sixteen and you should see her. Blazing inferno, that's what she is.'

'Just be careful – Briscoe won't take what's happened to him lying down. Boss would want you to keep a low profile for a while. If he hears you're taking E's again, he'll go crazy. Leo, are you listening to me? There's no pension scheme in this job and you're not allowed to resign. I'm not sure you're hearing me – there's a code of behaviour and I won't be able to bail you out if you decide you want to sink yourself with that shit. I'm looking after me.'

'Don't preach to me, man. Grandpa Briscoe got a taste of it last night.' He broke into a hysterical laugh, taking a gun from his pocket and caressing it lovingly. 'Comes near me, I'll blow his brains out ... bang!'

They got into the car, the engine cranked up and they glided out into the night towards the city of Boston.

As I arched myself slowly upwards from my stooped position, beep-beep signalled an incoming text.

Get yourself to a public phone and ring me. Don't use your cell phone or house phone. Paul.

I found myself in auto-mode, dressing frantically and running at speed down the driveway. Go faster, Ava, go faster, you're nearly there!

Banging violently on the door, Robert Compton catching me just as I fell. A wonderful sense of nothingness enveloped me, caressing me with its gentle cloud.

I blinked as light pierced through the curtains, signalling the beginning of a new day. Gingerly, I stepped out from bed and on to the landing, tuning in to the sounds, the chatter downstairs. The Comptons, Robert and Priscilla. Both jumped violently as I appeared barefoot at the kitchen door.

'Ava, you startled us. It's only seven thirty. You really should be in your bed. Dr Newbury is coming back over later this morning. She nearly admitted you to the hospital last night.'

I struggled to erase the blot that was my mind. It was as if everything caved in the night before the minute I saw the familiar face of her husband. I'd reached a place of safety and there was nothing left to give. I looked at them both, mystified, hoping that they would fill in the blanks without too much probing – it felt like my

193

head was going to explode. Robert picked up on it.

'You were beside yourself with fear when you knocked us up last night, Ava. Kept shouting that you were being followed. We just had to get Jessica over. She gave you an injection to calm you down.'

My thoughts slipped back to Paul's beating and the taunting that went with it. Your bit on the side is bats, Briscoe, raving mad. Like her mother.

I protested. 'But it's not true! I'm not insane. I'd better go and get dressed, see my lawyer.'

Priscilla was immediately by my side. 'We know you're not mad, Ava,' she said gently. 'Frieda rang – you weren't answering your phones. We were just on our way over when you came knocking on the door. She's filled us in on everything, Ava – you've been through the most awful time. Now you get back to bed, and I'll bring you up a cup of coffee.'

I trudged back upstairs obediently, a woozy feeling overpowering me just as I hit the bed. Sleep came quickly until I awakened once more to the sound of talking downstairs. Four o'clock, Monday afternoon. Hardly a foot out of bed in the last thirty-six hours. Tortoises, how do they do it, sleep through a whole winter covered in leaves? Not a bad one that. My lawyer is speaking in an imaginary courtroom. 'It is my client's constitutional right to hibernate. I'm seeking an adjournment until the spring.'

Soon, I'm back in the kitchen again, the calming voice of Priscilla a balm to my shattered nerves. Yes, the good doctor had dropped by again and saw I was sleeping. Left it at that, no more medication.

'Robert rang the office too, said you wouldn't be in. Your secretary, Laura, was hard to shake off, wanted to know why he was making the call. Chad rang immediately afterwards. Don't look so fearful, Ava. We said we didn't know where you were – Paul Briscoe's orders. He came by here late last night. Ran it by Frieda too and she agreed it was the right thing to do. No police and no lawyer, either – that's what this Paul guy said. I have to say I didn't like the look of him – he was all beaten up and bruised. Robert said to row along with him until you woke up. Paul went over with Robert to lock your house up. You must have run straight out, the front door was wide open.'

Why had Paul resurfaced so quickly, I queried my aching brain as I nibbled on some toast and scrambled egg. Don't touch your phones. That's what his text was saying. The nerve-jangling coldness of the thugs in my driveway, not the least fazed by the seeming threats of the senator.

'Do you mind if I shower, Priscilla?' I asked suddenly.

'You do just that. I'm just dropping over to old Mrs Wilson to check in on her. I won't be more than half an hour. She's, what, ninety-five now but insists that she's living out her final days on the hill. Oh, and there's a small graze on your forehead from when you fainted last night. It'll heal. Robert wasn't quick enough to cushion your fall.'

Within minutes, I was showered and dressed in

some of Frieda's left-behinds at her mother's house.

Two quick phone calls and I was in a taxi. I'd left a note for Priscilla.

'Chinatown, please, I've written down the address for you.'

The driver took it wordlessly before letting it float out through the open window.

He dropped me on the pavement and I pushed a twenty-dollar bill into his welcoming palm. I waved away his attempt to give me my change, looking up at the name above the restaurant door.

'Two Chinese beers, that's all I want for now. You can leave the menus – we can order later.'

The waiter looked dubious. 'But this is a restaurant, sir. Please, I must ask you to order.'

'My order is two beers and you can keep the change. Eight dollars for the beer, twelve for you. Now will you leave us alone?'

That settled it.

Paul and I looked silently at each other, our eyes locked together. Each trying to come to terms with the brutality of the last forty-eight hours.

I spoke first.

'I'm sorry for lying to you, Paul, I really am. I just wanted that baby so much I didn't even want to face up to the possibility myself that something might go wrong.' I could feel my voice faltering, a burning sensation all over my body. 'My doctor, she said I should go ahead – there was no reason–'

Paul cut in. 'You should have told me, Ava, and

you know it. I called your friend Frieda down in Provincetown. She's filled me in on bits I've not been hearing from you over the last few months. Finding out the Dimatos are not your natural parents...'

'Frieda told you that?' I said in surprise.

'Yes, well, not exactly. I put it to her as if I knew. Those guys were saying it to me when they were beating the crap out of me. I just had a feeling there was something to it. Here's your cell phone. I've taken a bug out of it and the one at your house. You can ring who you like now.'

I recoiled in disgust at the thought of the bugs. That had to be Chad, I thought bitterly. The senator was never so close that he could reach my cell phone.

'Just let me ring Mrs Compton. She'll be frantic right now.'

Despite the bruises, the cold, confident aura of Paul Briscoe had returned. He told me that when he sat a while with his wounds, the story his tormentors fed him about me didn't gel. Jed Byron had crossed his path briefly in the early eighties. Paul didn't know him personally but it seemed that nobody who knew Jed was in the least bit surprised that he ended up in a watery grave. A desperate character, he accepted the dirtiest of jobs in his craving for money and acknowledgement on the meaner streets of Boston. The police had confiscated his laptop from his home and the names of some of the more dangerous underground players in the city were on it. His family were devastated, thought he was engaged in mundane, respectable work.

'Ten years from now, this case will be marked "unsolved" – it could have been on Dimato's orders or about a hundred others.'

I told Paul about the two men in the driveway. 'They kept saying "the boss". Who do you think he was?'

'Don't know. That's standard practice among the bigger players. They never use the big names when talking, not even if they were out in the desert alone.' Paul stopped to caress his bruised jaw. 'Leo, who knows – I might run into him sometime, somewhere when he least expects it. Thanks for the name. I'm just glad it was your uncle who was pissed off with me, thought I was helping you find your mother. If it was this other guy, the boss, who was miffed, I wouldn't be talking to you now.'

The waiter accepted my twenty-dollar bill with gracious ease. Beginning to like the idea, I thought as I watched him slip the change in his pocket.

We had stopped talking in the dimly lit back room, nursing our beers, me contemplating the way a bright future was ripped brutally from my grasp. I knew by Paul's look that he understood, had most likely forgiven me but the landscape had changed dramatically. Somehow, I knew that even if we were to stay here all night tipping the waiter, it had to be said. I bit down hard before the words came of their own accord.

'I know it's gone, Paul, that it can't be the same again, ever.'

Christ, is he crying too?

Paul swallowed hard. 'It's just too much right

now … maybe, no, fuck it, I'm not being honest. I can't do it, Ava, I just can't.'

'It's okay, Paul, it really is. I'll cope.'

'Still telling lies,' he said softly. He rubbed the bruises on his face again and suddenly he was gripping my hands hard until they hurt as a steely fervour surged forth through his words. 'I'll help you find her. We're going to find her, your mother. She's out there somewhere and we're going to find her. And we'll find Ava too.'

21

I had listened resignedly to Paul's urgings, then politely declined his offer to dig up my past, find out who I really was. I was just spent and unable to cope with the prospect of further disappointment. It wasn't that he didn't sound very convincing – he, Priscilla and Dr Newbury had all talked about it at the kitchen table as I lay sleeping upstairs. It was something he wanted to do for me. Blind man walking, I reflected bitterly. What I really wanted was my own baby. It had been snatched away from me and people were sitting around the table deciding what next was best for me. Best for you, Paul – you get your revenge on Ben Dimato and perhaps purge some of your guilt at the same time. Lie low for a while, Ava, you don't need your lawyer now, that's what he had said. Inside information was that the Massachusetts State Police had struck my name from the list of suspects and were following up a different lead on Jed Byron.

Now, Tuesday morning, I was in Dr Newbury's waiting room, taking my place in the pew with a dozen or so ailing people. I'd thanked Priscilla for her hospitality and defiantly made my way into the city despite the doctor's offer of a house visit. A little cosmetics had rendered my scar all but invisible. Pity the inventors hadn't come up with something similar for the heart.

'Ms Dimato, Dr Newbury will see you now.'

I looked up in surprise and embarrassment at her secretary who by now was dealing with the reaction to my elevation up the queue.

'Appointments first, sir. Go sit down, that's our procedure here.'

I made my way sheepishly through the door.

Jessica Newbury was in her late sixties and was in practice with her older brother, Ivan, long before I was born. I'd started with the male side of the practice as he was the family doctor but switched over to Jessica in my teens. The surgery was on Sudbury Street near the Government Centre and they drew the majority of their business from the workers in these buildings. Ivan had retreated to the golf courses of Boston but not before his son was firmly ensconced in his chair.

'You really didn't need to jump me up the queue,' I said, aware of the hostility in my voice.

She paused momentarily, studying me through horn-rimmed glasses. 'Don't worry about that right now, Ava. What I want to know is how you are feeling – the truth – no bravado or denial.'

'Angry, seeing as you want to know. You've no

business discussing my past with the likes of Paul Briscoe or anybody else.'

'Okay, I'm hearing you. I was thinking of putting you on medication for a few days. They're Anxicalm and will help you get your balance, your composure back. There were other things I was going to talk about but they'll wait. You seem too agitated right now.'

I looked at the good doctor, obstinately conscious of my resentment of the medical profession right then. 'I'm not going down my mother's road, Jessica, and I don't want frequent visits back here to be part of my future. The best sedative you can give me is to tell me what you want to talk about, and I'll be on my way.'

Some fifty minutes later, I sat fingering my mug in one of the many coffee shops that surrounded the Government Centre. Jessica had gradually broken down my antagonism towards her and the world in general that morning. She'd won me over when she responded to her secretary's prompt that the man in the waiting room was getting troublesome about the delay.

'Oh, tell him to go and fuck off!'

We both burst out laughing at her indiscretion before she resumed.

'Now where were we, yes ... men.'

She had talked with Ivan last night – they even rang Doctor Benjamin together. Decided they were going to prioritise the current situation above my parents' right to confidentiality. 'More like secrets,' she said. And they had both passed on, so it was *me* who counted now – the living, as Jessica put it.

'It wasn't your mother that couldn't conceive, Ava. It was your father – he was sterile. He erupted into a fury when Ivan told him, swept all the papers off his desk, overturned furniture – you name it. That is over forty years back but my brother remembers it like yesterday. He was apoplectic with rage, frothing – almost deranged. Ivan got me to check in on Marie later, just to make sure she was all right.'

The café waiter paused as I came back to the present and I nodded my agreement as he refilled my coffee mug. What were the words of that song – yes, 'Silencio' an Italian song – means keep it all quiet, Maria, don't tell the world that the red-blooded Joe Dimato is firing blanks. You, Joe, get to screw all around you, no come-back, while your wife sits loyally at home, her spirit crushed, her identity robbed. Somehow it seems right that you were cremated. You've no right to lie beside my mother.

I found myself in the rest room dialling on my cell phone.

'Hello, is that Massey's Undertakers? Yes, this is Ava Dimato. I want you to send your engraver over to the graveyard. Yes, that's the one – do it straight away. It's my mother, and I want an error corrected. Her name is *Marie*, not Maria.'

Back at the table, the waiter was poised once more with his coffee jug. Yes, I would have some more and was that fresh baking I smelt? Two muffins, butter and blackcurrant preserves. Jessica had sent my mother on to a counsellor, but it was futile, useless. Her words resonated in my ears.

'Marie's counsellor would ring me. Said he was getting nowhere – it wasn't her that needed therapy, it was her husband. She was robust and cheerful back then, was Marie, but Joe Dimato broke her. She begged him to adopt, give a poor child a home, but he had other ideas. It's only now that Ivan and I appreciate fully what these ideas were. He just ground her down and all because he couldn't face telling the world that he needed to adopt. He wouldn't even have had to tell them, your mother was so loyal, devoted. It was just that he couldn't even tell it to himself.'

A vision of her swept forward, the night she passed away to eternity two years after my Ethan died. It was cancer that took her in the end and she lasted only two months after she was diagnosed. The least noticed death in the Dimato family. The least talked about, she died as she lived, in the shadows. Very few tears, even Jeffrey summoned up all of his willpower to be civil to Dad at the funeral. The creepy silence of her last hours, as I sat with her in her bedroom while she waited patiently for her time to pass. My coldness to her at the time, arranging the pillows methodically behind her head. Unable to give her a real hug, to say my goodbyes.

Later, I stood in the graveyard and nodded approvingly at the change to Marie. They've cleaned it up too. A tiny smile flickered across my face – Mum would have liked that. Sometime, the tears have got to come. Even to the most resolute, especially when your little boy lies to the left, cold. I wiped my tears and looked up again at the blue sky that was streaked with white clouds. I imagined my son and mother were looking down on me. She smiling approvingly, my son resting against her.

'I'm sorry, Mum ... I'm just so sorry,' I said through the tumbling tears.

22

'Sometimes, you've got to say fuck it, Mum.'

Now where did you hear that before, Ava? A TV show, a comedy maybe. Didn't know. Dusk was descending as I sat in the Garden in the Woods down at Framingham.

The trees stood majestically in the background as he approached and sat down.

'You look like the time I first met you, Paul. The bruises kind of help and I see you've stopped ironing your shirts again.'

He shifted uncomfortably, offering me a sandwich from a brown bag. Ham and chutney, one of my favourites. I surveyed this awkward man, momentarily content with the silence.

Honourable, dog-rough, but honourable all the same.

'Yeah, well, that's the way it is right now.'

'What does your wife think of the bruises?' There was still no denying the chemistry, the charged atmosphere between me and this man.

'Doesn't matter what she thinks, they'll still take the same time to heal.'

I resisted the impulse to suggest cosmetics. It wasn't the time to become overly glib.

'What have you got in mind, Paul? How are you, we, going to do it? I'm not really sure I want to go there.'

'That's what my fellow narks would say at the beginning. I didn't get to sit next to the throne at the Massachusetts State Police by being stupid. Right now, I don't know. But we start at the beginning, map back. Let's see – 1967 minus nine months to allow for all possibilities.'

'Okay, is there anything you want me to do?'

'Go back and talk to Mrs Compton. See if she's remembered anything. I'll be doing my own digging – I'll call you in a few days.'

Then he was gone.

I opened the door to my house at Beacon Hill and stepped gingerly across the threshold. I felt fired by Paul's resolve, his grim determination, but terrified too. The meal that I had prepared only last Saturday night still lay in the pots on the hob. My life was charted on a totally different course less than seventy-two hours ago.

Bruce's new-found dictionary shot to the fore: 'We can only live in the day, Ava.'

I wasn't interested enough to drop by the Comptons that night. I had just made my peace with Marie Dimato and the frantic erstwhile longing I had to discover my real mother had ebbed. It also felt disloyal: my brain was too busy recreating my images and perceptions of the mum I had for thirty-seven years. I'd dispatched my father to zero once I'd visited my mother's grave. It was the only way to deal with it – he wasn't even beside her. Specks of dust floating in the sea, bobbing outwards to be gobbled up mercilessly by the Atlantic before cascading to its bottomless floor. His soul sliding like slime down one of Boston's more ugly sewers – hopefully.

Chad's car purred up the driveway. Act casual, Paul had said.

'There is no need to knock, Chad.'

'Oh, I just didn't want to barge in here – you might have visitors,' he said while looking at the top of my head.

'Would you like a drink, coffee?'

He shook his head and plonked himself down on the sofa. His eyes trailed around the room like he was making an inventory.

'I just dropped over to see how you were doing. You haven't been in at work these past few days?'

'Eh, no, I'm sure I left a message on your phone.' I plumped a cushion and gave him a bright smile. 'Frieda was up the weekend. I had a bit too much to drink, had a small fall, cut my forehead.' Telling lies was becoming easier.

He leaned forward and stared searchingly into my face. 'Ah yes, I see it – the wonders of cam-ouflage. Jesus, you ought to be more careful, Ava. Bang your head in the wrong place and it's time out, permanently.'

Our eyes were absolutely locked.

He chuckled good-humouredly and shook his head regretfully. 'Sis, what are we going to do with you?'

'I know, Chad. It was just a one-off, a lesson learned. Say, that fellow who went off the road into the Charles River the other night. Just down the road from here. Jed Byron. Did you know him?'

He looked genuinely puzzled. 'Read about it in the local rags but no, I didn't know him. He was a private detective, wasn't he ... should I know him?'

'No, it was just that it happened so close. The gossip going round is that it was no accident, that this Jed Byron had annoyed someone important – that he was set up, snuffed out.'

He held my stare, brother to sister, so close that I could guess from the exhalation of his breath what he'd eaten for dinner that day.

'Could well have been. Ava – are you trying to tell me something, like he was connected with you, the company, in any way?'

'No, Chad, it's just that when it happens right on your doorstep it gives you the creeps.'

'So much of it going on too – life is so cheap to some people out there. Anyway, I came over for those old bits you were going to throw out after your revamp. You promised you'd keep them for me, remember?'

'Yeah, I kept them all – but you're hardly going to take Dad's old desk in your car, are you?'

'No, but the smaller things will fit in the trunk.'

'Fine – I'll just walk down to check the mail-box at the gate.'

I wanted to get away from Chad right then.

I took my time coming back, picked a few flowers.

'That's it,' Chad remarked, forcing the congested car trunk to close. 'Just the desk left. I'll be seeing ya.' Then he turned back towards me, his face filled with concern.

'D'you know – you do look well below par. I'd stay out of the office for the rest of the week. Let the scar heal.' He turned his car in the drive, looking just a little spurned that I hadn't offered him a coffee or something that would prolong his stay.

I watched his car merge with the other traffic. And wondered, if we'd had different parents, how different our lives could have been. I returned to my empty house.

I trudged reluctantly across to Priscilla Compton the following morning. I owed her that much – the courtesy of listening to what she had to say. What I really needed to do was tell the whole world to go screw itself. Then take a holiday, maybe go down to Mexico, maybe down to Tulum, look out at the Caribbean. On my own, no friends needed.

Priscilla was coming up to eighty and right now she was going off on one of her famous tangents, reminiscing about the past.

'Now you'll know my two boys, William and Francis. They're well into their fifties now. To think I was forty-two when my Frieda came along!'

I gave a wincing smile. Experience had taught me that you never rushed the Comptons – you only made it worse. She'd have to weave her path to whatever little snippet she had and it most likely would be useless.

'Now, William, he was an absolute devil in his

teens. He dropped by at my request yesterday – we'd spoken about it on the phone and I told him to get right over.'

It – very good, I thought, looking at the gilded carriage-clock on her mantelpiece.

'It was only then I remembered. You and my daughter are the same age. I'd just got the news that I was pregnant with Frieda. I was in complete shock and then Joe Dimato comes hammering down on my door, looking for William.'

'Why?' I prompted.

'You see, William reminded me last night. Robert had just bought him a camera and he was going round showing it off, the way he used to do.'

Oh, God, Priscilla, I urged silently, will you get on with it! *Dourpuss*, that's how Frieda described her older brother and here I was with his mother en route to one of her marathon recreations of her son's youth. But suddenly, the pace was to change.

'You see nobody knew where Maria was at the time – she was supposed to be over in Scotland. William had seen this girl on the grounds of your house once or twice and he was determined to get a closer look – it was hard to keep him away from the girls back then. Went round by several back gardens, including Mrs Wilson's.'

I could sense a small surge of electricity beginning to take hold. Don't interrupt, Ava.

'So he climbed up on the wall with his camera, and shouted at the girl, "Hey you! Snap! Gotcha!" He almost fell off the wall at her reaction. She dropped a basket of washing,

209

screamed and ran indoors. Then Joe Dimato arrived down at our house, threatening to cut my William's balls off – that's exactly the way he put it – if he ever trespassed on his property again. William never saw her after that.'

Priscilla was now opening a photo album.

'Me and Robert always kept records of the children growing up. God, you should see the amount of stuff that's hoarded in the attic! We always put the name, the date and place the photo was taken on the back. And I suppose William picked the habit up from his dad.' She pulled out one from the album. 'Here she is, that girl, the one he snapped in your garden. Look at the back of it, the date.'

My trembling hand accepted the ghoulish, macabre print. Black and white. I stared, mesmerised, at the brown-haired, pale-faced girl looking back at me. I fingered my own black hair as I looked for signs, similarity. Seemed sort of tall too, staring outwards towards the camera – a look of frightened alarm on her face. Semi-crouched, as the laundry basket tumbled from her hands. I cursed the nondescript, loose dark coat she was wearing – couldn't tell, I felt.

After an age I turned it over to view the neat handwriting: *1967/01/10 – Mystery Girl, Joe Dimato's garden.*

23

Born on 3rd July 1967, I'd missed American Independence Day by a whisker. 'Less than an hour,' Uncle Ben would say. 'Most people would give an arm and a leg to have that date on their job application form. Real door-opener, that one – gets the talk going, sways the bias towards you. Typical Ava! All she had to do was wait forty-five more minutes and she wouldn't – even making her own decisions that early!' He would continue, conjuring up his vision for one of Chad's orations from the rostrum. 'Think of it! *"As a proud American, I uphold the values of our Constitution and care for them deeply. I cannot forget them and if I do there's always my sister's birthday to remind me."'*

I'd taken William's cell-phone number from Priscilla, reluctantly conceding to myself that this kind old lady had no answers to the questions I was firing at her with reckless speed. Neither, apparently, had William – the photo was all there was. He'd merely heard her scream but not speak. I wished that I was back in the office with a giant blow-up of this photograph in the training and conference room. I peered once more at the woman in the photo, angling it around, futilely trying to get it to tell me if she looked pregnant. To no avail. You would have only been three months gone, wouldn't you? 'I suppose she looks a little like you,' Priscilla had said, 'but then again, how many people have mistaken you and Frieda for sisters?' No more than eighteen, probably younger, William had told her. Don't know about the looking alike, Priscilla – stop trying to console me. She looks tall and brown-haired. I'm five-four and dark. Wonder what Joe Dimato said when you dropped all the washing into the muddy snow?

I paced the floor outside the photographer's studio, silently urging him to come out from his darkened room. He didn't need to be in there what with today's technology, my mind raged violently. An elderly man, he was firm on that one – he had done it this way for years and he needed the serenity the darkness of the room. And the solitude, so no, I couldn't come in with him. He resurfaced just as I prepared to tempt fate by knocking him up again.

'There you go, Ms Jenkins – that's what you said, wasn't it? Four digitally enhanced images.'

I had busied myself outside counting the notes in my wallet. Two hundred and twenty dollars and I was pressing all of it into his hand. He looked at the notes briefly and was now pushing about half of it back where it came from.

'No, that's not the way I work and I'm not that keen on having customers who insist on hovering in my shop outside my studio door either. I won't take a cent more than my usual charges and, please, don't come back here again looking for instant service. You won't get it.'

'Okay. Say, Mr Graham, can you make me up a

CD of the photo once you have it on your computer?'

'Yes, I can. It'll cost you ten dollars. I can email it to you for free, though.'

'No, the CD will do just fine. I don't have email at the moment.'

He is back out again, wiping the sweat from his brow. Sixty-something, I reckoned. I was glad of the anonymity his fusty little shop offered and copper-fastened that by giving him a false name. He insisted on giving me his card and a reference number for my order should I need it mailed at a future date. I didn't want anyone to know about this.

Once home again, I fretted as to whether posting a copy to Frieda in Provincetown had been a good idea. At least it went from the street, gave it a kind of secrecy that couldn't be guaranteed at the office.

Paul's number flashed up on my cell phone. He listened patiently until I had finished.

'Mmm, so we have a photograph but nothing else right now. I've got no news except for a bit you won't like – won't like at all. The taps on your phone, the cell phone at least, were put there by someone working at your office. Laura Barnes, do you know her?'

'Of course I do. She's my secretary – *was*, as and from right now. I'm going over there to fire her. The bitch! Are you sure – how did you get to know this?'

'I'm sure and you don't need to know the details. And another thing, you're not going to fire her – not right now at least. You have to act like nothing's happened, it's the best way. Don't go alerting your uncle or your brother for that matter. Just act casual – maybe you should think about going back to work.'

Fuck you, Paul, I thought later. Treating me like a child, ordering me around. I can't even go over and throttle that lady, look her in the eye and tell her she's betrayed me. Can't even show the photo to anybody either – you don't want me to be showing it to anyone in the know who might tip her off, move her on. How in God's name are we going to find her? I looked at the telephone number Bruce had given me. Emily. She had been through this and had helped others track down people against all the odds, that's what he said. I just couldn't sit there.

Paul didn't even want us to meet, even to pick up a photo of this mystery girl. My head throbbed mercilessly as I recalled the billboard advertisements for a recent film. Yeah, *The Lady in the Lake*. Well my film would be *The Girl in the Garden* and I wasn't going to hang around waiting for a man who didn't want a photo of my girl.

I sat quietly observing the woman with her back to me at the self-service counter. Why does everyone I meet these last few days have morals, I wondered. First the photographer, now this Emily, turning down my money and then even insisting on buying me a coffee though she's between jobs.

'You'll really have to check this habit of offering

214

people money, Ava,' I whispered, chastened by the reality that not all people could be won over by the flash of the dollar. My face had flushed with indignation at her level response.

'I don't want your money and I find it distasteful for you to offer it. Bruce asked me would I talk to you and see could I help out. That's what I'm doing.'

I watched her with her faded jeans as she chatted away with the lady at the counter. She seemed to have eaten the same dictionary as Bruce ... the Narcotics Anonymous *family*. Bruce stayed over at her place the night he came past my house. Surely, it's all not so pure. I cringed as a vision of this ethical woman getting it off with my former husband surfaced. Now there was a man who loved a blow-job – he'd find it hard to lie on the couch on his own in your grimy little apartment with your firm little butt just a few strides away in the bedroom. She was back with the coffees.

'Counselling, that's what I'd recommend as a first step. Some people I've known that plunged straight in came out totally ravaged by the experience. Couldn't handle their new families, the rejection.'

'Yes, Emily, I'll think about what you said. Only, I thought you might have a little more on how I might find them.'

She surveyed me for a moment, looking a little offended. Again.

'Well, I don't. Bruce gave me some of the detail. He says you have a birth certificate saying that the Dimatos are your parents – and they're not able to tell you anything now. You've a brother and uncle who won't.'

Self-consciously, I passed the photograph back once more, glaring at the couple who were casting glances from the adjacent booth.

Emily was talking away, speculating. 'She could be from anywhere, apart from a few obvious places, Africa, China and that – she's kind of pale, isn't she? But then the photo is very old, faded. Have you stopped to think that there might be an innocent explanation? That she might be just someone who dropped by your house?'

'No, I'm convinced this woman, this girl, is my mother,' I replied, my hostile stare finally inducing the nosey-parkers to get up and leave. The obsession was beginning to grow again and I didn't want Emily to dampen it. 'No, she'd hardly be taking clothes off the line if she was a visitor.'

'Maybe a maid,' Emily said. 'I mean your family, the Dimatos, probably weren't short of money. Ooops, sorry – didn't mean to be cheeky.'

'Don't worry about it,' I gritted the words out. 'No, it's the right time, everything fits and I'm sure they wouldn't hire a maid that young.'

'Okay, if you say so. I can't say I see the resemblance. Have you put this alongside photos of you at that age? This one is no more than seventeen, tops.'

My eyes rolled heavenwards. 'Yes, of course I did. Look, I'm beginning to think this is not such a good idea...'

'Suit yourself. If you want to call me, feel free. I might be able to put you in touch with some

216

agencies.' Soon she is standing, putting back on the sweater she'd removed. 'I'd best be going. I'm off to a meeting of the fellowship. I hope you find her if that's what you truly want.'

She offered her unmanicured hand and I shook it warmly. Somehow it was hard to imagine her with that needle searching for the vein that would plunge her towards the depths. She was talking again.

'I don't know if I should. say this ... but ... have you thought about how you might react if she doesn't want to know, won't even meet with you?'

'No, I didn't. I suppose I'm so caught up with finding her, I didn't stop to think.'

She sat back down at the table, grasping my hands, her whole features intensified. 'It's not just about her, it's about you too, finding yourself. Finding Ava. See that counsellor.'

Several coffees later, I wandered dazedly out the door. Emily would most likely be standing up now in the inner circle, telling how it was and how it is now. That's the drill. I recalled my own selfishness when Bruce was in therapy, refusing to go see him, do the concerned relative bit. I wondered would he be there right now, watching her talk, confident that he would be in her bed soon. Let go of your bitterness, your cynicism, Ava – you're so confined, limited. Do you not believe in true friendship any more? You've only had one true friend yourself – what's that saying about you? I looked backwards at the name above the door. The Black Crow Café. Jamaica Plain. I reflected on all the clandestine meetings

217

of my life, my trysts with Paul included. It's easy to hide out in Boston. So many options, I could do a bloody good job as a tour guide.

Two days passed and there I was, sitting in limbo. Not a word from anyone, except Laura ringing to see how I was. Chad had told her.

'You poor baby, you were never one to knock it back. I've never seen you drunk in all the times we've been together. You weren't celebrating ... there's nothing wrong, is there?'

'Not a thing,' I replied stifling my resentment at her betrayal. You'll be looking at the job ads one day soon, lady — thirty-something and no reference. It's going to be kind of hard for you, isn't it? Not a nice feeling at all. Living on the one wage with a big mortgage to pay. What will your husband Terry think when he hears you've been fired — with your children and your plans for another baby? I let her prattle on. She'd moved on to the children now. The usual.

'No, I'm not up to meeting for coffee. I'll be in next week.' The doorbell is ringing.

'Say, Laura, got to let you go. There's someone at the door. Bye.'

Paul Briscoe. Something about the look. A brief embrace.

'I think we've got something, Ava. In fact I'm near sure. I need to ask you a few questions, just so that we don't, go off on the wrong track, follow up on the wrong lead.'

'What is it, Paul? Have you found her or what?'

'No, nothing like that. Questions first, though. But if I'm right you'll need to consider packing your bags. Going on a journey. A long one.'

24

'Ireland.' I seemed to repeat the word endlessly. Dundalk, Ireland.

It was about all I could muster. My head had been a complete blur as I sought to answer Paul's questions earlier. No, I'd never heard mention of Dimato Pharmaceuticals setting up business in Ireland. My dad was, in fact, wholly bigoted against the Irish and steadfastly refused to employ them at the white-collar end of the business. Keep them on the building sites or at best the factory floor, he'd say. It now looked as if the true motivation lay in keeping his secrets, the skeletons in the broom cupboard. Even though the chance was remote, Joe Dimato was not going to risk the possibility that someone from the past would turn up and oust his stealthy dealings from the closet. Paul nodded in agreement.

'Thought so. I had a friend check it out with the authorities over there. They call them county councils, in this case Louth County Council. Also the Industrial Development Authority. Their records for back then are either old or non-existent but some old timers, mostly retired, are certain they would remember if Dimato Pharmaceuticals applied for grants. And they don't.'

Could it possibly be that my father's craving for money would lead me to my mother? I mulled it over as I digested what Paul told me. Dad held the taxation system in utter contempt – he would not listen to any argument that government had the authority to pocket as much as a cent of his hard-won earnings. He combated it initially with aggression and intimidation of officialdom but soon learned that stealth and evasion were much more convenient options. Thus, the first rule that was etched into the brain of all Dimato executives was that taxation was the devil to be avoided at all costs. Paul was interrupting my thoughts.

'I had to speculate first, think about what he might have been doing back then,' he said a little vainly. 'Adoption was not a possibility but purchase was.'

I let the cruel word go as my fascination with what he had unearthed sat above any insult the world might hurl my way right then. You're talking about me right now, Mr Briscoe, and you're saying that someone bought me like an add-on trinket, a piece of flesh-trading across the counter at the butcher's store. Button it, Ava. Listen on, say nothing. Paul continued.

'I had friends in the Department of Taxation and in your company – insiders or snouts, that's what we call them in my line of business – go over Joe Dimato's records between 1966 and 1968. Bless the taxation office, they never throw away anything. They've always been at battle with your company over its exorbitant claims for expenses to be offset against its incomes. We've identified two payments, each £20,000 Irish money, to the Bank of Ireland, Dundalk, in January 1967 and

July 1967. You'll see the significance of these dates yourself. Here, have a look, these are copies of the records – they're really cheque payment stubs.'

I glanced at them briefly and went to switch on the gas fire, feeling a chill sweep through my bones at what Paul was telling me. Didn't I know only too well about the Dimatos' creative accounting practices? I was brought up on them – they were ingrained in the psyche of all senior managers, including myself. It suddenly felt tacky. The interior redesign of my house had cost $72,000 and a receipt made out to Dimato Pharmaceuticals was already nestling in our accountant's file. The interest-free loans that Dad gave to workers by paying directly for their holidays in faraway exotic places were all reclaimed under the guise of research projects or customer hospitality. Even the workers incurred a two-per cent administration charge on their loans – just to cover the costs of staff employed to operate the scheme.

'So, it looks like my father went out and bought me in two instalments. A down-payment and the second half on delivery of the goods. The goods being myself, of course. Then passed me off as his own child and filed a claim for expenses with the tax office,' I said grimly.

'I'm afraid that's it, Ava. Gruesome stuff. My mole at the tax office is continuing on with his work. There's no easy way of putting this. He expects to be rewarded, a back-hander, so to speak. Every bit as corrupt as your accounting practices but very useful, nonetheless. I had to give him guarantees so as to get him going, motivated.'

'That won't be a problem,' I said stiffly. 'And I suppose the same applies to your inside man at Dimato Pharmaceuticals. I'll be paying someone who already works for me and draws down a salary?'

'Woman.'

'Laura?'

'Look, it's confidential. But, no, I went a different track here. This one's got form, a colourful history, you might say. She doesn't want it exposed. I blackmailed her. Don't look at me like that, woman, or start getting all moral with me. You're at it, they're at it, she's at it – why not me too? It's life, Ava. Way I look at it, there's only been one honest man in the whole world and they went and crucified him.'

'All right – you said twenty thousand Irish money. What would that be in our own?'

'Then? It would be $50,000. It was two-and-a-half dollars to the pound those days.'

So it was down to Dundalk, Ireland. I looked at the website addresses that Paul had written down. Get me familiar with the place, he said.

'The trail goes cold after that. I couldn't track down the account on the far side of the water. The reference numbers are meaningless to them – they changed them all when they went computerised over there. I was so fucking close to getting you a name for the girl in the photo – well, maybe not, but a name for the bank account, at least. But you're down to one town, maybe the county, and a photo. That's assuming she's still there.'

'Yeah, okay – listen, Paul, could I hold onto the payment stubs?'

'I'll make copies for you. But what do you want them for? I've told you they're useless apart from confirming that the bank is in Dundalk.'

'No reason,' I lied. 'I'd just like to have them – the original stubs.' I was propelling myself towards fantasy-land, visualising myself standing above a shame-faced woman, humiliating her with the evidence of her betrayal. It might not be traceable on modern banks' records but surely it would have left an indelible stain on the greedy woman's soul.

There was a slight pause, a moment's hesitation. 'Oh, here – take the originals. I'll give my man some excuse – say I lost them. Listen, I've got to run, I'll be in touch.'

You do that, Paul, I grated silently as his car sped out onto Beacon Hill. Run. Once business was discussed he couldn't wait to get away. Scared I might want to talk. It hurt like hell but I couldn't wallow in it. It struck me then how similar he was to Joe Dimato, how I had managed to pick another unfeeling man to fill the void in my life. Hopefully I would learn from this. Wasn't every experience supposed to teach you something? Paul was probably eyeing someone else, maybe even fucking her already. This was exactly how my father treated my mother. I wanted to quell the piercing pain of rejection with a stiff drink. That was what my dear mother had done and look what happened to her. Somewhere along the way I had heard the words 'this too shall pass' and I knew that I just had to hang in there. Be strong and stay focused. A tiny smile flittered across my lips as I thought of Paul and Laura together. That was cute of you when I suggested Laura as a name for the insider at the company. Clam up on me, talk about confidentiality. Maybe you and her – I mean, she'd take them off for almost anyone in the old days. What to do now, Ava?

What will I wear? Isn't that the big question, the crisis every good woman faces every day as her eyelids flicker awake as light shines into wherever she is, signalling the dawning of another day.

Doesn't matter if you're alone in your home between fresh cotton sheets or lying in some motel room bathed in stale sweat from your gyrations last night with the man sleeping next to you, the odours of his seminal fluids dispatched inside of you still hanging in the air. He'll get up when it suits, shave, throw on the same stuff. But you must face up to it, stay calm. What will you wear?

This time it would be different, though. I'd be meeting someone I'd never met before. I'd got to get it right, look the part.

That's it, I reflected. All packed up and ready to go. Not as hot as Boston, prone to the occasional shower. Weather usually good in August but no guarantees. Not like Disneyland, Florida, where they'll promise you ten hours, nearly put it in the contract for you. Yeah, some jeans, shirts and jackets and the usual personal things will do. I could always adapt, make purchases once I got over there, watch out for what *they* wear. Blend in. Paul hadn't mentioned anything about him coming over with me. But 'I'll help you find her' – that's what he said when he kick-started all of this. I was damned if I was going to ask him. The intimacy was broken and he now seemed to be looking on it as business. Not looking for any money, a freebie for old time's sake. He hadn't said it but that's how it seemed.

Now, where did I put that passport? I distinctly remembered putting it in the filing cabinet in my bedroom. Had the cabinet hand-made to match the other furniture in my bedroom – I didn't want it to look like an office. My searching became a little more urgent. I had it as recently as my flight from Provincetown. Ever since 9/11, they insist on seeing it, even on internal flights.

Sure, there's my flight ticket that I put in alongside it. Going to claim it as an expense. Dimato habit.

You've been burgled, Ava. Someone's been in your house. The night you ran over to the Comptons, the door left open. But nothing else is missing. Surely a burglar wouldn't let a gilt-edged opportunity like that slip. Walk through the open door of one of the best addresses in Boston, Beacon Hill. Go straight past everything to my room, take my passport and leave. Chad ... you're the only other possibility when you stuffed your trunk...

'It's going to take four days and that's the best I can do,' the stern-faced official at the passport office said. 'That's our procedure.'

Yes, he knew I had my driver's permit, my birth certificate, had the form signed by the Massachusetts State Police. But I was going on a trip to Ireland, a holiday. No connections over there, nobody sick or dying. There was no emergency and he had his procedures to follow

What if I had to go on some internal flight within the next few days? But I didn't have to – I'd said so myself.

'Yes, I am listening, Ms Dimato, but are you hearing my response? Four days.'

William and I had arranged to meet at the Bull and Finch Pub on Beacon Street. He was now a bespectacled fifty-four-year-old accountant and a grandfather to boot, looking a long way removed from the mischievous teenage boy who dared scale Joe Dimato's wall. He was carrying a flat parcel wrapped in brown paper that would have looked like a gift for someone but for the dullness of the cover. The choice of bar above coffee shop was deliberate – Frieda would say about her brother that it was usually the third pint that transformed him from mute to chatterbox.

'Did you know that the *Cheers* bar was designed exactly to match what's here?' he said suddenly.

I'd chosen early morning to avoid the hordes of tourists that would later surge through its doors. William was well known to keep himself topped up during the day in the many bars that surrounded Boston's financial centre. He'd carefully wedged his parcel between his and an empty seat so it would not fall. Something

226

fragile, like a sheet of glass, maybe?

'Everybody from Boston knows about *Cheers*. I have to say I never bothered myself with watching it. We could have done this over the phone, Ava. You want to ask me questions about something that happened thirty-eight years back. You have your photo – that's really all there is to it. Not much more to add.'

'Dad doesn't like talking,' his twin children, Nicole and Dylan, would say when they came over to Beacon Hill to visit. They were seven years younger than me and Frieda and, years ago, when they came over in their double buggies our dolls were quickly abandoned. These were the real thing and we could do the proud mother bit as we strutted up and down the tree-lined avenues soaking in the admiration of neighbours who stopped to look. I'd even emptied the money from my own piggybank into a sock and had written *Nicole and Dylan* on it, perching it on top of the hood so that neighbours would get the message. Frieda stopped boasting about being their auntie once she came to understand, aged twelve, that real aunties had perms and spoke in garbled languages, cooing and twitching their faces into absurdly ugly shapes as they sought to amuse the little mites. No, cousins sounded more hip, with it. That way, she'd get presents back, too.

'Aw, come on, William!' I said. 'This is about someone who could be my mother – don't shut down on me now. Look, I'm having another coffee – you fancy another drink?'

The trick with this reticent man was to get him

to relive his boyhood days when he was known to be the scourge of most parents who watched over their daughters on Beacon Hill. His sister would say that the transformation was quite sudden – somewhere along the line he had converted from an impulsive, fun-loving young man to what he was now – 'strait–laced and boring' were the words she used to describe him. Alcohol now played the part of retriever – it was his animation, how he brought to life the bygone days and summoned up the dregs to bolster him, remind people that he was once a free spirit, carefree and appealing. It was only his rigid convention that kept him away from the drying-out clinics. Come nine every evening, he would suddenly stop as if some unknown force was guiding him home-wards.

Right on cue, once the third pint was emptied and the barman was signalled again, the tongue began to loosen up.

'You're having a drink with me, no more of that coffee. Now where were we – the girl in the garden...'

The first time he had seen her was in December '66 when Ben Dimato had driven her up the driveway of our Beacon Hill home. Just got out of the car, went into the house. Nothing much to say about that. She was wrapped up in a coat and scarf but it was enough to get his curiosity going. Definitely taller than me, he said, reacting to my prompt. About five-foot seven, decent height for a girl. Her walk was sort of graceful, intriguing, but it was the silence of it all, how she waited by the car without a word as Joe came out and removed the luggage from the trunk. It was the stealthy nature of the comings and goings at the house that was to captivate him, hook him in. He and his dad never bought into the story that the Dimatos were spending all their time in Scotland, setting up the new factory.

'I mean, your dad had set up in Turin and Munich in the previous five years and there was no upheaval to coincide with those. Why for Scotland?'

Why indeed?

'I'll never forget the way she looked at me the day I sat up on that wall and took her photo. She just stood there robot-like, mechanical, once she dropped the washing – could have been a garden statue but for the eyes. Dark brown they were and saturated with fear. I never believed that it was *all* because there was a young guy on her wall, capturing her on film. Most of it was already there, like she was very troubled about something... I don't know... Then Joe roared at her to get inside and she took off like a frightened rabbit.' His voice trailed away.

Suddenly, he was fumbling open the parcel on the floor.

'You'll need to come round here alongside me to see this. It's a painting of the garden that day – how I saw it, using the photograph and my memory of things that the camera didn't capture. I know it's not very good. I've been dabbling at painting these last few years – I find it sort of hard to sleep after five in the morning. I always thought the picture only depicted one person's fear that day but there was more – I was scared

229

too, your parents. Yes – even Joe Dimato. There was something in the atmosphere that day, you couldn't put your finger on it – but there was something wrong.'

God, you've no need to be modest, William, I thought. Boston in winter, the Dimato gardens covered in a fine film of snow, Mystery Girl looking up at the figure of a young man falling backwards off the wall, his camera flying upwards in the air. The washing she had dropped strewn across the garden. Joe Dimato emerging like a raging bull through the French doors.

'It's perfect, William, really it is. The house, the grounds, you've got it spot on.'

William was jabbing at the picture. 'That's me there, fell straight into the bushes in the next garden, Mrs Wilson's. She's at her door, asking me what do I think I'm doing. Pulling thorns out of my behind for the rest of the day, that's what I was doing.'

I looked at the small kitchen window over on the right. A face was visible, looking through. I started. 'But the person in the window, who's that?'

'Your mother, Maria Dimato, who else? You see, when your father came to our house throwing a fit, he made no mention of me taking photographs at all. I don't think to this day that he ever knew I took that photo. The girl, she was too frightened to understand fully what was going on. Or maybe just didn't say. No, what really bothered your dad was that I saw *two* women that he didn't want me to see that day – the girl and your mother.'

230

I was stunned. 'But you didn't tell your mother that!'

'No. I never told anyone. Not after Joe Dimato's threats. I almost chose not to tell you, even now.'

We both sat side by side as we examined the picture in hushed silence. I was struggling to restrain myself, hoping he would speak first. It was as if the spark that had disappeared from his public persona was flickering to life in his sketching, his drawings. He coughed briefly as if he was making a momentous decision.

'This one's kind of special to me, too. I did it over a two-year period, erasing things I got wrong – trying to get the two faces right, the girl and Joe, and imagine how I'd look falling off a wall. Mrs Dimato was too far away to capture the face – see how she felt about it all but, even then, her lurking in the shadows like she's cowering away from something, it kind of fits in, doesn't it?'

Surely does, William, I mused, that would be her. Silence again, each wrapped in the moment.

'Frieda spoke with me, told me things only recently after you came to mother's house the other night in a panic. I suppose deep down I knew – that it wasn't Maria Dimato that was with child – it was her, the girl. That would mean that you're in the picture too, wouldn't it?'

'I don't know, William, I really don't.'

Suddenly the words I was hoping for came tumbling out.

'You take it, keep it. It's more about your life than mine, though it's quite significant to me also.'

I bit down on a phoney protest at his big-hearted gesture. I could feel the wrench and didn't want to risk a withdrawal of the offer, a change of heart. It was not a Picasso but the flaws made it real, incapable of being copied because only he, William, was *there*.

'Thanks,' I whispered, while blinking back the tears. 'Look, I can see it means a lot to you so I'll only take it on loan. See how things work out, how I feel about it later on. Do you mind?'

'Not at all. Do you fancy another drink?'

'I'll just have one more with you, William. My round.'

Another drink in the company of this deep, complex man seemed a small price to pay for what he had given me. Somehow the term *Cheers* did not fit in with him and I wondered what significant occurrence had strangled the reckless abandon of his earlier years. Always lost in something, Frieda would remark, whether it be figures, some deserted bar or the early morning easel.

Paul listened as I told him over the phone about William's painting and then described my experience at the passport office.

'That makes it next weekend you'll be going.'

The *'you'* shone out like a bonfire, burning through to my heart. He was not coming, I'd be doing this alone.

And I was not to ask Chad about my passport either. I felt like all my power was slipping away from me, out of control into the hands of others. Cannot confront anyone these days – Chad –

Laura – Ben. Following orders from Paul Briscoe like a sheepdog. Hiding in terror behind the curtains in my own home while two thugs outside have a casual chat in the driveway – huddled in a smoky café with a needle-saturated junkie desperately picking up titbits that would help animate a still picture of a young woman, bring it to life. Give it meaning, give my life meaning. Society girl following orders from some shabbily dressed ex-cop who's cast aside the number of times you've had his hardened manhood between your legs, your lips, without so much as a thought. When this is all finished...

'You still there, Ava?' he enquired at the end of the phone.

'I am, Paul. I take it you're not coming to Ireland, then?'

An uneasy silence.

'Eh, you go over first. It's kind of personal – intimate, this stuff, finding your mother. You'll have your photo. People are nice over there, but a little suspicious. Two Americans bearing down on them, shoving photographs in their faces, might do more harm than good. Use your womanly charm on them – I'll always be at the end of a phone, help to keep you on course. I have my contacts – you'll be fine.'

I'll have to be, I thought gloomily. It made it worse knowing that he was right. Paul had helped me narrow it down from the universe to a small county in Ireland in a matter of days. The redundant bank account was the end of the line for a man in his trade. We were back to a level playing field. I could hold a photograph in front of someone's face as easily as he could. Maybe better. I'd have to make friends over there. What was the name of that film – the 'Yank' going over there to claim his inheritance and getting killed by some deranged Irishman? Oscar-nominated. *The Field*, yes. Better a woman go alone, I reasoned, unable to accept Paul's rejection.

Tuesday. My flight booked for the following Sunday, I paced the hardwood floor relentlessly as elation and fear took its grip simultaneously. There must be something I could do in the meantime while the clock ticked slowly down. Don't let them think you know anything's wrong, that you know anything, where you're going. That's what Paul had said.

I heard the phone ringing at the other end and dialled the extension that I knew by heart.

'Good morning, Dimato Pharmaceuticals, Sales Division, Laura speaking.'

'Laura, Ava here. How are things going in there?'

'Fine. Everything okay with you?'

'Yeah, listen, I was wondering if you'd like to go out for a drink, maybe a bite to eat – girl time.'

'Oh, I don't know ... the kids ... oh, why not? You're on.'

'We'll meet in the cocktail bar outside the door of the building. Five thirty, say?'

Replacing the receiver, I grinned manically at my mischief. Let her think everything is okay. That's what I intended to do. Sack her when I get back. A born social-climber and a sucker for status was Laura. A night in with the kids or to be seen out on the town with a partner in a global company? There was no contest. One of those who can recite the ins and outs of good parenting but will dump the offspring at the drop of a hat when something more attractive than their whooping and bickering comes up. No loyalty to either side, willing to eavesdrop on my telephone conversations yet fit to dump shit on the Dimatos while helping Paul out.

I spent the rest of the morning searching on the internet. County Louth. Population one hundred and ten thousand. Dundalk has less than thirty thousand. Not as popular as the west coast, Paul had said. You'll get accommodation quite easily. It didn't turn out that way and I quit, exhausted and dispirited, after numerous booking rejections. Best ring, I thought.

'Carrickdale Hotel – Alison speaking. Yes, we do have vacancies. No, I wouldn't say there's anything wrong with the internet sites. It's just that there are the National Community Games Finals that weekend. Everywhere is booked out and the place will be teeming with children. We're a bit further away so we don't get as many. You'll like it here, though. That's Monday August 22nd to Sunday August 28th. With an option to extend. Yes, that looks okay. No, you don't need to go back on the website and we do take American Express.'

I left the Louth site two hours later, my head a jumble of confusion. You're going to have to learn it all over again when you get there. Hopefully something will turn up in Dundalk, I thought, not relishing the notion that Mystery Girl might be hidden out in the larger county. You won't be

235

a girl now, though. In your fifties, if William guessed it right. I peered again at the photograph, running a finger across the clear features of her face.

'Ava, what are you doing standing out there in the street?'

I jumped to see Isabel behind me.

'You look weird looking up at your own office block like you're seeing it for the first time. Come on, I'll buy you a coffee, I've loads to fill you in on.'

Jesus, you would have to turn up at the wrong time, wouldn't you? I longed to say it. Instead I rang Laura from the lavatory of the Coffee Dock.

'Can you make it six, Laura? I've been held up. See you then. Okay?'

I put oh my saccharine-sweet smile as I approached my sister-in-law. The bags, Giorgio Armani, Chanel, Jasmine. This lady was one serious shopper when she got down to it. Had all the cards: American Express, Mastercard, you name it. Chad had tried reasoning with her but it was no use. Always had an excuse and flavour of the month now was that she had to look the part as the senator's wife. Let's wait until November and see if the people of Massachusetts will have him as congressman first, Isabel.

Right now, she was eyeing me up and down disapprovingly.

'Just looking at you coming back, you haven't put a pound on since you were twenty-one. The clothes though – they're cute but are they you?'

Blunt as you like. I looked down at my Ralph

Lauren polo shirt, faded denim jeans and white casual shoes. Talk about making you feel inadequate. Suddenly, I was embarrassed by my choice.

'Look, I didn't mean to insult you, I'm sorry. It's just me and my mouth. It's nice – just very laid-back, casual. Never saw you wearing anything like that before, that's all.'

Well, you wouldn't, I thought as my mind lapsed into the past. The Dixie Dude Ranch, Texas. Me and Paul had done three nights over there two years back. I'd been nagging him to set up a week somewhere. Three days riding on horseback, swimming in outdoor pools, it turned out to be an exhilarating experience. The outdoor hot tubs provided solace to my aching joints.

Isabel was talking again.

'Actually, I've been doing a bit of shopping myself.'

'How unusual for you,' I said cynically. It was a bit too late to rush back home and change.

'No, I mean, but this is different.'

Sure it is, Isabel. Keep on telling yourself that and it will be okay.

She continued in a lower voice but loudly enough for it to resonate in my brain. 'I'm pregnant.'

I could feel the pounding of my heart, my face reddening.

'Congratulations, Isabel.'

'It's a bit down the road yet. I'm just two months gone. I was wondering if you'd be fit to take a few days off at the time. It's just that Sam and Sabrina are fussy about who minds them –

they're still talking about their last time with you. You're so practical, Ava, I've always said that. You just fit in with them like you were one of them. Wish I had it...' Her voice trails away.

'I'm getting myself a drink,' I said suddenly, leaping towards the bar. 'Sea breeze, please,' I said to the barman.

'I'll bring it right down.'

'No, I'd prefer if you gave me one right here – you can bring another one down to our table.'

Downing it in one gulp, it was all I could do to stop myself going back to Isabel and swinging at her. Talk of tact and she wanted to be a senator's wife! The barman and an old-timer drinking a Budweiser at the bar exchanged knowing looks.

Back at the table I gulped down my second drink.

'Well, that's great news, Isabel. I'm delighted for you. Must dash now, though.' I started rummaging in my bag.

'But, hold on, Ava – I want to go through the detail of Saturday's do at our house. You haven't been over since we finished the renovation. Chad really wants this party to go right. He's hoping you can be there to give a hand – he's told Ben to leave you alone.'

'Okay, I'll ring you tomorrow about it. I've really got to be going...'

'You go, I'll pay, including the one you had at the bar. If you're in such a rush...' she said, giving up on the vain hope that I would give her some news to bring home to my brother.

25

My cell phone started to ring as I rushed out into the street. Laura's name flashed up.

'Ava, are you standing me up – hold on, I see you now.'

The noisy drone of traffic hummed along the Boston streets, almost grid-locked. My phone was crackling – her voice came, then disappeared. Laura waving, gesticulating towards the cocktail bar. Thumbs up from me. Cars honking at me as I navigated my way through the crawling traffic.

She was inside, two drinks in front of her. The suited businessmen stopped to stare. Some of them Dimato Pharmaceuticals. Executive women dressed smartly in their office suits.

'What's wrong with everybody today?' I asked, seated opposite my secretary. 'Go on, you say it, you're looking at me too. I've just had an earful from Isabel. You might as well get it off your chest, too.'

'The outfit – are you going somewhere special?' she asked.

'Jesus, I've been just across the street with Isabel and she's saying the same thing.'

Laura had done as I expected. Ran off home once lunch came and was now resplendent in a pure linen beige suit, white blouse and the whiff of Yves St Laurent hanging in the air. Didn't expect her boss to turn up looking like this. I gritted my teeth.

Bad fashion mistake, Ava.

'No, I'm not. I'm just going casual. Do you not remember, in the old days we used to have "dress-down" Fridays and we'd hit the pubs after work. I didn't expect you to be so dolled up.'

'Oh, it's nothing. I had to run back home at lunchtime. Small problem at the house. With the plumbing and all. I decided I'd change. Joe Dimato never liked those dress-down days, did he?'

Her eyes averted suddenly, her face reddening. I became aware that I was piercing through her with my stare, recalling. The gold watch – bought that last Christmas, wasn't it, with the company bonus – the 'loyalty bonus' as Joe Dimato would call it, the size of the paycheque determined by how long you endured the place. It'll look good at your next job interview, won't it, Laura? Hopefully I'll have you sorted by the end of the year – out there in the job queue. Save on paying you the bonus. Not now, though.

'Look, Laura, can we drink up and go somewhere less formal? I'm tired of all the looks I'm getting.'

We were out in the street, the noise deafening as people desperately tried to wind their way back home. The sticky heat had converted to a heavy downpour and my view ahead was blurring as the alcohol sent little waves rippling towards my brain. Laura was shouting behind me, damp patches starting to appear on her light-coloured suit.

'Have you any idea where we're going?'

'Brookline. We'll hop on the Amtrak, get there quicker.'

'Yeah, this is more like it – don't you think?'

'Ava, have you gone crazy? What are we doing out here?'

'I don't know what you mean. Isn't it fine?'

The pub was dense with workers coming from the building sites, fighting to get attention from the harassed staff behind the bar. Orders for fish and chips, bowls of soup and homemade bread flying about.

'Nothing, it's just that they're ... I don't know...' Laura was now fingering her suit questioningly, wondering.

'Just that they're Irish, is that what you were going to say? You'd be right. Matt Murphy's Pub. Isn't it great, different? Look, there's a little recess over there. You go sit down. I'll get the drinks and some menus.'

The men parted at the bar to let me take up a position. The banter started in the background. 'Let the lady past, boys – she's ordering for her boss as well – looks a bit snobby sitting over there. No, we like this one, don't we? Give me a pair of jeans on a woman any day!'

'Or off her!' came a voice from behind.

Guffaws of laughter all around.

A drink-fuelled surge of bravery flowed over me. 'A pint of Guinness and a Long Island ice tea, please, and two menus.'

'I wonder who the Guinness would be for then? The one in the corner doesn't look up to it. I'd say it's this one.'

'You'd want to be having manners now, Jimmy. Ye were at the same craic last night, annoying other folk.' A thick Irish brogue indeed. Melodious, kind of pleasing. 'You'll be out on your ear, barred, if you keep it up.'

'Don't mind him, love. That's his usual chat-up line. Pretends he's looking out for you, then pounces. One to watch, stay away from him.'

I made my way back to our seats.

Laura tugged at my sleeve, muttered, 'Let's get out of here, Ava. I don't like it, the way they leer at you.'

'Come on, you've spent too long listening to my father's prejudice about them, shredding their job applications as soon as they hit your desk. We need to change that policy. Be a sport, I'm having an Irish Stew. It's different, a change – you were always game for a laugh.'

'Well, okay, I'll stay for a little while,' she said hesitantly. 'You recommend something. I don't know what we're doing here, I really don't.'

Soon I was tucking into Irish Stew while Laura had a Shepherd's Pie.

'God, you know it's not bad, not bad at all,' she said. 'And the crowd has quietened down a little. Funny the way they go. Minute someone comes in the door, they go all raucous and jeering for a few minutes, then settle down again until the next one comes. Must be a custom over there.'

'I think they call it a *fáilte* – a welcome, yeah, that's it?' I was drawing on my Irish internet crawl. I tried hard to stop wincing as I sipped on my Guinness. How can they like this stuff? I

242

should have stuck to my favourite – a glass of chilled white wine.

'You seem to know a bit about this crowd – how's that?' she asked. 'I've never seen you go to an Irish pub before this.'

A memory of Bruce comes swimming up to rescue me. 'Hey, didn't I go to the Ireland versus Italy game back in 1994 with my ex-husband? Met up with a few of them afterwards.'

Laura paused and started again in a faltering voice. 'Speaking of ex-husbands, don't say a word about this to anyone but Terry has moved out, left me.'

My evening's drinking was starting to take hold. Poor Laura, office slut turned model mum. Terry was from Australia and worked as a pharmacist at the Massachusetts General Hospital. He'd come over from Sydney twelve years back and dropped his CV in at the office. Laura was in my office the following morning waving his tanned face under my nose as she fervently made a case for the man she'd met less than twenty-four hours earlier. Got all his qualifications, she said, jabbing her finger at the Education and Training Section. Big into surfing, he hung out on Bondi Beach during his summer vacation from college. The film *Point Break*, the one with Keanu Reeves – if you look closely enough at it, you'll see Terry in it as an extra. Exactly the right stuff for Dimato Pharmaceuticals.

'Leave it with me, Laura,' I had said firmly. I recognised the lustful look and was not going to let her hormones determine who went on the payroll. Good-looking, nice mop of blond hair, I

243

thought looking at the passport-size photo stapled to the form. There would be no harm done in giving him an interview. I rang only to be informed that he had left the Boston YMCA.

'I'm afraid your friend is gone, Laura, left without giving notice. Can you file this form in the applications-withdrawn section?'

'No, no, he's not gone – he's around all right.'

'Laura, give me a break. I've just rung the address. Your friend left suddenly yesterday evening, no explanation. Just removed his stuff from the dormitory. He'll be halfway to New York by now. Makes you wonder why he bothered to fill out the form. No number to contact either.'

'No, you don't understand. I can contact him for you – during lunch. I could get him over by the afternoon.'

My firm stare told my secretary I wanted the full story.

She just felt sorry for him. He'd have to leave the hostel next week when the students came back and he was down on his money anyway. It'd be a mean thing to do, leave him out on the streets so far away from home. Letting him stay over at her place for a few days until he got himself set up.

'Your apartment – it's a one-bed, isn't it?' I was revelling in her discomfort, watching her squirm.

As it turned out, Terry didn't need us in the end. Got himself fixed up with a job at the hospital that very morning and took Laura out to Nauset Beach in Orleans that weekend as a thank-you. Taught her how to surf and how Australian men do other things. Now, eleven years and two children later, he was walking out.

'Men, who needs them?' I giggled in a slurred voice.

'Ava, it's not funny. Someone from his past just waltzes in from Australia and he waltzes out of my life with her after eleven years. Eleven fucking years – as casual about it as you like. "Her name is Alice and we're in love."' Laura was now mimicking his Aussie accent. 'Wendy and Elliott are devastated and crying all the time ... when is Daddy coming home ... our mortgage and all ... I don't know how we're going to manage. He just doesn't seem to care even when I tell him I'm buying our children's clothes at the thrift shops, other people's castaways.'

Easy prey for Ben Dimato, I reflected bitterly. Probably knew she was strapped for cash and now she was in his pocket. Once he knew she was compromised, he wouldn't have to pay her anything at all – just threaten to reveal her as a traitor to her boss and friend. Anyway, Paul had unearthed her deceit and she already had lost her value to my uncle. It was hard not to feel sorry for her. A few days from now, I'd be flying out from Boston and I'd wait and see how I felt towards her when I got back.

We ordered more drinks and Laura continued her tale of woe.

Eventually, much later, I glanced at my watch through reddened eyes. Midnight. I'd had my first drink some seven hours back. I had a head full of Laura's troubles with an increasingly blurred vision of the people at the bar.

'He blames me for it all, said we were doing fine

245

until I started talking more babies. Ava, are you listening to me at all?'

I was on my feet, tottering unsteadily.

'We'll go one last round, lady. A toast to all men. Especially your Terry and Bruce Prefontaine – that God may remove their balls!'

'No, leave me out,' I heard Laura reply. 'Where are you going now, Ava? Your drink is being brought over.'

'The rest-room – you wait there. I'll be right back – right back.'

As I emerged some time later the barman was shouting. 'Cab outside for Ms Dimato! You watch how you go there – don't worry about the broken glass. Your friend – she rang you a cab and then she left suddenly. I'll walk you outside – sure we all get smashed once in a while. No, I don't know much about Dundalk. Opposite end of the country – Cork, if you ever heard of it. There you go now ... can you watch her bag, sir ... she was nearly leaving it behind.'

The front-seat passenger passed it wordlessly over to the driver and the car moved out into the night. I felt like I was going to get sick and stretched out in the back seat, my eyes squinting at the thickset figure in the passenger seat. Double-jobbing – these night-time cab boys are always on the make. Only one meter but two fares. Stay awake, Ava.

'So it's Beacon Hill first, then?'

A vaguely familiar voice cut in ahead of me. 'No, we'll be taking a detour down here, turn right at the next set of lights.'

Obviously has no consideration for ladies first

and all that shit. If only I could put a name on the chauvinist prick…

'Okay, and where to after that?'

'I'll tell you as we go along. You just do the driving.'

'Okay, Ben, you're the boss.'

A cell phone started ringing.

'Ben, did somebody say Ben?' I mumbled. 'Is that you, Uncle – what are you doing here – where are you bringing me?'

The men in the front continued to talk, ignoring me.

'That's in her bag, Ben. Here you go … aren't you going to answer it?'

'No, it's only Briscoe. Looks like he didn't get the message from the boys as clearly as I would have liked. He'll have to wait, won't he?'

'You'd wonder, though, what she sees in him. In his fifties, a grandfather, hair going missing rapidly. Someone like me now, I'd be much better for her… If she got one from me, she'd not want to go near him again.'

'Drive the car, you asshole. That's my niece you're talking about.'

'All right, you know I'm only joking. I know the limits. You were never one for the women, were you?'

'Turn left up here, then right, up the hill.'

'Your house. I was beginning to think you were dropping her off at Chad's. He lives around here too, doesn't he?'

'That he does, just two minutes away from me. Now, will you get a move on!'

'Strange that, her getting zonked out with the

Paddies. Went right out of her way to get there too. I mean, I'd never think of going over that way, especially to an Irish bar. No connections, it's strange.'

'Quit the talking – Ava – are you awake back there?'

'Hm, hm – what are you doing here, Ben? Why won't you two talk to me – tell me what's going on?'

I heard his voice sliding slowly away through my alcohol-filled daze.

'Nothing's going on, Ava – nothing at all.'

26

'There you go. Geez, lady, you really gave it a lash last night! Can you let us in on what you were celebrating?'

I blinked my eyes open as the hulking figure at the end of the bed gradually took shape. Ben ... what was he doing here? I sat bolt upright and the coffee that my uncle was holding sprayed violently across the duvet cover. Christ, I'm not even in my own bedroom, my own home.

'Don't worry about it, I'll get you another. Martha will come up later – put the bedclothes in the washing machine.'

'No, don't, I'll get up – I'll be downstairs in a minute.'

My mind raced frantically. I was at Ben's house. How did I get there? I scrambled out of bed as he left and locked myself in immediately. My bag, my cell phone, I needed to ring someone to come and get me out of here. What did Ben want with me ... where was my damn bag? At least I was sleeping in the clothes I wore, for once welcoming the stale sweaty feeling. It was much better than the thought of my uncle's paws all over me, undressing me for bed. Discarding them on the floor, I showered quickly in the en-suite and I was soon peering round the door of the kitchen.

'Sit down there, Ava, I'll scramble you up some eggs. Easiest thing to eat after a night on the tiles. I rang Chad – he's coming by on his way to work,' Ben said.

Sounded like family conference time. I reprimanded myself for not listening to Paul. A low profile – and there I was letting it all go in an Irish bar! Maybe I should have taken out a page in the *Globe*, let them all know.

'How did I get here, Ben? I was in the bar at midnight – then it all got terribly hazy – you and some other man – then nothing.'

'You can certainly say that. I can tell you, you mightn't look much, standing next to me. But try carrying you upstairs, you had me gasping. I'd say you were about eight years old the last time I carried you.'

I suddenly felt like retching and sprinted quickly to the downstairs toilet.

Ben was happily making circles with a wooden spoon at the stove when I got back.

'Nearly ready, honey. These, I like them just done, a little soft maybe. You'll probably like some toast – wholemeal, white?'

'Ben, will you stop rattling on and tell me how I got here?'

'Laura, your secretary. She tried to ring Chad first but couldn't contact him. She just thought that I'd be the next best bet. Didn't think it right that you go home to an empty house. She said you had a fall recently.'

My faithful secretary, I thought mockingly. Access to the senator, even in the middle of the night.

'Do you know where my bag and cell phone are?'

'On the coffee table in the living room. What took you down to Brookline, to Matt Murphy's? An Irish pub of all things?'

Divine inspiration needed to come from somewhere and it did. 'Well,' I said coyly, 'I'm seeing someone and he's Irish – only it looks like he stood me up last night. That's why I want to get my cell phone, ring him.'

'I'll go get it for you. So you're seeing a Paddy? Funny, Laura didn't mention anything about that. We'd love to meet him, Chad and me. Does he have a name, this guy? Why don't you ring him up there – get an explanation why he left you in the lurch last night?' His bulbous eyes showed that he was really enjoying my embarrassment.

'Eh, I'll leave it for now. He works on a building site. He'll have it switched off until evening.' I looked at my phone. Six missed calls. Five from Paul, one from a private number. I was to pick up my new passport today. I really needed to get away from this house. The cell phone rang again.

Paul – fuck you, go away!

'Aren't you going to answer it? Could be your Irish friend. It kept ringing while you came over in the taxi last night. Paul B, that's what kept flashing up.'

I felt cornered, trapped, right here in my uncle's home, my whole body feeling wet and clammy despite my recent shower. The phone stopped ringing. Ben was now gazing intently at me, a thin smile on his lips, but the eyes were cold, stone cold.

'Ava Dimato, my brother's daughter ... dear, dear, what has become of you? Paul B, I'd say that would be Paul Briscoe, ex Massachusetts State Police. Me and Paul go back a very long way. Fine guy, very helpful when he came on the force first. I think it was back in 1970. Got a few promotions very quickly, then forgot who was behind them. You're sleeping with him, aren't you? Now, I don't mind that but what I wouldn't like is if he was helping you with your wild-goose chase. I wouldn't like that at all.'

I heard the door in the hallway open.

Ben got up. 'That will be Chad. We're going to sit down as a family and talk this over, the three of us.'

Then his face dropped suddenly as the kitchen door opened.

'Martha! I wasn't expecting you over until the afternoon – what are you doing here?'

Martha Jones, this portly smiling woman, was standing at the kitchen door.

'Ava, my baby, it's good to see you,' she said once she got her breath. 'I was dreaming about

251

you last night.'

I gave Martha a pleading look, hoping she'd pick up on my need to escape from Ben.

'Now, Martha, don't go starting on again about your dreams,' Ben chided. 'Look, there's not much going on today – you take yourself off home.'

Martha glared at Ben. 'No, thanks, Mr Ben – I'm not going back to sit on my own in that apartment for the rest of the day. I'm going straight back to the grocery store to buy some apples because I'm going to make a pie. Remember, Miss Ava, you used to love my apple-pies.'

Ben looked baffled as he looked from Martha to myself, wondering what had he missed. It took all of my power to hold myself from hugging this two-hundred-and-fifty-pound Jamaican lady. Right now, she was my saviour, my opportunity.

'No, don't go, Martha. I'll go for you. Have a cuppa first. Say, Chad was talking to me the other day about your pension fund. Said it had built up nicely over the years.'

Martha was looking at me, nonplussed. 'What are you talking about, lady? I'm not going on no pension, retiring. Mr Ben, you say something – you're not letting me go after all these years?'

I was in before Ben could speak. 'No, Martha, not at all. Jesus, my big mouth! I didn't mean to alarm you. It's just money that's owing to you after forty years of service.' I turned to look at Ben. 'You tell her, Ben – Eagle Star, wasn't that where you invested for her? I even remember Dad talking about it – he felt he should throw a few dollars in too.'

Martha's smile was broadening while my uncle was rendered momentarily speechless. She whooped loudly and slapped him hard on the back just as he lifted the coffee cup towards his mouth.

'Well, good Lord! You might be one big bear, Ben Dimato, but a cuddly bear that's what you are! You were looking out for old Martha all along.'

I picked up my bag. Ben's face looked like it was going to combust into a raging fire.

I flung my arms around the big lady in gratitude. 'Martha, I'll go and get those apples.'

'No, you can't! You have to wait!' Ben hollered.

I flew out the door and out of the house and down the hill, then swung around to see Ben pumping after me, face reddened, his eyes bulging, and Martha with her arms thrown out dramatically, shrieking my name.

I sprinted flat out down the hill.

I seemed to be running for an eternity when the Massachusetts Bay Transportation Authority sign loomed ahead at Harvard Square. Nobody behind.

Ticket accepted, I paused to draw breath on the train, sucking air into my lungs, retching. Nobody seeming to notice or care. Packed like sardines on their way to work. I disembarked at Government Centre and ran for the nearest café. Once in the toilets, I opened up my cell phone to check for bugs. Nothing there.

I rang Paul.

'Ava, where are you? I'm over at your house.

Where the hell have you been?'

'Can it wait? I'll explain when I get home.'

'No, it can't, I want to hear what's going on. Stay where you are. I'll pick you up right away.'

Paul came within minutes and listened quietly as I told him what had taken place the previous evening before exploding into a rage.

'Here I am, running round after you, removing bugs from your home, trying to protect you from Ben Dimato and what are you doing? Calling up your secretary, who happens to be in his pocket, and then you go off to an *Irish* bar, right on my doorstep, and get yourself unmercifully tanked up! Is it that you want him to know or what?'

He paused for breath and an angry retort formed in my brain but not soon enough to beat him before he resumed his rant. 'You've also booked your flight over the internet and have been checking out hotel sites in Ireland on it too. For Jesus sake, Ava, are you trying to tip them off? Looks like we're going to have to get you out of here – tonight. You're going to fly over to Ireland tonight. Now we'll go and get that passport. Then I'll go back to the house – get your stuff.'

Chastened by this man once again, I felt violated, almost raped. He'd wiped my computer clean of all files and messages, didn't have time to be fretting over what was important to me. Was bringing it over to his house until all this was sorted out.

'But I'm booked for Sunday. And how were you able to get into my house?'

'Leave the booking as it is for Sunday – you can

take the loss. They may have accessed your password – it will do no harm to let them think you're on that flight. It also gives us a bit of time, space. There's a late flight to Dublin tonight. Still plenty of availability, there won't be a problem. We won't book it until the last minute, at the airport.'

There was no arguing with him. I sat silently and meekly in the car across the city. A strange sense of anti-climax and fear came over me, enveloping me like a shroud. I wanted to scream out at the world – Paul – my pseudo-family – everybody. There was too much pain, espionage and intrigue. What was it to Ben Dimato that he so badly wanted to prevent me finding my mother?

First I stopped at the bank. 'Ten thousand euros!' whistled the cashier. A lot of money to be carrying – this was Boston after all. What was I going to tell him – that I was working to instructions, had lost my power completely? Cash for everything from here on. Had technology moved so fast that if you flashed your American Express Card in China for a pair of silk panties, someone logging on in Boston would know immediately?

Wordlessly, I handed the money envelope to Paul and went in to pick up my passport. Same smarmy official.

'Now, here we are, Ms Ava Dimato,' he said looking at the photo, then me. 'Definitely you, I'd say. Enjoy your trip.'

I glanced at my watch. Three o'clock. Go over to Downtown Boston, South Station, and hang around there until about eight o'clock. Paul was keeping my luggage and cash. I was to get on the subway for Logan International Airport around eight. Flight to Dublin was at eleven o'clock. Don't check in – he'd meet me there at the main entrance. I was to ring him as soon as I got off the subway. In the coffee shop at South Station, I had plenty of time to regret not taking Emily's advice. See a therapist, a counsellor. Maybe I'd ring one – they could come over and while away a few hours until I boarded the train. We could talk about loads of things. Maybe she'd recommend I get my biological mother on one of these television shows where I could confront her in front of a worldwide audience, tell them she'd traded her baby, her soul for money. How I wished I could be Chad instead who didn't seem to give a damn about where he came from as long as he could grasp the reins of power. But then he had other things: a pregnant wife and two children, for example.

'G'day to you, Ava Dimato. Can I join you?' I looked up at the tanned face, the mop of curly blond hair.

Terry Cahill, until recently husband to Laura, my betrayer.

'I suppose you can. There's nothing stopping you from doing what you want these days.'

Terry sat and got busy slicing through his bagel, buttering it up like he hadn't got a care in the world. Eleven years since he hit Boston – the man from Bondi Beach. He'd gone back there on a once-in-a-lifetime family trip to Sydney last year. His parents had been killed in a road accident when he was just three years old. His

256

aunt had taken over the rearing of him and his sister.

Laura was walking on air for months before they went and had broken her one-hour-per-day TV rule to let Wendy and Elliott watch all three *Crocodile Dundee* movies, one after the other. Six wonderful weeks later, she would entertain the office endlessly with her stories of Sydney Harbour, the Opera House and how no surfing facilities down at Cape Cod could hold a candle to Bondi Beach. In Matt Murphy's Bar last night, though, it had transformed into the holiday from hell, a complete metamorphosis. He'd called up Alice, a beach groupie, as Laura spitefully called her, and there she was still on the shelf, primed to snatch her Terry away from her. Bits of last night's conversation started to resurface.

'He's going through a mid-life crisis, Ava. I read about it and he has all the symptoms. The kids are devastated after all the fun they had over there. We did all the must-do's for kids – the Bridge Climb, Harbour Cruise and the Blue Mountains. Wendy's burned all our photographs – she's terribly upset. As for her father, he's gone completely into himself, can't get him to communicate – he just stands there dopily saying he loves this Alice. You should see her! I'd say she's had more shots fired at her than that dartboard over there.'

What is it about women and rejection? Always ready to blame the other woman, even themselves. Only last night, Laura was saying she should never have proposed another baby. That was when he started working extra hours at the hospital laboratory. Or so she thought.

Terry wiped cream cheese from his mouth with a serviette. 'There you go. That was nice. Never talk while I'm eating. Yeah, I hear your animosity – very hurtful and all. I thought you'd be more broadminded.' The smile on his face was the giveaway – Terry didn't give a shit. 'It was just bad luck, for Laura I mean, that I ran into her when I was bust, nothing in my pocket. She took me in, we had eleven good years but once I saw Alice back in Sydney, I knew I'd made a mistake. Life's too short and I wasn't going to carry on refusing to acknowledge it to myself.'

'But this Alice, is she going to be happy to spend the rest of her life in America?'

'Won't have to. I'm going back to Australia. The kids can come and visit when they want to.'

I resisted the temptation to enquire about how this might affect his children long-term. Somehow, I felt I might end up in a police cell for assault using the boiling hot coffee in front of me. I had a flight to catch and I was not going to let this strutting egotist spoil it. Six o'clock. I decided I'd while away my time in another of the station's restaurants.

'I think I'll leave you alone in the wonderful little world of men that you have woven for yourself, Terry.'

He flashed me a brilliant white smile as I recalled Frieda's assessment of him: definitely got hit on the head by a surf board at some point – most self-respecting Aussies would disown him.

My cell phone started throbbing in my jacket pocket, its tone inaudible amongst the heaving

258

masses on South Station. *Private Number* started flashing up. Don't take any calls whatsoever, another of Paul's rules. Better eat something before you go, Ava. Those TV dinners you get on air journeys never quite did it for you. A quick Chinese would do nicely and kill off these last couple of hours.

Eight thirty. I was at the main entrance of Logan International Airport about to dial when I felt a tugging at my arm. No need, there was Mr Briscoe with my luggage, assuming control once more, summarily removing the phone from my grasp.

'You go buy your ticket. The 23.15 to Dublin. There are still plenty of seats available. I'll wait right here for you.'

Paul inspected the tickets on my return. I'd be landing in Dublin in the afternoon on Friday, with the time difference allowed for. My new cell phone nestled in my pocket. Paul had transferred just two numbers from the old: his and Frieda's. He'd hold on to it until I got back.

I just had to take a stand. 'No, Paul, give me my phone back. I'll use this new one you gave me, keep the other one switched off. I'll only check it for messages and texts. I won't make or take any calls on it. I'm tired of all this paranoia about surveillance, the supervision. I'm only going looking for my mother – it hardly counts as a national crisis. Now, hand it back.'

I got it back on one condition. No contacting the American Embassy when I got there. Too close to the political system. I nodded my consent, rolling my eyes heavenwards. I was too exhausted to be fearful any longer, too tired to care if my uncle and brother turned up with the CIA alongside them. I was boarding that plane to Dublin and they could come along for the ride if they wanted.

Enough time for a quick Budweiser in the airport bar before I headed through the departure gates. We sipped our beers slowly.

'Paul, thanks for all your help, getting me this far.' I flinched at the formality of my voice, like I was congratulating a sales executive on improved figures. The bond that we had together seemed severed and it hurt. 'It's not just for old time's sake, though, is it? There's something between you and Ben Dimato ... even eight years back when my apartment was burgled, your venom towards him shone through. But of course you've known him for much longer than that.'

'Thirty-six years, to be exact. Look, can we talk about something more interesting than your uncle?'

The announcement in the background came to the rescue.

My flight was called. My heart fluttered with sudden panic. What was I doing? I could still change my mind.

The bag-handler disapprovingly pushed my case on to the conveyor belt.

'Your passport and boarding tickets, Ms Dimato.'

Wordlessly, I ran back to the rugged man standing at the departure gates. I rubbed my hands across his receding hair, planting a kiss upon his nose. He looked awkward and I sensed emotion trembling through his body. He was about to speak but I placed a finger on his lips.

'Last word to me,' I whispered and walked backwards through the gates.

In the departure lounge, I thumbed through the latest edition of *Oprah*, trying to find reading material between the advertisements. Wasn't always like this, I thought. We'll hardly have left the ground by the time I'm finished with it. Doctor Phil was consoling some woman who lost sixty pounds and her husband didn't even notice – another woman lamenting the demise of her marriage once her husband started to live at home regularly. Up until then, he'd spent three-quarters of the year travelling – 'a blissful arrangement' she called it. Even Doctor Phil got in on the advertising act – smiling alongside his latest book, *Love Smart – Find the One You Want, Fix the One You Got.*

The announcer's voice droned in the background. Time to embark on my journey. If Sweaty Man had not come to such an abrupt ending, he'd most likely be hovering round like a sewer rat, taking worthless snapshots of me. Unlikely ever to be solved, according to Paul – that is, unless someone wants to escape from the underworld, trade information for immunity and a new life and identity somewhere else. Doubtful. My *Oprah* magazine was quickly snapped up by an alert old lady waiting for me to put it down. In like lightning, looking a little abashed.

'You don't mind, do you? It's got so expensive these days.'

261

I nodded my approval silently, not wanting to engage with her. I wanted some peace and quiet on this flight – I'd have enough connecting to do once I got off at the other end.

Soon the aircraft was gathering speed down the runway, humming louder and louder until it soared skywards to the sounds of clapping and cheering.

'Land of our fathers, here we come!' shouted an inebriated voice from the rear. Perhaps for you, sir – we'll have to wait and see, though. At least for the moment, I'd managed to escape the choking interferences of my next of kin and, despite his help, the oppressive work-to-rule ultimatums from the scowling Mr Briscoe.

27

'Ladies and gentlemen, we are now over the west coast of Ireland and will be landing at Dublin in less than thirty minutes. It is midday in Ireland, twenty-one degrees, nine cooler than Boston. Thank you for flying Boston Airways and we hope you enjoy your stay in Ireland.'

The plane started its descent towards the runway and a faint sense of anticipation started to claw its way above my more recent sluggishness. Time to get up and go, Ava. Hit the ground running. Eight and a half pounds at birth, that's what I weighed when I was brought from the Dimato home into Massachusetts General

Hospital. Bang on nine months, Dad would tell me. It was a difficult birth for your mother – she doesn't like talking about it. That would put it around October '66 when I was conceived. The results of a night of passion between a teenage girl and some unknown suitor. Didn't even need to be a night, as I drew comparison with my shoreline initiation with Jason. It could have been her first time like me, the difference being that she was waiting on a period that never came.

The plane was now braking towards a halt and I stood up to collect the hand luggage above my head. The stewardess frowned and the announcement boomed forth.

'Ladies and gentlemen, please stay in your seats until the aircraft is at a standstill. Thank you for your co-operation.'

A little girl looked at me admonishingly. Carrying almost ten thousand euros in my handbag had left me feeling vulnerable and on edge.

In the airport, I switched on my new phone, searching for Frieda's number to ring her up, tell her where I was. A quick glance at my watch put that call on hold. It would be five in the morning in Boston. My text to Paul telling him that my feet were planted on 'Irish soil' was returned not delivered. Some code adjustments were needed to acknowledge that I was in a different country right now and I whiled away my time fiddling with watch and phone until the first Boston bag appeared on the luggage conveyor belt. Travellers had resorted to all sorts of tactics to counteract the dreary similarity of mass-produced suitcases and a whoop of triumph echoed round the airport as the first cases were removed from the belt.

My Louis Vuitton suitcase pushed its way through the flaps and began to wind its way forward along the oval path towards its owner. It was only then that it hit me that I was not due at the Carrickdale Hotel until Monday and needed to find some place to put my head down for the next two nights.

The lady at the Boston Airways desk was not long about putting that right and I was booked into Jurys Inn on Dublin Docks. Go there immediately and pay up, they prefer credit-card bookings, was the advice.

'Boston,' the taxi driver remarked as he swerved through the bulging traffic. 'Never been to America – I've got two kids in Los Angeles, though. Their mother is constantly nagging at them to come home – we're on the rise here, you see. People never had so much money. They're pouring in from other countries to take up jobs that are not good enough for us any more. You go into any restaurant in Dublin these days and you'll be hard pushed to find an Irish person working there. Here's your stop coming up. Sixteen-sixty on the meter.' I discreetly pass him a twenty-euro note from my roll and make my way into the hotel.

The large bedroom was bright, clean and functional and a welcome sight after the receptionist insisted that I wait until three o'clock to check in. Nothing bright about the view, however, as I looked out over the canal at the sombre high-rise buildings and the building work in progress.

Unpacking my case, I became conscious of how rushed my departure from Beacon Hill had been. No toiletries, scarcely enough clothes to last me the 'week that had become ten days' trip. Ten days to find my mother or return to Boston as I left it, not knowing Ava and resigned to never knowing.

For the moment, though, I lay face down on the pillows as I contemplated once more the Mystery Girl – the results of William Compton's ardour-filled trespass through the back gardens of Beacon Hill to capture in still life the image that would lead me towards my destiny or fate me to live a life of not knowing, continuing to wonder who Ava was. I shut my eyes as I re-enacted my last meeting with William.

Right now, his painting lay in the sleeve of my suitcase as I drifted off to sleep, while outside folk bustled their way along Dublin's Docklands in the pleasant warmth of the afternoon August sun.

28

Slowly, I stretched myself awake while adjusting my eyes to peer around the darkened room. Quarter to six. Still bright enough outside. I bounded from my bed and switched both light and kettle on. My little snooze had rid me of some jet lag and I needed to get onto Dublin's streets to get a feel for the country that fate had brought me to. Thankfully, the Dimato business had brought me around the globe and I reasoned that London and Edinburgh had to be close enough in culture. I could blend in unnoticed. Showered and towelled, I sipped on my coffee as I considered what to do with the large envelope of cash that I was carrying. A phone call to reception confirmed that safety deposit boxes were available and I peeled several fifties before running downstairs to deposit the balance. Back at my bedroom door, my cell phone was ringing inside as the door card refused to co-operate.

One missed call. I examined the number closely before it jumped violently in my hand, the beep-beep signalling that I had a message to read. Nothing earth-shattering, just Paul checking in on me, don't ring back, he was off out and would call again tomorrow.

Armed with directions for both Henry Street and Grafton Street, I turned right out of the hotel and towards O'Connell Bridge. The conservationists have not been very effective here, I thought as I passed by an eclectic range of buildings while tracing my map. The beauty of the Custom House counteracted by the gruesome nature of Liberty Hall as it looked down not so majestically on Dublin's streets. Nondescript shopfronts abounded until I crossed the road towards the pedestrian area looking backwards at the Spire.

'Watch where you're going, will you?' came a voice from behind. An irate-looking old man was facing me, a walking cane in his hand.

'I'm so sorry, sir, I was just looking at your monument – what's it about?'

'Don't know, not sure anyone else does. If you can work it out, you should go into the Tourist Office and explain.' He waved me out of his way, muttering something barely audible about 'Americans' as he prodded his stick aggressively at the path with each stride down the street.

Two policemen with the word *Garda* emblazoned on their caps were moving two beggar children on. The boys looked scarcely ten years old despite their colourful range of foul, abusive language. It seemed that the police were loath to arrest them – nowhere to put them, most likely, no different from Boston. It seemed that the capital of this land of saints and scholars had become as cosmopolitan as most big cities. The streets were not quite as multi-ethnic as home but they were getting there and fast. A visit to Marks & Spencer yielded some underwear, jeans, soft shoes and sweatshirts and I picked up a rain jacket at Champion Sports in the Jervis Street Shopping Centre. My rumbling stomach reminded me that I had not eaten that day. A tub of fresh juices at a Zumo stall would fortify me until I got back to my hotel later. Fate took a hand first, though, and a wrong turn left me atop a hump-backed bridge wondering where I had gone wrong. Looking around in exasperation, I spotted the ugly Liberty Hall building reaching up towards the evening sky – at least it was useful as a compass pointing towards my resting place for that night.

I couldn't resist being drawn towards the red and blue bird-shaped neon light that shone in the dusk above the Eliza Blue restaurant. The early-bird menu was in full swing and I chose French onion soup to begin with and a duo of salmon and cod as main course. Outside, people were teeming by and a pang of uncertainty set in as I visualised myself out there in the County Louth streets with my photograph. *Excuse me, sir, can you take a look at this photo? It's my mother. This is her thirty-eight years back and I need to find her. Do you know her?* Desperation and gnawing doubt cropped up together, almost in chorus. A fraudulent tax claim by Joe Dimato had narrowed the task down from billions to the *Wee County*, as the website nicknamed it, in days but it remained a daunting challenge. All those missing-person posters about the city didn't help either. I knew I needed a big chunk of luck if I was to make some progress. An irate customer glared at me as she nearly fell headlong across the shopping bags that I'd carelessly left the wrong side of my table. The waiter was quick to intervene and removed the bags to a safe place while I ate my meal.

Back in the street, I savoured the lingering taste of quality fresh fish as I walked easily back to my hotel. More than made up for the soup – maybe some day I'd test it in Paris, just to see if they'd got it right. I'd declined the waiter's offer to strike it off the bill – just an experiment on my part that had gone slightly wrong.

The bar in my hotel had filled up nicely and a raucous male crowd had spilled over into the foyer, leering and jeering triumphantly. A stag party. The duty manager was negotiating a little bit of order with one of the less boisterous men, who was now rounding up the group and leading them out the main door.

I felt lighter in myself, like I was walking on air. It occurred to me then that in this city I was anonymous. No one knew me and it was a thrilling feeling. The down side to this discovery was that I could disappear without trace and no one would know or maybe not even care. If Paul really cared he'd be here with me. Though Frieda was my best friend, she would miss me but it wouldn't be earth-shattering – her life would continue. That brought me back to the Dimatos – would Uncle Ben or Chad care if I disappeared? I doubted it very much.

I stepped into the lobby, a bright smile on my face. I wasn't going to give out any negative vibes. Perhaps I could pass some time watching a DVD in my room.

'I'd say you'll have to buy, what with you passing through and that. Game Stop on Henry Street is very reasonable. You'd want to hurry, though – it'll be closed within the hour,' the receptionist replied to my enquiry.

The two little beggars had reclaimed their territory next to the shop and I wordlessly dropped some coins into the tin. Some of them are professionals, Chad would say when I succumbed to their haunting, pleading eyes on Boston's meaner streets.

Inside, I flicked idly through the titles. All the hard nuts, Stallone, Willis, Gibson – they were world-wide. Still, Gibson could diversify the odd time and get soppy. There's *Forever Young*, brand new at ten euros. I recalled watching it with Bruce back when we were happy to cuddle up on the couch with a bottle of wine and watch the latest releases. Early nineties, that was.

The shop assistant coughed apologetically, looking up at the clock. Make that choice, Ava. In the end, I hastily plucked a title – *Derailed* – from the shelves, feeling obliged to buy something to compensate for the hanging on.

Back in my room, armed with two quarter-bottles of red wine and a glass, I settled in to watch my movie but my eyes kept rerouting, unable to escape the figure in our back garden all those years ago. Poised there on the dressing table, a moment captured forever in time, never to age. I'm not going to find you, am I? William's artistic ability and camera are going to be my sole memoirs. Just like Gibson, you're going to remain forever young – I should have bought that one. I decided it was useless to continue watching, the focus just wasn't there. I chastised myself for not being out there searching for my mother.

A thought occurred to me.

I called up Frieda's number and was glad to hear her pick up at the other end.

'It's going to be very hard, Frieda … I'm not really all that hopeful of getting anywhere. Like, it's only when you're here that it hits you. All I have is a forty-year-old photograph. Look, this might sound silly but I came across that film *Forever Young* in a store earlier. Do you remember how he aged quite suddenly in it? I've a gut feeling that I read something about technology being used by the police to project what people might look like down the years. It could have been *America's Most Wanted*, where they are still chasing down big-name crime figures gone to ground. Maybe they could do something with Mystery Girl's image, bring it forward to what she might look like right now?'

'Mmm, I think it can be done all right. Do you want me to check it out for you – though, is this not something you should be asking of Paul Briscoe?'

'I'd prefer not to involve Paul.' I fiddled with the business card that I'd taken from my bag. Perhaps Frieda was right – this work was right down the detective's avenue but I was tiring of his controlling ways. 'Listen, I've got the telephone number and email address of the guy who worked on the photo over there. Walter Graham, that's his name. A reference number also. Can you call him up – ask him to mail it over to you? He mightn't even be a bad one to ask if he can do anything with the images. He's old and irritable but seems to have kept pace with all the changes. Frieda, if you could do this for me I'd really appreciate it...'

'Are you crying, Ava?'

'Yeah ... it just came over me suddenly.'

'Hey, that's wonderful – a good cry is great. You'll feel much better after it.'

'Yeah, thanks. Well, I'll hang up now so I can get on with my cry.'

I went off into a fitful slumber punctuated by nightmares as William's painting floated upwards in my brain. I was fighting so hard to escape my mother's womb, run away from the danger that beset me in this snow-covered garden. Dad with a gun shooting at my best friend's brother until he collapsed dead off the wall – my mother running for the gate only to collapse, blood seeping from her wounds into the snow.

I was awake again – my watch told me it was four o'clock, still dark as the drunken stag party arrived back at the door of Jurys Inn, rather subdued and compliant, thankfully. The black waters of the soundless Liffey provided contrast against the brightness of the streetlights. I boiled up the kettle once more, afraid of returning to sleep and turbulent dreams.

A text message came in from Frieda: *Walter wouldn't do it. Knows how all right. Paul Briscoe's name came up – small world, isn't it? Met him and gave him the hard copy. Knows someone in the MSPD. He'll be back on to me, sort out delivery arrangements. Bit old, isn't he?*

I texted back immediately. *Text me when you've got them. I'll go into one of the internet cafés ... see can I get someone else's account and password that you can send them to. Thanks.*

It was Saturday morning, nine o'clock, and I nodded approvingly that sleep had claimed me shortly after my last text to Frieda. Getting into the fresh bed had done the trick. I'd given way resignedly to the reality that I'd need Mr Briscoe when dirty work needed to be done: After all, I was here to find my mother, maybe my family, and it would be foolish if I let my disappointments with Paul lead me away from using his knowledge to find them. And knowing the man when he got the bit between his teeth, I might have something before the day was out.

The Irish weather had swung off in the opposite direction during the night and the rain pinged against my window as I laid a change of clothes out for the day ahead. I reclined in the hot bath and dialled the Carrickdale Hotel.

'Yes, I have your booking. You're coming down to us on Monday 22nd, two days from now.'

'I was hoping to come down this evening – I got into Ireland earlier than I expected.'

'Gosh, I'm afraid we're booked out for tonight. Two wedding parties. But there's no problem with tomorrow night and I can give you the same room. Okay, I'll adjust your booking ... yes, I'll change your contact number right away.'

Another night in Dublin. Two consecutive weekends of National Community Games had gobbled up almost every bed within forty miles of the venue. 'You're right beside the train station, where you are,' the receptionist at Jurys had said. 'Trains go there and back every hour.' I could always go there on a day trip if I was finding it so bad in the city. But tomorrow would come around quickly, always does.

I made my way up to St Stephen's Green and sat down to watch the passers-by trundle along. Each woman that looked the wrong side of fifty got special attention. If only I had my prediction back of what Mystery Girl looked like right now, I could start making comparisons. The darkening skies encouraged me to abandon my surveillance and I hopped into an O'Brien's Sandwich Bar just as the heavens opened. Munching a bacon and sausage breakfast combo, I listened to the messages on my old phone. Chad telling me he was worried about me and to ring him back – Ben had told him I'd been drinking and behaving strangely. Martha Jones, gasping grotesquely, asking me why I ran off, telling me to call her back at Ben's house. Can't do that, Martha. A large load of business trivia followed and I deleted them as they came up. One from Laura – she knew I'd bumped into Terry and wanted to know if he was asking about her. I stiffened as I listened to Detective Ramon Hawkes: he was outside my door at Beacon Hill with his partner Dan Jefferson and they wanted to talk some more about Sweaty Man. Hadn't we agreed that I'd let them know if I was going away? Fear and anger surfaced together. I had visions of being apprehended in a foreign land and flown back to Boston to be handed over in handcuffs to the Massachusetts State Police.

Paul was unable to shed any light on it when he phoned.

'I wouldn't worry about it. Jefferson, in particular, thrives on that type of intimidation. Most likely, he wouldn't have clearance to call you up. A mole tells me that Byron recently lost a consignment of drugs belonging to one of the city's big movers in the trade. Keep me updated if anything significant happens.' The line went dead.

'Paul, what about the photos–' I paused in mid-sentence, realising I was talking to nobody. Didn't Frieda say he was handling it? That was it – his male ego was bruised because I hadn't gone direct to him with it. Never had you down for a sulk, Mr Briscoe.

29

'Got them, Ava!' Frieda was at the end of the line, sounding excited. 'Ended up back with Walter ... Paul had given him the nudge. All I have to do now is email them to you.'

She seemed to really have taken to the old guy. Old and crusty he might be, but he certainly knew the ropes. Also said to tell Ms Dimato that his services were wholly confidential. He recognised me the day I walked in his door. Frieda's dad knew him well. Said Walter would know more about technology and photography than the all the whiz-kids in America. He'd recreated images of the 'girl in the garden' twenty years on and ones for the current day. He'd also factored in the possibility that the lady had been unkind to her body over the years and done a separate set to demonstrate the effect that alcohol and cigarettes might have had.

'What's with the twenty years?' I asked, the answer immediately dawning upon me as I spoke. 'Well, what does she look like at thirty-seven?'

'Can't say there's any great resemblance – she's sort of athletic, graceful, isn't she?' Thanks for that, I glowered silently. Nothing like best friends to reassure you, boost your self-esteem.

She continued. 'Look, this thing about sending them to email accounts – I think Paul Briscoe's paranoia is over the top. What matters is that you get them. Your uncle will have gone through all the permutations. He'll know this woman, her origins, most likely where she is right now. He'll already know you're gone from Boston – all that's left is for him to speculate that you might be getting close to her right now I'll stick a read receipt on my message – you text me too.'

'Send them on direct, Frieda ... I'll talk with you later.'

Made sense, it did. Also, I was dying to stick two fingers up at the hold my uncle's supremacy had on people's imaginations. The clout, the muscle – being intimidated by what he *might* do. And Ben knew it too, I told myself as memories began to surface. One of the summer garden parties at the Dimato household, coinciding with Chad's twenty-first.

'Hey, Joe, I'm talking to your boy here, mentoring him for office. Come on over, I'm telling him it's all about image, style. Saying the right things, being seen in the right places.' He paused for breath. 'Have your opponents think they might know you but worry that they might not.'

Mmm, that's what it's about, Uncle. Being enigmatic, mysterious – living in a cocoon in awe of your own power. Insulating yourself against your own stupidity, your ego preventing you from seeing that it's your money and the convenience for some of having a bent senator around that counts. You don't count, Ben – even the thugs in my driveway could see that. They'd snuff you out quite handily once they decided they didn't need you ... like when you take a step back from politics and these corrupt committees. Not major league at all.

The internet café also did photographic services and its Indian owner looked on disinterestedly as the prints rolled out. Leave them to dry for a few minutes was the advice. The place was abuzz with foreign languages and hardly a word of English, even with an Irish brogue, to be heard. Other faces glued to screens, alternating between smiles and grimaces as messages bounced back and forth. Families in distant lands, fathers and mothers desperately forgoing the comforting bonds of family and home to be part of twenty-first-century Ireland. Some over-enthusiastic commentators were eulogising it as a global economic power. A complete turn-around from the fifties and sixties – a reversal of fortune just like the film. No more books needed about the Irish in America.

The prints were a bit of a let-down as if the air was escaping from my soul at slow-puncture pace. It wasn't the quality, just the chilly sensation that a programmable package immune to humanity had produced a cold forecast, an assessment. A technological wonder maybe, but lacking the reality of William's spontaneous efforts. Only time might tell how good they were. It was the eyes, I decided – somehow I felt that they lacked expression. I bit my lip as I looked at the gaunt features, the greying untidy hair. Walter wasn't predicting any weight gain for the woman and he obviously felt that she wouldn't be one to spend too much time in the hairdresser's chair.

How could he know that – she could be fat with a perm in her hair by now! My faith was receding.

I keyed in two extra names and numbers to my phone book from the *Golden Pages* – from under Cars and Detectives, each listed with Dundalk addresses. Glancing at my watch, I went into the Eason bookstore and the sales assistant was soon back to me.

'This one – *Do Penance or Perish* – might be what you're after. Yeah, it goes around them all – Cork, Waterford. It's a good thing they're all closed now, terrible places.' She was becoming animated. 'I'm a single mother myself – I've got a little boy, John, he's ten. I'd never let anybody send me to one of these places. We're in a flat in the city but we're happy – the Corporation is going to give us our own house any day soon.'

'Thanks,' I mumbled. 'I'd better go pay for this.'

Later, back in my room, I set aside the book, my eyes red with tiredness from scouring the statistics in frustration. Imelda, that's what the sales assistant's badge said, and I'd had to escape as quick as I could from the proud mother bit. Imelda and John. Let it go, Ava, a voice whispered in my ear.

Next morning I disembarked from the train at Dundalk Clarke Station and soon I was sitting behind the wheel of a zero-four Volkswagen Golf. A portly man was standing outside observing. Very anxious to do this deal, didn't even give me the chance to ring him. I was barely on the platform when he called. Seven hundred euros for eight days seemed very pricey. I knew I was being hit on.

'I know you're wishing the steering wheel was on the far side and was automatic but, give you twenty minutes driving it, and you'll be right as rain. Will I put your case and bags in the boot? Loads of space, even for a hatchback.'

'I'll take it, Mr Malone – there's no need to persevere with your advertising mission. I'd say it's way above the going rate but it's Sunday morning and the rest of Ireland is still in bed. You've got your deal and we're to meet back here on Sunday of next week when you get your car back and I get my deposit.'

Inside at the rail station the paperwork was completed, cash exchanged. My man was up and gone before I could entice him to come for a spin round the local town, settle myself in. Only one detective agency had been listed in the *Golden Pages* with a Dundalk address and it was a cellphone number. Setanta Private Investigations. He arranged to meet me downtown at the Imperial Hotel within the hour.

'And your name is Ava Dimato. I'll have your name hailed at reception when I get there.'

As it happened, 'Matt' got there first. He listened patiently in the foyer of the hotel as I came down to earth from my first driving experience on Ireland's roads. I hadn't reckoned with the power of the Catholic Church, what with cars being literally abandoned at all sorts of angles as people made their way to Mass. Then I got down to my main purpose and soon I had acquainted this stranger with my reasons for coming and my fears that I was on a hopeless quest working on my own.

'I did have a detective, ex-Massachusetts State Police, who helped me narrow down the possibilities to Ireland and payments made round the time of my birth to a bank in Dundalk. Apart from that, all I've got to show is this photo thirty-seven years old and computer-generated predictions as to how she might look today. The bank couldn't help with tracing the owner of the account.'

Matt wasn't talking right now but I could sense his feeling that this wasn't the type of case he was accustomed to solving. He felt it was important that I get an idea of his own background before committing to hiring him. He was aged forty-two and had been in the detective-agency business for nine years. Pensioned off on disability grounds aged just twenty-nine from the Gardaí after being rammed at high speed by thieves who had hijacked a Securicor van. He had spent two weeks hovering between life and death on a ventilator and it took almost four years of physiotherapy, traction and treatments he could not even remember to get him living a normal life again.

'The bulk of my work revolves around compensation claims, maintenance cases and cheating partners. I've done some missing persons but never one where there was no name to begin with.'

'Are you saying you won't take it, Mr...?'

'You can call me Matt. But my surname is

Smith, just in case you think I'm hiding it.' He spent a while staring at Mystery Lady before speaking again. He scribbled nonchalantly on the newspaper he was carrying. 'The chap who took this – you say he saw her more than once. Did he ever say what age she looked or what age he thought she was?'

'He put seventeen on her – he's convinced she was no more than eighteen.'

'Mmm, and you will have shown this to a few close friends. What do they think, including you … don't start getting aggravated, this is important.' At least he's perceptive.

'Seventeen, that's what almost everyone said.'

'And that's what I've written here so there's a fair chance it's right. I'll take your case on, Ms Dimato, but you'll need to know my charges first. Four hundred and fifty, euros that is, per day and I cover my own expenses and additional costs within Ireland. I'd say that's cheaper than your investigator in Boston.'

I felt my cheeks burning instantly. He'd never believe it was for zilch, measured in financial terms. How close I was to letting this whole thing go on the basis that my 'investigator' and I were going to have a baby together. He was probably right, though. In a rare display of affluence, Paul had once taken me out to the ridiculously expensive Julien in Downtown Boston. Feeling kind of flush, he had said, just picked up twenty-five grand for two weeks' work. All he had to do was pin down the wealth of a particularly elusive Scrooge who was claiming inability to support his estranged wife. Accountant's work really, but

281

his client would get a multi-million-dollar settlement owing to his handiwork.

'Okay, Mr Smith ... Matt. I'll go for it. I'll need to see some sign you're putting in a real effort on my behalf, though.'

'You will because you'll be with me.' He pointed at his evidence. 'Let's begin by assuming that this girl was a secondary-school student in Louth in the mid-to-late sixties. We're all saying she's seventeen, remember. I remember my old school-days and every year from Baby Infants up to my Leaving Certificate, there would be a class photograph taken. The schools will have them on their files, especially the nuns. This lady might be in one of them alongside forty other witnesses. That way, we'll put a name on her for sure. A name and a current address, assuming it's within Ireland. The schools would look like the best place to start – we can look at the unmarried mothers' homes after but I'm hoping we turn up something at the schools. Those homes – some of them were called Magdalen Asylums – they're gone now.'

'Yes, but the buildings are still there and the nuns – some of them would still be about?' I ventured hopefully.

'They would – but they're not easy people to get information from. Don't worry, we'll do them if we have to. Schools first, though – okay?'

I nodded. Impressive, I had to concede. Tall and slim with tight-cut flint-grey hair, Matt Smith exuded an easy air of calm efficiency about him. He'd collect me at the Carrickdale Hotel the next morning at ten o'clock and we'd start our tour of the schools. I'd turned him down flat when he suggested that we put a photograph in the local newspapers – a 'Do you know this lady – this is a picture taken in 1967' idea. I cringed at the thought of it – she might have deserted me but I wanted to protect her despite that. There was so much fear and alarm in her face – didn't matter that they could blot out the background, the basket of washing – I wasn't willing to humiliate her in what was most likely her home county. This evening, I was to go through the *Golden Pages* and jot down all secondary and vocational schools that were listed under County Louth. Phone numbers too – the nuns wouldn't make us welcome if we were to drop in unannounced. Chances were that she went to one of the convents and it wouldn't matter that it was school vacation. The nuns never went away.

Makes it sound easy, I thought, as I joined the motorway going towards Belfast. I'd had all sorts of other crazy notions as to how I would go about it. Visions of me approaching people in the street asking them did they recognise her, know her – this is her nearly forty years back: please take a look. Mystery Girl adorning every shop window in Louth. No, that was the same as the newspapers. I didn't want to scare my mother off after coming so far to find her. A sign at the end of the motorway pointed left for my hotel and signalled the beginning of two-way traffic along a narrow twisting road. Bostonians would say that the roads and transport system were the blight and ruination of many an idyllic trip to this beautiful atmospheric island and right then I understood fully what they meant. A queue of irate horn-tooting motorists had lined up behind me, hemmed in by their leader's snail-crawl pace. Little wonder that road traffic is ticked in surveys as one of life's more significant stressors, occasionally knocking death, divorce and moving house from the top slot. Mostly, you get to experience these traumas once or on limited scale, but the driving, it's a continuous experience.

After what seemed like an eternity, I was in the hotel car park and decided that a visit to the leisure centre would be the ideal recuperation from *that* experience. Another check-in for the much-travelled high flyer completed, I relaxed briefly in my room with the obligatory coffee sachets that are renewed daily. At least Matt Smith would be doing the driving tomorrow – hopefully, the county's archives of past pupils would be as good as he anticipated.

Now he was phoning me, telling me to check out under Convents too – some of the smaller outlying schools would have shut down during government cutbacks in the eighties. He remembered the street protests, the one-agenda candidates at local election time. Nothing like government belt-tightening exercises to bring to the surface your average Irish person's sense of injustice and oppression. Patriotism, he called it. He'd show them to me when we visited the schools, cartoons of learned men on the run from the 'Crown' stopping off in the nineteenth century at 'hedge schools' to wide-eyed children seeking to equip themselves with the basics – reading, spelling, adding it all up.

I found myself laughing at his infectious enthusiasm. This guy was kind of cute. Same profession as Paul but that's where the similarity ended. You didn't have to deal with the in-your-face ego all the time. I was assuming that his ring-less fingers were a true indicator of his bachelor status.

'Don't let yourself get distracted from your main objective, Mr Smith. If we get an early result, find my mother, say tomorrow – we can renegotiate, decide if I want to continue with you as a tour guide, a historian and an activist to boot.'

'Activist?'

'Yeah, I think I get a sense of republicanism coming from you – that's why us Americans love you all so much. It's a positive thing, Matt – don't go getting offended on me now. I don't like sulky men.'

'What'll you be doing for the rest of the evening?'

'Checking out telephone directories, you've decided that for me. I'm also on a seven-day package here that includes evening dinner. I was looking forward to a visit to the leisure centre but I haven't packed any sportswear. I'm not going to risk life and sanity by taking to those roads again this evening.'

'I think they have swimwear for sale at that gym – I use it myself occasionally. Anyway, I'm off. See you tomorrow.'

'You'll be walking below the road outside, just follow the signs.' That's what the receptionist said.

Now I was staring intently at a selection of swimwear held up by tiny pins on the wall. The well-built male assistant seemed slightly amused at my predicament. His voice was very different from the coarse banter that I'd witnessed at the fruit stalls down Moore Street the previous evening – melodious and somewhat easy on the ear. His eyes were twinkling and swept upwards and downwards as if he were contemplating how I would look undressed. Twenty at most and with an arrogance to match his youth.

'I'd say you're a size twelve at most, definitely not a fourteen – and you don't want a bikini. Doesn't leave you with much choice, I'm afraid. We only keep a limited stock, don't get many buyers.'

Put an end to this, Ava, the guy is enjoying himself a bit too much. 'I'll take the plain black one,' I said stiffly.

'Okay, and have we agreed on a twelve? That'll be forty euros, please.'

His audience of young girls was giggling stupidly in the background. Hangers-on.

'I guess you'll be lonely when they go back to school next week, Teddy,' I said.

'It's Edward,' he countered, tapping his name badge indignantly.

An hour later, I emerged feeling refreshed and invigorated, tingling from the contrast of sauna and plunge pool after half an hour of vigorous lane swimming. The near-empty facility confirmed that exercise was not high on the agenda of the Irish on a Sunday evening. I skipped past my earlier tormentor unnoticed as he entertained two stage-struck teenagers at the small coffee and juice bar.

The receptionist laughed as I recounted my embarrassment below. 'Put it on your comments card at the end of your stay – the only person that takes Edward seriously here is Edward himself. Nobody else does. He'll be showing off his "pecs", that's what he calls them, to the girls down there. Indefatigable ego but we have to make do with him – it's hard to get people for those jobs these days. Eight o'clock for dinner, then?'

I always kept a laptop in my suitcase for travelling and soon I was busy upstairs typing in the details of all schools and convents in the county. Leave the 'Nationals' alone, Matt had said – junior schools – and I was glad of that. No end of them – it looked as if there was one for every village. With my information saved to my memory key, I was now back at reception as the printer obligingly produced confirmation of my evening's work.

'There's my place, Saint Vincent's,' the receptionist exclaimed as she handed me over two copies. 'Are you doing some sort of book on them?'

'Eh, no, I have an Irish friend in America who is thinking of doing a big reunion of past pupils in Dundalk. I'm just helping her out, picking up names and addresses, that's all.'

'I see you have the Grammar School listed for

Dundalk. Toffee-nosed shower going down there all right. You'd want to have your elocution right before they'd let you in. MTV watchers wouldn't last too long in there.'

30

Seven thirty on a Monday morning and I was back down that tunnel towards the swimming pool again. My appetite, usually good, was no match for the helpings that were put on my plate the previous evening in the hotel dining room. I was already force-feeding myself by the time I had finished my first course of goat's cheese on garlic bread with salad. A fillet steak followed and I had to decline dessert, though the sweet trolley looked very impressive. The place was very full but the floor staff appeared unfazed by it all, showing no sign of a stressed-out environment that usually accompanies such thronging masses. All done in a quiet, unobtrusive way. The waiter most apologetic when enquiring whether I would join the other lone diner in the room, no other table free. An elderly man. I was beginning to think I was destined for a series of blind dates with people from the Lonely Hearts Club. He was easy company, though his habit of consulting his newspaper every few minutes irked me. 'Most of them come from across the border, families, not short of money. We're only a few miles from the North – you should look in on Newry during your stay.'

I had to deflect his curiosity as to what a young American woman, as he put it, was doing sitting alone on a Sunday night.

The upshot of my over-indulgence was a restless night spent tossing and turning. Simultaneous feelings of excitement and fear came to the fore. What if I found her and she didn't want to know me? What if she was dead? What if I found out something really unpleasant ... maybe ... no, I couldn't even entertain the thought. They'd never kill someone, would they?

I donned my new swimsuit, shivering at the clinging dampness that followed from the previous evening's effort. Perhaps I would tie it in a knot around the side mirror, let it dry in the breeze as Matt sped along the county roads. Thinking of him brought a smile to my face. He was a nice guy and very different to Paul, or Bruce for that matter. I shook my head to get rid of that line of thought. I finished off my strenuous efforts immersed in the freezing plunge-pool until I convinced myself that I could face something more sustaining than the obligatory morning coffee. Matt was sitting in the foyer as I made my way back across the building towards my room.

'Matt, I'm sorry, I thought you said ten...' I glanced at my watch. Nine fifteen.

'And you're right but I've not had breakfast yet. Thought it a better idea to come over here and have a bite than join the builders in the supermarket queue for one of their breakfast rolls.' He was standing up now, perhaps six-two, those azure-blue eyes blending in with the steely grey hair and the rather formal navy suit. Explaining how these rolls would stink a car out for days afterwards and would I mind if he joined me for breakfast – we could look over my list of schools. Got to be single, forty-two, he had said. Unlikely to be living with his mother, either ... she wouldn't have let him out of the house on an empty stomach, not an Irish mother, would she?

'You wait there, Matt, I'll be back down in minutes.'

I chose some grapefruit segments, muesli and toast while my dining partner went for the famous 'Full Irish' that adorns many an advertising board outside taverns in Boston. The waitress came back to recheck.

'Yes, it's Room 315, three-one-five, you got it right first time.'

She departed with a puzzled frown to engage in hushed chat with her colleague. Suddenly, we were both laughing as we realised the source of her vexation.

'She thinks me and you – that I slipped you in on a freebie last night. I'm only registered for a single – you haven't told them – oh, my God, what will they think?'

'What do you care what they think – they'll be getting paid for the breakfast.'

Our eyes met and I felt some colour come up in my cheeks as my own imagination started to roam.

'If you want me to say something I will, but I don't even think they'll be interested.'

I shook my head. It didn't matter and it wasn't

worth fretting over. I'd been down that road with Paul so often, and even in the most freethinking of cities, you'll always get the waitress who's lived the sheltered life checking for one or more wedding bands that will concentrate her mind, enable her to make judgements.

'Let's look at your list,' he said urgently. 'I'll go outside, get my map.'

Matt pored silently over my list, talking mainly to himself as he went along. 'A bank account in Dundalk doesn't necessarily imply that the person is from County Louth. You should see all the tribunals going on – you'd be amazed at the lengths people go to in order to conceal their wealth.'

Still, he was taking it that this was a person of habit and convention so we would continue on this road.

'One thing strikes me, though, Ava. It would be very rare for a teenager to have a bank account those days. Post Office books were the status quo for your more prudent youngster back then. It was more likely to be paid to her mother, her father, perhaps a donation by your Boston family to these homes for single women in trouble back then. They say childless couples often went to these homes. Sometimes they were Americans. They'd flash the dollar at the sisters who'd then go and do the convincing on the vulnerable young girl. There have been TV programmes on it – the nuns could be bitches, no feelings at all.'

My whole body shook with revulsion as I chewed over the possibility that my mother might have someone, maybe parents, who would stoop

291

to making a quick buck over her plight. However, greed and poverty tended to bring out the worst in people. Stories of women renting out their bodies to childless families, taking the seed of the male donor that his partner cannot accommodate. Rich lesbian women getting involved in all sorts of things in order to fulfil that maternal craving. I thought about how I had broken the trust I had with Paul Briscoe to meet that same craving. How what we had was unlikely ever to be retrieved – how I'd gambled and lost a partner and a child.

Matt was talking again. 'Doubtful whether it was one of those institutions, though. They certainly used to export babies but I've never heard of one where they exported the mother. But you never know. Money is a powerful persuader. A rich American ... a rich *Catholic* American... Look, I rang some of the convents in Dundalk last night. They can be a bit unforthcoming, suspicious – I had to tell some lies. Anyway, two of the bigger ones, St Vincent's and St Louis, will have to wait until later in the week when someone has the time, as they put it. I think we should do Drogheda today, if it's only to eliminate it. Parents living halfway between the two big towns – it would be the school bus service that would decide where their children went.'

Back on the motorway going towards Dublin, Matt had gone quiet once he popped a CD into the player. Classical, I noticed, and nice. His car was a Mercedes – five years old, though, he was quick to remind me. He'd bought it earlier in the summer, a bargain at twenty thousand euro. He'd sold a Toyota Avensis for fourteen, so all in all it meant that he'd only forked out a few thousand to plonk his behind in one of the world's prestige cars. I think I'll write a book after all this is finished. *The Lives and Tastes of Private Detectives.* Paul Briscoe, Matt Smith ... Sweaty Man. I looked at the cover of the CD. *Inspector Morse...* Matt noticed.

'He died about two years ago – the actor, that is, John Thaw. A police series set in Oxford, the English university city. Liked his classical music did the character, Morse, and so do I.'

Eliminate. That was the word he used, wasn't it? It seemed that the convents and schools were quite accustomed to this sort of thing and viewed such occasions as an opportunity to wave all sorts of sponsorship cards in front of the visitors' noses. Matt confirmed that such gifts were not included in his daily rate.

Eliminate all of my money, more like – and not so much as a whiff of Mystery Girl. My eyes burned red in my head from all the photographs we had examined. Somehow, I knew that I would recognise her when I saw her and I waved away one or two suggestions of likeness by my travelling companion.

'You note their names down, if you wish, Matt, once you've confirmed them with the Reverend Mother.' There was a bite, a sarcasm to my voice that I did not like but it was how I felt right then.

Now I was sitting in his car at the end of a fruitless, exhausting day while he shook hands with the cloaked figure outside the Holy Family Convent. Five o'clock – I had spent a whole day in and out of the car around Drogheda looking at picture albums of complete strangers, digging my hand into my pocket as we went along. I declined Matt's offer of lunch earlier, preferring to shop for some sportswear for the gym back at the Carrickdale. I also needed a break from the monotony of his introductory ploy. *'Good morning sister, I want to introduce you to my friend Ava. She's from Boston and she is doing some research on Drogheda schools in the late sixties. I wonder if you could facilitate us by...'*

The nun had looked carefully at Mystery Girl. Then, 'No, I'm sorry, not one of ours.'

'Still not hungry?' he enquired as we sped back along the motorway towards my hotel. 'You know, there's going to be more days like this. We just have to knuckle down, keep our focus. If she's from the area we'll match her up before the end of the week. I'm certain of it.'

'Has it occurred to you that she might be a school dropout, mightn't be in the school line-outs at all?'

'Yes, I've conjured up lots of scenarios and possibilities in my head but right now we are *searching* for her. We have St Louis Convent in Dundalk tomorrow. Apart from that the only possibilities in the area are Ardee, Dunleer and perhaps the other St Louis in Carrickmacross.'

'Is that all we're doing tomorrow – just one school? It's not a lot – is it?'

Matt looked taken aback, offended. 'I'm still waiting on a call from the Vocational Schools –

they're not live-in like the convents and it's the summer holidays.'

'All right, Matt. I have copies of the two payments to the Dundalk bank in 1967. They're in my case. Maybe I'll bring them along tomorrow?'

'Yes – we can go in there, talk to the manager. Maybe I – we can try to persuade him to do a detailed search.'

We continued in silence until we reached the Carrickdale. Perhaps I'd been around Paul Briscoe for too long but I sensed he'd have a few more tricks up his sleeve, a different modus operandi than this formal, seemingly shy Irishman. Things had a habit of happening much faster when the rugged Bostonian was around. A voice in my head reminded me that only recently I was cursing the American for his domineering ways. Finding faults in men seemed to be the flavour of the day right then.

'Ten in the morning so,' Matt said. 'Are you going to leave the Volkswagen sitting there for the week? You could always leave it back – get a refund.'

'I doubt it somehow – he didn't look like a guy who'd let go of money easily once he had a grasp of it. I'll be seeing you.' I trudged wearily back into the hotel, pent up with frustration.

I unpacked the sports gear I'd bought in Drogheda earlier. Forty-five minutes of gentle jogging, cycling and stepping it out in the gym appeased the tensions of a most difficult day. I had to remind myself that saying sorry to Matt about my bad mood would also have a calming effect. Still one hour to dinner, I noticed, retrieving my trusty iPod from the suitcase, and soon I was listening to the sound of classical music fanning gently across my ears. Pity they didn't have Inspector Morse, I thought.

31

I snapped shut the last album of the St Louis Convent selection in Dundalk. I shut my eyes tight – all I wanted to do was bathe them in a soothing lotion for the rest of the day. Another wasted morning – we'd pored over hundreds of uniform-clad girls. I was beginning to get familiar with some of them as they cropped up again but no sign of Mystery Girl. I nodded at Matt – why not show the sister our photo? Come to think of it – why didn't he think of doing it? He was supposed to be the detective. I noticed her shake her veiled head and thought she looked old enough to have been around in the sixties.

I walked resignedly towards the hall and then out of the door – they'd gone off to the dining room together to pass the picture around the other sisters.

Matt was soon out, an apologetic smile on his face. He seemed about to say something and then lapsed into silence.

'Did you make an appointment with the bank manager?' I asked, a cutting edge to my voice. I was beginning to boil over.

'His assistant will see us, said we can drop in

anytime – she'll be there all day.'

Vera Knowles, assistant bank manager, handed me back my stubs and placed the photocopies in her work tray.

'It's a long shot but we'll try – I'd say that we could come up with something. But before the end of the week? I'm not so sure. We've traced older ones than this – you'd be amazed the amount of accounts that lie untouched for decades, then someone comes in to claim the money.' She looked at me. 'You say you don't want to claim the money, Ms Dimato – that's if there's any. But you still have to fill out the form.'

Matt intervened. 'The person could still be alive – let's not jump to conclusions.'

'Could well be, Mr Smith,' she smiled, showing a set of gleaming white teeth. 'But as you don't know who that person is, the bank will not be giving you the name of the account-holder. Even if we find it.'

'That's fair enough,' Matt replied evenly. 'But you will confirm if the account is still active and the address is Dundalk? No names.'

Vera's eyes turned towards me. 'We shouldn't even do that under normal circumstances. But I sense Ms Dimato really needs to find somebody. So I'll do that much. No more. I'll take both your phone numbers.'

We were back in the Imperial where we met first a couple of days back. I was supping from a bowl of vegetable soup and nibbling listlessly at a chicken salad sandwich.

'So, that's it for today,' I said, blinking back the tears. 'We've got appointments with the convents in Carrickmacross and Ardee tomorrow and nothing for the afternoon.'

Matt shrugged his shoulders defensively. 'You don't have a name, Ava – that's a huge drawback. I know you came over here thinking this place is only a fraction of Boston's size. Say this woman came to me saying she knew an Ava Dimato and only gave me all of America to go on. I'd have you rooted out using databases in no time.'

I sat quietly for a while before conceding to myself that there might be no other way. 'All right, we'll go to these schools tomorrow and if we come up with nothing you can set up that appointment with the *Dundalk Democrat* for Thursday. Get her photograph in the paper for the next edition. We'll think up something vague. Say someone who met her briefly wants to link up with her again only she doesn't have a name.'

'I'll write one up for you later – why don't you just take a rest from it until tomorrow? There's some beautiful scenery to be explored up on the coast. I'll take you around, if you'd like. We could take the photograph, maybe show it around. It's quite close to Dundalk – Carlingford, they call it.'

I glanced at my watch. 'I suppose there's nothing more we can achieve today.' I yawned resignedly.

Matt stood behind me as I looked out across Carlingford Lough and marvelled at its beauty. This was a magical place and it thrilled me that he had brought me to his own special retreat.

This was where he came to relax, whether it was going fishing or walking along the Táin Trail. He'd gone back briefly to his house and was now dressed in polo shirt, jeans and walking boots with a soft jersey tied round his waist. I had sat in the car outside his semi-detached house, regretting that I hadn't said yes when he suggested that I wait inside for him. Franklyn Park, that's what the sign had said at the front of the estate. Neat-looking and that went for the gardens too.

Now, the small village of Carlingford rose majestically in the background and it was clear that this place had not sold its heart and culture to developing Ireland. There were some signs of the boom but new house building was discreet and shielded away in small cul-de-sacs that did not obscure or even feature in the magnificent views.

The middle-aged man behind the bar at the Carlingford Arms shook his head when I showed him the photo.

'It's not a very good one, is it – from the sixties, you say. I would have been around, a teenager myself then. No, can't say she rings a bell – I mean I don't know her. Maybe you don't use that phrase in America?'

Matt had persuaded me to have a go at a rock-climbing expedition.

In the end, I capitulated and he departed to make the booking. Soon he was back, looking around the door.

'Come on out into the sun. We'll walk part of the Táin Trail. Be well back by five o'clock for the rock climb. Plenty of time.'

My walking partner strode effortlessly ahead of me as I huffed and puffed my way up the near vertical slopes.

'Jesus, Matt, it's ferociously steep! It's knocking all the wind out of me – I'm finding it easier to walk backwards, less pressure on the lungs and back.'

I found myself making comparisons. No chance that Paul Briscoe would ever come up here – even into his fifties, he clung like a leech to smoke-filled bar-rooms, reggae and jazz clubs. Rarely surfaced before five in the evenings, and his forays into upmarket restaurants would be a lot rarer but for the fact that he was sleeping with Ava Dimato.

The road levelled off briefly and we sat upon a wall looking down at the bay.

'Matt, I don't know but there's something about you that doesn't fit as a private investigator. I mean, I know so many of them back in Boston and they're a completely different genre to you. You'd never get them up here or listening to your music either.'

His gaze met mine for a moment before he replied. 'I hate the damn job. It was just something that I fell into as I recovered from my injuries in the Gardaí. There was an old geezer, he's dead now, that would do a bit of snooping round at this and that. He started to give me a bit of work and it went from there. It's a seedy business and I hope to get out of it some day.'

Matt had been recommended for promotion to detective when it all fell apart one fateful morning on Dublin's North Circular Road. He had been working through the night and had only remained on duty as a colleague failed to turn up for work. He responded to a call to intercept a robbery and ended up being lifted straight through the air and across a garden wall by a van. His colleague died instantly and the only good thing was that Matt remained unconscious while they cut him from the wreckage. Often had nightmares that he'd lain beside the corpse of his friend in that car. He could have taken up a desk job when he recovered but it was not for him.

We started to walk again.

'I guess I just took the money – the compensation, the pension – and ran. It was a bad, bad decision. I was due to get married at the time and I couldn't resist the lump sum – just what we needed to buy our house at the time. I took several years to knock myself back into shape and to be fair to the authorities they would have waited. Think – I could have made at least Superintendent had I stayed.'

Funny, I thought as I listened. So many parallels with my friend Mr Briscoe. He had his chip that he didn't get the biggest prize with the Massachusetts State Police. Eventually, I dared ask. 'And the girl you were due to marry, Matt? What became of her?'

'Never happened. We bought the house, or rather I did. We fell out during my recovery period – she said I was impossible to live with. Ended up getting half the house, which I think was wrong. We weren't even married but her solicitor put together a marvellous tale of her nursing me back from death's door and the judge fell in with it. Simple as that – I couldn't risk any more money on an appeal.'

No name, I noticed. Too bitter to identify her as a person.

Matt had gone back to evening school a couple of years back and had got his law degree the previous summer. That was only the start of it, though. You needed to have it to begin with but he had to do eight more exams before he could even approach a legal firm to look for an apprenticeship.

'Yeah, they're called the Blackball Place Exams. At the minute I can't see a way of mixing this job with all the studying. I was absolutely knackered after finishing my degree. I really don't know where I'll take it from here. I'd find it hard to make ends meet on my pension.'

Quite suddenly our conversation was interrupted by a herd of sheep coming straight for us on the steep incline, their eyes full of terror and dogs in pursuit. I found myself being deftly scooped into the air by Matt's strong arms and he stepped to the far side of the wall until the mêlée had passed. Our eyes met briefly.

'Mmm, not bad for a guy on disability ... are we going to carry on like this for the rest of the walk? How chivalrous of you for volunteering!'

He put me down gently and we walked a while in awkward silence.

Suddenly he dug me playfully in the ribs. 'You're making me morbid, woman, digging up my past like that. I've had some great times too. Not many chaps around that have scaled Mount

Everest but I did, and lots more. In the meantime, though, we'll do a deal for the way back down.'

'And what might that be, Mr Smith?'

'You're going to tell me about Ava. No more Matt, just Ava ... who she is ... what she's done ... what she's going to do. Let's start with your first boyfriend.'

'That's definitely not something I want to repeat,' I said aloud as the small party of rock climbers descended the path towards the village.

The youthful tour guide was from New Zealand and his storytelling hit the right spot with awe-struck children who gasped as they visualised what a climb of six thousand feet would look like. I couldn't even manage half of the fifty feet of quarried rock that was hewn from the cliff-side and abseiling from its top was no less intimidating. Thanks but no thanks, was my final say on the matter.

Now, this day was drawing to a close and the easy sharing of life's experiences and feelings that took place along the Táin Trail was being swallowed up by the numbing recognition that this was just an interlude – a respite from a grim search.

'Can you wait a minute, Matt?' I said as I noticed an elderly lady close the door of the tourist office. We were down in the car park at the front of the village. 'There's a likely person to ask. Where did I put that photo – Christ, I think I put it in that rain jacket they gave me at the Adventure Centre – it was one of the copies.'

Matt hopped from the car, waving down the

woman as she started up her car. He was showing her another one of Mystery Girl's prints and she looked distinctly displeased at being intercepted.

Soon he was back in the car. 'Wow, I wouldn't like to meet her every day – devoured me for walking out in front of her, said she'd report me to the Gardaí. I hope she's more civil when she's behind the counter dealing with tourists. Anyway, she didn't recognise her – I see you've found yours.'

An awkward silence surfaced as we made our way back to my hotel. The shutters were back up and we almost didn't need to confirm that we would rendezvous in the car park the following morning and take our magnifying glasses back on the scent of a woman who might have graced the Wee County's schools all those sunsets ago.

Matt's Mercedes melted southwards into the evening sun as he headed towards Dundalk.

Same-time feelings of relief and disappointment quarrelled for space within my brain, perhaps my heart. *Be glad that he's gone, Ava,* said the brain. *Follow your heart,* said my spirit. *But what are you following?* said the two. The common strand that was infused in my contradictory cravings of late was that I wanted to fit in – to belong. But to whom – a mother, a lover, a child? Perhaps them all.

Once more I would be eating alone and I imagined that he would be doing much the same. Over the next few days, Matt Smith would either lead me or not to my mother and he would wave his goodbyes as he stuffed a bundle of euros into his trousers. He would have had many an opportunity to console scorned women as he tracked the finances or mistresses of wayward husbands. What better retribution could a spurned woman wish on her man than to let him know that a handsome stranger had helped her to screw him financially and also want to screw her in a much more pleasing way as he went about it? Was I attracted to this man because I felt discarded by Paul Briscoe, who shied away from his promise once he knew the risks? Or simply because he was the man's opposite? Perhaps I just wanted someone to hold me if my mission resulted in failure. Impulsively, I decided to skip the feast that was dinner in the dining room that evening. I reasoned that my soup and sandwich in the Imperial Hotel earlier was enough to sustain me and my nerves were too threadbare to submit them to an evening of quiet meditation in my room.

Matt's phone was on answering service.

'Matt, it's Ava. I'm at a loose end up here so I'm going to do Ardee and Dunleer this evening. I noticed the signs for each earlier on the motorway. I've rung ahead for both places and they've agreed to meet with me. Will see you in the morning.'

I knew Matt would be annoyed about Ardee – me bringing forward the appointment – but he wasn't the stranger sitting alone in a hotel room.

The heavy oak door of the Mercy Convent groaned open slowly and a middle-aged lady greeted me warmly as she held the door ajar.

'I bet you're Ava. I'm Patricia – no, I'm not a

nun, God forbid. I'm the live-in housekeeper. I was talking to you on the phone earlier. I'm going to put you in this room to wait on Sister Cecelia. She'll be a few minutes – she's winding down on the prayers. Cardinal rule here is that you don't interrupt the good sister during her conversations with God. Even kept the Minister for Foreign Affairs waiting there recently when he turned up on the door with news of money for some little project she was chasing. So don't despair – you're not in bad company.'

Patricia was back quickly with tea and sandwiches.

I'd struck Dunleer off my list with a near cursory examination of their late sixties records. Even into the twenty–first century it was male-dominated and the 'stills' from forty-odd years back confirmed that only a handful of brave girls ventured through its gates back then.

'So you're looking up someone from the sixties? That's when the Beatles were on the go. I've got every one of their records. They're down to two these days, what with George's cancer and one of you Americans shooting poor John. Best band of the lot.'

I was struggling to keep pace with this bubbly woman's conversation. 'So what time will you sign off for the evening, Patricia?'

She looked at me for a minute, bemused before letting off a hearty laugh.

'Sign off? You Americans are so funny. I signed in here sixty years ago, the day I was born, and I'll sign off the day they carry me out in a wooden box.'

'So you've lived here all this time?'

'Almost and loved every minute of it. I was left on their doorstep and they took me in. Used to get fostered out in the early days with all sorts of weird families but I'd keep coming back here. Sneaked a look at my file one day when the social worker left the office for a minute. "Problem child", that's the label they put on me – their official excuse for not doing their jobs. Anyway, I came back here permanently when I was twelve and here I am now at sixty, only two weeks back, and don't I look great?'

Soon, she was showing me her room upstairs and her Beatles collection. In and out of this room during her first twelve years, she was finally able to call it her own once she came back as a boarder. Only one who got her own room, she declared proudly. She had to go on the council housing list recently with so many convents closing their doors and selling up. Dreaded the thought of moving out, she said – even gave Minister Ahern an earful when he came visiting.

'I told him I'd go down to Saint Brigid's – that's the psychiatric hospital down the road – unless he did something to keep this place running. I'd get the reporter from the *Dundalk Democrat* in to do an article. Throwing old women out of their homes!'

I braced myself at the mention of the newspaper, thinking how I might find myself forced down that route very soon. 'But you're not old, Patricia...'

Back she came, this time with an American twang. *'But you're not old, Patricia!* 'Course I'm not old, but have you never told a lie so you'd get what you wanted? Didn't I win the karaoke at my sixtieth birthday! Cecilia came down to the pub with me and there they all were. A surprise party, they said. They had forgotten they did it on my fortieth and my fiftieth so I don't know why they thought it would be a surprise. Anyway, I sang *Yellow Submarine* and I won, told the little upstart to turn off his stupid machine and I'd do it my way. Have you ever heard it? It goes like this.'

There was no stopping her. I had to listen through it. Awful, but infectious none the less.

Social Welfare had given her a weekly payment and a free travel pass for looking after one of the more fragile nuns and whenever she had a row with one of the battleaxes she just took herself off to Dublin for the day. Give the old wagon time to cool down in the same skin she'd heated up in. Last time, she went to Dundrum Shopping Centre – biggest in Europe.

I found myself confiding in her that I was looking for only one person – it was not about a class reunion or a special project.

'Give us a look ... no, she was never here, that one ... no, I don't need to take another look – I'd have been about twenty-two then. Didn't I have to go into the classrooms every evening and scrub their chewing-gum off the floor? No, I'd remember her if she was here.'

Back downstairs Sister Cecilia confirmed with one look what Patricia had told me. Never at Ardee. I was disappointed but also enchanted by the harmonious ambience that pervaded the place. I also felt relieved – their certainty convinced me that I could excuse myself the ordeal of trawling through endless more snaps of gymslip girls. I threw caution to the wind and we sat sharing Irish coffees and chat until my watch said it was time to go. Patricia let me out at the front door, hugging me closely as I left.

'Just one thing, Patricia. It's just you saying you belong here, have no interest in the past. Why didn't you just go and join up, become a nun?'

Her voice lowered a few notches and the bubbly personality seemed on the wane – it was like she was tugging against something that was causing her distress.

'Me, no way. I wouldn't have been much good at that chastity thing, especially in the sixties. Oh, the lads came round all right... I tried living in flats for a while but it was too hard. Social workers always sticking their noses in – but that's another story. Look, I'd better let you go. I hope you find whoever it is you're looking for.'

The door shut suddenly and I resisted the impulse to ring the bell again. I felt I'd crossed a boundary, removed all the jollity of the evening with one stray remark. Patricia, the clown who made everyone else laugh – but not herself. It was as if my last question had reminded Patricia of her past and apologising was not going to do any good. I'd touched a raw nerve, including my own.

Was it always going to be like this – on my own again? That sounded familiar, like words of a song.

I pressed harder on the bell and a light switched

on upstairs. Matt was at the window, looking downwards.

'Ava, it's one in the morning – what are you doing here? Is something up? Hold on, I'll come down... Jesus, you're shaking, what happened?'

'Nothing, Matt, nothing. I just want you to hold me.'

32

It was kind of slow to begin with but once I'd let my hands wander inside his *Simpsons* T-shirt, he knew it would be okay. Consenting adults, that's what they call it. *Simpsons* boxers too, there was certainly a little boy inside – not physically, I noticed that straight away – but in spirit. Hold on, he had said – this is kind of unbalanced, unfair, me with nothing on and you fully dressed. I pushed him backwards onto his bed.

'Let me take care of that for you, Mr Smith. You get to watch – for free. No surcharge, no taxes, though you're going to agree I'm worth a lot more than four-fifty.' I undressed slowly, provocatively in front of him and I could see him harden further at the sight of my breasts. Slipping off my pants, I started to manoeuvre him inwards, reassuring, holding his hands down. A finger pushed to his lips.

'Quiet ... you do it best when you do nothing at all, Mr Smith. There now, I can certainly feel you, you should know I'm ready ... are you ready,

Matt, can you feel me?'

Lying there afterwards, the only disappointment was that Matt had not bought the *Simpsons* outfit himself. And they were *pyjamas*, at least that's what his nephew had told him. A Christmas present. Darren would be at the Community Games at the weekend in the under-thirteen basketball finals. I could come down if I wanted to. I'd frightened the 'bejasus' out of him. Didn't know what that was but it hardly mattered with my head now placed on his chest, twirling my fingers in the soft downy hairs. Sleep came easily though I awakened again at six.

'Matt, I'm going back down to the Carrickdale – just to swim, change, freshen up.'

He was sitting with his elbow propped on the pillow and the morning sun cast just a little light on his earnest, searching face. 'You're not having any regrets, are you?'

I was lying face towards him on his bed. 'No, of course I'm not. Are you?'

He chuckled. 'No, I just thought you were way out of my league.'

'Oh, Matt,' I said, marvelling at his honesty.

'And you remembered where I lived too, what with all the turns and that?'

'I took a note of the name on the way in – anyway it's not just your cell phone that's listed in the *Golden Pages*. You should take a look.'

A self-satisfied grin spread across his face. 'Sounds like you knew you were coming back. Must say I'm flattered.'

Suddenly my impulsiveness of the previous night gave way to embarrassment. I turned to

311

business, filling him in on my expedition to Ardee and Dunleer.

'It's not that I don't trust you – I find it hard to stay in the hotel on my own and time is starting to run down. You were to do up the advertisement for the newspaper?'

'I've got it downstairs – do you want to see it?'

'Not right now – I need to get back to the hotel. Bring it down with you.' A great urgency took hold of me to make a fast exit. Things were complicated enough. 'The pool will be open around seven, so I'd better leave now – we've a long day ahead of us.'

I found my shoes in the hall downstairs exactly where I stepped out of them the previous night. It would have been nice to stay and have breakfast, perhaps make love again, but I needed to be on my own.

Back at the hotel I sped upstairs to get my swimsuit. I swam with a ferocity that morning, feeling a sense of elation that something was going to happen that day for certain. Thoughts of Paul Briscoe flashed across my brain. Our affair was over and being with Matt last night confirmed it for me. Was it too good to be true that I had connected with this wonderful man? Would it all end in tears? I had to remain positive – no matter what, the now was just blissful.

Matt arrived at reception as I was walking across the foyer. I pinched his butt as I passed by.

The receptionist looked on, her baffled face following us as we made our way to the dining room.

Once Matt had outlined our itinerary for the

day, we both decided to go for the Full Irish breakfast.

'I wasn't going to leave Ireland without doing this at least once,' I remarked as I thrust a piece of black pudding into my mouth.

Matt was in a flirtatious mood, his eyes twinkling. 'But the lady has done it more than ... oh, you mean the breakfast. How stupid of me – that's what I'm like if I don't get the full eight hours' sleep.'

Matt had decided that the St Louis Convent in Carrickmacross was to be our first stop that morning.

'This one is outside County Louth but it had a reputation as the region's premier girls' boarding school in those days. Many parents from Dundalk sent their children to St Louis in the past to keep them away from the temptations that were emerging in the urban areas: alcohol, pot and the like. They're expecting us down there about noon. There's a retired nun, Sister Eugenie, who handles all the historical stuff. She's already pulled the records between 1963 and 1970 in readiness for our visit.'

We arrived just in time and were ushered into the waiting-room that seemed to be obligatory in all these convents. Sister Eugenie arrived with a flourish minutes later, her diminutive figure being counterbalanced by a fierce, unrelenting stare. Eighty-six, Matt had told me, but she looked early seventies at most. She cast a condescending eye over each of us before she spoke.

'So it's Ms Ava Dimato from America and Mr Matt Smith from Dundalk and you're doing an observation of the school from a historical perspective.'

Matt had advised me in advance that we would have to go the scenic route towards the school photographs.

Sister Eugenie was renowned for her attention to detail and first stop was their website where she could commence her eulogy to the St Louis Secondary School.

'We're a very progressive school here, Mr Smith, always have been. This year, we opened the new Sports Dome, May 2004, with the first sod only laid in September 2003.' Women didn't seem to count with this reverend lady.

'Sister, you see that one,' I said. *'Reunion 1965–1970.* Could you click on that?'

A haughty quiver of her eyebrow told me that she did not welcome the interruption.

'Well, all right, if you must. All that's there is a list of names of people who, in 2001, attended a reunion of Leaving Certificate classes between 1965 and 1970. There's about fifty names on it so you'll see that a rather small percentage turned up.'

After endless visits to the websites including Sister Eugenie's dogmatic insistence that I accept copies of her students' recipes, she relented by showing us the yearly school-photograph albums and the ritual disappointment ensued.

I wiped away a tear as Sister Eugenie packed away the albums, saying to Matt, 'That's nearly all the schools – we'll never get round all of Ireland by the end of the week. How many of those unmarried mothers' homes are there?'

Matt shrugged. 'Were – they're mostly all gone now – only the buildings remain. I'm not sure how many of them there were. Seems like it's over here at least. Look, we'll just go down to the Sports Dome, then make our excuses about a bus, a flight or something. This old bat thinks we have each room in the place to go around yet.'

Eugenie was now leading us in imperialistic pose towards the Dome. What a contrast to Cecilia the previous night! I doubted that Irish coffees would be made available at the end of all this.

The Dome was now empty, though I imagined it would be a hive of activity once school recommenced the following Tuesday. Throbbing with pubescent girls sharing their summer experiences with each other while I would most likely be resuming my executive duties back in Boston. The voices of my companions were fading into the background as I scanned triumphant teams carrying cups aloft at varied sports over the years, Eugenie echoing in the background.

'We take great pride in our sporting achievements over the years, Mr Smith. Basketball, volleyball – more recently hockey has been undergoing a revival. When students come in here to play their games they get to see the successes of their predecessors. It motivates them. What many people, including parents, forget these days is that sport is a *discipline*. It's not for the fainthearted – you've got to fight for each ball.'

'Bitch will have an orgasm,' I muttered acrimoniously as I continued my offhand perusal of Eugenie's 'achieving girls'. Must have been their mentor herself, I reckoned, while more ancient achievements revealed younger versions of the notorious nun as I navigated my way around the hall and down the years.

Voices in the background.

'Shall we move on, Mr Smith? Your lady-friend, where's she gone now ... oh, I see her down there ... she's been on edge since she came. She's searching for something, isn't she?'

I was rooted to the spot, utterly motionless apart from the slightest nodding of the head. Yes, I am – I mean, I *was* searching. In front of me was a photograph titled *St Louis Secondary School Hockey Team 1966.*

There she was – standing tall in the back row, smiling broadly out at the camera back then. There was no need to compare. I just kept on with my robotic nodding, a silent gasp escaping from my lips. Thank you, Matt, thank you, Paul, and William too.

Matt only needed to look once. There was no doubt.

'What will we do, Ava? I mean, do you want to ask her yourself or will I do it?' Even the detective looked in awe at what he had found.

'I don't know – I mean, yeah, of course – we'll do it together. But, notice – Eugenie is not in the photo. She's in most of the other ones but not this one.'

A voice boomed from the centre of the Dome. 'Mr Smith, Ms Dimato, it is terribly rude of you to go off like that and then start whispering. I think it's best that we terminate this meeting immediately.'

Matt was trotting back to her, speaking in a pleading voice. 'Sister Eugenie, Ava – eh, Ms Dimato, my client – has come from America searching for someone that is missing from her life for so many years. She believes that person is on a team photograph at the back of the hall. Could you look at it with us, please?'

A long pause followed before Matt pulled Mystery Girl from his pocket, handing it to the perplexed nun. Now the three of us were staring at the hockey team together, our voices lost as the nun's eyes darted at a rapid pace from the wall to our picture and back again.

Eugenie broke the silence. 'I am baffled, completely baffled. I don't know who she is. I went to the missions in Africa between 1965 and 1968. But I know everyone else in the picture. They're all fourth and fifth years. Most of that team were sitting their Intermediate Certificate exams the year I went off to Africa – but not this young woman. She's definitely the same person as the one in your picture.'

She sat down on a spectator's bench and seemed lost in thought for ages. I felt agog with excitement but our host was floundering helplessly.

'It's things like this that make me feel my age. Poor Sister Genevieve, she took over the sports while I was away on the missions. That's her there – she died last year.' She looked at me directly. 'You're adopted, aren't you? You should have told me from the start what you two were about. I'm not sure I could give you her name even if I had it. Some of that team are still around here.'

I felt overwhelmed as we went towards the exit. Even the imposing Sister Eugenie was suffering a crisis of confidence as to what she might do next. Matt had lapsed into silence. It was as if we should let her reach her own decision.

'Sisters Bernadine and Alphonsus drove up to Dublin today. They were both here in 1966. They'll know her, no doubt. Alphonsus was the principal – they called it Reverend Mother back then. Can you come back in the morning – it's just that they're usually late, sometimes near midnight. They crawl along in that car, oblivious to the angry motorists behind them. Leave it until nine o'clock in the morning. Oh, and can I take that picture from you, Ms Dimato? It's a better one and it will save me removing the other one from the wall.'

Matt was standing at the back of his Mercedes. 'Just as well I keep a case in the boot – we won't look so obvious, will we?'

We were parked in the grounds of the Nuremore Hotel. He had tried reasoning with me – it was only a short distance from Dundalk, Carrickdale, wherever I stayed but I was not budging. I was not leaving town right now. The only concession I made was a grudging agreement that I would not go knocking up the convent at midnight. A double room was available and I took it unquestioningly. Matt stood in the background, his empty case in hand. My initial shock and euphoria at seeing her picture was starting to beat a retreat, giving way to nagging fears.

318

Hello, Mrs/Ms Whatever – and is this your husband? My name is Ava, your daughter ... remember we were in Boston together? It'd be thirty-seven years ago now. Can you tell me why you abandoned me? I want nothing from you, just the truth ... no more lies. I'm a tough lady, I can take it. I won't crumble or make a scene or go hysterical. Just the truth.

Upstairs, we sat on the corner of the bed together. It was like a pin had deflated all the pent-up energy I was storing. Matt made the coffees and we sipped slowly together, Matt occasionally squeezing my hand.

'Ava, are you okay?'

I nodded while holding back the tears. 'So much has happened in a few days, Matt.' I heard myself laugh a little manically. 'I mean we only met on Sunday. We've become lovers within three days, now this. Come next week, I'll most likely be back in Boston. I'm scared, just plain scared, of what tomorrow is going to bring, I really am.'

Matt gave me a reassuring hug. 'Just let the morning come along, Ava. You haven't eaten – I haven't eaten all day long. We'll go down and check out their dinner menu, maybe have a few drinks.'

'Yeah, okay, it's still only five o'clock. Could you drive me back to the village, just so I can get a change of clothes?'

Matt sat in the car while I went into the boutique. I wanted to look my best tomorrow but did not know for what or whom.

'Let's start with the shirt and shoes,' the sales assistant said. 'White cotton and black-patent leather. There are any amount of well-tailored suits available in a wide range of colours. You can pick skirt or trousers or both to go with the jacket.'

I hadn't the heart to tell my driver that I'd just spent eight hundred euros when I reappeared with my bags. Instead, I opted for a glib, 'Couldn't pick up any Bart Simpson pyjamas for you in there, Matt.'

My sense of anticipation and dread over what might happen the following day hung like a black shroud above us that evening. If Matt had a hunch, he was keeping it to himself. He was so unlike Paul and this was what I loved about him. There, I had admitted it: I was falling in love with Matt. In Ireland I felt like a different person. I no longer had to act the tough lady. If Matt knew the real Ava Dimato, would he even like her, never mind love her? My stomach muscles contracted nervously. I really had fallen for this guy.

An awkward silence was growing between us. Somebody needed to break the ice so I decided to have a go.

'You see that picture of the Irish soccer team that's hanging up in the bar over there? That was in 1994 before they went out to the World Cup in America. I was at the match with Italy in the Giant's stadium in New York.'

Matt was smiling. 'I just put the weather up on Aertel when you were powdering your nose. There's rain promised.'

Soon we were laughing helplessly.

'I really believe we need to see a relationship counsellor, Ms Dimato. I mean I've suffered your mood swings for going on – let's see – eighteen hours. Things will have to change, Ava.'

The waiter interrupted our fun.

'Your table is ready now – may I lead you to it?'

We spent a very pleasant evening in the dining room of the hotel, tasting and sharing various treats such as swordfish and pigeon for starters, scallops and venison for mains and to wrap it up blueberry rice pudding. The tension had mostly evaporated and I remembered Frieda's words of wisdom for bad times – keep talking even if it's small talk: it'll click back in over the long run.

Matt and I made love slowly and tenderly that night and later I lay awake listening to his shallow breathing before an uneasy sleep set in, bringing with it angry black storm clouds that ricocheted large hailstones against my face. I was bathed in sweat as merchants of doom surfaced at every street corner to ostracise mother and baby. *Burn in hell, you wicked woman! That child is not for you!* I lashed out wildly as I felt myself being taken away, pinned down, and the voice echoed in the distance.

'Ava, it's me, Matt, you're just having a bad dream, that's all. Sit up now, you'll be okay.'

'I don't know, Matt – what is it – six in the morning? A few hours and we'll have a name for the face – no need to meet the newspaper.'

'You just lie back there. Don't rule out the newspaper just yet – we still need to find out where she is *now*, today. I'll make you a coffee, run a bath for you, it might help you relax.'

I supped from my cup, the water gushing in the background. So close, still no name but not for

321

much longer. We both had lapsed into silence, coming back to the present abruptly.

'That sounds like the bath overflowing, Matt.' I bounded from the bed. 'Got it in time – floor's just a little wet.'

33

I was blow-drying my hair when Matt's cell phone rang and he went outside to escape the whirring noise of the drier. Minutes later I was putting on my new grey suit, opting for the skirt and a pair of black stockings. Dressing up for the nuns – they never approved of trousers for girls, now did they?

Matt came back and he was looking concerned.

'That was the school, St Louis. Sister Alphonsus. She says she wants you to come alone this morning. Unyielding, she insists that it's a family matter. She won't meet with you unless you agree to that condition. I have to ring her back.'

'Tell her I agree. You drop me there and we'll meet up later.'

I'm back again in the visitors' room, my shoes tapping incessantly against the marble floor. Stop shaking, Ava.

The door opened and two elderly women entered, one of them cloaked in the regimental black and white. There was no sign of the crotchety Eugenie and immediately I felt less assured, like I had to start all over again.

The nun offered her hand first and clasped mine in hers momentarily. 'I am very pleased to meet with you, Ms Dimato. I'm Sister Alphonsus. This here is Eileen Burke.' She gestured for us all to take seats. Then she continued. 'Yesterday must have been a terrible shock to you. Sister Eugenie has told me everything. Unfortunately, she's had to go off to Dublin for a few days. As soon as I got the news last night, I rang Eileen here.'

I looked at the elderly woman, baffled. She was too old to be my mother.

Sister Alphonsus continued. 'Eileen here is your grand-aunt if what you say is true.' Tears rose in my eyes, preventing me from having a good look at my grand-aunt. I roughly wiped them away.

'Here's a tissue,' the elderly woman was saying.

I muttered an incomprehensible thank you. Suddenly I was thinking of my father Joe Dimato. I found myself sitting up straight and squaring back my shoulders, preparing myself for whatever news I was going to hear.

Sister Alphonsus was speaking again. 'Last night on the phone I told Eileen – that an American lady had recognised her niece in the hockey-team picture. Eileen was very upset about it all but she agreed to come down and talk with you. We apologise for excluding Mr Smith but it is a family matter. I just came here to introduce you. I'll be withdrawing from the situation myself. You may stay here and talk if you wish or perhaps take a walk down to Eileen's home.'

Eileen's eyes looked reddened, as if she had been crying. 'I think I'd like to take Ava down to my home – it's a little more personal, private. Can you drive us down, Sister? I just feel so tired.'

Eileen Burke's cottage was an unfussy two-bedroom affair on the edge of town. If my grand-aunt had received Dimato money surely she'd be living in a better house than this? I felt obliged to be patient with her as we settled into talking about the past.

'I got such a shock – I was in bed when Sister Alphonsus rang me last night. She said that you had come to the school with a picture of my sister's child and you said that she, Catherine, was your mother.'

'She is my mother, Mrs Burke. I have no doubt of that. But I need you to tell me everything. What was her full name?' I was pushing her but I needed to know immediately.

'Her name is Catherine Loughnane and I agree that she must be your mother. I'm *Miss* Burke, by the way. Catherine came here in February of '68 and was gone by November the same year.'

'Do you know where she is right now, Miss Burke?' I asked urgently.

'Well, it's a no and yes situation. Catherine discovered she was expecting a baby, that's you, I mean – well, obviously, you wouldn't have come here otherwise – in November that year. She went down to one of those homes in Cork to have her baby but disappeared while there. I've never seen her face to face since. Thirty-eight years nearly, so I guess I'll not ever see her again at this stage. I've spoken to her over the phone twice in the past twenty years and that's the height of it. It's about eight years since she last called. She's living somewhere in Australia and says she's married with four children. Won't even give me a number to ring her back on, not even her husband's name – maybe she doesn't want him to know about her past.'

She stopped to drink some tea as I sat aghast, seeing all that I'd followed slipping away from me. The word 'Australia' hit me like a jackhammer in the chest. I gulped to take a breath. I'd come so far only to have it snatched away from me at the very last minute. Ava Loughnane, daughter of Catherine, who'd removed herself to the farthest corner of the globe.

All that was left of the Loughnanes in Ireland was Eileen herself, her bachelor brother James having died five years back. Under different circumstances, her voice would be termed soft, even dulcet maybe – but what she was saying made it grate remorselessly into my brain. Birdlike, like the woodpecker as he pierces his way relentlessly forward until he can see right through to a gaping hole.

'Catherine was the only child of Teresa, my sister, and Frank Loughnane. They lived in Creeslough, Donegal. It's right up on the northwest coast. Frank died many years back and Teresa only last year. Think of it – she'd be your grandmother. Anyway, Catherine didn't come to either funeral. She mightn't even know but it's only because she doesn't care. She was always difficult–'

'Could you stop it, please, Miss Burke! That's my mother you're talking about.'

'I'm sorry – but things weren't easy. Her parents wanted her to have a good education. She was bright but her results were poor.' Eileen stopped to clear her throat a few times. 'There's no easy way to say it, Ava – can I call you that? But she got an eye for the boys much too young. Nobody could stop her.'

I was beginning to feel waves of nausea creeping over me and I had to remind myself that I hadn't even met this scarlet woman. I was finding it hard not to judge her. She'd always run out on me, hadn't she? First time it was Boston. Then, as soon as I track her down to Ireland, I find she's as far away as she ever was. All I got was an old woman's reminiscences about her.

She talked on until I suddenly rose and said, 'I think I need to go outside for a while – get some fresh air. I'm not going away, Eileen – no, I just feel dizzy.'

A difficult child. Don't the wise old women of this world have a wonderful habit of labelling people once they don't conform to whatever it is that the elders have laid out for them? Yes, most likely each time my mother ventured into the street the chorus of wisdom would kick in. *There she goes, Catherine Loughnane – problem child.* Banished to Carrickmacross from Donegal in 1966 owing to poor Intermediate Certificate results – wasn't that what Eileen called them – and common knowledge that the red-blooded males in the locality found her to be a most willing type of person. Put her in boarding school, close to her aunt who'll take her at weekends. That way she'll have the best of both worlds with the added bonus that her Aunt Eileen was a national-school teacher. That perfect combination of boarding-school discipline and the kindly aunt who would throw in free grinds at the weekend. Almost certain to ensure the right Leaving Certificate results except it didn't work out like that. News of her willingness got carried on the back of a stiff western breeze all the way to the boys of Carrickmacross and I could picture the inevitable coming to pass as Catherine spent her mornings racing from classroom to toilet. She probably even managed to drive a wedge between the two sisters, mother and aunt, who couldn't agree where the dastardly deed had taken place. *Bad girl.*

Eileen was standing beside me in her front garden.

'Your garden is beautiful,' I remarked.

'Thank you, Ava. That's a beautiful name. Are your adoptive parents keeping well?'

'They're both dead.'

'I'm sorry to hear that. Please come back inside. I have something for you.'

'Yeah, but hold on – I haven't said I was adopted – what do you mean by that?'

Eileen's face was flushed. 'Well ... I said Catherine rang me afterwards. It was from America the call came. She said she had a baby girl and she'd arranged good parents to look after her, you. I took it to mean adoption.'

I felt myself tensing unbearably. 'Eileen, my family in America made two payments into a

Dundalk bank account before and after I was born. Do you know anything about that?'

'No ... surely you don't suspect that I was involved – that I got money out of it?' She was looking highly indignant at this stage.

'No, but it's strange. From what you say, if it had gone to a Donegal account, that would make sense – but Dundalk?'

'I'm sorry – I just don't know. Do you want to see what I have for you?'

Back inside, Eileen Burke handed me an old photograph album.

'I started this last night. I just couldn't sleep after what the Reverend Mother told me. Started putting it together about six in the morning. I just thought you might like to have it, maybe not. I've just removed my own stuff – there's her home place, Creeslough village in Donegal overlooked by Muckish Mountain.'

Her head looked downwards as she expertly shifted some pictures into a more meaningful sequence, as she called it, a *This Is Her Life* caricature laden with dates, events, memories.

'There now, I'm getting old – I thought I had them in the right order but it's lined up properly now.'

'The house, Eileen – is it still there?'

'Yes, it is, but it's lying idle. It's a council house but the site is owned by the Loughnanes. The Council want to buy out the site but they need to track down Catherine first. Frank, your grandfather, worked as a fisherman and money was very scarce.'

'It must have cost a lot to send Catherine to

boarding school.'

Money, the easy answer. I saw the similarities with my adoptive family. I was brimming with animosity and I just couldn't find a way to hide it. 'Look, I'm sorry, I will take the album with me and thanks. All of it explains why she never made it to the classroom photographs. She only had three months here before she had to go again.'

'Yes, to Cork, as I said earlier. Sister Alphonsus might be able to tell you about that. Catherine went off to one of these homes to hide out – she was to stay there until her baby was born. They used to describe it as "falling from grace" at the time. Only Catherine can tell you what happened down there or perhaps your parents in America told you about that.'

'No, they never mentioned it,' I intoned sullenly. 'Was it Alphonsus that brought her down to Cork?'

'No. They hired the local hackney service at the time. The convent paid for it, though. Look – you could always stay over the night, that's if you want. I have a spare bedroom – you're more than welcome. You didn't get to see her classroom – she etched her name with a compass into the wooden seats in the laboratory: it's still there to this day. I've kept a little poem she wrote. I'll put it into the album for you.'

I didn't answer her immediately – there were so many questions racing through my brain.

'And there was no regular boyfriend? I mean, surely yourself and your sister had some idea as to who she might have been with?' The frightened girl in William's photo, the painting –

I found it hard to accept that she wouldn't have told someone.

'No – her father, Frank, he was a poitín drinker. He went about both Creeslough and Carrick-macross accusing people but it didn't do him any good.'

The doorbell rang.

'That will be my home help. She comes round for an hour every day.'

'Uh huh. I'll just go walk for a little while – maybe buy some food. I noticed people setting up stalls earlier.'

This wasn't really Catherine's home. Crees-lough was but there was nobody left up there. And I was due to fly out to Boston on Sunday night.

Matt listened as I talked over the phone to him. I felt it best that he go back home – most likely I'd follow him down later. No, I hadn't forgotten that he was going to cheer on his nephew in Mosney at the weekend and, yes, I'd like to come. Hearing Matt's soft, melodic voice was comforting, I longed for him to hold me. Damn, I really had it bad!

'Maybe we could go back-packing in Australia for a few months, Mr Smith. We'd have to renegotiate terms, though. I'm not sure I could afford to pay you four-fifty a day. I'm just joking, Matt. I think I've reached my journey's end here – maybe I'll get her address somehow, write some day. Otherwise I'll leave her be – it's clear she doesn't want to be found.'

The market stall buzzed with activity on this

bright Thursday morning and I filled my grand-aunt's basket with salad vegetables and fresh-baked brown bread. I stopped over on the way back at a butcher shop and picked up some cooked ham, noting the quaint bicycle parked outside the door. I resolved to be pleasant to the old woman when I got back. She had provided my mother with a haven when her parents discarded her and it wasn't Eileen who'd impregnated her.

I wondered if he was walking the streets of Carrickmacross right now – probably sixtyish, brushing past his daughter as he collected his provisions at the stalls.

Eileen had wrapped up the album in formal brown paper when I got back. Touch of William there, as I recalled his depiction of the girl in the garden. She gave me a type of contrite smile.

'Standard paper for covering books at school, it is. You'll be able to look through it in your own time.'

We ate together silently and I helped her wash up at the kitchen sink.

'Eileen, do you have the name of the place she went to in Cork? You say the school paid for the cab. Then they'd know where they dropped her off, wouldn't they?'

'I'll get it for you,' she said resignedly. 'Only, it's closed now – luxury apartments, that's what's there now.' She disappeared into the bedroom before coming back with a slip of paper. 'Here it is, for what it's worth. Look, I've told you all I know – I'm old and I'm not able for this. I can swear to you I got nothing but heartache from it

331

and I never got a penny out of it. I know I mentioned your staying but maybe it's not a good idea.'

'I'm going to be going shortly, Eileen. I wasn't going to take you up on your kind offer. I've only a few days left and I want to do other things before I go.'

I sensed her relief; the sooner I was gone the better. I took a minute to compose myself, fearful that the words might wobble in my mouth.

'Give my best wishes to Sister Eugenie and tell her she's not so bad. And, thank you.'

Suddenly, I am back self-consciously knocking on her door again.

'Eileen, there's just one more question I need to ask of you. Catherine – she was good and healthy, wasn't she? I mean – did she have any illnesses, diseases?'

'God, no. What do you mean – she was a strapping young girl. Very fit and healthy.'

'Oh, it's nothing. Well, then, I guess it's goodbye … thanks for the album.'

'Goodbye,' she said as she closed the door in my face.

I looked in the bedroom window from the garden, imagining my mother sleeping there – living with her aunt but alone with her fears. The old four-poster bed. There was only so much morbidity you could take and I didn't want any more of it.

As the cab came into view at the end of the road, I wished I'd accepted Matt's offer to stay until I was finished – that I hadn't told him to go on home. Always trying to appear strong, in control. Eileen could have asked me back while I waited, but no. She'd done her duty, given me the photos – I wasn't family despite the connection. Back in Boston, Emily had hinted at it happening like that. Was this how it was for Catherine thirty-seven years back, head bowed in disgrace as she waited to be chauffeured off to the home? Perhaps some leering driver bored with the long journey ahead goading her for information as to what local boy had put her in the family way. No surprise that you wouldn't want to come back, Mum ... none at all.

34

Wouldn't insomnia be so awful
If the swans were not here to see?
So early in the morning
I can pretend the lough belongs to me.

In daytime it's so bustling
You cannot hear the seabirds sing
But I know come dawn tomorrow
Once more my heart will sing.

CATHERINE
31/10/1966

I squinted my eyes to adjust to the Irish way of recording dates. You would have been 'with child' Catherine, with *me*. I wonder did you know then, when you wrote that? Waiting for the period that would not come…

'Could you take me to the Carrickdale Hotel, please?'

'Jesus, missus, you could have told me earlier. You said Carlingford first.'

Angry motorists making their way home hooted their horns violently, braking to avoid his sudden reaction to my command.

He left me in the car park, muttering a grudging thanks for his fare and tip. I could not go back inside – I needed to be alone, to think. I started up my rented car and was soon disembarking from the car at Carlingford.

I made my way back up the steep incline I'd twice climbed with Matt only two days back. Mildly inquisitive eyes of walkers, kitted out with rain jackets and walking boots, followed my path. Nothing unusual about walking in these parts but doing it in a business suit while carrying a parcel would get you attention if you wanted it. I was glad that Matt had shoved my other bits into his showboat suitcase. The tour guide was completing his descent into the village as I made my way up the cliff-side to pause right next to where I'd abseiled down not too long ago. My reward was to be the solitude, apart from a few prying sheep that roamed near to me. I could have grown up here; this could have been my home. I breathed a long sigh of relief. It was over. I had met a family member and I felt sickened that her reception felt so cold. She was ashamed of me. I buried my head in my shaking hands. Now I could permit myself to cry. Only the tears wouldn't come. She didn't even hug me nor shake my hand nor ask me about my life in Boston.

My real mother knew where I lived in Beacon Hill, yet she never made any effort to contact me. I had come to the end of the line. Maybe it was for the best. I had to surrender to the fact that there was nothing more I could do. From my vantage point I looked down at the tranquil sea. I felt so lonely and yet I didn't feel alone. Just last Christmas, I'd sat through three and a quarter hours at the Kendall Square Cinema in Boston as King Kong looked out in splendid isolation from his vantage point on Skull Island on the edge of the world. I wanted a not dissimilar remoteness and I had it so I could be alone with this pictorial biography of my mother's life until she departed into the unknown once William had snatched his still shot of her.

Eileen had pasted my mother's little poem just inside the cover. Nothing about her baptism but there she was propped up against lace cushions on her first birthday – 25th November 1950. You had not reached sixteen when you wrote that poem, Catherine, when you conceived your first-born – me, Ava Loughnane. There is *Teresa and Catherine, Creeslough 24/07/1958* – the mountain, Muckish is what Eileen had called it, rising spectacularly in the background. Indoor photographs of Communion and Confirmation, my grandparents smiling as she blew out candles with other adults and children looking on. Eileen's words came back to me.

'What with me and my brother not marrying

and she an only child, it was akin to a rent-a-crowd situation when these social calendar dates came up. Frank was partial to the odd drop of poitín so he had no trouble getting people to turn up.'

A replica of the picture of the hockey team from 1966 at the Sports Dome. This was most likely the last time she faced the camera in Ireland. A final that was held over from the previous season, couldn't be played for some reason or other.

The little things that a search can turn on – a delayed match was the difference between me having the name of my mother or going back empty-handed to Boston. But my heart was near empty – the elusive lady had cheated on me again. A picture, a drawing – a name. But no mother.

There was little more that remained left to do.

The beep-beep signalled an incoming call and soon I was sharing my news with Frieda.

'So, you've found her,' was all that she could manage to say.

'Well, I suppose I have, yes, but she's gone and taken herself to the far side of the world. Word is she has four children, so I guess that's it. Matt says I can't go forcing myself on her. He reckons it mightn't be that hard to find an address for her in Australia. She'd have a social-security reference number out there and you could feed her date of birth, birth surname and nationality into it. Even in a country of that size, she would most likely be the only exact match.'

'Who's this Matt you mentioned?'

I hadn't intended letting that slip out and my silence told Frieda it was time to close in on her prey.

'You're not about to tell me that you found time for a little romance out there, are you?'

Far too perceptive was my friend. It was too late to extract myself with a plausible explanation – she was going to get her information. Much too good at pouncing on the stray word and how it is spoken.

'He's just a private dick that gave me some help at this end. What was I to do ... stand outside in the street with a placard?'

'A private dick with a dick, I'd say. What's it with you and that trade? You're a junkie ... Matt ... the minute you said it I knew. Are you still off the pill?'

My cheeks were reddening furiously. Making love with Matt was something that happened and I was not going to acknowledge that any part of it was related to the maternal instinct, even the subconscious one. 'Look, I haven't said that anything happened but, yes, I'm still off the pill.' It wasn't *her* sussing me out that mattered – she was bringing my conscience into play and that conscience was telling me that Matt needed to be told. I made my excuses with her and started thinking of getting myself homeward bound. Home being the Carrickdale Hotel for now. I was glad that Paul Briscoe had not rung – he could be just as insightful as Frieda. Or was it just me wearing my heart on my sleeve?

Back once more in my room, it was time to engage in some accounting exercises to see how

337

my ten thousand was faring. I set aside three thousand that I felt I owed to Matt and that left me with less than three to cover the next few days. That was if I kept to Paul's rules – no plastic cards. Anyway, his advice had been rendered redundant by events since. Ben Dimato could relax – I was not going to expose him, never was. I just wanted to know for myself. Where was the compassion in this so-called Christian country? It certainly didn't hover around my grand-aunt.

Was my father Joe Dimato trying to protect me? A single tear slid down my cheek, and I wiped it away. This was painful. I was tempted to ring Chad up and tell him. What good would that do? Trying to get through to Chad was futile. He had his own agenda. I knew I had done the right thing in coming to Ireland – at least now I had nothing lurking in my background. I felt more fulfilled. But that's your choice, dear brother. Finally I can say to myself. *I am me.*

I went though a variety of messages and texts on both phones. Nothing of significance there. Matt to say that he was at home if I wanted to call him. 'Feel free.' I knew I was no company but texted him back to thank him. Chad enquiring casually where I was and how I was. It seemed that the intensity had somehow gone out of it. I smiled as the croaking voce of Martha Jones came across the line.

'Ava, honey, I've been worried sick about you since you ran from the house – what is it – a full week ago now. I'm here alone at the house this morning if you want to ring me. I sat your uncle down after you left and gave him a right earful that he'd have Martha Jones to answer to if he ever upset you again.'

It was really comforting to know that Martha loved me warts and all.

The phone rang out at Ben's house and eventually she answered breathlessly.

'Hi, Martha, it's me, Ava. Just ringing to say I'm okay.'

'Great! The cantankerous old so-and-so is here right now, talking election nonsense with your brother. Came back unexpectedly. I'm glad you are fine. I always pray for you during our services. The Lord always listens to Martha when she prays – everyone will tell you that.'

I giggled as memories of Martha's fondness for the Bible came back to me. From Monday to Saturday, she would slog her way round in anonymous grey tracksuits and drab, colourless smocks. Come Sunday, that would all change and she would attire herself in the most colourful of costumes and hats and take herself off to church to practise her Baptist faith. She had once nearly lost her job when she took Chad and me off to their weekly sermon where the baptism of a child was also taking place. It was Chad who let the secret slip.

'You should have seen it, Dad, loads of funky music and then they took this boy, he was older than me, and laid him out in a full tub of water. Everybody was clapping and singing. Can we go there instead of church from now on? Ours is so boring!'

It didn't help matters when he heard that she

had capped it all by taking us over to the tenements in Tent City to continue the celebration. Chad had got talking to Dwayne, the boy who was baptised, and had a whole catalogue of questions for him – was he not scared, was it cold? At fifteen, Chad had chosen as his high-school project to compare the Baptist and Catholic faiths and came down very heavily in favour of the choice and self-determination of the former. So vehemently that his teacher had contacted Joe Dimato. Chad rebelled by refusing to attend Mass and the home atmosphere was laced with friction as Dad sought to impose the heavy hand. Chad wasn't having any of it.

'I'm making my own decisions – your religion is such a load of crap, going round preaching, telling everyone to "do this" and "do that". I'm not going any more and that's it.'

Joe needed a counter-strategy and it was about then that the 'charismatic' uncle began to wield influence in my impressionable brother's head. Religion was subsumed by politics and it didn't take too long for them to mould him back in their images, only this time he didn't know it.

'Has he come up with anything on your pension fund, Martha?'

'Yes – he says he's working on it. I don't think he would be only you forced him into it. Thanks. We'll talk soon. Gotta go now. Bye.'

Carefully, I pasted *The Girl in the Garden* into the album that Eileen gave me. The room was fast darkening as the late evening sun disappeared into the night. Underneath the photo, I wrote my thoughts down.

It's as complete as I can make it, Catherine, Mum. You'll know that I am out there, just waiting for your call. I really liked your poem – maybe some day you'll explain it to me.

35

'Room service, Ms Dimato.'

I looked at the clock and saw that it was morning. But room service?

'Hold on, I'll open the door in a minute.'

Outside there was nobody and I peered around the corridor to see.

'Yes? Reception. Is everything all right?'

'I don't know – I thought I heard somebody knock on my door, calling room service. I didn't order anything.'

'You didn't ... weird. It could be some child playing a prank. Look, let me know if you get any further annoyance.'

She was gone when the hand reached out and she would not have heard my piercing yell.

'Jesus – Matt – what *are* you doing – how did you get in here ... and under the bedclothes? You scared the–' Suddenly I was laughing.

'Yeah, that's it – get it out, you need to bring that word back to America with you. I scared the *bejasus* out of you, just like you did to me Tuesday night. Now, what happened afterwards – I've decided I'm going to forgive you for that.'

'Should you not be out earning some money,

341

building up your resources until you have that sign above the door: *Matt Smith, Attorney at Law?*'

'Right this minute, there's something else building up and it's not my career.'

'Matt, it's eight thirty in the morning and you're a trespasser. You can't just walk into a lady's room like this. We American Catholic girls have morals...'

'That's okay, but Sunday is fast coming and those morals seem to have gone out of the window as recently as the early hours of Wednesday morning. Accosting a committed bachelor like that *and* in his own home. You'll be on that plane and you'll be saying if only me and Matt had done it one more time...'

'Well, seeing as you put it like that...'

Lying in his arms afterwards, I chided myself for daring to think that this was more than a holiday romance. To be fondly remembered when all that's left are memories.

I had sealed his money in an envelope the previous evening.

Though I was scared with what unpleasant information might come my way, my few days in Ireland could only be described as blissful and the reason was simple – Matt.

'What are you thinking about?' Matt broke into my thoughts.

In a dark corner of my mind there was that tiny but nonetheless irrefutable uncertainty that this was not quite right.

'Oh, nothing.'

'You're a funny one. I thought women loved to

be asked such questions.'

'Right now I just can't put words on it – my mind is whirling round with so many thoughts.'

We showered together afterwards and, once dressed, I passed Matt the money he had earned.

'I don't feel quite right about taking this.'

'No arguments, Matt, take it.'

'Right. You've twisted my arm.' He pocketed the envelope. 'Oh, by the way, I rang the bank. They've failed to come up with a name for the account number.'

'No surprise, really.' I sighed.

'Cheer up – we're going to the Community Games today. First game is tonight. His family are staying with me in Dundalk.'

'Mmm, I'm beginning to see now why some boys were so lecherous this morning. You already knew there would be nothing for Matt tonight. I'd love to go to it – that's if you're still asking?'

'I am.'

I drove into the Buttercrane Shopping Centre in Newry at noon. I reasoned that I ought to get some value from my car-rental agreement – a woman always has to justify herself for shopping, of course. Exhaustion had led me to accepting what Eileen Burke had told me – my mother was in Australia and my father was in the 'unknown file', a John Doe. It seemed that there was nothing more that could be done. Going down to Cork to view an apartment block seemed pointless right then. Plus, I had three thousand euros burning a hole in my pocket and I didn't want to lose money on the currency changeover back in Boston. I was just past the door of the Kylemore when Alison the receptionist hailed me from inside.

'Ms Dimato, Ava – if you're looking for a seat, there's one here. I'll hold it until you get around.'

I motioned towards my lips with an imaginary cup and the nod came back.

'Well, fancy running in to you!' I said as I joined her. 'I've just left the hotel myself. Are you on a day off?'

'Yeah, I did a swap with Imelda – she wanted Sunday off for some reason or other. Anyway I said okay and here I am. I love browsing around the place, even when I don't have the money – which is most of the time.'

'And how many do you have to shop for?'

'Just meself and me boyfriend. I'm tempted to throw the fucker out. Apart from the sex, he must think I'm his mammy. I'm with him eight years now and he's a pet but they redefined the word "lazy" when he came on the scene.'

'And does he work?'

'Oh, he does – George is his name by the way – he's a carpenter and a good one. He'd have his own business if he wanted but he prefers the thirty-nine hours a week and no risks, just the pay packet. He's not washed a dish or lit a fire in his life. Does do one thing – once a week – a ceremonial placing of the rubbish bin at the gate. The fanfare that goes with it... "Alison, I'll put that bin out shortly"... "I'm putting it out now"... "It's out".'

'Boy, George sounds like a handful.'

'Oh, he's no Boy George, I can assure you that.

No, if he brought an attitude problem into our bed, I'd tell him to hump off with himself. I put up with enough of him, I wouldn't take that. What are you looking at me like that for? Oh, I get it ... you didn't really mean what I thought.'

With Alison's help I picked up some gifts at the centre to bring back home – clothes at Adams for Sam and Sabrina and various creams and soaps for Frieda and Isabella. I hadn't given Chad his shirt and tie from Cape Cod yet so there was no need to be overloading myself. It was only a short walk to the Quays for more variety and I made some purchases at Benetton and Debenhams. Alison was looking wistfully at a necklace and earring set at OR Jewellers, reluctantly putting them back under the disdainful eye of the assistant. More coffees followed and it was time for us to part company.

'I'm just down the road here in Newry in a flat with himself. I suppose I may see you Sunday before you go.' Her eyes widened as she recognised the little box I pushed in front of her.

'No, jeez, I couldn't ... wow ... well, I could actually. When did you buy them – when I went off to the loo, I guess? They're beautiful! Thanks!'

I felt a smug sense of satisfaction as I saw the sign for Mosney looming up on the road. Once inside I rang Matt.

The basketball was starting in twenty minutes. The brochure identified the games as Ireland's Premier Sporting Event for Children and they literally teemed all over the place pushing, running – general bedlam. I felt a tug at my heart

when I thought that Ethan should be there –
maybe soccer if he took after Bruce ... or ice
hockey if he'd his grandmother's eye for the
smaller ball. In the past, I would have succumbed
to my fear and run away but not today.

Matt waved at me from across the floor.

'Ava, I want you to meet Jack, my brother, and
Sarah Jane, my sister-in-law. This is their
daughter, Gina – she's five and she's come to
watch her brother bring home the gold medal for
Carlow. Darren is over there with his team.'

Jack smiled and shook my hand warmly. Hardly
twins, I thought – he's taller, a little more
rounded at the waist. His wife looked vacantly at
me, then turned her head away. Nice to meet you
too. Mrs Smith, I fumed silently.

The teams were formed into a circle, their arms
clasped tightly around each other's shoulders.
They broke apart with a loud ritualistic roar and
the chosen ones took up their positions near the
semi-circle to face their opposition.

Sarah Jane looked despondently at her
husband. 'He's on the bench again – he'll go
mental, Jack.'

Within a short time, it was clear that there was
not going to be a gold medal in it for Darren's
team as the bigger opposition raced into a
commanding lead. The Carlow team coach, a
slender dark-haired man, remonstrated furiously
with his team, the referees, occasionally with
himself, while Sarah Jane examined her rings, her
watch, as she lapsed further into boredom. The
coach seemed to give up the ghost, sending on
most of his bench in one substitution. It was then

that Sarah Jane changed, once Darren stepped out on court. I had to step backwards from her high-pitched yells lest she damaged my eardrums permanently. Was this what I might have become had God spared my Ethan so he could take his place in the sporting arena? I closed my eyes briefly as the pain of seeing other people's children frolicking happily hit home and my quarrels with God resurfaced and all connected with Him for allowing my beautiful child to succumb to the cruel soil. The staunch Catholicism of my womanising father as he pontificated about the will of *The Great Man*. I caught Matt's eyes fixated upon me – yes, Matt, you know some of it: that my little boy died. But if only you knew the void, the pain of it all. The team fell further into arrears and came off court soundly walloped. Sarah Jane came over smiling.

'Ava, I'm so sorry about my manners but these occasions get right under my skin. I just can't deal with it – I go into a trance with the tension of it all. God, I'm glad it turned out so well.'

I looked towards the scoreboard and she picked up on my confusion.

'Oh, that. I wouldn't worry about it at all. Darren got more than half a game. He's involved and he's happy, that's what counts. I overheard you speak. You're American, aren't you? Let's go get some coffee while I find out what my brother-in-law has been up to lately.'

I looked across at Jack. He and Matt were twins after all. They'd slipped off for a beer and were propped up against the bar. Jack raised his Budweiser bottle in acknowledgement. It was everywhere, that drink – I wondered if you'd get one in the Sahara Desert.

'Gráinne that's the girl Matt was going to marry, she was one of my best friends. We were both nursing at Temple Street Children's Hospital and met the boys out on the Dublin club circuit. You wouldn't believe it – that first night, I thought Matt was hitting on me. Think of how easily things might have ended up differently. He'd have been a bit too sophisticated for me, what with his meditation and his music. It all started seventeen years back but it wasn't to be for them. Turned very sour, it did. Anyway we're out of here for tonight – we're going down to Matt's. Are you coming down?'

'Eh, I wouldn't say so … I'll talk to Matt in a minute.'

I said my goodbyes to the children and Jack, and Matt and I rubbed noses at the door of my car. Their last game was at one o'clock tomorrow and once that was over, Matt was a free man. So that meant, round about four o'clock, a lady should look her best. I squeezed his hand tightly and made my way off down the road towards the highway. My chat with Sarah Jane meant that I would have lots more probing to do, get to hear about his meditation and yoga. There was that look too, across the basketball court, when his eyes intruded upon my pain, my yearning to hold a child once more. Maybe he understood, felt the same himself, that longing...

I looked briefly into the hotel bar on my return and decided I'd make do with a sandwich and a glass of wine. It was thronged, and the thought of scoffing down cheesecake and coffee after midnight did not fit into my plans. A slim dark-haired lady, in her forties, I guessed, was chasing a young boy around the foyer. They'd been down at the basketball –the little lad had notched up a few points for the beaten team, hadn't he?

'Seán, you've got to quieten it ... where have the other two got to ... and put down that golf stick. You can't go waving it around here ... okay, okay, a pitch and putt stick – but put it down all the same. I wish you'd say something to him!' She turned to the tousle-headed man sipping his Guinness nearby.

I spent some time cramming the 'want-nots' for what was left of my trip into my suitcase. I'd have to wait and see where Matt wanted to park his head tomorrow night, before I completed the job.

The sounds of people traipsing back to their bedrooms diminished gradually and I felt myself lolling towards a peaceful sleep. That was until the phone rang. In my trousers pocket on the damned floor. The ringing tailed off and the beep-beep of an incoming message ensued. It'll do in the morning, I decided obstinately. I'm not getting out of my bed. But it only could be one of three who have the new number: Matt, Paul or Frieda. Jesus, folks, you've got me nosy now. I stumbled out of my bed to listen to the message.

Ava, it's Paul. I've been trying to reach you all day. I've just discovered that I was dialling your old number. Ring me the minute you get this.

Not like Paul to raise a fuss. I dialled immediately. Paul got straight down to it.

'Get yourself a pen. Take these details down.'

'Uh huh, got one, what is it, Paul?'

'My friend in the Department of Taxation carried on rooting after he traced those old payments. Came across another one for ten thousand Irish "punts" in 1996 into the same bank, different account number. We've got a name for this one and what's more it's the same person who got the money all those years back. The old reference numbers were recorded in free text on the new account. My friend here managed to pass himself off as somebody who is involved with all the tribunals and investigations that are going on over there. I've got you a name and address, are you ready?'

My head was going into overdrive, my brain already transmitting the information towards the tip of my pen. Loughnane, definitely, but which of them had made profit from my mother's misfortune – and mine? The poitín drinking Frank? Maybe his wife? Then there was Eileen – she needed to recover those boarding-school fees, didn't she? Please don't let it be Catherine, Paul – I know she might have needed it so that she could get away, but she's my mother. That would be just too much to bear.

'Yes, Paul, I'm waiting – you shoot.'

36

Mr James Ellis, Tholsel Street, Carlingford, County Louth, Ireland.

'Text me those details, Paul, in case I lose them.'

This was how our transatlantic conversation ended at two in the morning. Now, three hours later, I reconsidered the information for the umpteenth time. *James Ellis.*

Paul's cautionary advice echoed like drums thumping loudly in my ears.

'Don't go barging in on him immediately – there's something very peculiar about it all.'

By the end of our phone call, I resolved that if I never saw a private detective for the rest of my life it would be much too soon. The cold analysis, the clinical nature of it all. I was to consider all of the possibilities ... that it might be an unrelated matter, nothing to do with Ava – or Catherine. Paul had also insisted that I note down the two account numbers. Maybe a blackmailer, someone who'd unearthed Joe Dimato's dastardly deed of baby-trafficking and decided to make a quick buck or 'punt'. Could even be a 'fixer', a sort of agent who preyed on the difficulties and emotions on both sides – the all-consuming need of Joe Dimato, the panic and terror of Catherine Loughnane. The only thing to do was find out first who this man was.

I'd filled Paul in on how I had traced my mother, leaving out the Matt Smith part. Impressive, very impressive, was how he put it.

There remained only twenty-four hours to have this done and dusted and I was first into the dining room at seven thirty. Breakfast was tea and toast with a small side-plate of bacon and grilled tomato. Come nine o'clock, I was docked in the small car park next to the tourist centre in Carlingford. Back again, I mused silently over our earlier unwitting visits. Well, it was apparently the pride of the east coast, a reminder to the west that all of Ireland's beauty was not on their side. Catherine's poem – the lough. How close I'd been – how close I was to walking away not knowing. Prior to coming to Ireland, I had visited the census website to see how the one hundred thousand plus population of the 'Wee County' was distributed. The information I was now holding showed Carlingford as having just under thirteen hundred people. Most likely, I had looked down on James Ellis when I came here to be alone while looking at the pictorial history of Catherine Loughnane. Maybe not, though. It had been over eight years since he got his last cash injection – he could be out there in the graveyard. Discreet signs advised that the Carlingford Oyster and Jazz Festival was taking place that weekend.

The village was still silent and I was left to stroll down the road towards Omeath – to ponder how and where this beautiful little village fitted into my life. The marina was near full with boats though there was little sign that the occupants had risen from their slumber to face the day.

Once again I passed by King John's Castle and upwards towards the winding village streets.

'Here for the festival?' enquired a voice from behind. An elderly man stopped alongside me. 'I'm sorry if I alarmed you – you were lost in thought.' He peered through the locked gates. 'A monument to ancient times – cause any offence to Her Royal Majesty in those days and you ended up locked in that little cell for the night, to be hanged the following morning.'

'Yeah ... this is Tholsel Street, isn't it?'

'That's what they've called it for as long as I've been around. Very few locals living in it now.'

Definitely a 'Paddy' as the Bostonians would jest. Up to one hundred thousand of them in the city, most of them had made it big. This chap adequately captured the spirit of the few that didn't. Guinness-stained clothes that were most likely slept in – definitely a candidate for the league of unfortunates who never got to grips with enough of the US dollar. Still part of the fabric, the culture or as they would say 'the craic'.

'Do you live on this street, Mr...'

'I do, and I'll be glad when this bloody festival is over so us folks can have our street back. Fuckers, banging away on this jazz music until all hours last night. Meself and me son hardly got a wink of sleep with them.'

'That's terrible, you should complain, Mr...'

'That I'll do, but right now I'm off down to me local for a few, bottles of stout. I'd normally not go until the afternoon but this particular weekend is different. I couldn't sit there listening to them city slicks, coming in from Dublin and Belfast later on in their BMWs and Lexuses.'

Then he shuffled off down the road tapping his stick as he went along.

The shop higher up the road was open and I stopped by, picking up the *Irish Independent*.

The words are suddenly out: 'Would you know a family by the name of Ellis on Tholsel Street?'

The shop assistant eyed me for a moment as if she were considering whether she should tell me.

'I do. Jimmy Ellis and his son Fintan. Why do you ask?'

'Oh, friends back in America mentioned him to me. They were over here last year, stayed over with Jimmy for a while.'

'I'd doubt that somehow ... what confuses me, though, is why you didn't put all of this to the man himself when you were talking to him in the street a few minutes back.'

James 'Jimmy' Ellis had taken up his place at the bar in O'Hare's Pub and was carefully pouring a bottle of Guinness from a trembling hand. The barman handed him back some change.

'You had a skinful yesterday, Jimmy. Pension day, of course – I'll have to talk with you again about abusing the customers, though. It can't go on or I'll have to bar you.'

A long lingering swallow of his Guinness before Jimmy speaks. 'It's them you should be barring, not me. Bloody tourists – didn't they try to pull down that ornament you have outside the door?'

'The antique petrol pumps ... they did, all right. I had to bolt them back in place earlier. Anyway, sure now you have the travel pass, you don't have to hang around looking at them – you could always take yourself off somewhere the festival weekend.'

'It's not me that should be moving out. I'm damned if I'll let them shift me out of me own town. This is me own local and you'll get a lot more money from me over the year. Don't look at me like that. I know I owe you a few bob and you'll get it, for sure. I'm going to put in an objection for next year. They should have left it alone. We had great peace when they quit it a few years back and now they're at it all over again. It's just a money racket, that's what it is.'

He paused to look at me standing near the doorway.

'You again ... you've got a customer back here, PJ.'

I took up a seat away from the bar with an Irish coffee to continue my surveillance of the old man. The bar lapsed into silence apart from the sounds of PJ stocking his shelves. What was clear was that I was going to have a long wait for this man to go home. Just the two of us, strangers to each other but bonded together by some inexplicable force that persuaded Joe Dimato to deposit large sums of money into this man's bank account. Another man entered the bar and PJ swiftly produced a pint of Guinness on the counter and responded to a signal to uncap a bottle for Jimmy.

'Settling in for the long run, boys,' the bartender commented. 'I don't know what sort of livers God gave ye – but you two are a mighty pair of lads, no doubt. And you, Jimmy, it's taking you a while to get rid of that cane. How long will it take that hip to heal? You'll most likely break the other one before it does.'

Jimmy bit back. 'I wouldn't be so slow that I wouldn't hit you with a few swipes of it before you'd get near me.'

The Carlingford Arms Hotel gave me the perfect look-out point so that I could observe comings and goings from the pub. The backward glances of Jimmy and his drinking companion had persuaded me to relocate across the road. I interrupted a series of coffees with a bowl of sea-food chowder served with brown bread. Christ, will the man come out, go home – his friend seemed to be footing his drinking bill, no sign that he's still carrying round any of the Dimato money.

A text came in from Matt: *Won the bronze medal but Darren not too happy … only got five minutes near the end.*

Best that I reply.

Matt, something's come up. I'm not so sure about tonight. I'll call you later. Sorry. Bye.

I was about to order another coffee when Jimmy stumbled into the street. Almost five o'clock. His gait was less certain and, hurriedly, I rushed towards the door.

'Your newspaper, ma'am...' the voice trailed away.

I was running down the street.

Jimmy was fumbling with the key of his door. After an eternity, it swung ajar and I bounded through the open door before he could even turn to close it.

37

James 'Jimmy' Ellis stood poised in his hallway, his cane held aloft in the air. His eyes burned bright with fear and indignation. A musty stale odour hung in the air, dark brown patches of dampness marking the peeling wallpaper. A dog yelped loudly in the kitchen, scratching furiously at the door.

'Come near me, woman, and I'm telling you, I'll give it to you! What do you want with me? I see now you've been following me since morning, in the street, the bar. I've no money. I'm an old man. My son will be home soon. You'd better get out of here before he comes. You go now or I'll let this dog loose on you! I'll call the police too – I mean it.'

My heart was beating wildly as I struggled to find the right words. The rehearsals across the road in the Carlingford Arms: *Mr Ellis, my name is Marilyn Briscoe from the Massachusetts State Police. I am investigating the embezzlement of funds from a major pharmaceutical company that ended up in your bank account.*

It didn't come out like that at all.

'Mr Ellis, are you my father?'

The instantaneous slump of his shoulders told it all as his cane clattered to the floor. The fight, the rebelliousness that characterised his aggressive behaviour earlier, dissolved in an instant. His eyes desperately sought to look elsewhere but in the narrow hallway there was nowhere else to look. The skeletons in his closet were about to come to life and he took on a glazed expression as if he was unwrapping the layers of his earthly existence in front of me.

'Mr Ellis, my name is Ava – Ava Dimato. You've heard that name before, haven't you? I know you have.'

Slowly he picked up his cane and a small package that had fallen with it.

'Do you mind, I'll put the dog out to the yard first. He's only a little whelp but he's nipped the odd person in his day. He'll be a bit excited by the noise.'

After a bit of commotion and cursing behind the door, Jimmy was back.

'I suppose you'd better come in, sit down. You're likely to have loads of questions. I'll do my best but I'm old now. It was a long time ago.'

I bit my tongue on the more recent payment. That would have to wait. Let him tell it himself, I thought – that way, I'd get more.

We went and sat in the living room. At least that's what it looked like but the place was a right mess. It looked like a week's pile of ashes in the fireplace and unwashed dishes were everywhere.

'I'd prefer if you told it yourself, Mr Ellis. How this all came about? Am I looking at my father or am I not?'

'No – yes – I mean, I don't know. If you're Catherine's daughter, then you're mine too. And the Dimatos – that was the name. It all fits.'

My rage was starting to bubble along nicely.

Just like that – yes, I could be your father, in fact I am.

He was rambling on but I couldn't make out the words.

'Would you mind talking to me, Mr Ellis? I don't need to sit here listening to you mumble to yourself.'

Jimmy suddenly buried his head in his hands and sobbed. 'I can't get started! Honestly, I can't. It's over and done with. God, if I could undo it I would! To this day it still haunts me.'

'You can tell me and you're going to. I want to hear it from you. I've come a very long way and I'm not leaving.'

'No – it's me nerves – oh, God. I need a drink. I'll go and get a few bottles – then I'll talk. I just need something.'

'Tell me what you want and I'll go and get it for you.'

Somehow, as I ran frantically back to O'Hare's, I knew he'd stay there for me. For James Ellis, the running was over.

'I did a wee bit of cleaning while you were away. Sparked a small fire – it's kind of cold, isn't it? Dark too, not much light gets in, even in summer.'

I gave him a bottle of Guinness, which he poured into a mug, after retrieving an opener from under the armchair. Wouldn't be his first fireside drink in his lifetime.

'They called you Ava – that's nice.'

'Yes.'

I felt my heart expand in my chest as I waited patiently for him to begin.

'Your mother Catherine was fifteen; I was twenty-seven. I'd got a part-time job driving the school bus into Dundalk during school term. Catherine would be on the bus, going in to St Louis.'

'Carrickmacross?'

'No, Dundalk, but there's another one up the road in Carrickmacross. She went there too for a short while. I was married to Patsy at the time and we had two children, Fintan and Clare. She had this post-natal depression, Patsy did, after Clare and things were very hard. Very little money and we were always fighting.'

'Fintan, he's the one that lives with you now?'

'Yeah, he came back from England eight years back. The women, Patsy and Clare, that is, are still over there. Patsy never forgave me over your mother. Catherine lived out on the Omeath Road with her mother, Mary Mallon.'

'Mallon?'

'Yes. Catherine's name was Mallon. Didn't you know that?'

'No ... go on, Jimmy.' So much for Loughnane.

'Well, I used to go walking on the beach in the mornings and Catherine would always be there. Even at six in the morning, rain, hail or snow, she'd be there looking out over the lough. I'd always stop, chat.' He laughed nervously. 'She used to be writing little poems while she was there, ferocious shite, they were. One about swans in the lough, swimming in pairs with their young in a line behind them. Everybody knew that the swans swam on the canal, not the lough. She said she could see them, though, made me close my eyes, imagine – and, do you know something, I could see them meself too ... but that was her...' Jimmy's voice began to wane.

I was tempted to pinch myself to make sure this was not some dream. The face of Eileen Burke loomed large in my brain as her story of a poitín-swilling fisherman grandfather on the north-west coast of Ireland disintegrated. How could my grand-aunt lie to me? The transmutation since I watched Joe Dimato die was near complete: from Dimato to the girl from nowhere and onward to Loughnane, Mallon or maybe even Ellis. Like fish changing colour, camouflaging themselves on the seabed to escape being seen, being easy prey.

'We began seeing each other in secret, we did. Down at the beach. I took her off in the school bus one night. Her mother reported me and I was sacked. The guards, they warned me off too, saying that she was under-age. Mrs Mallon then packed her off to the boarding school in Carrickmacross but we kept on meeting – I just couldn't stop meself at the time.'

I passed him another bottle of Guinness and went to the kitchen to boil up a kettle. I retrieved a stained cup from a sink full of dirty dishes. The frying pan seemed to have the remnants of about a month's eating in it. Squalor was how you would describe the conditions.

'It was Hallowe'en. Catherine came back up from St Louis. We met down at the lough, the usual place. It was then she told me that she was pregnant. I was in a terrible state but we needed to do something fast. We were to meet that night. Catherine was going to get the keys to her mother's car and we'd be on the boat to England from Dun Laoghaire before anybody knew. She didn't turn up but her mother did. With the guards – they said they'd have me in Mountjoy – the prison, sure you wouldn't know – within twenty-four hours if I ever came near Catherine again. Mary Mallon was the school principal and had a habit of getting her way – still does.'

Best to keep your mouth shut, Ava, I said to myself when another period of silence ensued. This man had wronged me badly but I was witnessing his inner struggle as he sought to summon up the courage to tell me the complete story. Being in his company was not easy but my need to know overrode all.

'A couple of weeks passed without me seeing Catherine and then I got a letter from her. She was down in Cork in one of those homes. She really wanted to get out, said they were nice to her but she still didn't like it. I left it a few days until I got some money together and then I went down. I'd decided I'd take her out of the place – sail out of Rosslare. We could live in England until the baby was born – you, that is.'

With a muttered apology he shakily got up and went off to the toilet.

It was six o'clock and my chances of meeting up with Matt were fast receding. I took the opportunity to text him.

Matt, I've met my father. It doesn't look good for tonight. I might delay my flight back until later.

Matt replied immediately.

Ava, tell me where you are and I'll come to get you. XXX *Matt*

I noted the kisses and felt a warm glow growing inside me. It was nice to know that he cared.

I shook my head at Jimmy's offer of a ham sandwich as he unwrapped his small package, mumbling something about PJ always setting aside the previous day's selection for him.

My cell phone started ringing, Matt's number flashing up. News that I'd found 'Dad' must have come as a shock to him.

'Aren't you going to answer it?' Jimmy asked.

I shook my head. I didn't want to lose the moment. I had to prompt him to continue.

'When I got down to Cork, things had changed. Catherine was packing up to leave – she was going off to America to live with a childless couple and they'd adopt the baby when it was born. She'd changed too: she was very hostile towards me – they'd poisoned her mind against me. Or maybe it was the glamour of going to America that had turned her head.'

I cringed inwardly as I reflected on the small things that decide fate – the Dimatos could have come to Ireland a little later or could have been attracted to some other desperate individual. That would have left me, a baby, in some dingy flat in London with a teenage Catherine Mallon and Jimmy Ellis as my parents. That's if Jimmy even lasted that long.

'This American guy was there,' Jimmy went on, 'driving one of the old Ford Granadas and he was going to take her off right there and then. There was a struggle – we had a right fight there at the gates of the home.'

'Was there a woman with him, Jimmy?'

'No, he had a driver with him – that was it.'

So, Marie Dimato did not even get to choose her 'child's' mother. Suddenly, I longed for her to be alive. To talk to me – tell me how the two 'mothers' got along while I grew in Catherine's womb.

A brief smile flitted across Jimmy's face as the light dimmed further. 'Gave me a right few digs, he did – I hardly got a decent swing at him at all. I did manage to rip his jacket off, though. So that was it – Catherine was gone.'

My anger began to surge forth as this weedy creature began to divert himself from his dreadful betrayal by romancing about street fisticuffs, casting himself in the role of spurned suitor, a hero indeed.

'Do you know what I think – I think you're leaving a very big bit of the story out, Jimmy Ellis.'

'No, I'm not – I'm telling it as it happened and I'm getting to something I'm very ashamed of.' He got up and started rummaging in the cupboard, taking out a stained yellowish business card: *Dimato Pharmaceuticals*. 'I searched the pockets of his torn jacket and this is what came out. He was already back in America when I rang. I recited the details of his business card to him and told him to send Catherine back. Otherwise he'd get to hear from the Boston police about what he had done. It was then that he made his offer. Forty thousand pounds for my silence. In two instalments – it was a huge amount of money, back then, and I took it.'

By this time I was laughing cynically, unable to

conceal my disgust.

'Forty thousand pounds, Mr Ellis – wowee! I believe the dollar back then was eight shillings of your money so that means you would have got a hundred thousand dollars from the man I thought was my father. Tell me, Jimmy, did your *real* family make any gain from it all or would they have even known? I mean this dump, was it bought with your slice of good fortune?'

My father just bowed his head slightly, looking at the floor. Nothing to show for his opportunism and betrayal. The only dignity he clung on to was that he was not making excuses.

'The house we're in right now was my mother's. My wife took herself and the children off to England. Small neighbourhoods can be so cruel – she felt people were looking at her, deciding that there had to be something wrong with her that drove me to take up with a schoolgirl. No, she got nothing – the pubs got it all.'

Funny the coincidences that life throws up. On the day Catherine brought me into the world, Jimmy was before a magistrate in London who barred him from going near Patsy over there. He'd spent three months in a bed and breakfast and once the Irish pubs in Cricklewood closed, he'd go over to her place pleading to see the children. Slithering back, falsely contrite, to the woman he had betrayed. Looking for another chance. He had given his house back to Louth County Council in a fit of arrogance while the feel of Joe Dimato's money in his pocket led him into believing he could conquer the world.

'And that was the end of it, then, Jimmy?' I prompted. 'Once your forty thousand was gone or *my* hundred thousand, depending on whose currency you're looking at, you had to get back to earning your own. You don't mind me talking about the money in *my* terms, do you – because if there was no Ava, there'd be *no* money, would there?'

I passed him another bottle of Guinness – there was no point pulling the plug on him yet.

'No, it wasn't the end of it. It was back about eight years ago when Fintan came back to Ireland. I was down in O'Hare's. This American fellow left a newspaper behind him – it was the *Boston Herald*, I think, and there *he* was on it.'

'Who?'

'The senator, the fellow that gave me the hiding all those years back in Cork. Not Joe Dimato, as it said on this business card, but Ben.'

Well, well, well. Uncle Ben. How about that?

'I just saw an opportunity – Fintan had got a job in Dundalk but had no transport. So I put the squeeze on the senator and he paid up. Ten thousand pounds – I gave three to Fintan and I kept the rest. A few months later, I went back for more. He said to give him a little time. I heard nothing until I came home from the pub one night and when I got in, this guy was sitting right there where you are now. A younger man than the senator. Fintan was on night shift.' Jimmy was starting to cry as he remembered. 'He put a gun in my mouth. He was American. He told me that the senator had given orders that I was to be killed but he couldn't make up his mind if he should do it. Even asked me what did I think. He said he'd be doing me a favour, that I was scum. I knew it wouldn't cost him a thought to pull that trigger – he had a look in his eyes that would freeze you with fear. He made me repeat over and over again that I would never contact the Dimatos as long as I lived.' Jimmy was convulsing in great big sobs. 'Then he hit me across the face with the gun – I got over twenty stitches in my skull and a broken nose. Me ribs too, when I fell. I nearly died. I was in the hospital for two weeks. The locals wouldn't believe my story – they were convinced it was just another drunken fall.'

I stood up and a dreadful feeling of nausea gripped like a vice. Pins and needles shot up through my face as if all my gums reverberated with electricity from a thousand dental injections. Somehow I knew immediately. I don't know how. Sheer instinct, I guess. I put a trembling hand inside my jacket pocket and pulled out my phone. I selected *Camera* with fingers that were slippery with sweat.

'Jimmy, Jimmy, take a look at this photograph.' I held my old cell phone up towards his face. 'Look at this man here and tell me – come on, Jimmy, I need you to look – is that the man who came to your house?'

'Let me see ... yes, it's him. It's those eyes – I'll take them to my grave.'

'Oh, Jesus, Jimmy, Jesus...'

38

'Where is she now, Jimmy, my mother – Catherine Mallon?' He poured from the last bottle of Guinness into his cup.

He seemed deep in thought and I was about to ask him again when he spoke.

'I really don't know. I've never seen Catherine since she looked out the back window of that car as she drove away in that Ford car down in Cork.'

'Would you have stayed with her, Jimmy – had you made it to England? No, forget I asked that.'

Jimmy had gone to England anyway to catch up with his first family and caused nothing but trouble for everyone. He had come back to Dublin after two years and spent his time getting what work he could on the building sites and dropping into quayside pubs on his way home to his bed-sit.

'My mother would come up from here once a week on the train to see me. I'd meet her at Connolly Station and we'd go about together. She was widowed very young – I was just a baby. That's a picture of her over there – and she liked a drop of Guinness too. There was no point in me coming back here at the time – the locals would have nothing to do with me. And you had always had Mary Mallon to remind them whenever there was a danger they'd forgive and forget.'

I looked at the portrait of the stern-faced

woman on the wall, imagining her making the weekly pilgrimage to Dublin to see her outcast son. Jimmy was talking away – like clockwork she was, would never miss a Saturday. A bundle of clean clothes packed in a plastic bag – he would hand over his new washing – that was the cycle. Then one Saturday, she didn't come.

'That was 1981 and she didn't have the phone. She'd never missed before – I went back to the pubs for a while but I knew something was wrong. So I came to Dundalk on the evening train and hitched a lift out here. She was in the bed – stone cold, she was. Looked kind of peaceful, like she was asleep. Only fifty-nine, it was the heart.'

Jimmy had come back to Carlingford for her funeral and stayed. He'd been exiled long enough and everyone in the village except Mary Mallon had come up to sympathise with him.

'I suppose they wanted a look too at the returning sinner but I soon settled in and people forgot. Things were changing anyway and gossip has a much shorter lifespan these days. There was one strange thing, though: Mary Mallon came to my house about eight years back, looking for some blood samples or some such from me – that Catherine wanted them.'

Not so strange, I thought sadly. Jimmy had agreed and she had arranged for him to go to the hospital to give the samples. That was the last he heard of it. He couldn't remember why she'd needed them – maybe he never knew – he'd just got the cash injection from Ben and alcohol was the priority then.

So, it seemed the Dimatos had made an effort to help Ethan after all and did not want him to die just because they had secrets.

It was strange but I had no anger left to visit on this pitiful man that was my father. He was still only sixty-five but a lifetime of drinking had taken its toll. His daughter Clare would drop in whenever she came home to visit but Patsy had never made her peace with him. Fintan was in his forties and, apart from work, his two loves were fishing and drinking – he'd probably arrive in the wee hours. I became conscious of the cold snap of the house.

'Jimmy, maybe we'll go down to O'Hare's, anywhere, for a last drink. It might help you sleep.'

'Yeah, maybe we'll do that. We'll go somewhere quieter, though. The crowd will be out on the street at O'Hare's. You're a strange one, you are. I thought you might want to knock all my teeth out.'

'I've seen too much violence lately and it solves nothing – just don't expect me to call you Daddy.'

I'd booked in for the night to the Carlingford Arms. I had one last person to visit in the village and after that I would head back to the Carrickdale where I would meet up with Matt. I was not leaving Ireland on the Sunday night.

The bar was only half full and, while he made no attempt to introduce me to anybody, it was clear that he was very proud to be seen out with me and was getting a great kick out of their inquisitiveness.

Jimmy's hatred for Mary Mallon, my grand-mother, burned brightly and it became more evident as he topped up his day's drinking with a few Jamesons. Yes, Frank and Teresa Loughnane actually did exist and had died up in Donegal. Teresa was a sister of Mary Mallon. That was cunning of Eileen, making up a family album for me – I had fallen for it, thinking she was trying to be helpful by filling me in on the past. It was now clear that she'd been leading me away from it and I was sorely tempted to go back to her after the way she brazened out the deceit.

Well past midnight, I linked Jimmy up the street and he promised to dig out some photos for me for the next day.

'Did you say something about having a fold-away bed at your house?' My attention was turning to my half-brother Fintan. He was closer to me than Chad, I reasoned. It would be worth waiting until he came in – the wee hours, Jimmy had said. I wouldn't cancel the hotel – I'd go back there to freshen up in the morning.

'Yes, I can pull it out any time.' His face bright-ened suddenly. 'You're going to stay?'

'Well, yes – but I'll go walking early in the morning. There's no need for you to get up. I'll see you after my walk. Oh, and Jimmy...'

'Yeah?'

'That poem about the swans. I read it and it's not shit. I think it's very good.'

'Maybe ... maybe. But what would I know?'

I knocked briskly on the dark red cottage door on the road to Omneath and an elderly woman

371

answered almost immediately. My heart skipped a beat – it was the woman from the Tourist Office who had torn into Matt for walking in front of her car. Our eyes had met as she drove by then but she was showing no marked reaction now.

'It's you – you'd better come in.'

Before closing the door she looked up and down the road quickly as if she had just admitted a wanted felon into her house. The inside was as immaculately kept as the garden and the smell of fresh-baked buns filled the front room.

'I am afraid I cannot offer you tea as I am going out presently.'

'Carlingford Arms does a good breakfast,' I said curtly.

'You made a wise choice when you decided to stay there. You would need to be fumigated if you stayed in Mr Ellis's house. So you met with your father down in the village pub – that will have been nice for you.'

Something about the syllables, the way she spoke. Robotic.

'You saw us – how did you know who I was?'

'I did not see you and I do not go to pubs. I heard it after Mass this morning. Mr Ellis and an American girl. It wasn't hard to work out, after you had been down in Carrickmacross upsetting my sister Eileen. She has been unwell since.'

The ease with which this old woman's sister had spun her web of lies a few days back had left me gob-smacked and drained. The similarities were very easy to spot – each small and tidy in appearance with near-white hair pinned back in a bun. The difference was the steel in this

372

woman's eyes. It was quite easy to imagine Eileen taking instructions over the phone in the dark of night from this lady – someone who was prepared to write herself off as dead rather than face up to how badly she had let down her own daughter. I had confronted my father less than twenty-four hours earlier and had found a human being – badly flawed, opportunistic, wickedly selfish. But you could reach him – find his conscience, experience his remorse.

'I suppose the album was your idea – feed the American girl something plausible that will bring her probing to a halt? I just came here to ask where my mother is. That's all I want to know and I'll leave.'

'I do not know where she is. I haven't seen her in over thirty-seven years. After you were born, my daughter Catherine was booked on a flight from Boston to Dublin. She never turned up and I have not seen her since. Nor had any contact with your American family.'

Unemotional, impassive, frigid. I was in the company of a woman with ice in her veins. Part of me had considered asking for a picture of herself and Catherine for the album, real mother and child, but it didn't seem right.

'You're lying. How did you get to know about my little boy, Ethan? You went up to Jimmy Ellis to ask for marrow samples. You told him they were for Catherine.'

'They were not for Catherine. They were for the Dimatos. I arranged for him to meet with a doctor in Dublin who carried out the procedure. The samples were sent direct to America. I was asked to help and I helped. That is all I know. Otherwise I would never have gone near him. That man, your father, violated my daughter, took advantage of a child. He should be in prison.'

'Do you know what, Mrs Mallon? It seems you yourself found it hard to accept her as a child at the time. I could easily understand why your daughter would not come back to see you. I'm sorry I came to see you and it's a pity that I'm leaving Carlingford with such a bad odour in my nostrils.'

'So you are off, then. Well, just take with you the reality that your mother was a slut. She was reared to do better than she did do, breaking up another poor woman's marriage. I will never forgive her.'

'I think you should realise, Mrs Mallon, after thirty-seven years of absence, your daughter, my mother, is neither looking for your forgiveness nor your company. Sad, isn't it too, *Grandmother*, when you get to thinking of Jimmy and his little fleapit up there and you down here with your pristine little cottage – *his* son came back to him for all his drunkenness and trickery. Still, I hear you've got your tourist office, historical society and committees to keep you going when you're lonely.'

The fire in Mary Mallon's eyes was becoming fiercer as she faced me directly. 'Do all of you Americans start off by threatening to leave and then outstay your welcome by blustering on about God knows what?'

'Yes, I am off, now. I believe you were the headmistress of the local national school, guardian of Carlingford's young.'

'That is true – I was headmistress for twenty-three years – and what of it?'

'My God, Mrs Mallon – doesn't God bring such suffering to little children at times?'

I felt myself being drawn back to Tholsel Street to talk again to my father and see if I could meet up with Fintan. I'd lain restlessly on the foldaway bed in the living room until five o'clock in the morning but my half-brother never came. Eventually I'd plodded back to the hotel to grab a few hours' sleep.

The windows were open and he had been putting in something of an effort to clean up the house. The kitchen was at least functional and the pots and pans were washed. Clean cups too – a bit of scouring powder, he said apologetically. Loud snoring was coming from upstairs.

Jimmy had obviously given himself a bath and he was dressed in a sombre grey pullover and black trousers. His eyes were red and watery – maybe it was the previous day's drinking, who was to know?

'Ava, you asked for some photos. I don't have many of them but you can have them.'

'Thank you, Jimmy.'

We drank some tea and it was time to go. The hug was short and awkward but it was warm and a welcome relief from the refrigerator on the Omeath Road.

Jimmy spoke falteringly. 'I suppose this is it then, we might never...'

I put a finger on his lips. 'Don't, Jimmy. I just can't say right now – it's too hard. I'm extending my stay a couple more days and I'd love to see Fintan too – only there's no point stirring him right now–' my thoughts turned to Matt, 'and there's someone that I have to get back to at the hotel. We'll have to wait and see. Bye.'

I was glad to get away for fear he'd see the tears. I watched him in the rear-view mirror, standing there, just looking on until I disappeared.

The tour guide from New Zealand was leading a group of children up towards the cliffs to do their rock climb. The little boy, Seán, from the basketball and the hotel, was zigzagging between the cars, his mother heaving sighs of resignation as she followed him on the footpath. Life carrying on.

Matt, it's 3 p.m. I'll be back at the Carrickdale in half an hour.

The foyer of the hotel was packed with people – all eyes glued to a football game on TV. Alison waved from reception and I could see she was wearing her new earrings and necklace.

'You should have seen George's face when he saw my jewels! Once he was satisfied that I hadn't splashed out money on them he began fretting as to whether I was having an affair. I'm not going to make him any the wiser, keep him on his toes for a bit.'

'That's the spirit, girl! But what's happening? I never saw such a crowd.'

'It's Dublin and Mayo. Our national game – the All-Ireland Semi-Final. We had to take a TV down here from one of the bedrooms. Too many in the bar. I thought you were leaving today.'

'I have to talk to you about that. I hope to stay at least another night, maybe more. Is that okay?'

'It's no problem. A lot of guests check out on a Sunday.' She checked her computer.

'Yeah and you don't need to move rooms either. I'll stick you in for tomorrow night too. If you don't need it, it'll be okay?'

I opened the door of my bedroom to find a sealed envelope on the floor.

Mrs Dimato. I waited for over an hour at Clarke Station this morning where you were due to return my car. You are not answering your phone. I'm writing this at the hotel. Please ring me.

Denis Malone

One phone call later and the car was secured for another two days. My deposit was no longer guaranteed.

Text from Matt saying that he was held up.

I went back down to the foyer where the audience was getting more and more agitated. A crescendo of heartfelt cheers went up and the team in the green and red jerseys were hugging each other, crying, laughing while the blue shirts plodded dejectedly off the field.

'They beat the Dubs, Mayo beat the Dubs!' a middle-aged woman said.

39

'Sorry to disturb you, Ms Dimato. You've got a gentleman that's come asking for you – what'll I tell him?'

I jerked. my eyes open as I came down to earth from my reverie in the hotel jacuzzi to the sight of the pool attendant leaning over me. Matt had his nose pressed to the glass outside and was pulling funny faces. He pointed towards his watch.

'Thanks – I just nodded off. Tell him I'm getting out – to wait for me.'

I wasn't going to explain to the pool attendant that I wasn't asleep but trying to revive my brain cells and de-stress from recent nerve-wracking encounters and confrontations. What with Jimmy Ellis, the Mallon sisters and seeing my true mother pinned up in the Past Heroes Gallery at the Sports Dome, I was sure that I didn't need any more excitement for the moment. I was just looking at the immediate future and how I might entice my new-found lover to linger awhile in my life. And it had come to me as I lay in the foaming water.

'Matt, I've been checking out the return flights to Boston and I've got a seat back for Tuesday night. In fact, there are plenty of seats and that's what got me thinking ... how I'm going to miss you and that.' I knew I was blushing but it was out now and the rest was easier. 'So, maybe you'd like to come over to Boston for a few days with me – a sort of a thank you for all you've done – you might want to think about it.'

'Not much thinking to be done, Ava – I'll go. It's not every day a chap gets an invite to Boston – add a so-so-looking woman to the package and you've got a nice little offer, all right. So it's a yes.'

'So-so, Mr Smith? You'd want to withdraw that or you might get left behind.'

'Shuah, ma'am. I just know it's going to be wicked good.'

'Well, begorrah and bejaysus, shur we'll do it then!'

I had fallen for Matt – it was as simple and complicated as that. Trust me to fall in love with a man who didn't even live in the same country as me. Would he want to get involved? A casual invite to come Stateside was very appealing but what would happen after the holiday was over? The sensible thing to do would be to just say our goodbyes – that way I could save myself a lot of heartache. And yet I couldn't do that – I harboured the dream that Matt wanted the same things as I did. Hadn't he already indicated that in Mosney when our eyes met across the crowded basketball courts? Surrounded by children and none to call our own. It seemed obvious that, at forty-two, he would want the same thing so there was no need to ask him, was there? I opted to disregard Frieda's warnings about mapping out other people's lives – better to wait and see what might happen in Boston.

'You can't decide what's best for others, Ava. These are life-changing decisions – it's not something trivial, like if you'll buy that dress, eat in or eat out. Paul has the right to know if you're scheming to make him a father.'

I had snorted derisively at her advice.

Anyway, it was *different* with Matt, wasn't it? A week or so together on Beacon Hill, a little bit of probing with law firms and he might see a chance of fulfilling the dream. Become that attorney that he always wanted to be and learn that he was going to be called Dad. It would be perfect, wouldn't it? Then there was Paul Briscoe and him wanting to know when I got back so he could pick me up at the airport. Oh, Paul, I almost forgot – this is Matt Smith.

I'd gone back tongue in cheek to Alison at reception to enquire if it was okay to have an unofficial visitor in my room for the night.

'Of course. I'm glad to see you're enjoying our Irish hospitality.'

All that remained to be done before our departure was for Matt to pick up some things at his home. It was time to show my partner that I could drive too – let him enjoy a few pints with his oysters and brown bread.

'Not bad at all,' Matt murmured his approval as I parked once more facing the lough. 'Will "the family" be expecting you back?'

'No, I sort of wanted to get away earlier what with Mary Mallon and that. Imagine she'd have known as far back as Tuesday that I was around – when you intercepted her leaving the tourist office. She'd lots of time to prepare others – Jesus, that Eileen! I'd really love to hit her, but what's the use? But I never got to see Fintan and I keep getting drawn back towards the old man. I think he's told me all he knows about Mum, though.'

I locked the car and was looking up the road to where my maternal grandmother lived.

Matt broke into my thoughts to say, 'I'm really sorry, Ava, that it's turned out so badly for you. At least now you know why your mother never came back.'

'You've obviously been listening rather well. I like that about you.'

Matt was looking outwards at the expanse of water, the mountains and cliffs encasing the village in a protective shroud, making its own emphatic plea to leave nature be as intended. Beautiful and unspoiled. I linked my arm in his.

'Think, Matt … imagine. We could nearly be them, act it out – bring it back to '66. I'd be Catherine, coming down at all hours of the morning to escape my gruesome mother, think up my poems.' I threw my head back, swooning mockingly towards my man. 'And you are the lecherous Jimmy, prowling the beach – ready to pounce on me, a poor innocent girl. Except you haven't said what's stopping you from sleeping, what you're running from.'

'Responsibility, most likely, and I'd need to see this Jimmy before consenting to the comparison. D'you know what I'm thinking? I think they duped us at St Louis in Dundalk. Seeing as Catherine went there, they must have had photographs. That nun in Drogheda must have known her and contacted Mary. Do you want me to ring them? Ava, are you listening?'

'Sure I am.' But I felt a kind of resistance in me, as if I was afraid to open up to hope again.

'Hey, we're getting drowned wet here – have you noticed the rain, Ava?'

The droplets were trickling down through my hair and on to my face and I gratefully accepted Matt's tissues.

'I was just thinking ... the mother thing ... Catherine. I don't know, Matt. Do you know – after all the chasing, if she was to appear out of a genie lamp right this minute, I'd want to vanish down another one. Can you imagine that?'

'Could do – sure, you've had, what is it, four surname changes over the past few days. If she was to turn up right now as Mrs Somebody – that'd make it five. So that's it, then? You don't want me to contact Dundalk?'

'I do. Ring them up. I'd be back in Boston and regretting it if I didn't look in again on the place. That's where Jimmy drove her each day.'

We were back up in Tholsel Street.

'We'll go into O'Hare's, see if that rogue is there. I'd like to settle, consolidate for the minute. I've had enough surprises and you deserve a pint for listening and not complaining once.' I squeezed Matt's hand. 'We'll have our time alone later.'

Jimmy's eyes shot up from the little group of locals converged in the corner. Hadn't he moaned about the tourists invading their little 'winter alcove' once the sun came out – how their counter strategy was to squeeze up near to them until they were forced out by their perseverance. It looked like he was on a loser on this particular day. The sight of Matt seemed to halt him in his approach until I motioned to him to come over.

'I didn't think you'd be back this way so soon,' he said uncertainly. 'There's not something wrong, is there?'

My companion was getting the once-over and Jimmy was making hard work of finding the right words to say. He shook Matt's hand while averting his eyes towards me. 'You're after going and spoiling it for me now. The locals and the village gossip in the newsagent's were having a right bit of banter about my American girlfriend except you've come back with some competition.'

Matt's eyes were twinkling merrily as he looked downwards at my father. A larger man was now casting a shadow in the background as he shifted from one foot to the other as if waiting for an introduction. I took the lead.

'Fintan, I presume,' I said, leaning forward to kiss his stubble. He took a step back, blushing. Black hair, five-ten. I'd have to ask Matt later if he saw a resemblance.

'That's me, and Dad's filled me in.' He looked towards Matt. 'I've seen you about the place before – ye do yer share of fishing, don't you?'

It conveniently turned out to be the icebreaker and soon the two men were chattering away about the one that got away.

Fintan was forty-two and seemed a genial enough chap, unfazed by the fact that this was a very different Sunday evening than what he'd expected. I'd have to wait and see what he might be like away from the tongue-loosening ambience of his local. I wondered if he blamed me in some way for tearing his father away from his family. Four years old – that's how young he was when his father's affair with Catherine ripped his family apart. From the way Jimmy had told it, it was to be near on thirty years before father and son united again – and only then when Fintan was down on his luck with no place else to go.

Only got to hearing about me after his father was beaten up and left in the hospital – he'd been suspicious when Jimmy seemed quite happy that the Gardaí had no leads on his attacker.

'Fintan, would you mind going outside for a minute – your, eh, our father too? I've got a camera built into this phone – I'd like to take a few memories back to Boston with me.'

Outside, I snapped busily for a minute or two. Then Jimmy requested that Fintan should take a few shots of himself and me.

'Yeah, I've got you right there,' Fintan said as he pointed my cell phone towards father and daughter. Then he handed the phone over for us to admire ourselves and winked at Jimmy as he went back into the pub. 'I'd keep it in my private collection, though, if I were you!'

Still out in the street Jimmy Ellis paused before asking, 'Why did you come back down, Ava? I didn't think you'd come this way again.'

'I don't know. I sort of ran away this morning – wanted to blot it all out, move on. But now that I'm here – do you mind looking at *that* photo again?'

384

I needed to satisfy myself that there was no doubt. It was eight years back but pain is a raw commodity. I didn't need to be running over to the Gardaí or the Health Board hospital to confirm that what he was saying was true.

I showed him the picture that was stored on my cell phone.

Jimmy was staring at the image. 'This man, I get a feeling you're close to him – that you know him very well. Yes, it's him, no doubt.'

I stared a moment longer before answering. 'I thought I knew him, Jimmy – only I'm not so sure any more. It's getting a little cold out here. I'd like to go back inside now.'

Matt had made the phone call the previous evening and he was told to be there the following morning at eight. No negotiating. He was sound asleep when I drove out of the Carrickdale.

The previous night I had been forced to abandon the idea of getting closer to Fintan as I watched the pints of Guinness mount up steadily. Jimmy had noticed my disappointment.

'He never calls his sister from one end of the year to the next – he's sort of awkward around womenfolk,' was Jimmy's explanation.

The door of St Louis Convent swung open and I stood back in surprise as I was met with the erstwhile stern features of Sister Eugenie. This time, she was smiling.

'Don't be too surprised, Ava – it is me again – this is the same order as Carrickmacross. I've been expecting you – they said you were coming.'

I nodded approvingly and wasn't going to ask if

somebody had loaned out a smile to her on this grey morning. I was just glad that Mary Mallon hadn't been able to manipulate her into a cover-up. She passed me over an envelope containing a few photographs without ceremony and looked a little dejected when I put it directly into my bag.

'Won't you stay for a cup of tea?'

'Oh, sorry, no. I need to go. It's not that I'm not grateful, Sister. I just feel like I'm at my journey's end. It's been very hard – I'll look at the photos later.'

'Of course, I understand. The nuns here, they were too embarrassed to face you – that's part of the reason I'm here today. Mary Mallon's presence is felt in these corridors and they were afraid to say anything without her permission. She had put pressure on them years ago, warning them to keep quiet about Catherine, anticipating just such an event as this. In the interest of privacy, she said. Luckily for you, the one in the Sports Dome at Carrickmacross escaped her scrutiny. And I hope you don't feel too badly towards Eileen Burke – she was working to orders from your grandmother, felt there was nothing she could do.'

'Look, maybe I do have time for that cup of tea after all.' I removed the pictures from my bag.

It was clear from looking over the photographs together that Catherine Mallon had a great interest in sport. There were some sheets of paper in the envelope too – some more poetry apparently, something to read on the journey back.

Eugenie was talking. 'I'm amazed she escaped

my attention what with all her participation in sports and that. I'd have been canvassing to get her down to Carrickmacross earlier – that's the way we were those days, always trying to pick up the fittest and the brightest.'

Yes, I reflected – it wasn't just Americans that had spawned the survival of the fittest theory.

I prodded at a curly haired girl.

'It looks like everywhere Catherine went, this girl is right beside her, sharing the same school desk and all. Do you know her?'

'Well, I do, but I am conscious that you want to let things rest for now. Maybe I could put you in touch some other time.'

I could feel that something was starting up all over again. I looked again at the curly-haired girl – best friend, had to be. The body language almost told it – just like Frieda and me at high school in Boston.

'No, Sister – you might as well tell me now.'

'Her name's Heather Conlon. She's married, living over in London now. Eileen spoke with her – she felt she had to try and make up for her lies.' Eugenie passed me a telephone number. 'She's been told to expect a call from you. Just one thing, though – she's lost touch with Catherine herself. You've had a lot of disappointment lately, so don't go building up your hopes on this.'

'Thanks, Sister. I'll most likely ring her before I leave. I feel like I've been putting together a jigsaw from the moment I read Joe Dimato's records – I thought I'd reached the end of it when I saw her on the wall in Carrickmacross, but no. So I don't think this phone number will wrap it up either – just another piece.'

'Maybe she'll come to you herself one day – it might even be nicer that way.'

'We'll have to see. Better go, Sister – and thanks.'

Mr Malone was in the hotel car park when I got back. He was sighing repeatedly as if the inconvenience of it all was registering high scores on his stress-radar. He stared fixedly at the car as if I was bound to have done something terrible to it. Matt's Mercedes was still in the car park.

'I suppose it looks okay – sometimes you need to take them up to the car wash to be sure. It's then that you get to see the little nicks and scrapes that the dirt conceals. It's all the bloody roadworks, you see – leaves all sorts of grime on them. You'll know about that, coming from Boston. You're near the end of the 'Big Dig' over there, aren't you, and about time – near ten years since you started?'

'More or less, Mr Malone. Can we wrap this up?'

'How are you getting back to the airport – you're sort of stranded out here, aren't you?'

Obvious this man is in no hurry at all, maybe eyeing an opportunity to squeeze a few more dollars from his American tourist.

'I'll be fine, really I will. Good of you to ask, though. I'll just double-check your car, make sure I've taken everything out. It'll give you time to calculate how much you owe me back.'

Minutes later, he pushed three fifty-euro notes and a fistful of small cards into my hands, speaking with an exaggerated flush of generosity.

'Look, I know you kept it a day longer and then you go changing your mind again. I wasn't expecting it back until tomorrow so I'll just take one-fifty off your deposit and that will cover everything – including me coming out here and all.'

'Wicked – awesome. What can I say, Mr Malone, you've got me near speechless. What can I say?'

He looked at me confusedly before laughing out loud. 'You nearly had me there but that's Boston-speak, isn't it? You can call me Denis – it's what everybody calls me. Could I ask you to leave some business cards at the airport stands? Just tell them to ring Denis if they have any enquiries.'

40

The aircraft continued its ascent as I looked out at the concrete jungle of Dublin gradually disappearing below. Matt had lapsed into silence, his face pale and ashen as he gripped the hand-rests tightly. His passport showed him aged thirty-four, with a fuller head of black curly hair. Well-travelled did not apply here and the sole evidence that he had left town was a single stamp that I was scrutinising closely but could not decipher.

'Tibet,' he said helpfully. 'I went to the Himalayas eight years back to climb Everest. Fund-raising effort for the National Rehabilitation Centre. I'd much rather climb it again than go up in one of these things – this is my first time to fly since Tibet. Seven-and-a-half hours of torture, I should have gone out and got plastered.'

It was reassuring to know that Matt had cared enough to come. I hadn't told him about Heather Cordon and my telephone call to her. It was only when Matt got stuck in conversation with one of the airport police that I summoned up the courage and dialled her number.

'Never thought I'd see the day I'd get talking to my best friend's daughter. I've gone on your company's website from time to time. I've seen you on it – Head of Sales, aren't you?'

'Yes, that's me, all right. Do you know where my mother is right now, Mrs...?'

'Doyle, that's my name now. No, I don't – I haven't heard from her in over six years but I do know that she went over to Boston about eight years back when her grandson, your boy, was very sick. There was nothing she could do. She was very distressed – she only rang me once or twice after that and then nothing at all.'

I gulped down on my shock – the Dimatos had spirited my real mum into Boston to see if she could help my Ethan out. Did they prevent her from seeing me – or did they not need to? Catherine would have had thirty years to explain – she mightn't have wanted to face her daughter.

Talking with Heather brought me that little bit closer to Catherine – the photographs, the name, the family and now her best friend. My mother had turned up on her doorstep in London ten years after I was born, skin and bones, chain-smoking and barely recognisable as the girl she had last seen in '66 during the Halloween break. Heather knew about Jimmy Ellis and her friend's pregnancy.

'The worst decision I ever made was to tell Mary Mallon that her daughter was pregnant. She merely thanked me, cool as you like, almost if I'd told her someone had thrown litter in her garden. Catherine disappeared immediately afterwards and I ended up on an official warning at St Louis for "spreading rumours" as they called them. It was like they threw up a wall of silence so they could save face for Mrs Mallon – none of them seemed to care about Catherine.'

The bitterness in her voice came out loud and clear. My mother went on to stay the next seventeen years in London but just wouldn't talk about where she'd been. After a year spent recuperating at Heather's place, she went to work as secretary in a dental surgery. She was briefly married to a Scottish man, Kenny, but it didn't last.

'To be honest, you couldn't live with her – she was no longer the girl I remembered from my school days. She was prone to terrible mood swings – everything got broken, Delft was her specialty...'

'Did they have children?'

'No, there were no more children. Then she just upped and off again eight years back – at least we knew why that time.'

The elusive Catherine Mallon. My mind

flicked back to my history lessons at high school, my mother now taking the place of the Scarlet Pimpernel. *She seeks her here, she seeks her there, poor Ava seeks her everywhere. Is she in heaven or is she in hell, the mysterious Southern Irish belle?*

'I suppose that's about it, Heather. I'll give you my home number in Boston. You ring me up if you hear from her again.'

'Of course – but there's one more thing. Do you know of someone called Martha back in America?'

I felt that another tidal wave was about to descend on me and was amazed when I heard myself saying no.

Heather continued. 'I've told you about the mood swings. From time to time, Catherine would get it into her head that I'd plotted with her mother to take her baby away from her. She was back on that topic when she rang me from the States eight years back. Screaming down the phone, absolutely hysterical she was. There were all sorts of noises, like a struggle in the background. Then this Martha, black I'd say she was, came on the line and said it was okay – everything was under control. Line went dead and that's it. It's not much help to you, but it's all I know.'

All I could do was thank her, continuing the pretence that I'd never heard of Martha Jones.

Now I surveyed Matt with his eyes shut tight, beads of perspiration forming a film across his forehead – nodding wordlessly when the flight attendant asked was he all right. What is it that you're seeking, my friend, that makes you challenge your fears in this way? *Two* suitcases for the trip ... a little fashion conscious, aren't you? The Americans will like you with your Marlboro jeans and shirt but will the Marlboro Man vanish down Boston's mean streets once he gets there, another alien gone to ground among three hundred million souls? I was back on the edge once more – poised at a crossroads, contemplating what road I'd go down. Too many options, directions.

Heather, trying to explain that there was a difference between finding and meeting, that it wouldn't be fair to walk right up to my mother and say hello. Didn't it matter that her daughter might have waited, most of the time unknowingly but still aware of the void, for Catherine Mallon to do just that ... walk up and say hello? A struggle in the background, that's what she had said – to what lengths would the Dimatos go to make sure that the ghosts of the past remained silent? Sweaty Man might have been able to tell me that, only he couldn't now.

Frieda could be so annoying at times. I simmered quietly as I remembered my last call before getting on the plane.

'There's far too much going on for you, Ava – you're back up in the air. This Matt is coming over to Boston to get *away* from what he does and it looks like you're going to keep him in detective mode. He'll be back on that plane and don't forget you'll have some questions to answer to another private dick on this side. Yeah, Paul. Wandering men are more jealous of their mistresses than their wives. That's what attracted them in the first place – the mistress is a temptress, prepared to play by a different set of rules. Wasn't that why they strayed – seeing Ms Dependable in the baggy jogpants, food stains on the T-shirt, yelling at the offspring to get in the car for school?'

Now I'd never look like that because I stayed in mistress mode *and* that's where Matt Smith came in.

'Bullshit, you're such a crap-artist, Frieda – you should leave it to the shrinks. Anyway, Paul would have no right to make things difficult for Matt.' I was red with indignation.

'Truth, Ava – that's what it is. And I've met Briscoe – he's an arrogant man. Lots of charm and magnetism but still full of a sense of his own importance. I could even see his eyes wander all over me as he chewed his gum. No, he regards all his competitors as eunuchs – he won't be able to take it that his bit on the side has moved on and so soon. He's hardly left your bed and you've replaced him with another detective.'

I'd bought a larger album once I left the convent in Dundalk. Eileen had compacted it all nicely but she hadn't foreseen that I'd need space for Jimmy Ellis and for the real Catherine to fit the shoes of her story-bound mermaid that drifted in from the coast of Donegal. There was a grim satisfaction in thwarting the two school-teacher sisters' vile deceits, their loathsome plotting. Maybe I'd get back to the Carlingford Arms one day, have a big celebration to celebrate the second coming of Catherine Mallon, maybe write a book – no, frame my mother's poems, have them framed and mounted on the walls of the beautiful village. Imagine the immortality of it all – we'd all be lying cold as the historians gathered their audience to hear the story of the *Fallen Woman* who'd returned triumphantly to challenge her oppressors. The penitent sinner no more – in the land of *The Táin*, the Red Bull that was Mary Mallon vanquished. I rummaged in my hand luggage, realising that I was not going to get much conversation from my travelling partner on this trip.

The plane felt like it was hovering in a still position above the Atlantic despite the reality that we were scything forward relentlessly towards America's east coast. I waved away the offer of food for myself and the unfortunate Matt and returned to my task of transferring and rearranging the pictorial biography. And then there were the poems, written in fountain pen: those were the rules in the sixties – write it out in anything else and you got marked *zero* straightaway. Do it twice and you were talking about detention. I recalled Eugenie's lament. Now they're coming in with their portables and the art of good handwriting is completely gone! She could only talk about my mother second-hand but all were agreed that Catherine Mallon had that prose, her own writing style, even though she was barely into her teenage years. Always made it into the school yearbook, nearly took the publication over with her short stories and odes – one spiteful student had suggested that it be renamed *Catherine's Chronicles*. A really funny one called *Flour in My Schoolbag* that captured her hatred of Home Economics. A liberal dose of curry powder in some chocolate buns had saved her from the monotony of the convent kitchen. I stifled a laugh at the thought of my mother's nose against the windowpane as the reverend sisters paused to consider their post-dinner treat.

This one looks interesting, I thought, as another tract unfolded from the pack.

I'LL 'SEA' YOU SOME DAY, DAD

They took my dad away that day
Said SHE to me, just sit there, pray
It isn't fair, I should have cried
Can someone tell me WHY he died?

I'm back again in Donegal
Looking out across the wall
All heads counted, back ashore
Except for Dad, he is no more

He'd read me stories into the night
I've just stopped hoping that SHE might
Now, you'd think SHE'D know why I wish
That I had never seen a fish

Catherine
27/07/66
PS. Love you, Dad, always

With a dominatrix like Mary Mallon, it was inevitable that something insignificant such as a husband would get swept under the carpet. Once we hit Dublin, Matt had travelled over to the

Health Service Executive at St James Hospital to pick up a copy of Catherine's birth certificate. You never know when you might need it, was all he said. And true enough, in mid-air, here I was already reading it.

Brian Mallon, fisherman.

'You okay, there?'

I leapt violently. 'Jesus, Matt – you startled me. Not a word from you for hours, I'd written you off. Phew!'

'You look like you're deeply engrossed anyway.' Matt was nodding towards the album. 'You're not going to be able to let go of it until you find her – that's about the gist of it, isn't it?'

'I don't know, maybe. Do you mind, think I should leave it or what?'

'Me? No, I don't mind. I'm sure you don't need any more advice than you've already got. There's enough wise men and women in the world waiting to dish it out without me having to join them.'

I cursed his knack of being able to detach himself the minute I asked him for his opinion on what I should do. Only recently I was cursing Mr Briscoe and the Dimatos for being the opposite – controlling – and I'd now got the exact contrast, the Laissez Faire Man himself. Momentarily, Frieda's analysis of men and their mistresses felt more appealing – at least you were wanted whatever the motivation. I don't mind being shoved round a little bit, boyfriend, if it's only to show that you care – that I'm not just somewhere for you to park your equipment. It's that Gráinne, isn't it, and you making sure that nobody will get that close to you again?

'Why did you come over, Matt?'

His reply was interrupted by the deafening self-possessed voice of the captain travelling down the passageway.

'*Ladies and gentlemen, we are beginning our descent into Logan International Airport. It is thirty degrees and the sun is shining in downtown Boston. Thank you very much for your cooperation and for flying Virgin Atlantic.*'

Thank you very much, Mr Captain – me or the other few hundred would never have guessed that this is Logan airport. I mean that's why we got on at the other end. And your timing – just when he was about to tell me.

'So this is it,' were Matt's few words as we looked out from the plane.

'Yeah, here we are. Are you okay, now?'

'I'll be fine. Starving though. Will we deal with that first? You didn't eat either.'

41

Home again at Beacon Hill and the sounds of a bath running upstairs as my jet-lagged Irishman prepared to soak away his phobia and jet-lag all in one go. He'd looked towards the floor embarrassedly as he enquired where he'd park his suitcase contents.

Less assured than when he'd crept up on me in my hotel room – he was obviously better equipped to deal with home games. It wasn't just Matt – having him in my house brought home the difference and I was cursing my neediness, my impetuous nature that brought him across my porch. It's about living together – a little different than loving together, though it all helps. Here – in my private sanctuary.

I led him up to my room with its en-suite bathroom. I was glad that he had agreed to wait on eating until we got back to the house – I hadn't ruled out the chance that Ben would resume his tracking once I set foot back in Boston. Paul Briscoe was a possibility too, wasn't he?

And there was Martha Jones to consider. Thoughts of Emily surfaced. Some of the things she'd said – that I'd rejected at the time. It wasn't just about finding my mother – locating people, places and things might turn out to be the easiest part. It was about taking it on, creating the space where you fit in to it all. So many walk away, wishing they hadn't bothered – others can't or won't walk but still wish they could. God's greatest curse was not letting people choose their own families. So much wisdom fitted into those tight jeans, Emily.

Matt's stuff was packed away into my walk-in closet – I reasoned that there was no point in my becoming demure and virginal at this late stage. I telephoned the MSPD, just to keep myself occupied. Dan Jefferson or Ramon Hawkes, either would do.

'Mr Jefferson, I've just returned from vacation. You were trying to see me.'

There is a silence at the end of the line, before he speaks.

'Was I now … I'm not so sure. There's so much going on.'

'Mr Hawkes and you. You came to my door while I was away. Left a message on my answering service when you couldn't get a reply.'

'Not me, I'm afraid. Say, you haven't deleted the message, have you? I'd like to come over and listen to it, if you don't mind?'

'I'll recheck, see if I have it … most likely I deleted it. I'll ring you back if it's still there. Have you made progress with Jed Byron's case?'

'You ring me back first. I've left that one with Ramon. It was *he* spoke to you on this message, was it?'

I wasn't going to tell him that Ramon Hawke's staccato droning had left an indelible mark that would not easily be erased. Sounded too like his sidekick was fond of solo-runs. Best that I take a page from the Briscoe best-practice manual – do plenty of listening and only enough talking for the gobshites to know you're not a mute. I was going to have to level with Matt – let him in on the reality that there was a whole lot of unfinished business that needed dealing with. Back down to the kitchen then, open a bottle of wine – it'll help get the conversation going; he'll be able to understand.

'Spaghetti Bolognese – looks good I must say. Were you expecting me?'

'Paul … what are you doing here, how'd you get in?' My mind raced frantically, composing 'I've been meaning to tell you' speeches or simply wishing that Matt had fallen asleep in the bath upstairs.

'Well, that's a nice welcome, lady – you've set up here for two, except I don't see anybody else right now. I've been keeping an eye on your house for you – in fact, disabled a spying camera set up at your gate. All *the boys* still want to know where Ava is.'

The alluring nature of his voice, like a magnet working in perfect harmony with the bright smile that didn't feature once you looked upwards of the nose at the cold glint of his eyes. Frieda had noticed it – the way each part operated independently. 'Soulless' was how she described it, not creepy in the perverted sense but feral, almost heartless.

I had to think of something quick.

'My attorney, Gayle Fairbanks, is on her way over. You know we passed out at Harvard together. More of a girl meets girl thing, catch up, the usual.'

I was giggling stupidly. Paul was laughing with me.

'You're a howl, Ava – really you are. You just get off a flight from Ireland after all that drama and you call up your lawyer immediately. For a girls' night out – sorry, evening in.'

I felt my cheeks beginning to burn at his arrogance, his unspoken statement that he had a right to know it all. The relationship had changed but there was a new one in place and it involved me keeping him informed. And Paul Briscoe had no interest in shooting the breeze. He wouldn't hang around waiting on worthless gossip: he was only interested in the need-to-know stuff.

'I'm thinking of pulling out of Dimato Pharmaceuticals completely – I've had enough of the way they operate and I want out. I might even go back to Ireland and Gayle is coming over to get the ball rolling, get me the best deal.'

I was surprised at what came tumbling out as if it had been lurking at the back of my brain. Maybe not the Ireland bit, but escaping the clutches of Ben and Chad for good looked very appealing. I could easily do without the pervasive presence of this man and all of his espionage and his 'life on the edge' lifestyle. He was smiling again but with irony.

'Now, there's something you'd need Paul Briscoe to sit in on. Best way of getting a man to up his offer is to whisper a few of his secrets to him. Now, I'm not sure that Gayle would–'

It was time to cut this short.

'Paul, it's not that I'm being ungrateful but I want to get away from the feeling that I'm living in Boston's politics *and* its underworld. You left my bed once you knew there might be commitment and risk. Some of it's my fault for cutting you too much slack but you're no longer in my bed, Paul. So, if it's keys that you used to get in here, I want them back. You can put the damn camera back up at the gate if you want – if people want to watch me come and go, I don't give a shit. They'll get fed up eventually. Now, just go, please, will you?'

A voice comes up in the background, Matt coming up to my side.

'I think what Ava is saying should be clear to you. You should be off about your business now.'

We hovered in silence for what seemed like an eternity before Paul spoke.

'Well, if she hasn't gone out and brought herself back a Pat – sorry, you might like Paddy better. I think the season's potatoes are already picked, friend.'

'I'm not interested in making friends with you. Now, if you'll excuse us we were about to sit down to eat. Maybe some other time, but there isn't enough for three.'

The cold amusement is still in Paul's eyes but he is not finding it funny.

'Are you going to tell me what your new friend does, Ava, if it's not potato-picking?'

'He does the same as you, Paul – private investigations. His name is Matt – Matt Smith – and he's ex Irish Police Force. I would've introduced you, but it seems you're in no mood to be civil.' I could see through his macho posturing that he was hurt, confused, even looking a little old. There was no need to humiliate him. I motioned Matt to leave the room with my eyes and I resumed talking softly, tears in my eyes.

'Life has to go on, Paul, and I still have so much to do. You walked away and it hurt, remember? I do. Can't you just go now – we'll talk again, I promise.'

Paul was going out backwards and his smooth baritone had disintegrated into stammering laughter as he tried desperately to save face. His attempt at a dismissive wave was grotesque, his twitching neck muscles providing the contradiction. The door clicked shut softly and Matt was back.

'He's gone then – do you want to talk?'

'Yeah, but we'd better eat first, Matt, or we'll die of the hunger. I just get the feeling that there's trouble around the corner.'

I hoped that Matt wouldn't get to learn that Paul did not like being upstaged by anyone.

Matt took it all calmly and in his stride. If he'd been fazed by Paul Briscoe, he certainly wasn't showing it.

'I couldn't help overhearing,' he said gently. 'Very recent too – you said he walked out but he was acting like he owned you.'

'Well, he doesn't and he knows it now. It's good to have it out of the way.'

'Do you think he'll leave it at that?'

'Oh, he will – I'm sure of that. He's very proud; he won't make a fuss.'

Matt put Ethan's picture back on the mantelpiece and soon was prodding me playfully.

'So, it turns out that my rates are dearer than your American gumshoe's – all of four-fifty per hour dearer. What would that be in dollars, now that I need to adjust?'

'Forget about that now and tell me why you decided to come over here. You were scared shitless on the plane. There must be something pushing you badly when you faced something you were so afraid of.'

'I'm afraid of flying *and* my life passing me by. Second one won out this time and the company is not half-bad either. And you've seen how long it took me to take to the skies after Tibet. What was it, eight years? Now do you think you could put up with me that long? Because I think it will take that amount of time before I'm up to flying again.'

'I don't know, Mr Smith. I'll have to settle for your one-liners for now – I'm just trying to remember which of the spare rooms I unpacked your clothes in.'

'Oh, there's something I forgot myself – it's another one of these damned phobias. I'll just have to seek help for all my fears but it's a little late tonight.'

'And what's this one, Matt?'

'I never sleep alone on my first night in a strange country.'

'And how did you make out in Tibet?'

'Just think about sitting in the nude at the North Pole and you'll see why it didn't come up.'

I know you're fond of your quips, Matt, helps keep that little bit of distance that you're intent on maintaining.

Best to sleep on it all.

It was only a few short months since an idle reading of a medical chart had changed the course of my life completely, laying bare all the assumptions and the myths that went beforehand.

'There's no need for you to be asking questions these days,' Frieda had admonished. 'They're coming along nicely of their own accord, aren't they, making a habit of finding Ava before she finds them?'

It wasn't Matt Smith who was afraid of being alone in the dark and I listened to his even breathing as he slept serenely in the dead of night on Beacon Hill. Two short weeks ago, I'd connived to get someone else between the sheets – most unlikely that he's at home with his wife right now. More like the Back Bay, drowning his sorrows at the clubs, setting up his next acquisition, that notch on the bedpost.

42

'You're in the *Boston Globe*, Ava.'

I'd surrendered to tiredness just as the blackness of night was ebbing back to that grey interval before dawn when the serious bustle would herald another bright new day for Boston. Last time I woke up in the city, it was down at Cambridge to the sight of Uncle Ben as my head throbbed violently from my escapades in Matt Murphy's Bar.

Now, another Irish Matt was doing the honours with a tray of coffee, toast and fruit juice by my bedside.

'What time is it? You've obviously been out...'

'It's near eleven. Popped to the nearest shop to get the paper. Check out the *Situations Vacant* columns.'

'You're eager.'

'Joking ... about you being in the paper as well. It's your brother and his election campaign.'

'Give me a look at what's going on in Boston.'

The feeling of being back home again hit me

full in the face as I scanned the front page. There was my brother basking in the afterglow of yet another keynote speech, Uncle Ben at the front table leading the applause. Audience photographs on page two – Isabel, Sam and Sabrina towards the front. All seemed to be going smoothly.

I braced myself upwards in the bed as I read the headliner: *Senior Glaxo Executive Recruited by Dimato Pharmaceuticals*. Chad stepping aside as Chief Executive so that he can devote his full energies to representing the people of the state of Massachusetts.

Germaine Patterson was taking over. She was thirty-five and her ascent had been nothing short of meteoric in the industry. She started out as a counter assistant at the CVS Chain Drugstore. Quit at high school, she was a shining example that you did not need a piece of paper from Harvard to make it in life. Was Ava not interested, Mr Dimato? No, in fact it was she who recommended Germaine. Hadn't she increased profits at Glaxo by several percentage points each of the last three years? Sometimes you have to acknowledge that a good woman is the right man for the job.

That should shovel up a few more votes for you, Chad. That was neat of you too, escaping the wrath of the Dimato stars who were entitled to believe that their time had come by putting the blame on me – ask Ava, she'll explain why she did what she did.

I'm out of all that.

Matt was leaning across my shoulder. 'She's got

looks too. A bit stuffy, though, like a younger Hilary Clinton, perfectly groomed. Where does that leave you?'

'Right now, in my bed talking to you – but I need to get out of it and quick. You probably heard me dropping my attorney's name, Gayle Fairbanks, to Paul last night. Well, I'm going to have to call her now – I was thinking about it anyway. I'm not going to work with Germaine Patterson.'

So, the Dimato bandwagon was relentlessly rolling forward on all fronts. It wasn't like the *Globe* to drool over an individual so slavishly. There's one from the archives, Uncle Ben and my youthful brother at the start of the Big Dig project, the first sod being dug. And more recently at the mouth of the tunnel, smiling out at the world as if the pair of you had spent the last fifteen years with your shovels and wheelbarrows, over and back to Boston harbour. Saving the city beyond the twenty-first century. Wicked pissa, that's what you are, boys – wicked pissa.

I got off the Red Line with Matt at Harvard Square, ignoring the Red Sox banter from a group of loudmouths chanting in the background. Pass for twenty-something. Matt had nodded approvingly as my pinned-up hair vanished beneath the baseball cap, a pair of Ralph Lauren shades completing the transformation. Down to one-twenty on the scales, my keep-fit routine on the Emerald Isle had paid off handsomely as I patted my flat stomach in front of the panelled ceiling-to-floor mirrors of my bathroom. I'd assured myself that vanity was a woman's privilege and wholly different from the preening figure of my brother as he rehearsed from the *Life Coach's Rulebook*. That was the difference – a woman could do it for herself – and I strode haughtily out into the Cambridge daylight in my Gant jeans and soft shoes. They'll help, I mused, should I need to attempt breaking my PB for that mad dash from Ben's house to the subway last time around.

We parted at the station, deciding that we'd make our way separately to Ben's house.

The beep-beep signalled an incoming message on my spare phone.

Your map is good. I think that I'm across the street from it right now. Black BMW in the driveway. I've disabled the CCTV and the one next door.

I texted back.

Don't you move yet. Be there in ten minutes.

I got to the back door as the doorbell jangled repeatedly outside. I smiled in wicked satisfaction as I watched Ben cursing as he surveyed the blank screen on his security system. He was in the kitchen, looking exasperatedly at the debris as he dialled a number on his phone. Most likely Martha, get her down to clear up the mess – the aftermath of yet another late-night examination of the state's electoral registers and maps. The political cronies most likely tucked up in their beds, Chad too. Looks like you'll have to clear up the Bud bottles yourself, Uncle – she's not coming, is she? I ducked back behind the trees as he opened the French doors to let out the stale odour of pizza and chips. He was now out in the hallway, peering out through the spy-hole.

'Who is it? I can't hear you. *Speak in through the intercom.* If this is to do with the election, can you go back down to The Square? We have an office down there. My secretary will set up an appointment.'

Nice of you to leave the back door open, Uncle, I thought as I sped upstairs. I heard the heavy oak door opening in the hall.

'Can't you bloody well hear? I don't do interviews at the house. It's my nephew that's going for election, not me.'

The man in the bright orange polo-shirt and off-white chinos smiled brightly.

'Thank you very much, Senator – I wouldn't have bothered you only the ads say that it's okay to call by at your house.' He offered Ben an extended hand. 'Do you mind if I come in – I'm Matt Dalton from the *Boston Phoenix*. I'm interviewing all the candidates in the upcoming elections on behalf of the city's gay and lesbian community. There is still so much prejudice out there, sir, even in twenty-first century Boston.'

The senator was muttering some incoherent explanation about Chad only doing interviews for the mainstream newspapers. Just keep him a few more minutes while I get out, Matt.

'I'll be making a complaint to the Media and Broadcasting Standards Office. You can't be coming round invading on people's privacy like this. Irish, aren't you – I'll be reporting you, for sure I will.'

410

The garishly dressed Irishman was holding his hand up as the anthem music on his phone declared an incoming message.

Got them. Now get out of there. I'll meet you back at The Square.

'Can you hold on, Senator, sir? It's a message from the office – I'm afraid I have to cancel. Can we do this again sometime? It was really nice meeting with you.'

On my way, Daisy. That was fun. I have to look for Charlie's Kitchen, isn't that it?

Ben's phone rang repeatedly as I sat in the booth waiting for Matt to link up. The pouting waitress decked out in the tightest of black miniskirts glared at me as she bustled about the place carrying greasy plates of food back and forth.

'D'ya mind switching that off? It's really wicked boring watching ya staring at it and that woeful tune banging on.'

Three calls, three messages. C, Ramon Hawkes and House. Chad just linking in, wanting to do a post-mortem on the previous night. The unmistakable voice of the MSPD detective telling Ben that they need to cool it– *'Jefferson smells a rat – he has his sights on someone else for the Jed Byron murder and he's asking why I went round to Beacon Hill alone. Ava is back.'*

Matt was sitting into the booth.

'Catch this one,' I whisper as we press our heads close together.

'Listen, you guys, one of you drunken pricks has got my cell phone and my address book too. Bring them back down to the Pru with you. I'll be there later. Had a skid from The Phoenix at the door already.'

'A skid? What does he mean by that?'

'You're a low-life, Matt Smith, but I could have told you that.'

'Best to switch it off as soon as we can,' Matt said before copying the directory. 'It shouldn't take too long for it to dawn on Ben that he's been hoodwinked.'

The leather-clad tartlet was back again with her notebook poised at the ready. Over cheese-burgers and chips, we looked through Ben's address book and phone. Nothing extra recorded under Jones or Martha. I'd seen her with a cell phone only once. It looked like our theft was pointless apart from my enjoyment of my uncle's misfortune.

'Don't shut off his phone yet, Matt.' Another one coming in from C. 'That's Chad, my brother.'

Matt looked on quizzically.

'Ben, I've just been speaking with Hawkes. He tried to connect with you – why aren't you answering? She's back, some guy in tow. Ramon couldn't get a shot of him and they've fucked up the CCTV. You need to find Martha, get her out of the way, Ben. The boys are still staking her house but she hasn't shown up. She's been cracking up lately – we can't afford any slip-ups now – I'm going to ring you at the house.'

Matt's phone started ringing, flashing up *Private Number*.

'Wrong number, just hung up – don't know who'd be ringing me over here?'

Private Number was flashing up again as the waitress scowled her disapproval, throwing her arms aloft in frustration.

412

'Just how many phones do the pair of you need?'

The manager apologised. 'She's just having a wicked bad day – she's okay most times. Go out the back, Phoebe – have a cigarette, cool your jets down for a while.'

Suddenly, I snatched the phone from Matt. 'Hey, that's *my* phone you're holding. Someone is trying to get through to *me*.' I answered.

'Ava Dimato?'

'Yeah, this is Ava, you've got the right number. Donovan … I'm not sure … oh, yes, the Baptism, I remember. Dwayne, that was his name.' I could scarcely forget it – Martha nearly lost her job over it, well past twenty years back.

'She's not down at Jamaica Plains – she's staying with me and Merlene over at Tent City. She's very afraid, Ms Dimato, and wants to talk with you. The senator is saying that Martha could be deported.'

43

I glanced at my watch anxiously as I hovered outside the agreed meeting place in the Back Bay. Matt had yielded to my insistence that I was going alone. I was not to go near Tent City or Jamaica Plain: it was back to where Martha felt safest and that was where she was closest to God – the First Baptist Church on Commonwealth Avenue.

There was a cruel irony to my presence on the street and I felt a chill of rage envelop me as I looked furtively up and down the streets through my dark shades. Most likely the woman who had worked her whole life for Ben was making her way towards the church in the same clandestine manner, terrified that her employer might have her whisked away to the deportation lounge. Wasn't it right here that the brainwashing of Chad began to the point that I could no longer distinguish between brother and uncle?

I had taken heed of my father's admonishment and did not go back around Dartmouth Street again to mix with the Jamaican community or go near the church. Chad chose to defy it and was becoming increasingly rebellious at high school as he sought to assert his transition to adolescence. 'He'd want to firm up pretty soon, Joe' the high-school principal had said. 'He's risking his place at Harvard by continuing to behave in this way.'

And now the transition from rebel to tyrant was complete. I jumped suddenly as a hand was placed on my shoulder.

'Ms Dimato – Martha is inside in the church. She's been waiting on you. It was only when you walked past a few times that she recognised you.' The minister was in his forties with wisps of receding sandy hair pasted across a balding pate. 'I'll leave you two alone now. All the doors are shut so you can talk without being interrupted.'

I took my place in the pew alongside her and listened in silence as her whole body vibrated with heaving sobs. 'I'm sorry, Miss Ava, I'm so

414

sorry – it's always so peaceful in here but I am so sad today, I just cannot stop crying. I was just so afraid. I did not want to go back home.'

'It's okay, Martha, it's going to be all right.' Tears were stinging my eyes. 'No matter how bad it is I want you to tell me everything – it will be all right, I promise.'

That morning all those years back, Martha had taken down the Christmas decorations at my uncle's house when she got the phone call. Went over on her ankle rushing to pick up the phone but Ben was in no mood to listen to her sob stories. She was to stay over there until the senator got back – there was an emergency. Ben and Joe Dimato arrived over later that evening with a young Irish girl in tow. Both brothers confirmed that there was to be a change to Martha's working conditions and she was to be a live-in housekeeper from there on. This included looking after the young lady. And the other condition was silence, complete silence.

Martha paused briefly, sniffling into her handkerchief. 'I tried to protest but Ben said he was cancelling the rent on my little apartment on Jamaica Plain if I didn't fall in with his plans. I either took the new arrangements or I was out on the street. Catherine – funny that they didn't make up a name for her – she sat quietly in the kitchen while all this was going on, never uttered a word.'

And that was the way it started. Catherine and Martha lived together at Cambridge for the next few months. It was during that time she became familiar with the names Jimmy Ellis and Mary Mallon almost to the point she felt she knew them intimately.

'She was so young. I was twenty-three when I made my way here from Jamaica, but here she was barely turned sixteen. Sometimes at night, I'd hear her crying and I'd get out of my bed and go over to her. I'd ask her if she wanted to go back home but the answer was always no. It was as if there was something worse over there – the only reason she'd go back was if her father was alive, but he wasn't.'

I was loath to interrupt Martha – here in the quiet hush of the church, there was a near-supernatural feel to her retracing of the time between my mother's emergence in the snow-covered gardens of Beacon Hill and the inevitable climax to her account. But the lure of finding out a little more about Catherine's father was too much to resist prompting.

'Her dad, yes, Brian, that was his name. Her eyes lit up whenever she spoke about him. She never quite said it but I got the feeling that he did not live with them. He was a fisherman up on the north-west coast. She spent school-terms with her mother but she spent all of her Easter and summer holidays up with her father. I just can't remember the name of the place.'

'Donegal – Creeslough,' I said softly.

'Yes, that was it. Mrs Mallon never seemed to have any time for Catherine. It really hurt her that her own mother couldn't make time for her once the school vacation came up. A *teacher*, Catherine would snort, and she with the whole summer to herself. It sounded like she wouldn't let Brian come home – something about not wanting to be shamed by having an unemployed husband about the place.'

'Sounds very much like her,' I murmured.

'You've met her? Occasionally, the nightmares would get very bad. Catherine even took to sleep-walking, really screaming for Brian, her father – she felt she was drowning, just like him. I'd make her hot cocoa and then, one night, she told me. She was only twelve and had just finished up before her Easter break. She hadn't slept at all the previous night – so excited about going up to see him but it never happened. What really got to her was that Mrs Mallon brought his body home to ... oh, I don't know what it's called.'

'Carlingford.'

'Well, she laid him out in the living room and everyone filed past looking at him. She never forgave her mother for that. She wouldn't have him at home when he was alive – then they all got to ogle him when he was dead just because there was "procedure" to be followed.'

It had carried on like that through the winter and into the summer, Ben barely acknowledging Catherine's presence in the house. It was only when the birth was approaching that Joe Dimato began to show up and it dawned on Martha what was happening.

'I said to them, you cannot do this – it will not be your baby – but they wouldn't listen. There was going to be a home birth and they would bring the baby to the hospital afterwards. Catherine pleaded with me to leave it – she had

417

nowhere to take her baby. I just couldn't take any more. I said to Ben, okay, but I'm not going to be in the house – I'm taking some time off and I did. Only I came back that morning... Ava, can I take a rest?'

The sandy-haired minister nodded quietly as I stepped outside into the evening air. I smiled approvingly as I noticed the man sitting up the street on a bench in beret and dark glasses, a sweatshirt concealing his dazzling polo shirt. Taking heed that corrupt people like Hawkes were about and had noticed his presence. Matt had come to Boston to leave behind the not-so-intriguing pastime of shadowing people that others were interested in but, for now, it wasn't working out that way.

'I've been coming down here for over forty years,' Martha reminisced. 'You'll remember Dwayne, the boy who was baptised here – Donovan and Merlene are his parents.'

It was kind of hard to forget what with Chad inviting him around to Beacon Hill on his fourteenth birthday. The hush that descended when Dwayne walked in with his brightly parcelled present. Joe Dimato was too dumfounded to protest – he would feel well vindicated, however, if he were around to notice that the Jamaican boy had slipped into the drugs culture while his 'reformed' protégé was setting out on the trail to the White House.

'It was Independence Day ... I knew I would be in big trouble if I did not drop by to help the senator out – he never let *that* day go by without

418

putting on some sort of do at the house. There were up to four cars in the driveway. The minute I opened the door, I knew it had happened – you were only hours old, but Lord, you could yell.'

'I was probably protesting, Martha.'

'Well, your mother certainly was. She hadn't said a word in objection previously but she was shouting something about the deal being off. They were encouraging her to get into the car outside – they were all going down to the hospital, Maria too. Only she was travelling with the baby, not Catherine. They duped her into a following car and took her somewhere completely different. I don't know where that was but it wasn't the hospital. And that was the last I saw of her, right then.'

The pictorial history of Ava Dimato's first years saved Martha the ordeal of further explanation. The Dimato cameras had swung into action from every conceivable angle, the bonny baby being star of the show at the christening – the displacement of the young Irish mother swept under the carpet without a mention. Maria had begun the cycle of hospital admissions within six months. Post-natal depression, it was obvious, wasn't it? The camera also showed that a further surrender had taken place, the Jamaican lady taking over the mothering in the early years. Even Frieda had been taken in but she was only five then... Mrs Compton was able to capture it well...

'Mummy, shouldn't Ava be a little bit black – her mammy is *really* black.'

'And to think they relived it all over again with

Chad,' I mused.

Martha shook her head emphatically. 'They didn't. You could see that Joe was affected by it all – he wouldn't have gone back down that road again. Most likely it was a more normal kind of adoption arrangement – though still not by the proper legal channels.'

'Martha, did you see Catherine again after that?'

'You remember the newspaper cuttings that your uncle used to show you – the time you were nearly snatched down at the Public Gardens? I was there that day too. That was your mother – Catherine. I do wonder how often she hovered around that place watching you grow, not able to approach you. The Dimato boys, they specialised in putting the fear of God into anyone who crossed them and they had lots of help with their enforcers – some of them in the MSPD too.'

How often had I heard about the day my uncle had gone into the kiosk to emerge with his Superman cloak to ward off my kidnappers? How they would have demanded a big ransom – Ben pointing out the most evil pictures in the Marvel comics when my childhood innocence demanded that he come up with a description of the man he warded off heroically.

'There was just Catherine – nobody else. I'll never forget her pleading eyes *and* the abuse I got from the senator,' Martha recalled bitterly. 'He only took you down the parks as a photo opportunity – it was him who left you alone, wandered off to make some phone calls. I'd gone over to an ice-cream van with Chad. And then there was the policeman and the way he roughed up your mother ... easy to see how he got his promotions.'

'Who's this you're talking about, Martha?' My instincts were working again, my nerves beginning to stand on edge.

'Oh, I don't know, I was never one for names. I'd say he was new, just a boy himself at the time. He was around in no time and had Catherine in handcuffs. He'd often drop in on Ben over the years and then it all stopped. God, I should be able to put a name on him but I can't. He's retired now. I think he does private investigations.'

We walked out of church together and stood beside Donovan's ramshackle car. She said she felt relieved but I knew there was pain in acknowledging that she would not walk through the gates of the senator's house again. There was the status too – the community from Tent City down to Roxbury all envied her position as *personal aide* to the senator. More recently she'd been bragging about the pension windfall that was coming her way thanks to my intervention – we all have our vanity, she reminded me. The Reverend Minister would not approve of it in the Lord's House, though. I hugged her tightly before we parted, assuring that she'd done nothing that needed forgiveness.

'No, I should have told you, Miss Ava,' she said as we parted. 'I've often asked the Lord to forgive me. It's a bit late for you to be hearing this.'

'You were afraid, that's all – but it's more than enough when it's the Dimatos who are doing the scaring. I'm not angry with you, Martha – I promise.'

I pointed up the road at Matt and he waved back.

'What's he doing with a wool cap on in the heat of summer?'

'That's what I keep telling him. Dreadful dress-sense but he's an Irishman – what can you do?' I whispered in her ear: 'But the good thing is that he's an expert in legal matters – specialises in social security, pensions and immigration, just what you need right now.'

'I suppose he does have that *je ne sais quoi* look about him. He'll have to take the disguise off if he's to go into immigration, though.'

'I thought Spanish was the second language on Jamaica Plain, lady?'

My journey had taken me full circle. Perhaps the reason I had to go to Ireland was to find Matt. I had set out to find my mother and ended up finding love. I knew my mother had loved me and I knew when the time was right we'd meet.

God be with you till we meet again. Wasn't that the signature tune that was played at the end of each prayer meeting and worship? Despite her sadness and uncertain future, Martha seemed restored as she departed for Jamaica Plain.

'I'm glad I told you, Ava, and right here, where God could hear my confession too – he'll be able to forgive me now Doesn't matter if Ben has somebody waiting outside. I'm going to walk right past.'

There was no point in debating religion with her and I squinted upwards at the mural of figures carved into the tower summit. It was the Italians that did them, Chad would argue when he was going through the faith-questioning phase. I shook my hair loose from its bun and pocketed the cap and sunglasses. Matt could abandon his disguise too. We could go back to Beacon Hill hand-in-hand together, that's if forty-something Irishmen weren't embarrassed by the like. Suddenly I was animated, alive in the street.

'Come on, Matt, no more secrets. Remember, you let *me* unpack your case. You know you were missing something in Ireland – you just wouldn't have packed your qualifications and job references otherwise. Live with me on Beacon Hill, Matt, there's no need to go on pretending it's for a few days, unless you intend to go missing among the ex-pats in Boston.'

That's where good girlfriends come in, I thought as Sarah Jane's number nestled comfortably in my phone book. Rang me the minute she knew her brother-in-law was off to Boston. Jack had bought the Mercedes from him. Besotted, that was her description of him – she'd noticed the way he'd looked at me across the floor in Mosney. Wasn't he a twin so I was getting advice from the expert who happened to share a bed with the other half? All he needed was a kick-start – a nudge to get him going...

His worried features melted into a relieved smile. 'I was waiting for you to ask, honest – I just wish you were the penniless side of the duet. I didn't want to be part of the folklore, the charming Paddy coming to America to loosen the purse strings of some lonely middle-aged woman.'

I let his impudence go and resisted the impulse to suggest that a certain Mr Briscoe would locate him quite easily in Boston's underbelly if he decided to run off on me. In the meantime, he'd need to get moving to safeguard the interests of one Martha Jones. *He* was the detective and the would-be lawyer, I reminded him, when he put on the little boy lost look. Best way to find your way around Boston was to go around Boston.

Back at the Seven Ales House on Beacon Hill, Matt supped on his Guinness as he continually shook his head.

'I just don't get you, Ava Dimato – look at you now, all carefree. A while ago you were a cat burglar racing round the senator's house looking for clues that will fit in the last piece of the jigsaw – your mother. You were reckoning that she might be in Boston ... well, is she?'

My eyes misted up as the remnants of Martha's confession echoed in my mind.

'No, she's not, Matt – but she's safe now and I need to let it go. It just wasn't meant to be. Look, I've arranged to meet somebody back at the house. You might like to stay a little longer here – talk to your Irish buddies. I'll be fine – you come on up later.'

Dan Jefferson replayed the message on my house phone and the one I'd thieved earlier from Ben. His fists clenched as he listened to his partner mention his name as he brought Ben up to date on events.

'That's them both taped and I've got that

message from Leo Brubaker too. That's loose of the senator not to have it disconnected yet – that is unless he is trying to track down who is using it. Do you mind if I take it from you now? This could be very useful. And you're sure Brubaker was the man in your driveway?'

'Absolutely. When someone takes a gun out like he did, you're hardly likely to forget him, are you? I'll give you the phone provided you do me a tape of the conversations too.'

Later, I listened to the comforting sound of the Irish brogue thanking the cab-driver profusely in my driveway. Two in the morning – I wouldn't want you out this late every night, Mr Smith. Soon, I was drifting off to sleep.

44

'Now, let's run through this again, Ava. You want me to sell up Dimato Pharmaceuticals and split the proceeds fifty-fifty with you. Why should I do that?'

'Aw, Chad, I just thought it'd make sense. If you get elected, you'll have to devote your energies full-time to politics. Now that you've got Germaine Patterson in, wouldn't it be a good time to off-load the company to Glaxo? She's very highly regarded over there.'

Chad was sitting at my desk, dressed in a navy pin–stripe suit and plain maroon tie. Clock-watching already, even though he hadn't seen his sister in weeks. I'd stopped by with Gayle Fairbanks and she'd listened wide-eyed as I outlined my plan. Forget it, was her advice, there's no basis, you'll never pull it off. Not so sure, Gayle, I reflected grimly – you don't have all the information. Neither does Chad – yet.

'You've been over in "the land of the leprechaun" these past two weeks, haven't you? I think it's affected your judgement, sister. Did you manage to track down your mother while you were over there?'

I shut my eyes, trying to block out his scorn and derision. God, how foolish I'd been, completely misreading my brother. A wolf in sheep's clothing, more lethal than his blustering uncle – only mildly amused at my proposal.

'I can see you've lost your tongue for the moment, Ava, and I've got to dash. When you log on, you'll see that you have an email to deal with from Germaine – to report to her as soon as you turn up for work. You *are* back for work, aren't you?'

I felt that my plan was slipping away from me: intimidating people was not my specialty. I should have left it to Briscoe, maybe the MSPD.

'Chad, I want to sell my share – I'll take my twenty per cent. I won't work with Germaine Patterson and want nothing more to do with you either.'

'Well, that's a pity because you need each partner to agree on it and I won't. Read the fine print. You do own twenty per cent but cannot sell it off without my consent. Now if you don't mind...'

'Oh, but, I do mind, Chad. It's a little more complicated than that. We'll do this the fucking hard way, so. I brought you back a photograph from Ireland. Take a look.'

My brother's colour started to change and he seemed to be propelling himself backwards in time. Jimmy Ellis and his sister Ava. He started to loosen his tie.

'Here's a copy of the reports from the hospital, Brother. Fractured skull, broken nose and badly bruised ribs – you certainly left your calling card, you bastard!'

Now, he was giggling manically, his voice raised several decibels.

'Now, you're not going to get all moral with me about a scumbag blackmailer ... hold on. This piece of shit ran out on you thirty-eight years ago and you're in here giving me the third degree because I went over and gave him a few punches?'

'He got lots of encouragement to walk out, no end of muscle. Dimato Pharmaceuticals no more belongs to you than to me. It's back up to fifty-fifty, Brother. You pay me half its market value and you can keep it. There's a police file labelled "Unsolved" over in Ireland.'

'Look, maybe you don't get my drift. It'll be my word against that of a blackmailer and a drunk. He can't even remember yesterday, let alone eight years. You'll come out of it worse.'

'He nearly died, Chad. The file is also marked "Attempted Murder – Grievous Bodily Harm". This was 1996. They've stopped being leprechauns over there a long time ago. They have fingerprints, brother...'

I heard his office door slam shut. He was sulking. Same old Chad. It gave me little satisfaction seeing him acting like this. There would be no heart to heart.

He came back into the office, his tie now discarded completely. I'd watched him from the window as he paced outside on the sidewalk, phone hung from his ear.

Back inside, he gulped his fourth cup of water from the dispenser.

'Look, Ava, I've been trying to ring Ben. You can't demand an answer right now – you have to give me a little time.'

'You've been part of a cancerous secret for God knows how many years, Chad. All the time you knew about me and you left me helpless. Two days, that's all I'm giving you.'

'Please, Ava, you can't–'

'Two days, Chad, or you can kiss your political career goodbye. I want out and I want half. You'll be walking away with a multi-million dollar gain and the political career that you crave *or* you'll be facing an attempted murder charge. Come Thursday, the *Boston Globe* could be writing a totally different type of article. It's your choice.'

I walked out through the main office – it seemed that the staff had taken the cue and departed to the coffee shops in the street below. Germaine was coming out the elevator door, launching into some patronising oration about Ava being the very person she needed to link up with. The broad smile on her face faded as the lift door started to close and she was left with her arms clutching empty air as I rebuffed her offered embrace. Hugging the new chief executive was not on my list of priorities right then. The bond that existed with my brother for thirty-five years had begun to unravel as I sat with the ailing Joe in Mass General only a few months back. It was now a full-blown rupture and I knew there would be no going back to the pharmaceutical industry and that my detachment from the flawed and corrupt existence at the Dimato household was complete. I'd leave the treacherous Laura in the hands of her new boss, recognising that she too had been exploited by the predatory nature of the opportunists surrounding her. Digging up the dirt was the Dimatos' specialty; lying in wait to pounce on people's secrets and weaknesses counted as normal behaviour. I didn't need to look upwards to confirm that Chad's eyes were following me down into the hub of Boston. Let him score his sister out of ten for rivalling him and Ben in dishing out intimidation when it was needed.

45

'Are you sure you want to go in alone?' Matt asked. We were back outside the gate of Uncle Ben's house, a frown furrowed into the Irishman's brow

'Yes, Matt – I want to look him in the eye and tell him that I've got a new life now, that there's

no scaring Ava any longer. I'm going in alone –
I'll ring you as soon as I come out.' This was
something I needed to do for myself– confirm
once and for all that the spell of the senator was
broken. I was about to press the bell when the
voice rang out.

'Door's open.'

Ben was sitting in the kitchen, a small case
beside him. An empty bottle of Redbreast
whiskey was perched on the table. Twelve noon.
Ben liked a drink but not at that time of the day.
I reasoned that Chad had phoned him to tell him
about my ultimatum. He looked towards me with
a wistful smile.

'I hope you haven't come over here to threaten
your old uncle. I've had more than enough
threats for today already.'

I was tempted to remind him of how good he
was at dishing it out but I was wholly unprepared
for the changed man before me. I was expecting
a tirade, a face-down about my ultimatum to
Chad – but nothing. This was the man who
snatched me, still in the womb, from my Irish
roots all those years back and right now I was
supposed to be giving him hell for it. Yet, nothing
was coming. It was somehow as if he'd reached
journey's end himself. Ben's only surviving close
relative was his sister Laverne and she had
removed herself to Naples forty years back,
embarrassed by her brother's scams and schemes
in search of the dollar. She was not one to have
her head turned by money and was not going to
spend her life acting as her brothers' moral
guardian, in constant rebuke at their excesses.

'Ben, has Chad told you – I want out of Dimato Pharmaceuticals, a clean break. He hasn't taken it very well.'

'Yeah, well, things have got a lot worse for your brother since then. I've had a friend of yours around, Paul Briscoe – take a look at the two files over there.' Ben nodded towards two manila folders. 'Identical files. One for me, one for Chad.'

Silently, I flipped over the cover and it didn't take too long for me to discover that my former lover had seen another opportunity as his mole steadily built up a damning profile of how the Dimatos handled their tax affairs over the years.

'At least he remembered it was my birthday – it was he brought the whiskey.'

Seventy today, I thought silently. 'What do you mean things have got worse, Ben?'

'He wants me to resign from the senate, Chad to withdraw from the race for Congress – or else. Simple as that, and he means it.'

It seemed like too much of a price to pay. All I wanted was to be out of my uncle's and brother's lives, to tell each of them that I didn't need them any more. My hands weren't so clean on tax matters myself.

'It wouldn't be like Paul to snitch to the taxman – I'll talk to him and tell him I don't want it to go this far.'

Ben laughed ironically. 'And he'll listen – will he? He's not going near the tax office. He's made a deal with our political opposition – approached them, telling them he had information that would persuade Chad and me to get out of

431

politics. He had two conditions – it was going to cost them and they didn't need to see it. Just the result and the way clear for them to profit. They jumped at it – knowing that we have no strong candidates to step in at short notice. Home and dry, that's what they are – and they're sure to add a few noughts to Mr Briscoe's bank balance for his trouble.'

It was time to change the subject. 'The kidnapper in the park, all those years ago – that was my mother. Have you no soul, Ben? You and Paul – he was in on it too, wasn't he?'

'He only got to know who she was very recently and, yes, it was her.' Ben was breathing harshly. 'I did it for my brother, Ava – not having family really cut him up and he was my family. Wouldn't hear of adoption so gradually we came round to thinking of something different. Funny thing is, I'd gone to Cork to bring over someone else's baby, already born, but the mother opted out at the last minute. It was then I saw her – your mother, Catherine – she was sitting on a wall in the gardens. One of the nuns took her in and we talked. Her own mother came down the following day to help persuade her that it was the best thing for everyone.'

'Well, it wasn't, Ben. Look at all the pain you've caused – for Catherine, me – we could have got help for Ethan earlier.' I was crying openly. 'Why did you do it, Ben? You should have gone back home when your first plan fell through!'

'Joe was my brother and I tried to help him – how was I to know it would turn into such a bloody mess? And she agreed to it at first – then turns up in the park four years later thinking she can pick you up and walk away with you. She dumped you too – it wasn't all us! Joe loved you. He gave you a home and he couldn't have predicted how sour it would turn.'

'Catherine was a child when you pounced on her, Ben – sixteen. You just came, saw and took what you wanted and that's what you've always done. If you thought of other people for once, the predictions would have been easy. I'm done talking with you now – you're a pathetic old man.'

'I'm sorry, Ava. Look, I might be able to help. I haven't heard from your mother in a good few years but I'd say I might be able to contact her. Last I heard, she was–'

'No, you'll leave things as they are. I'm exhausted by the searching for now.'

I emerged into the autumn sun to find Matt pacing the street. He rushed towards me expectantly.

'You were in there a long time – I was nearly going in several times. You look so pale.'

'Let's go home, Matt.'

'Matt, what do you say we drop down to Emmett's later on? I've had a call from Paul Briscoe – he's down there, wants to make his peace.'

He looked at me in some trepidation before replying. 'I'm not so sure you, I mean we, should be mixing with him. I don't like him – we need to get away from people like him.'

I came up behind him, putting my arms around

his waist. 'It's so nice to hear you saying we, us, Mr Smith, but I didn't know you were jealous – I like that. I'd never have met you but for him and he knows he's history as far as my bedroom is concerned. Anyway, I came out of it better – you're much younger and better-looking.'

'Yeah, I was thinking about that bed. I think we should change it – it creaks a bit, doesn't it?'

'You *are* a jealous so-and-so, aren't you? No, you needn't fret. He never made it to *that* bed.'

I whispered a silent prayer for Sweaty Man and hoped that his demise was not linked to his futile invasions into my private life.

'Okay, sure it can't do any harm – only if he starts on about potato-picking, I'll deck him, for sure. He's likely to be sloshed, too – it's only three in the afternoon. What's he doing picking Emmett's – an Irish bar of all places?'

'Oh, he'll have a reason, only nobody will know it except him. And it's unlikely that he'll be "sloshed", as you call it – no, he'll wander out from time to time: a burger, maybe a newspaper…'

'You liked him, didn't you? What about his wife, how does she feel about his lifestyle?'

'I've never met her, even seen her – the invisible woman, something like Catherine.'

The incoming message on my cell phone brought me back to the reality that there was also loss and hurt in the situation and I hoped that Sam and Sabrina would some day understand.

Isabel was the sender: I was a bitch and I was to go ahead – gloat at seven this evening, get a few televisions, CNN, Fox – they'd all have it.

Never come near her or her children again.

Better to watch it on the national network, I thought. Less detail – able to look at it in the broader context, get it over and done with.

Clever of Ben that, bringing the old ticker back into the equation and on his seventieth birthday. Recuperating at the Mass General, stable – drinking with Paul earlier that day would've pushed up the blood pressure a few notches, got him admitted. Chad had all but claimed that he had some form of spiritual experience – they were expecting their third child and his wife had never been that keen. The deal with Glaxo had been done several weeks back and bringing Germaine in was all part of it, keeping the value of shares up. Somehow, it fell flat – not near as polished as Ben.

Emmett's was well full as we passed through the door with no end of government workers speculating as to what would happen next in Boston's politics. Some more inebriated souls would be claiming they had the inside track, no doubt, but Mr Briscoe had come out of it all with his sense of mischief and timing intact. One or two politely enquired about the day's events but it was one of these places where life went on and the barman was making sure of that.

'Who wants to watch the Red Sox whup ass?' he bellowed loudly across the floor.

A huge whoop of approval went up. Things like the Fenway Park outfit reclaiming the World Series after an eighty-six year wait were far more significant to the greater Boston populace.

We sat in the corner together as the Guinness

slowly broke down the barriers between my Irishman and the Brookline Brawler.

The barman was back asking if we'd make do with sandwiches, maybe some cocktail sausages. He was short a pair of hands and couldn't do the cooking and the bartending.

Matt excused himself, sensing my need to speak with Paul alone.

Paul didn't waste any time.

'Ava, I was the cop that roughed up your mother in the park that day.'

'I know.'

'I figured you might: you've got good at this detective game.'

I shook my head regretfully. He was trying to reel me in but it wasn't going to happen.

Then he told me about his visit with my Uncle Ben earlier that day.

'He won't be hassling you again.'

Our eyes met and momentarily I was drifting back. Then the moment passed.

'I hope you didn't put him in hospital.'

Paul finished his drink and didn't reply.

'Thank you, Paul.'

Matt was back with another round.

Paul raised his glass. 'To happy endings and all that shit!'

'Cheers!'

We three clinked glasses.

'Now that I'm finished with Dimato Pharmaceuticals I'm thinking of opening my own agency. Help other people looking for their biological families.'

Paul's face brightened. 'Yeah, we could look into

it. I'd only do it on a consultancy basis, though – swore the day I signed off from the State Police that I'd never be an employee again. No, you'd only need to call on me for the hard ones: that's when you need that bit extra – that bit of experience, the edge. And you, Matt, you'd agree with that?'

Matt refused to take the bait 'Well, I could give it a go, only I've had my fill of following adulterers – if you can agree to that, I'd be happy.'

'And no fighting?'

'You know me, Ava – I'm not one to let my hang-ups about shanty Irishmen to get in the way of the dollar.'

'Yep, I've only been around for forty-eight hours and I'm not above mucking out with Massholes – drinks, everybody?'

Matt winked at me. A definitive win-win. Paul kept his ego and Matt kept the woman.

46

The evening sun was setting on Boston Common. Matt had taken Aoife over to Beacon Hill under orders to start preparing dinner. All I could see was Brian's button nose peeping out from the woolly blankets. Boston in April can have its chilly moments and this was one of them but they couldn't reach my heart. I stopped to sit at the park bench, looking closer to see my little boy's restful sleeping. I looked at my watch. Time to read that letter again.

Beacon Hill
Boston
03/17/2007

Dear Catherine,
I hope that you will not find my letter too upsetting.
I'd better say from the start that I am Ava. Martha
gave me this address nearly three years ago but I was
too frightened at the time to make contact. Funny
that – I'd even been to Ireland looking for you, ready
to knock down walls to connect with you, and when
someone hands me an address and a telephone
number, I chicken out.

Up to three years ago, I knew nothing about the
circumstances of my birth and then Joe Dimato died
and I got to know that I'm Ava Someone Else. I
fought hard to find who that someone else was and if
I mention the names Ellis, Loughnane and Mallon,
you'll know how far I took it.

I'm still living in Boston. I fell out with my 'family'
a few years back – we had a big business, all over the
world it was, but we sold up because I wouldn't work
with them any longer. Now Chad, my 'brother' won't
talk to me – Uncle Ben does, but it's not the same any
more.

But I've got a good life now. When I was over in
Ireland, I ran into this guy, Matt Smith, and brought
him back to Boston with me and we got married. I
had to ask him myself – he had this terrible poor
boy/rich girl thing going on in his head, afraid to say
he loved me for fear that I'd take it to mean he loved
my money!

I'm Mrs Smith now and I'm hoping to stay that way because I've had a lot of names in recent years and Matt's name is not half-bad at all.

When I was looking for you I was surrounded by private investigators and policemen – so I got the idea that I'd set up this investigatory company. We don't do the standard stuff like going round finding out who's having affairs or employers wanting pictures of someone lifting something when they shouldn't be lifting anything. We managed to wangle Matt into Harvard so he can be a proper attorney – that's what he always wanted. We call ourselves Boston Advocacy Services. It's not just about getting information for people – sometimes they need a bit of a dig-out, support to get where they deserve to be.

We had Martha working on reception but that didn't work out. I walked in and there she was giving Matt a demonstration on how to iron a shirt properly. She drops by most days – at least Ben fixed her up with a pension so she has a bit put by.

Me and Matt have two babies. Aoife, she's one and a half and Brian – well, he's just two days old and that's sort of why I'm writing, to say that we're going to christen him sometime soon and that I'd like you to come.

So I'm going to say goodbye now – you'll know the right thing to do and we'll wait and see.

Love,

Ava

'Well, hello, you really look lost in thought.'

'William – thanks for coming along. I'll just put this away.' I folded my letter neatly into its addressed envelope. He adjusted his scarf to speak as he peered into the pram and the customary smell of alcohol wafted forward across the frosty air.

'He looks a great little man, Ava, really does. Two children, and in two years – it's all turned out so good.'

'He *is* a great little man, you mean. Yes, it has turned out good – and you'll be coming to the christening, I hope?'

'I will be delighted to but I doubt you brought me out to Boston Common just for that,' William said.

'No, you're right. I was looking at your picture again last night and it's beautiful, haunting. But I have my two babies now and I see too much anger in it, fear. I don't want them to be reminded of it – come to think of it, I want it to be in my past too. So, I hope you'll take it back – it's in the tray below the pram,' I said, nodding downwards. 'It was never mine.'

'And what about Catherine – that was her name, wasn't it? Frieda was saying that you've got an idea where she is now. After all the searching you did, it just seems funny for you to stop.'

I was conscious of the letter in my pocket. Soon, I'd be depositing it in the first post-box I met on the way home. Best to keep it quiet – it was now only a part of my life, a much bigger, joyous life. 'Not so strange at all, William. It's about letting go. I've my own two babies to look after now. Now, are you going to take your picture?'

'Back in the brown wrapping too. You know, I

440

missed it myself – why I don't know. It was no fun watching Joe Dimato coming charging at me like a bull.'

'Mmm ... that was the Dimatos for you. They were either charging at something or running away from it.' I paused to replace Brian's soother in his mouth. 'You take care now, William, I'm off home.'

Epilogue

Catherine Mallon sat in the quiet café down at the Amadeus Hotel in Budapest. This was part of her ritual for the past seven years and she had come to like the anonymity that the Eastern European city gave her. She had felt a little insecure when the business started advertising in the Irish newspapers but to date no customer had turned up from the Wee County that recognised her. Anyway, she felt that forty years on it was most unlikely, Heather apart, that anybody would recognise her. She'd looked in the mirror that morning and felt that at fifty-six she could acknowledge without conceit that she would pass for a woman ten years younger. It wasn't like that eight years back when she had abandoned a sixty-a-day smoking habit but a dramatic change of lifestyle had gradually restored her to good physical health and a feeling of self-worth. Her elevenses coffee break was her sole departure from a diet of fish, vegetarian meals, fresh mineral waters and herbal teas. This morning was no different and the waitress deposited the customary mug of frothy hot chocolate and lemon cake without question.

She looked at her watch, noticing that her boss, Adolf, was running late or, more likely, cycling late. Each Friday morning, Adolf went for the 'burn', the ultra-distance, and trips of 180 kilometres were not unknown. Catherine generally opted out at eighty so she was leaving him to it for today.

She looked out the hotel window towards her fourth-floor apartment and nodded to herself in quiet satisfaction. It did not have the views of Carlingford Harbour or Donegal but it was *hers*. She was satisfied with her simple, ordered life and the confined comfort of her job, her apartment on its doorstep and her daily treat at the Amadeus. She avoided the bustle of the city and enjoyed her summer morning cycles with Adolf and the meditation exercises he had taught her.

She had first met him fifteen years back at a London dental practice when he'd presented a copy of an estimate from another surgery and asked for another quotation.

'You will have to make an appointment, Mr...' she said, noticing that there was no name on the bill.

'Adolf, just call me Adolf,' he replied in stilted English.

She resisted the impulse to ask him if he was Hitler as she noticed with bemusement his gleaming white teeth and the lengthy list of

'Work Needing Doing'.

'I'm sorry, Adolf, but one of our dentists would need to *look* at your teeth. He may feel that you need different work, maybe not as much as what's listed here.'

It was then that he told her he was doing some research, was hoping to set up a practice in Budapest and wanted to compare costs. Catherine prepared the estimate on her own initiative and in return got his business card – give him a call if she ever needed work.

She had made that call eight years ago and credited Adolf with the dramatic changes that had taken place in her life. Slowly she was able to put down the cigarettes, the anti-depressants and come to terms with the misfortunes that life had dealt her. My *maharishi*, my spiritual leader, she would jest occasionally. The relationship was purely platonic but she sometimes wondered if, at ten years her junior, he was ever tempted to take it to another stage.

Right now, he was running late and she resumed reading the letter.

'Adolf, I didn't see you come up! How far was it today?'

'Not so far. I think my body was telling me something so I did the shorter route. You could have come but then you couldn't. You've been absorbed by that letter since you got it. How many times have you read it?'

Catherine blushed, then smiled. 'Maybe once for every kilometre we cycled this year.'

'Oh, that bad?'

'Well now, I was thinking, Adolf – I've worked up a lot of holidays, right?'

'Right ... and now you want to go somewhere and what's more you're ready to go too.'

'Slow down now, Adolf. I don't want you going all spiritual on me. I'm afraid but, yes, I'm going.'

'That's great – hold on – I'll check the flight times.'

'I've done all that. You remember the insomnia I told you about – it came back last night so I checked all that out.'

'So decisive – I'm just going to retire, let you do your own thing from now on.'

The publishers hope that this book has given you enjoyable reading. Large Print Books are especially designed to be as easy to see and hold as possible. If you wish a complete list of our books please ask at your local library or write directly to:

Magna Large Print Books
Magna House, Long Preston,
Skipton, North Yorkshire.
BD23 4ND

This Large Print Book for the partially sighted, who cannot read normal print, is published under the auspices of

THE ULVERSCROFT FOUNDATION